MONUMENT

ANNIE FLANAGAN

Typeset in Minion Pro

Cover photo © Robert Phelps of RP Photography

Editing, design, typesetting and publishing by UK Book Publishing

www.ukbookpublishing.com

ISBN: 978-1-912183-72-2

"To teenagers everywhere:
I miss you. Stay safe."

Acknowledgements

There are some very special people I would like to thank for their support and encouragement in bringing this novel to life. Without them, I fear my courage would have failed and I would have ended up with a drawer full of manuscripts like so many others have in the past.

My original young "guinea-pig readers": Lauren Howarth – you were the first. Your reaction to Monument was what spurred me on to approach others. Thank you so much for your honesty and enthusiasm.

Erin Snaith – you gave me such detailed feedback I was astounded. I did change the ending, adding more detail, just as you suggested!

Dominic and Jerome Bramley – Boys, you received the book at a particularly busy time of year for both of you and still took the time to plough through it for me. I loved your observations, your commitment and obvious enjoyment of character, plot and setting. This is a novel designed to encourage boys to read and you have proved that it works successfully.

To Robert Phelps of RP Photography for the front cover image of our very special icon. It's outstanding and atmospheric, just what I wanted!

To the people of Fatfield and Penshaw. I have taken a few liberties in changing the layout of the riverside ever so slightly. Maybe nobody will notice? It's a wonderful spot with a fine sense of community spirit.

And finally to everyone at UK Book Publishing for all their wonderful publishing effort, particularly Ruth for her editing skill, Jay for design and layout and all of you for putting up with my regular meltdowns when my decrepit, elderly, steam-powered computer got the better of me, plunging me into darkness. We must all do it again sometime very soon!

Penshaw Monument

Visible for miles around in every direction, Penshaw Monument stands proudly on its hill, a comforting beacon to the people of the North East of England. On returning from a long journey, locals heave a sigh of relief at seeing its familiar presence welcoming them home. Built in 1844 as a testimony to Lord Lambton, the first Earl of Durham, a local land and mine owner, it has played host to many families over its years, holding picnics, concerts, egg rolls at Easter, fun, and exhausting days out climbing to the top of the hill to survey the world spread out all around. Share it with the cattle and happy visitors to the region who have been drawn by its majesty, as you sit safe in its shadow and enjoy the spectacular scenery.

To my knowledge, nobody has ever featured this famous landmark as the setting for a piece of literature. I have changed that. This is the place that acts as a security blanket for poor little Billy Higson. And yet, he struggles to come to terms with the memories it brings; he simply cannot confront them; he finds them too distressing. Can his new friend Frank help him find the emotional release he needs to move on? Can he climb the hill and find the freedom and the comfort he deserves?

The Monument represents Billy's fears, a huge, constant presence in his life: sometimes seen in sunshine, at other times surrounded by gloomy clouds and stormy weather. The Monument is also representative of the comfort and security Billy finds in his new friends, Dagger, Frank, Sue and Richie. Billy longs to leave his past behind him, to grow up normally, like the other people who love this local landmark. Can he put his past behind him and move on up that hill, to enjoy the view from the top?

Chapter 1

Billy Higson, twelve years old, was dying. Not dying quietly, peacefully or calmly in a hospital bed, surrounded by machines and monitors, with efficient nurses speaking softly and his mam sobbing at his side. No, he was dying in a panicking, choking, sweating and fighting kind of way.

It was black, the suffocating darkness pressing onto his eyes and filling up his nose and mouth so that he couldn't breathe – the weight of a phantom figure lying heavily on him. He thought he was screaming but no sound struggled from his tortured lungs. His fingers clawed and scrabbled aimlessly at the lid of the tomb enclosing him. His finger nails were ripped, bleeding and throbbing, but the pain did not register in his agonised mind. The need for air and light engulfed him as he writhed and twisted in his terror. He was in a hot, all-consuming hell, slowly losing consciousness as his survival instinct deserted him.

Desperately, he tried to calm himself, tell himself that this was not the end, that someone would come to his rescue before it was too late. But who? Who cared about him enough to do that? Who would even realise he was missing? He could be locked in this pit and this pain for hours, and then it would be too late.

As dust and cobwebs descended onto his face and hair, he began to fade into the darkness. Silent tears streamed down his grimy face as he gave in to his fate. It was his turn now. He had known it would happen at one point or another, just not now, not here, not at this young age. Black despair overwhelmed him.

*

"Ok everybody, if you'd like to get a chair from the side of the hall and come and sit in a circle, we can begin." Mrs Hardcastle picked up the high stool and sat in the middle of the large room, waiting for her year eight class to settle and follow instructions. Oh, but they were a lively bunch. Yes, they loved their drama lessons but was all this noise and confusion really necessary? "And please do it quickly and quietly!"

The class milled about her, one or two shoving each other around good naturedly, whilst others deliberately ignored her instructions so they could continue their enormously important discussion on who was the fittest lad in the year nine footy team and whether Mr Cooper from Science had really had a facelift over Easter. After five minutes of constant cajoling and reminders, with Mrs Hardcastle removing one or two likely lads away from each other and taking two mobile phones off a couple of sulky girls, the class finally came to order. *Ofsted would 'love' this lot*, thought the teacher. *If they observed me with them I'd be lucky to end up serving in McDonald's.*

Bring on break time and a nice hot cuppa in the staff room...

"Right class," she began. "Last lesson we... Carly, what have you got in your hand? No, I really don't want the details, just put it away and let's get on. Last week we considered how to... whoever is making that noise, please stop it. Now."

The class looked at each other bemused. What was she on about? What noise? They actually stopped their chatter for a second or two. Silence. Except for the draught whistling through the blind on the ill-fitting window.

"OK, who can remember what we said about the central character in... Michael, is it you?" Mrs Hardcastle was losing her patience now.

Michael, for once, was innocent. He was quite affronted by the accusation. Sam, three seats away on his left, took the opportunity to make a noise himself, because obviously something was going on here and he didn't want to miss out on the chance to cause some havoc. He made a sort of strangled quacking sound. At least the girls were entertained by it even if his drama teacher was not. Their giggles made him feel important and clever, for a change, until all the eyes in the class turned on him and he felt a bit of a tit.

Just then they all really did hear a strange wailing sound in answer to Sam's pathetic effort. *Ha! Whoever was making that noise had some nerve*, Sam thought. It was pretty scary really, more than he dared do, and in the large darkening hall it was actually quite eerie. The class fell silent, only their eyes moving towards each other in question and puzzlement.

"Right," sighed the teacher. "Just stop it now, whichever one of you is making that ridiculous noise, and let's get on with the lesson. It'll be lunchtime soon and I'll keep you all back to make up for the time you've wasted so far." Mrs Hardcastle was losing her temper now. *Little sods*, she thought. *I really don't want to spend any more time than I have to with them, but I've got to get to the bottom of this.*

"Miss, I think it's the seagulls." Jodie looked nervously about her. She was terrified of them at the best of times: always in the playground, waiting like vultures to swoop down on them to steal their crisps and sandwiches. They were as big as vultures, too.

"It's not the seagulls, Miss. It's the ghost of the dead caretaker, you know, the one they found hanging from the lighting galley after you did 'Phantom of the Opera' on the stage there."

Charlie was enjoying himself – it was a *drama* lesson after all! And there, there really was a noise, a painful, weird sort of wail, and this time everyone in the room heard it. The pupils gasped dramatically, their eyes widening in mock horror.

"Maybe it's rats?" suggested Leanne, clutching her blazer tighter to her chest.

"Is there really a ghost in this hall, Miss?" asked the one with specs whose name she could never remember, and who had released the floodgates.

There followed a chorus of "Don't be stupid, rats don't wail" and "This school is minging, they should pull it down" and "Miss, my house is haunted, you know…".

Mrs Hardcastle stood up from her chair and yelled at the noisy bunch around her, "Will you lot just shut up for one minute, for God's sake?"

She paused for a second to regain her composure before listening intently. The class actually did shut up. The teacher, who had honed her exceptional hearing over ten years in the trade, moved quietly towards the stage. The sound seemed to be emanating from on there, somewhere. Two of the bigger, braver boys stood up and followed her – more to make themselves look like protective heroes than anything else. The girls in the room held their breath.

"It's alright, Miss, we're right behind you," Ben told her, holding tightly onto Josh's hand, before they both realised it and made a huge show of letting go of each other and wiping their hands on their blazers.

There was that sound again. Mrs Hardcastle was up the steps now, almost silently gliding onto the stage. The class sat watching, mesmerised, on the edge of their seats. This was almost better than the time Mr Watson had fallen backwards into the swimming pool while ranting at them for being noisy and obnoxious.

Mrs Hardcastle padded about the stage, moving curtains and peering behind the scenery flats. There was nobody else on the stage. It was darkly deserted. She stepped back and almost fell over Ben. Both of them shrieked in surprised confusion. The class giggled nervously. One or two of the girls came quietly on stage to join them. Sally looked up into the lighting galley, half fearing and half hoping to see a spectral figure swinging up there. No luck. Kelly quietly looked behind a pile of chairs being stored in the darker recess at the back of the scenery store. Nope. Nothing there either. Down on their chairs in the main hall, the class – well, those who were still in their chairs and not on stage in the search – were agog, eyes staring, ears straining. In the distance the rest of the school could be heard, quietly going about their business. Chairs were being scraped; voices could be made out dimly, droning on in the Science department; a door clanged shut noisily.

But on stage, and in the hall, there was still that unmistakeable muffled wailing cry. Mrs Hardcastle stopped right in the centre of the stage, holding her finger to her lips, eyes begging her class to stop and just listen. And for once, they did, because they could hear it too now, every one of them.

By now, most of the year eight class were standing huddled together on the stage, some holding quietly on to each other in the dimness, ready to jump or scream at whatever might make an appearance. Mrs Hardcastle's eyes were drawn to the trap door at her feet. All the eyes in the room followed her gaze. Silence fell as thick as a blanket. Collective breath was held.

"Miss, I think it really is a rat down there." Sam spoke in hushed tones.

"Don't be silly, Sam; rats don't make noises like that," Mrs Hardcastle whispered back. One or two pupils were now crouching around the trap door, ears cocked as they listened intently.

"Do ghosts sound like that, though?" whispered Michael, glancing fearfully over his shoulder.

"Don't be silly, Michael, there are no such things as ghosts. Now," she began, briskly, "let's get this trap door open."

Some of the children gasped and stepped back, still holding tightly onto one another. Mrs Hardcastle gave them a withering look. Jodie was the nearest one crouching by the trap door.

"OK, Jodie, get hold of that handle and when I say pull, lift it open," the teacher told her quietly. Jodie was aghast.

"Me?" she squeaked. "No chance! You do it, Miss. You're the adult here."

Jack stepped forward.

"I'll do it, Miss. You just step back there and leave it to me." He puffed himself up to his full five feet one inch and almost swaggered towards the trapdoor handle. The noise came again. It *was* from under there!

Sally gazed at Jack with new interest. Actually, he did have very nice brown eyes. Funny she'd never noticed them before.

"He's so brave," she whispered to Jodie, swooning slightly with renewed interest in Jack.

"If it's a rat, I'm outta here, mind." Michael visibly shuddered, moving to the outside edge of the group, preparing to leap off the stage should the rabid rodent put in an appearance.

"OK, totally quiet now please everyone." Mrs Hardcastle glared at them with a warning look. "On my word, Jack, after three: one, two, *and lift!*" Jack lifted the trap door.

Nothing happened. All was quiet, and the class leaned forward as one person, quite disappointed that there seemed to be nothing making that awful noise. Suddenly, a face appeared. A dark, dirty face, twisted up as though in pain or anger. Tears had streaked through the muck making greasy channels, its hair was standing up on end and it looked for all the world like a grotesque smaller version of Quasimodo, or some terrifying little hobgoblin. The class screamed in unison, hanging on to each other's arms and shoving each other out of the way of this miniature mad man. Jodie fell over and lay on the floor, screaming, crying in pretend pain, adding to the drama of the moment, secretly hoping that Jack would come and pick her up. Sally saw through her plan, though, and slyly kicked her.

The creature shot out of the trap door like a rat from a trap and scuttled across the floor before leaping off the stage and making its sobbing, wailing way out of the hall, lurching and tearing at its hair as it went.

"Stop him!" yelled Mrs Hardcastle.

"Are you daft?" demanded Michael, still dithering near the edge of the stage. Just in case, like.

"Did anyone recognise him?"

"Miss, I think it's that odd boy from our year. What's his name, Jack? You know, the one you took the cheesy chips off last week."

Jack didn't dare admit that he was actually too shocked and afraid to look too closely. Plus, he didn't want to get a detention for pinching chips off a pupil.

"Never seen him before," he stated, trying to look hard and not bothered.

Mrs Hardcastle was trying to restore some form of order in the hall. She ushered all the pupils back to their seats and tried to calm their panic, and near hysteria in the case of some of the more lively girls. They were all still chattering and laughing nervously. They weren't really with her at all. Just then the door to the main hall opened and in strode the Head. *Great*, she thought. *Now he thinks I'm a complete numpty who can't control a class of thirteen-year-olds.*

"What on earth is going on in here?" demanded Mr Blythe. "Shouldn't you lot have a teacher with you? Sit down and shut up, and *one* of you stand up and explain yourselves to me!"

The class finally did as they were told. You didn't mess with this guy. He looked like an all-in wrestler and was known to reduce the *baddest*, maddest boys in year eleven to tears with just one look from those ice blue eyes. Mrs Hardcastle stood up slowly, raising her hand like a naughty pupil. Her face was bright red.

"I'm with them, sir... er, Mr Blythe," she stuttered. "We all just had a bit of a shock."

The nervous, nameless girl with glasses stood up quietly. "Mrs Hardcastle, I think that was Billy Higson who crawled out from the hole."

At the mention of Billy's name the class was reduced to sniggering, nudging and giggling once more.

"That is enough!" roared the Headteacher, fixing them all with his piercing death stare.

They instantly shut up and sat up straight. Some of them physically quaked, staring at their feet.

"You, girl." Mr Blythe pointed to the girl who had named Billy. "Go to his Head of Year and tell her what has happened to him. She may wish to send out a search party."

As he walked towards the main door of the hall, Jack took the opportunity to whisper "Aye, aye, cap'n".

Sally smirked at him and he smiled back at her. It was ok – the Head hadn't heard his nickname. Jack was safe and he was definitely her new hero.

The whole gathered group listened silently to his footsteps echoing across the shiny parquet flooring. Mrs Hardcastle attempted to start the lesson again, whilst the Head was still just about in the room. She desperately wanted to prove to his retreating back that she could handle this horrible little bunch of demons.

"So, finally…" she began. "Who can tell me, which is the evil character in 'Dr Jekyll and Mr Hyde'?"

"Jack Fletcher – detention, my office, 3.15 tonight," Mr Blythe called out without turning his head as he pushed open the door to the hall.

"Aye, aye, cap'n," sighed Jack, hanging his head.

Chapter 2

In her office, Miss Dorwood was making her visitors a cup of coffee. *Where is Billy,* she wondered. It was not like him to be late for an appointment. In fact, sometimes she had to prise his fingers off the door frame to get him to some of his lessons. He was always happy to sit in the quiet comfort of her room, away from the rest of the school, often with a book or his drawing pad in his hands. Miss Dorwood worried more about Billy than she did about the other pupils in her year team. She knew she shouldn't really. Lots of them had problems, but there was something about Billy's pale face and sad eyes, and the way his fingers were constantly twisting. Unless, of course, he was drawing. He rarely looked her straight in the face. He only ever spoke quietly and was always sort of shrunken into himself, like a tortoise too afraid to come out of its shell.

"I'm sure he won't be long," she said, handing out two cups to the men in her office. One, Davey, she knew well. He was Billy's case manager, the one who had overall charge of his file, but who rarely saw Billy. He had the rushed, stressed, pale face and harassed look of most of the social service workers who came into school regularly. The other, older, man was a stranger to Miss Dorwood. He was heavyset, wore glasses and had thick, greying hair. His trousers needed a wash and his finger nails didn't look too clean either.

The man reached forward to shake Miss Dorwood's hand; she took it gingerly in her own. He smelled of cigarettes and, as he sat back down, his tongue darted out and he licked his lips. Like a lizard. He even had light hazel, lizard-coloured eyes.

Miss Dorwood repressed a shudder. *Be professional*, she told herself.

"Hi, I'm Paul Costello," he told her. "I'm taking on Billy's case for a while."

Miss Dorwood raised her eyebrows in surprise as she sat back into her seat, indicating for the men to sit down, too.

"Yes, I know," Mr Costello continued. "Billy was doing well with Pamela Jackson, but she has family problems out in Australia and won't be back for some time. What can you tell me about how he copes in school?"

Miss Dorwood quelled the angry urge to demand if he had read Billy's file *at all. What would be the point*, she thought wearily. She wished that all her sad little cases like Billy would find some support and encouragement to make just an iota of progress in their quest for peace and contentment. Sadly, it rarely happened and when these pupils did actually reach a tiny high, there was always some little toe-rag ready and willing to burst their bubble before it had a positive impact on their lives. Looking at Mr Costello, squatting in his chair like an aging bull frog, she didn't fancy Billy Higson's chances much. *Poor little lad*, she thought.

"Billy's usually quite keen to come in to see me for a chat," Miss Dorwood told the men. "I hope he's ok."

Davey was helping himself to another biscuit. "It's a shame he's losing Pamela after making a good start with her," he told the teacher, "but there are a few changes afoot for Billy. His mam has to have a fairly big operation and she'll need some convalescence afterwards. But don't worry, we've got a good foster family ready for him, and they're fairly local, too."

Leaning forward earnestly, Paul Costello said, "It should only be for the summer. And with the end of term coming up, and holidays starting soon, Billy shouldn't miss out too much on his education."

Perhaps, he wasn't quite as reptilian as she originally thought. But it was unlikely that Billy would take much of a liking to this guy.

"Well, Mr Costello," she began, looking directly into the new case worker's face, "Billy doesn't cope well here or anywhere. We do our best, and there are one or two members of staff whom he trusts. But when it comes to dealing with other pupils, Billy just won't open up at all. He is wary of people and seems to always carry a heavy burden around with him. The other kids soon give up. Some resort to teasing him, but mostly Billy is happy to just… blend into the scenery."

Mr Costello and Davey exchanged glances.

"Is there much bullying going on here?" Mr Costello asked, raising a questioning eyebrow and shuffling his bulk forward in his seat.

Miss Dorwood could feel her hackles rising. "Absolutely not," she stated, perhaps more forcefully than she had intended.

There was a loud rap on the door. She ignored it for a minute.

Davey took her side, turning to his colleague with a determined expression on his face. "No, no, Paul. I'd say this is one of the better schools in the city when it comes to keeping the pupils safe. There are some schools who don't measure up, but Kingswood is fine. I can reassure you."

Miss Dorwood smiled gratefully at him. "I see Billy regularly and he knows that when he needs time out for any reason he can always come straight to me." Miss Dorwood began to get up to answer the now fairly desperate knocking on her office door. "Billy will be along in just a minute and I'll introduce you to…"

The office door suddenly burst open. A mousey-haired girl wearing spectacles rushed in, looking flushed and upset. She was panting and had obviously been running.

"Miss Dorwood, you've got to come quickly!" she panted. "Billy Higson's up on the school roof. I think he's going to jump off!"

*

Although everyone should have been in lessons by then, there was quite a crowd gathered at the front entrance to the school, all looking skyward and pointing. There was lots of laughter, and the obvious catcalls from some of the wags who decided this was a far more entertaining option than going to ICT or Geography.

"Oy, kid, see if my football's still up there, will you?" laughed one of the boys.

"And that mince pie the seagulls nicked off me yesterday!" called his mate.

One or two of the older pupils took this distraction as an opportunity to sneak off behind the Art block for a swift fag, but most were happy to stay with something so shocking and dramatic. They stared up at the small figure huddled and hanging on to a heating vent on the main roof. The crowd on the ground creaked their heads back, shielding their eyes against the glare of the sun. One teacher was pacing up and down talking into a walkie-talkie whilst other staff made their way to see if they could usher the bystanders back into their lessons.

They didn't have much luck.

Miss Dorwood had run to the scene, leaving the two male visitors to catch up as best as they could. Her heart was beating wildly as she arrived, her hair had dropped from its tidy little ponytail and her shoes were in her hand. She stood on the cool grass looking up anxiously towards the roof. Another member of staff approached her, shaking his head.

"Is that Billy Higson?" she asked him.

"Yes, I'm afraid it is. Isn't he the kid who's terrified of, well... *everything?*" he asked Miss Dorwood. "I don't know how you do it, Alice. You've got some right nutters in your year group, I tell you."

"Not helpful, Mick," she told him angrily. "How on earth did he get up there?"

"Well, he's obviously not scared of heights, is he?" He smiled.

Behind them, the group of pupils were slowly being ushered away by a couple of other staff who had turned up. One of the pupils had started lustily singing an old song, called 'Don't Jump off the Roof Dad', whilst the others began a slow hand clap. Obviously, they were a bit narked about leaving the scene of a potential disaster and they all wanted to appear on the front page of 'The Echo' that night, giving their invaluable insight into this tragic situation. Most of them knew Billy, and he had been a fairly consistent form of entertainment in the two years he'd been at Kingswood. If asked, these boys and girls would say they weren't *cruel* exactly… it's just that the kid was weird and good for a laugh. He brightened their dark school days. They weren't bothered that this lad sometimes looked… well, tortured.

Mick, the Maths teacher, was gazing expectantly at Miss Dorwood from Drama.

"How are you going to get him down from there, then?" he asked, crossing his arms and looking like he was in this game for the duration, too. "Police? International Rescue? Spider-Man?"

Miss Dorwood gave him a thump on his upper arm.

"Don't be silly, Mick," she told him. "I'll think of something. Do you think he can hear me up there?"

"Probably best if he can't," he said, watching the backs of the retreating, grumbling kids, strolling slowly and reluctantly in to their lessons.

"He must have gone up the scaffolding at the back," he told her. "I know they were doing some work on the boiler and central heating ducts recently. But he can't be safe, or comfortable, up there." He was squinting anxiously up towards the lonely silent figure on the roof. Glancing back behind them, Mick suddenly uttered a quiet "Oh no – here he comes."

"Shoot… The Head?" asked Miss Dorwood nervously.

"Worse. Look," said Mick.

Steaming across the lawn towards them, little bandy legs going ten to the dozen, was the caretaker, his moustache bristling indignantly in his haste.

"Oh oh," sighed Miss Dorwood. Really. As if she didn't have enough problems already. Mick from Maths decided that this was the right point to disappear.

"I'm off," he told Miss Dorwood before she could beg him to stay. She looked imploringly at him, mouthing "Nooo… don't leave me…"

"Got a class." He walked away, smirking to himself.

Mr Pettigrew, the caretaker, was beside himself with rage and almost incandescent in his anger. Miss Dorwood tried to pre-empt his bluster by smiling calmly at him and trying desperately to appear as if she knew what she was doing. She didn't, obviously. Hadn't a clue how to sort this situation out. But Mr Pettigrew wasn't to know that. Oh no. He'd hound her for half a term, daily giving her his opinion on how he would have never allowed the situation to arise in the first place. After all, it was *his* school. *He* was in charge here!

These teachers knew nothing about how this building ticked. Ha, they thought it all happened by some sort of magic. They thought fairies came in at night when they were all watching Emmerdale and got everything ready for the next day. And as for the bloody kids. Well, if it were up to *him* they'd show a bit more respect. Yobs and hooligans. Mr Pettigrew knew they weren't wired up properly but that could be sorted out. Get the little buggers into the Army. It didn't do *him* any harm. In fact, it had made a man of him, so he happily berated anyone who stepped onto his lawn, dropped a crisp packet or tried to sit on a wall, bellowing at them in proper sergeant-major style. He knew the kids had a cruel nickname for him, Mr Pottygrow, but by God he was proud of that allotment. Where did they think the runner beans came from in their school lunches, eh? And he'd heard worse, but he could give as good as he got.

"Who told him he could go up there?" he demanded of Miss Dorwood, pointing a finger aggressively towards the figure up on the roof.

The teacher sighed. "No one did, obviously, Mr Potty... er... Pettigrew. He took himself up there and I'm really worried. This is so dangerous..." she told the caretaker.

"Aye, you're right there, pet. Anything could happen. He could break that new skylight. Or damage one of them new heating units. And if he's scraped the paint off the new guttering there'll be hell to pay."

"I meant it is dangerous for the boy!" Miss Dorwood told the caretaker, exasperated at his bullying response to this awkward situation. "He could fall and hurt himself."

"Well, the daft little sod shouldn't have gone up there in the first place. What the hell's he playing at? Shouldn't he be in class, causing trouble somewhere?"

Miss Dorwood started walking away from the older man. She held her hands clenched in fists at her sides, worried she would hit him if she had to stand there a minute longer.

"And where do you think you're off to?" demanded Mr Pettigrew with his hands on his hips. The teacher stopped in her tracks and turned to face him.

"I'm going to get him down. It's Billy Higson," she explained to him, as if the name itself would help ease the situation.

"What? That dopey little kid who's terrified of everything? Well, he's obviously not scared of heights, then. And no," he told her firmly, "you're going nowhere, Miss."

The teacher had the distinct impression that he wasn't calling her Miss due to respect for her title or professionalism... The caretaker was being his usual unhelpful, uncaring self: demanding, demeaning and bossy.

Miss Dorwood turned to face him, her eyes and cheeks burning with embarrassment and anger. "Excuse me? That boy is in my care and if I want to go up there to help him, I will!"

The caretaker pulled himself up to his full five feet four inches and puffed out his chest. "No, you won't," he said. "You're not in the Union."

"What?" demanded Miss Dorwood in disbelief.

"You're not insured. And I'd lose my job if you went up there – without an 'ard 'at as well."

"Then get me a flaming hat, before half the school gets out here!" she demanded. She didn't like this guy at the best of times, and with Billy up there for nearly ten minutes already, her patience was wearing thin.

"What seems to be the problem out here?" a calm voice of reason asked.

Miss Dorwood and the caretaker both turned to look. *Great*, she thought, *the Deputy Head. Someone on my side to help.*

Miss Barrett. Elegant, detached and always in supreme control of any situation – partly due to the fact that she didn't actually teach any classes anymore. Miss Dorwood was starting to feel the relief at being able to hand this serious situation over to someone who was paid an awful lot more money than she was. She felt the tension ease a little.

"It's Billy Higson, Miss Barrett," she told her. "I don't know how or why he's up there, but if you can get him down I'll take over and have a chat with him. I can calm him down and get him back in lessons."

"Me?" the Deputy asked her, raising an eyebrow quizzically. "Oh no, he's all yours. We're in the middle of interviews and in ten minutes the candidates will be touring the school. You've got that long to get that boy off the roof before the Police arrive. Or worse, the newspapers."

"See, you should have let me buy that water cannon off the TA last term, when they had one going cheap. That would bring the bugger down." The caretaker was still staring up at the boy on the roof. "But *this one* wants to go up for him." He indicated with his thumb to Miss Dorwood for the benefit of Miss Barrett.

"I don't really care who goes up for him, but I want him gone off there before I start walking these Science candidates round with the Head," said Miss Barrett before briskly walking off, shaking her head.

"Well, thanks for nothing," muttered Miss Dorwood, turning towards the caretaker. And great, here were Sam and Jack, two year eight jokers who should also be in lessons. Jack stopped confidently in front of the two adults.

"Miss Dorwood," he began, "would you like me and Sam to go up there and drag him down? We're only missing English, Miss. We can do it," he continued, gazing up at the roof with quiet confidence and casting a critical eye at the brick work.

"Boys," she sighed, "that's really very kind of you, but I can't put two more pupils in danger."

"And you 'aven't got an 'ard 'at either, 'ave yer?" demanded the caretaker.

"Actually I have," Sam told him. "My dad got me one for my birthday. It's for when we go rock climbing."

"Ah, but where is it?" asked the caretaker smugly, rocking backwards and forwards on his feet. "It's not here in school, is it?"

"The Drama department's got one in the props box, though," Jack replied with just the same smugness.

"And there's a Policeman's helmet in there as well. That's a hard hat," Sam added, holding one finger up to make his point.

"I'm not having a couple of numpties running around my school roof, wearing a Bob the Builder hat and a Policeman's helmet, man!" The caretaker shook his head in disbelief. "I tell you, this job gets dafter by the minute."

The boys weren't to be beaten on a minor point of order, however.

"Ah, but... *you* said we could go up there if we had a hard hat on and..."

"No, what I said was you *couldn't* go up there *unless* you had a 'ard 'at on..."

"I'm sure there's a cowboy hat as well, would that do?" Sam was enjoying himself just a little too much.

The three of them squared up, arguing their case loudly, nobody listening to anyone else. In the confusion, Miss Dorwood slipped silently away.

Chapter 3

With her shaking hands becoming more slippery by the minute as her fear mounted, Miss Dorwood edged closer towards the crouching figure on the roof. There was a hand rail, of sorts, provided for the safety of any roof or heating technicians who had to access the various flues and tiles on the roof. She paused for a minute, trying to calm her ragged breathing. Wiping her sweaty hands on her trousers – thank God, she hadn't gone for the patterned summer dress this morning – she stopped to listen. Under the calls and laughing cries of the seagulls, she could hear a quiet voice muttering and mumbling. She couldn't make out what was being said but she knew it was Billy. She'd heard him do this before when he was stressed and she had never been able to make sense of it. Stepping further onto the flatter section of the roof, and trying to keep her eyes on the sea in the near distance, rather than the ground dizzying below, she called softly to the boy.

"Billy."

No answer; no change in the muttering.

"Billy, it's me, Miss Dorwood. Are you OK?"

Get a grip, woman, she told herself. *Of course he's not OK. Why would he be up on the school roof in the middle of the morning, if he was OK?* There was, however, a short pause in his mumblings. She edged closer to him. The boy was sitting with his legs astride a silver pipe which stuck out of the roof. He was hugging it and had his face pressed into its smooth surface, his arms reaching round it in a tight grip. Miss Dorwood thought she heard him mutter, "One hundred, fifty-three, seventy, eighteen."

"Hey, Billy," she began again, this time a bit louder, "do you mind if I come over there to join you? The sun's in my eyes here and I'm getting a bit blinded." The boy looked up at her, shading his eyes with one hand. "And wobbly," she added.

After a brief pause, Billy nodded, but again he began that curious mumbling. "One hundred, fifty-three, seventy, eighteen."

Miss Dorwood carefully weaved her way from the slightly raised section she was on, towards the flatter part of the roof where Billy was sitting. She felt slightly safer and a little relieved to be closer to the boy. Carefully sliding down beside him in a sitting position and trying to control her shaky breathing, she finally allowed herself to gaze around the town unfolding beneath them. The weather was glorious, and calm. *Thank God, it wasn't wet or windy today*, she thought. The sea sparkled with diamonds of light on the horizon, endlessly blue; to the north, she could see a white passenger liner waiting patiently for the tide to turn so it could sail into the Tynemouth harbour; to the south, she could see the smoking chimneys of the works in Middlesbrough, whilst all around her the parks and city gardens of Sunderland spread a beautiful canopy of jade, agate and emerald. It was actually quite breath-taking – a view of her city she had never seen before.

"Wow. Billy, it's just…" she breathed, but the boy seemed to ignore her, continuing with his strange litany.

"One hundred, fifty-three, seventy, eighteen."

Miss Dorwood put an arm around Billy's thin shoulder. He was such a nice kid with such a hard life, and she felt absurdly protective of him.

"You know, Billy, I can think of better places to do your Maths homework," she told him with a gentle, reassuring squeeze. The boy stopped mumbling and finally turned his face from the silver pipe to look at her, his large grey eyes asking a silent question.

"What happened, Billy? Why are you up here? Can you tell me?"

The mumbling got a bit faster and more incoherent.

"Onehundredfiftythree…"

"It's OK. You don't have to tell me just yet. Only, you and me, we've got to get down off here pretty soon before potty old Pettigrew appears beside us, probably dangling from a helicopter with a large grappling iron in his hand."

Billy took his gaze from her then, down towards the gardens, and actually smiled. It was a soft, sad little smile and it almost broke his teacher's heart.

Miss Dorwood went on before the mood was lost. "And, Billy, you see that seagull over there, the huge one? Well, I'm just a tiny bit terrified of it and I'd be really grateful if you'd help me get past it. Please?"

Right on cue, the seagull started up its raucous calling, bobbing up and down as it padded closer towards them on its flappy yellow feet.

"It's calling to its mates, Miss. It probably isn't very happy about us being up here in its territory," Billy told her, fairly matter-of-factly.

"It's flamin' laughing at us, Billy! Do you think we should move?" Slowly, Billy stood up. Miss Dorwood also stood up, but wobbled in a quite dramatic way. She grabbed onto the silver pipe, her eyes wide in surprise and shock. Billy reached forward and took hold of her hand.

"It's OK, Miss. You just follow me. I'll keep you right. All the way down." He started to lead her towards the back of the roof, towards the scaffolding. Now he could feel how terrified his teacher was. She was shaking like a leaf in the wind.

"You just keep saying the numbers, Miss. It helps, you know."

They had reached the edge of the roof and Billy was calmly climbing over onto the scaffolding board. Miss Dorwood froze. She couldn't do this. The football pitch and carefully manicured school lawns shimmered and moved dizzyingly beneath them. She felt sick to her stomach.

"That's right. Just repeat after me. One hundred, fifty-three, seventy, eighteen…"

The teacher closed her eyes for a second and started counting. Her voice wobbled as much as her legs, but she had to concentrate on the strange sequence of numbers.

"One hundred, fifty-three, seventy, eighteen…"

And the boy was right. It helped Miss Dorwood keep her mind occupied and her feet steady right until she got her last foot onto the ground. Somewhere, far behind them, the school erupted in a chorus of cheers and whistling. Miss Dorwood hugged Billy Higson and promptly burst into tears.

Chapter 4

Billy had gone quiet again now that he was back in the familiar Head of Year's office. Even the cheers and wolf whistles of the watching pupils, as he had walked with Miss Dorwood back across the yard, didn't seem to have penetrated his mind. He was dulled and introverted once again. *Just when I thought we were getting somewhere*, thought his teacher. She sat the boy down and switched on the kettle.

"Think we need a cuppa after that, don't you agree, Billy?"

She glanced across at the boy, huddled into the large chair as though he wished it would swallow him up. He nodded in a distracted way.

"I'd really rather have a large brandy, but I don't think Mr Blythe would agree with me on that, eh?"

Nothing from Billy. Two cups of strong sweet tea were made and placed on the table in front of the boy.

"Hobnob, Billy?"

Nothing.

"Go on, they're chocolate ones. Oats. One of your five a day. Treat yourself."

Billy slowly reached for a biscuit. *More to be polite and not offend his teacher than anything else*, she suspected. She sat down at the low table between them and studied Billy in a kind way. He was pale faced, whereas the other pupils by this point in the summer term had lost their zombie-like complexions and were beginning to look healthy and more alert. There was still dust in his hair and his face was streaked with sweat and grimy tears. He looked hot and distant, his eyes guarded. A clump of his hair was missing, as if it had been torn out. It was just behind his ear and the teacher was trying to remember if it had looked like that the last time she had spoken to him. He looked thin and uncared for. He seemed smaller than most of the other pupils in her year.

Miss Dorwood got up and found a pack of baby wipes.

"Here, Billy, wipe your face and hands with these. They'll make you feel better…" She paused, realising just how ridiculous that statement sounded in the face of what this boy had just been through. Regaining her composure, as Billy reached for a wipe and cleared his face and eyes with it, she asked, "Can you tell me what happened, Billy?"

Billy paused in the act, before continuing to hide behind the cool wipe.

"Do you know who shut you in the trap door on the stage?"

Behind the wipe, Billy started counting again.

"One hundred, fifty-three…"

"Please, Billy. I need to know who they were. I need to know their intentions. Were they trying to hurt you?"

Billy was rocking forward now, holding the baby wipe to his mouth. The teacher waited patiently.

"I want to make sure they don't do that again, Billy. To you, or any other child. Can you tell me?"

Billy slowly took the grimy wipe away from his face and folded it into as many pieces as he could. He kept his head down and his eyes averted. Miss Dorwood could see the cogs turning, weighing up whether to tell her anything about his ordeal.

"They were older boys, Miss. I don't know their names," he mumbled, his shoulders dropping as he sighed sadly.

"Could you tell me what they looked like at least, Billy?"

"One was blond and the other was Asian, and that's all I know. They tried to kill me. They were laughing, Miss."

Miss Dorwood sat back. How could she set his mind at rest? She was sure it was a stupid prank that had got well out of hand. Another pupil would have come bursting out of the trapdoor on the stage scaring half the school, or they would have been angry as hell, wanting to kick somebody's head in. But not poor little Billy Higson. He was simply too damaged to cope with daft schoolboy tricks. He nibbled at his biscuit like a mouse as the teacher watched, trying to break through the barrier that, as usual, had fallen between them.

Miss Dorwood changed tack.

"You missed meeting your new social worker, Billy. He seems…" She struggled here. How could she present the reptilian Mr Costello in an appealing way to this sad little boy? As if his life wasn't difficult enough. "He's… OK, Billy. Although, not as good as Pamela," she told him truthfully. "I know she had to go back to Australia, but she will be back to take on your case just as soon as she can."

Billy simply shrugged into his Hobnob: as if *he* cared what went on in his life or who tried to help him. He'd given up years ago.

The teacher went on, talking in a calm, soothing way. She knew that Billy hated raised voices, shouting and confusion. She had worked with Billy since he started at Kingswood as a damaged and depressed eleven-year-old. Of all the staff willing to give him some time and attention, she was really the only one who could raise even a glimmer of a smile. But that never lasted long. Billy's smile, when it happened, was sweet and sunny, yet fading quickly as dark storm clouds soon raced in.

"We'll set up another meeting very soon, Billy, but I do know that they've found you somewhere to stay while your mam goes in for her operation. And for while she's away recuperating."

Billy's head came up then, his grey eyes sharply focused, for once. "I want to stay in my flat, Miss. I don't want to go to stay with anyone else. I'm…" He paused. "I'm … safe in my flat, Miss."

Miss Dorwood shook her head. She had anticipated this response from Billy. *He's going to* hate *this*, she thought, *but he has to do it. There's no other option open to him.*

"Billy, you know you can't. The flat isn't suitable for your mam to return to for a while, all the way up those stairs. And you're too young to be home alone. You couldn't cope." She watched as his face fell, his head lowered, and he stopped nibbling on his biscuit.

"Look, Billy, it's only for a little while, and I know the house isn't very far away. It's quite local, so you wouldn't feel completely…" She was going to say 'abandoned', but quickly changed her mind. *Too close to the truth*, she thought. Billy wasn't an abandoned child, he had his mam, but she wasn't a well woman, and the way Billy denied everyone any access into his private life or his innermost thoughts, he did seem to be completely alone in the world. Not for him, the mad social whirl of *Facebook*, texting, meetings at *McDonald's*, scrapping in the playground and matey joshing about at home time. Billy moved through the world surrounded by a dark, impenetrable fog of his own making. No one was allowed to get close to him.

"Look, Billy, I bet that when you return to school after the summer holidays, you'll be like a different person. I think this change will do you a lot of good. Honestly. Your mam will be better and you will have tried new things and made new friends. Then you'll come back here," she told him brightly, her voice rising in happy anticipation.

In his chair, in front of her, even the top of Billy's head looked depressed. He had slumped so far forward in his seat that it was all she could see of the boy now. As the familiar number chanting started up again, very quietly, Miss Dorwood sat back and sighed deeply.

Chapter 5

Paul Costello's car was as lumpy, bumpy and scruffy as he was. He sat hunched behind the wheel, spilling over the sides of his seat. *Like a big bag of dirty washing*, Billy thought. Large, pale, sweaty hands gripped the wheel and occasionally he flicked back a lock of floppy grey hair. The car smelled of digestive biscuits and wet dog. There were empty crisp packets, some sandwich wrappers and, for some reason, one of those ridiculous flat pink bags which made a farting noise when you sat on it. Glancing around the car and over his shoulder from his front passenger seat, Billy had a vague memory of somebody he knew using one of those things for a laugh. He blocked out Paul's attempt at friendly chatter and tried to picture who it could have been. Certainly not his mam – she was too much of a lady to go in for a trick like that. Uncle Rob, perhaps? Maybe. He had been daft enough, in his day, but Billy and his mam hadn't seen Rob for years. Couldn't have been one of his neighbours. They rarely saw them.

Billy knew he was desperately trying to block out any recognition of why he was in Paul Costello's scruffy car, and where he was actually going. He tried to concentrate on the scenery, but after another sunny day a thick damp fog had descended and he could just about make out the halo-ed street lights a hundred metres away. The whole city seemed shrouded and muffled.

Not many cars were out and about. They were late anyway because Billy hadn't been able to tear himself away from his mam. He had tried desperately not to cry. He knew this separation wasn't for ever; he knew she was having her operation later this week; he knew he could go and see her in hospital; and when she had recovered, he knew that his safe, cosy life with just the two of them on the 17th floor of the city centre flats would be over. For ever.

"So, what do you reckon, Billy?" asked Paul, hunching forward over the wheel to see better through the fog. "Would the black Elvis suit, or the white one, be better for me? Eh?" Paul glanced down at the huddled figure beside him. Billy was fiddling with his fingers as usual, and had that pale, pensive expression on his face, despite Paul's attempts to engage the lad in conversation and cheer him up. On his lap, the lad had a battered and tattered sketch book. Paul watched as Billy constantly moved his hands over and around it, feeling for it constantly, whilst not really looking at it or taking it in. He knew this sketch book was rarely far away from Billy.

He was difficult, this one. Paul Costello prided himself on getting kids onside pretty quickly in their new relationship with him, but Billy Higson was a real challenge. All right, they'd met only three times, and the first one, after the incident on the school roof, had been pretty harrowing. But this little guy was going to be a tough nut to crack. Paul had years of experience with these kids. Usually, after a couple of weeks of his jokes and gags, he'd manage to make a little bit of headway. And OK, they had all been Newcastle kids, but really, being in Sunderland shouldn't make it any harder, should it? He'd tried all the usual tactics on Billy: the standard Geordie versus Mackems banter – nothing; his Elvis impersonations – nothing; his Donald Duck ordering a meal in KFC trick – still nothing. This lad was scared of his own shadow.

Paul patted his pocket, double checking he had all the documentation he needed to hand over to the foster carers who were taking Billy on for the summer. Not that it felt like summer, he conceded. This weather was weird and depressing, and Paul could understand how it made the lad feel even more lonely and isolated. Even this road he was on was lonely and isolated in this flaming weather, too. He had wanted to pull up to the house on a bright summer's night to drop Billy off. Maybe show him around a bit and settle him in before he headed back home. But this rotten weather was quite disorientating. If it brought *him* down, imagine how Billy must have been feeling.

Paul had hated dragging the lad away from his mam. Both mam and son had been tearful, clinging tightly on to each other, but somehow he'd got Billy down in the lift and out to his car. *It's a shame*, he thought, *I bet the views from that flat are amazing. Couldn't see a thing from up there tonight, though. Not from down here, either.*

"Where are we?" Billy asked, completely ignoring Paul's question about the Elvis suit.

"Just heading west, Billy, out of Sunderland. But it's not too far."

It could be Outer Mongolia, as far as Billy was concerned. He was leaving his beloved city centre flat, with its spectacular views, the peace of living almost in the clouds, away from prying eyes, noise and confusion. No one bothered them up there. Even the birds didn't usually fly as high as the living room window. At night, the city centre and its nightlife lit up underneath them, but Billy and his mam couldn't hear a thing. They both loved it. Billy was safe in the flat and wanted to live there for ever. He knew that it wasn't really suitable for his mam, though. She had a really bad back and had to have a big operation. She had struggled for years, her once pretty face becoming hard and lined with the imprint of permanent pain etched onto her skin. Billy helped where he could, carrying shopping for her and putting things away, but lately she had got so much worse. If the lift went out of order, which it sometimes did, Mam was trapped, often for days. The doctor didn't like to make a house call to the flats and their front door was rarely knocked on. That's just how Billy liked it, though. It was his cocoon, his refuge from a big scary world. That world was out there, seventeen floors below, and he had to go out for school or to the shops, but once he was behind that front door B, he heaved a huge sigh of relief and relaxed a little. Still, the suffocating bad dreams would come and get him, but mostly when he was outside. Or asleep.

Paul Costello's car made a right turn at a huge roundabout and they started to drop down a hill. Billy couldn't see any houses, but then, he couldn't really see anything at all. The world outside had gone, he thought to himself. If only that were the case. If only he could jump out of this car and roll all the way down the hill and get away from this stupid fat man. He bet he could find his way home, back to his mam and his beautiful home in the clouds. Safety on the seventeenth floor.

"Nearly there, I think, Billy. Should be just down here and on the right somewhere."

Paul was slowing the car as he peered out into the fog, looking for street signs or recognisable features like a pub or a church. Billy put his hand onto the door handle. *This is my chance*, he thought. *I could jump out now. I could.* His knees started to shake and his breathing grew faster and shallower as he imagined falling out of the car and rolling away under some bushes. It would hurt, and he might get injured, but it would be worth it. The thought of the pain brought him up short. *So what*, Billy thought. *I've suffered worse than falling out of a moving car.* His fingers gripped the handle, feeling it give a fraction of an inch. Billy held his breath as the car gathered pace, going down the hill in twists and turns.

At that moment Paul reached out and patted him on the knee.

"I know you're worried, son, but honestly, these are good people and they are really looking forward to having you. It's only for a while, too," he told Billy in a kind voice. And the moment was lost. Billy took his hand off the door handle and dropped it on his lap again. He shook his head sadly – he wouldn't have done it anyway. He was too scared. Nothing new there.

The car drew to a halt and Paul turned off the engine. For a moment, he and the boy sat in silence, listening to the quiet tick as the engine settled and cooled. They had stopped under a street lamp and in the dense fog it threw off an alien, green-tinged halo. Billy could just make out trees dripping heavily and silently around them. He was aware of Paul's eyes glancing in his direction. The man suddenly started rubbing his hands together as if he was cold, or very nervous, then he turned to Billy.

"Right, come on then, Billy. It's going to be fine, you know. We can't sit here all night. They'll be wondering where we are. And we're already a bit late. Out you get."

The car seat groaned as Mr Costello creaked his way out of the driver's door. Inwardly, Billy groaned, too. He hated leaving the relative safety of the smelly little car. At least in there he felt he still had some hold on his life. He knew that, as soon as his foot hit the pavement, his old life would be gone for good. He was terrified – of what this new house meant for him in the future, not just right now. Where would he end up? How was his mam feeling right now? How would they both cope? Billy felt tears start to well up in his eyes and throat. This was not what he wanted, but he had no control over his life. He was twelve years old. He was being held hostage. He hung back, scuffing his feet, head down, as the hot traitorous tears began to fall. Paul Costello stopped when he heard the now familiar quiet number mumbling. Coming back to the front of the car from where he had been taking Billy's bags out of the boot, he paused beside the boy.

"Let's just take a minute, shall we?" he asked kindly, placing one meaty hand gently on Billy's shoulder. Paul stood quietly beside the boy. He understood how he might be feeling. Being dragged away from the safety of your home and family and dumped in a totally strange environment wasn't an easy thing to handle at any age, but when you were a strange, almost silent little lad like Billy, well…

Mr Costello decided to lighten the mood a little in an effort to distract the boy and give him time to dry up his tears.

"I used to come here years ago, when I was a little lad, Billy. Bet it hasn't changed that much. It's a pity we can't see where we are in this flaming fog, but it's a pretty enough spot, I can tell you." Paul Costello put his head back and inhaled deeply, like a bull sniffing the air for a matador. Billy lifted his head to watch him, a puzzled expression on his face.

"Ahhh, smell that, Billy. By, that takes me back."

Billy tentatively sniffed. The air just smelled of wet leaves, grass and coldness. Around him everything dripped, the trees, the fence post next to the road, and the air was still strangely muffled and silent in the dense fog.

"My dad used to bring me and my brother down here, blackberrying, you know, Billy? We used to eat more than we ever took home, though. We'd end up filthy, scratched and happy. Then he used to bugger off into the pub and leave us outside with a packet of crisps and a lemonade. I remember it was always safe, and we had many a happy day down here. I loved it. Always wanted to come back, and here I am, all these years later, and I can't see a flamin' thing. Ee, well. That's life I suppose."

Paul Costello picked up Billy's suitcase, checked he had the folder of paperwork and looked down at Billy, who was at least looking up at him and had stopped that crazy mumbling he often did.

"Come on then, sunshine, follow me. We'll go in the back door cos it's just here." Once again, he put a protective hand on Billy's shoulder. *To guide the lad,* he told himself. *Or to stop him from running off into this fog,* a voice in his head stated. Together they stepped away from the car and approached the house.

Chapter 6

Billy stared ahead at the looming door. From what he could tell they were approaching a house in the middle of a small terrace. It had a long, thin garden with a shed in it. Looking up, Billy glanced at the house, taking it all in. The windows were new, the place seemed tidy and smart, and from what he could see, the garden was filled with flowers. There was a bike leaning against the gate, a wall separating this garden from the next, and lots of trees. Beyond them, he could see nothing in the gloom. Billy got the impression there was another row of houses some way ahead of them, but he was only going on the distant subdued glow of more street lights.

There wasn't a single sound. No birds, no cars, no planes. And that was fine by him – Billy was used to being seventeen floors up, where noise and neighbours were rarely an issue. Quiet was good.

Paul Costello knocked on the white double-glazed door. He smiled down at Billy. "Okay, son?"

Before Billy could answer, the door opened and a friendly face greeted them. A lady of about the same age as his mam stood back with a cheery smile and opened the door wider to let them in. Billy felt himself being gently steered into the kitchen and found himself momentarily dazzled by the whiteness inside after the gloomy night outside. The first thing he noticed was that this house smelled completely different from his own. Not unpleasant – a sort of clean washing smell with a hint of lemon and something very fresh in there as well. The kitchen was spotless, all white and gleaming, with flowers on a table and a kettle boiling away. In one corner, a washing machine swished quietly and rhythmically.

The lady and Paul greeted each other like old friends, Billy noticed, shyly glancing up from under his fringe: shaking hands and exchanging warm pleasantries.

"So, this is Billy," began the lady. He noticed she had short, fluffy black hair and startling blue eyes. She was slim, dressed in jeans and a plain T-shirt.

Her face was tanned and her eyes sparkled with interest and what seemed to be genuine affection.

"I'm so glad you found us all right. I've been so excited about you coming to stay for a while, Billy. It'll be lovely to have another man about the house. Someone I can have a normal conversation with which does not involve car parts or football," she told Billy warmly.

"Billy, this is Sue Render, and she'll be looking after your every need for the time you're with her."

Billy liked the sound of Sue's voice. She had a soft local accent, which he found reassuring. It made this house seem less of a threat to him, somehow. His attention was drawn to her earrings, as Sue sat at the table and took all the paperwork off Paul. Billy found himself fascinated by them. He actually moved a little closer to Sue to get a better look. As she chattered away happily, whilst talking to Paul, Billy turned his head questioningly to see the other earring. Sure enough, when she swung her head towards him with a smile, Billy noticed that her earrings were shaped like little artists' pallets, complete with blobs of coloured paint and tiny paintbrushes. He was enthralled. Then he noticed that the tips of her very dark hair were spiked blue. He tried not to gawp, but he'd never seen anyone so individual in his whole life. And here she was, chattering away to him quite normally. He almost forgot to be afraid.

Out of the corner of his eye he thought he saw Paul and Sue exchange a small secret smile, but he didn't know what that was all about.

Sue got up from the table and put the teacups into the sink. She paused beside Billy and dropped her eyes from his face to his lap where his sketchpad lay.

"Aha, what have we here, Billy?" she asked, raising an eyebrow and looking at it keenly. "That looks interesting, and very well loved, I would say."

Billy ducked his head down, awkwardly folding and feeling the tattered edges of his sketchpad.

Paul Costello smiled at him encouragingly.

"Go on, Billy, show Sue. She's an artist as well, you know."

When Billy made no response, Sue told him, "Well, when I get time I like to sketch, but it doesn't happen very often, and I bet you're better than me. Come on, round here, Billy, and tell me what you think."

Billy got up reluctantly and followed Sue to a short corridor, just off the main kitchen. He felt clumsy and lumpy in this immaculate little house. Lined along the walls were a number of paintings and drawings, all framed in a variety of colours and styles. And every last one of them was… well, wonderful. Billy was drawn to the wall, taking in the scenes before him: a boat, a waterfall, trees, a big old guy mending a net, a cat on a garden wall, and every one of them had been created with such skill, attention to detail and obvious love. Billy stared at each in turn, admiring the details, the fine lines, the perspective in each image, before he came to the last scene at the far end of the row. Sue stood back quietly, allowing him the time to look closely, watching his face come to life, and a tiny smile form on his lips. As Billy reached the end of the line, she became a little concerned as he drew in a sharp breath when he saw the final picture. She leaned forward to read his expression more closely. Billy's eyes were wide, his mouth forming a silent 'o' shape, and he had become completely still. He appeared to have almost stopped breathing.

"So, what do you think, Billy?" she asked him, concerned now and glancing over her shoulder into the kitchen at Paul. The case worker just nodded and smiled back encouragingly.

"Any good? I don't know if they're as good as yours, though. Maybe you'll let me see them, eventually, when you've settled in and found your feet?"

Billy looked her straight in the face, his large grey eyes wide.

"They're amazing!" He breathed quietly. "I love them. Who did them? You?" he asked in awe.

"Yes, me, Billy. But I don't have a lot of time lately. Maybe now that you're here, we can sit together and get really stuck in. What do you think?"

She watched as the boy reached up and traced one finger very carefully over the lines of the last picture. He turned to Sue and very quietly breathed. "The Monument." It was said almost silently, reverently. He seemed to be miles away for a second, lost in thought. Sue felt, rather than saw, a cloud cross his eyes, but Billy actually smiled at her then, a proper warm smile, straight from his heart and up into his eyes which glittered with light. Sue found herself unaccountably swallowing back a big lump which had formed in her throat. She felt the two of them had made a small connection here, in front of her work on the wall.

"Yes, the famous Penshaw Monument, Billy. It's a great subject, much easier to draw than that cat," she told him, pointing to another small sketch. "He never sits still for long enough, but the Monument… well, it's one of my favourite spots around here, anyway."

Billy watched her face closely, his eyes on her mouth as she explained about the picture.

"It's round here?" he asked her in a small voice.

"Oh yes, you can almost touch it from here," she said, smiling warmly down at him. *Funny little lad*, she thought.

Behind them, Paul Costello scraped back his chair and began gathering his jacket to leave.

"I think you're going to be just fine here, Billy," he told him, shrugging into a sleeve with a smile. "You've got my number and I'll be coming for you a bit later this week to take you to see your mam, after she's had her operation. In the meantime, you get yourself settled in and try not to worry about a thing."

Sue joined him at the back door, leaving Billy with the pictures on the wall. Glancing back at the boy she told Paul, "He'll be fine. He seems like a troubled little soul, but at least he's safe here with us. We'll take good care of him. Thanks, Paul. See you in a few days, then."

"Aye, you're just the person to bring him on a bit, Sue. Thanks a lot. Shame about this mad weather, eh? I can't wait to see his face when he sees it all in daylight. Ta-ra, then." And he stepped out of the brightness into the gloom of the dripping fog.

Chapter 7

Billy woke next morning fairly early. At first, when he struggled to open his eyes, it seemed as though he was still asleep. Huh? This wasn't his bed. The window was in the wrong place, that wasn't his clock, and there were *sounds* going on which he didn't recognise. He could hear a bird singing somewhere nearby. Not the raucous seagulls he was used to, but a proper bird. Then the seagull sounds started, and his rising panic settled a little. Now he remembered. He wasn't in his flat in the clouds; he was at Sue's house, quite a way from his home. He had fallen into bed after a quick visit to the immaculate and modern bathroom, stashed his things on a dressing table near his bed, and fallen instantly and soundly asleep. Now he needed that bathroom again, and fairly quickly. He stretched his eyes wide and wondered if he could find it. What if he went into another bedroom by mistake? The worry caused more pain in his stomach and he wriggled about in the bed. What if he got to the bathroom no problem, and *someone else* was in there. *A stranger.* Billy had a thing about only using toilets he knew and toilets who knew him. Would he have to cough, or whistle or something, on the landing, just to warn everyone else in the house that he was up. He lay for another minute, ears straining, listening for any signs of life from within the house. Nothing. His room was fairly dark because there was a heavy curtain over the large window, but his door was open just enough for it to be sufficiently light to find his way. Another sharp pain propelled Billy from his bed and out onto the landing.

He paused for a second or two. It was lighter out here because there was a small window at the end, looking out over the back garden. The bathroom was next to that window and, joy of joys, the door was open. No light on. It was free. Billy shot along the passage, glancing out into the sunny garden as he ran. He dived into the bathroom and started to pee, sighing with relief and looking all around himself as he did. It was a lovely room. It smelled of perfume and flowery talcum powder. Large buff coloured tiles, with the occasional picture on them of boats, rivers and willow trees. The shower screen over the bath was gleaming glass, patterned very subtly with gold markings. Billy was impressed. The sink, bath and toilet were large and square and clean enough to eat your dinner off. *Yuk*, he thought to himself. Who would? Stupid idea. He thought of his own bathroom at home. It was smaller than this and didn't have a window, so it was always a bit stuffy and airless. It was white as well, but it didn't shine like this one did. In the corner of the bathroom, there was usually a pile of Billy and Mam's dirty clothes, waiting for the laundry fairy to load the machine, as Mam would say. It rarely did. His towels were rough and old, but as Billy flushed the toilet, he noticed that the towels in Sue's bathroom were huge, soft and fluffy. Above the sink, there was a clear glass shelf with a range of toiletries, lotions and potions in soft pastel colours, all in a neat line of little pink bottles. Nice. At home, his mam had a bar of yellow soap and a ratty old facecloth.

He reached up and opened the window at the top because now this gorgeous room smelled of pee and unwashed smelly teenager. Billy hovered, uncertain. Should he just have a quick wash, now that he was in here, or should he get into that inviting shower? But then, if he did, this gorgeous bathroom would be trashed. His mam always complained whenever Billy had a bath that it looked as though a whole regiment had been in there with him. He couldn't do that to Sue's bathroom. And what about towels? He remembered that Sue had put one in his bedroom for him, but he knew if he left this bathroom now he'd struggle to go back in it again. Oh dear, life could be so complicated.

Outside, in the garden, he could hear Sue's voice. She was chatting away to someone out there, telling them that it was going to be a gorgeous day. Billy put the seat down on the toilet and climbed up onto it so he could hear and maybe see a little better. The lid was cool under his bare feet, but he was able to peer out of the top. Still couldn't see Sue, though, just the tops of the trees and a cloudless sky. Now she was asking this other person if they'd had their breakfast. Billy smiled. Sue sounded so lovely. She was caring and cheerful.

In the next sentence, however, he heard her tell this other person off and ask if they had left a dead mouse near her gate. What? What sort of person would do that? Sue was saying it had been the third one that week, and she was getting sick of it. She was demanding to know whether this character would object, if she came and poured her breakfast all over *their* gate. Porridge could be hell to get off once it hardened, you know. Billy got down off the toilet, amazed by what he had heard. What sort of weirdos lived round here, anyway?

Shaking his head, Billy didn't really look where he put his feet. He lurched sideways off the toilet, slipped, then grabbed out at the wall to stop himself from falling to the floor completely. There was a loud crash and a smash. Billy landed in a heap, unhurt, his face blazing with fear and shame, as he saw the broken glass on the floor and in the sink, pink goo oozing out everywhere.

Oh no. How could that have happened? He scrambled forward, grabbing at the shattered glass with his bare hands. He unrolled most of the soft loo roll, trying to soak it up with clumps of it, but the goo was too thick. It just spread it further around the bathroom floor. Billy was frantic. He knew he was holding his breath because he soon began to feel dizzy. *Would Sue chuck him out for this, after only one night,* he asked himself. Her beautiful bathroom: look at it!

He picked up a facecloth and tried to clean the floor with that. It was a bit better, not perfect. He started his number mumbling as he tried to clean up, grabbing a fluffy white towel to remove the final streaks. Downstairs, he heard the door open and shut, and someone, probably Sue, started to come into the kitchen. *Quick, get it sorted, you idiot,* he told himself. Then he noticed the towel. It was covered in blood. Billy dropped it on the floor, among the wads of used toilet roll, and the limp facecloth, and stared at his hands. He was bleeding, and now there was blood everywhere, as well as the pink goo. He sat back on his heels and allowed the tears to fall.

Out on the landing, at the top of the stairs, Sue was gently tapping on Billy's bedroom door. Having noticed it was open, she checked quickly, then headed for the bathroom. She stood outside for a second, listening to the strange mumbling going on in there. *Was he okay,* she wondered.

"Billy?"

No answer, although the mumbling stopped. Strange, it sounded like he was repeating numbers.

"Billy, are you alright in there? I'm making breakfast and the kettle's on."

Sue listened carefully. The door was slightly open and she thought she could hear Billy crying. Tentatively she pushed the door a little further open and stepped closer to pop her head round. She was greeted with a scene of such despair that she actually caught her breath. Billy was on his knees on the floor, covered in blood, wearing only his boxer shorts, surrounded by toilet roll, towels and a facecloth. He was sobbing and holding one of his hands, which was dripping blood steadily onto one of her best towels.

"Billy! You're bleeding! It's alright – here, let me help."

Sue knelt beside him on the floor. She gently took one of his hands to examine the damage. Helping him to his feet beside her, she ran his cut hand under the tap. Billy flinched and sobbed. He was shaking like a leaf in the wind.

"I'm sorry, I'm so sorry," he cried, leaning in to her. "I wrecked your bathroom. I broke your lovely pink bottle and when I tried to tidy it up I made it all worse."

Sue glanced at the broken bottle.

"What, that old thing? Honestly, Billy, it's about four years old. Richie got it for me one Christmas and I swear I only opened it once. Never used it, mind – it smelled like gloss paint. Think he got it off a bloke in a pub. It's hardly Chanel.

You did me a huge favour breaking it, actually." She gave him a reassuring squeeze. Billy wasn't buying it, she could tell.

"Honestly. Now he'll have to buy me the real thing, eh?"

Standing there all pale and blood-smeared in the bathroom, Billy watched Sue expertly gather up all the broken bits, the clumps of loo roll and the dirty towels, whilst at the same time turning on the shower.

"Tell you what, Billy," she told him. "You jump in there and have a good long soak. Use that other towel over there, and when you're ready and dressed, I'll have a cowboy breakfast waiting for you downstairs. Deal?"

Billy stopped his sniffling and tried a watery smile.

"Okay, deal," he told her quietly.

"Nice one, pard'ner." She grinned, before closing the door and leaving him to it.

In the sunny kitchen, with the door open to the garden and the radio playing cheerily, Sue busied herself making Billy's breakfast. *Poor little lad*, she thought. What a first impression to make, especially as she knew a little more about him now. He had lots of worries and troubles, and she knew that breaking her things and causing a mess would torment him for some time. Oh well, she'd just have to take things slowly with this one. She could hear the shower stop, and there were sounds of Billy moving around the bathroom and along the landing into his bedroom. She had made sure his clean clothes were on the bed for him, but she hadn't opened the curtains yet. Billy could do that when he was dressed and ready to come down to eat. She started dishing up bacon, eggs, sausage, beans and fried bread. The lad certainly looked like he needed a hot meal inside of him, so pale and scrawny he was. This should cheer him up a bit. On the table she placed a little vase full of wild flowers she had picked in the garden earlier. It looked like just the way to start the day for Billy, after his bother in the bathroom.

Upstairs, Billy left the warm comfort of the bathroom. He smelled much better and was feeling fresh. He shook the water out of his hair, rubbing it with the soft towel. Billy smiled when he saw his clothes laid out ready on his bed. He could smell something wonderful in the kitchen downstairs and his tummy rumbled loudly. He realised that he hadn't really eaten anything much since he left the flat yesterday afternoon. He'd been too chewed up. He thought of his mam, wondering if she was having her coffee and looking out over the city as she drank it. Billy would stand beside her, admiring the sky and the scene in the distance across the city, a bowl of cereal in his hands. Bending down to pull on his socks, Billy straightened his bed, plumped his pillows and went to open the heavy curtains.

Sue put the plate and a cup of tea onto the table in the kitchen.

"Billy, breakfast's ready when you are!" she called. Turning back to the sink to wash up her own cup, she thought she heard him exclaim before she heard him come thundering down the stairs. She smiled at him as Billy burst through the kitchen door and without a second glance flew straight past her and out into the back garden, a look of abject terror on his face.

Huh? Now what? she thought.

She put her cup into the sink, dried her hands quickly and went to follow him. Outside, in the sun, she stopped and looked about for him. No sign. She looked up and down the lane to her left and right, trying not to panic. Where could this lad have gone? He didn't know anyone in the area. And more to the point, why would he have just taken off like that?

Richie was just approaching the gate, coming home from night shift. He saw her standing there, looking confused. He walked down the path towards her.

"Morning, darling, I don't suppose you've…" she began.

Richie paused beside Sue to give her a kiss on the cheek.

"Morning, pet," he told her with a grin. He walked towards the kitchen door, smiling tiredly as he went.

"By, something smells nice. That for me?" he asked his wife, then looked up at the sky. "Oh, morning, Billy," he said, indicating over his shoulder to Sue. She followed his gesture. At the very top of the highest tree in the garden, the small shaking figure of Billy clung tightly to a branch.

"Is he OK, do you think?" asked Richie, scratching his head as he gazed up into the dense leafy branches. "Sounds like he's talking telephone numbers to me."

Sue and her husband craned their necks, shielding their eyes against the bright morning sunlight.

"Billy. You OK, pet?" she asked, calling up to the canopy.

After a few minutes of mumbling, it all went quiet. The tree stopped trembling.

Sue and Richie stared at each other and shrugged.

"Now what?" she asked him, mouthing silently.

"Billy, come on down and say hello. I'd come up and join you only I'm a bit wrecked after me night shift." Richie paused, waiting hopefully for an answer.

"S'funny," he continued. "That was always my favourite tree when I was your age. You can see the whole world from up there."

The tree began trembling again, and after a minute or two Billy's feet, then his legs, appeared, coming down. When he finally jumped down the last few feet to land on the path beside them, Sue was surprised to see that his face was no longer pale and shocked. He was smiling tremulously at her.

"OK, Billy?" she asked gently. "It's a great tree, isn't it, son?"

Billy nodded his head. He seemed unable to speak at first, then he told them, breathily, his eyes shining, "I can see the Monument from up there."

Sue glanced at her husband with a puzzled expression, placed her arm around Billy's shoulder, and together they walked down the garden and into the house.

Chapter 8

Billy sat in the sunny kitchen and tucked into his huge breakfast, whilst Sue cooked more for Richie. He stood with a cup of tea, his back against the sink, and watched Billy closely, though he pretended to be drying the dishes for his wife. On the unit beside the sink, he had glanced at the paperwork which always came with any foster child. He had quickly and expertly scanned the first page, detailing Billy's name and address, some of his personal circumstances, general health and overall concerns. There was a whole list of items which seemed to freak the lad out. Richie had seen the list contained blood, the dark, thunder, and enclosed spaces, but he kept up a constant stream of good-natured chatter as he tried to get Billy to open up to him a little.

"You ever been down here before, then, Billy?" he asked, sipping at his tea and scanning the page in his hand.

Billy shook his head, pausing with his fork in the air near his mouth.

"I've lived here all my life," Richie told him. "Sue as well. We wouldn't live anywhere else, would we, pet? It's really calm and peaceful down here."

Billy stared at Richie, his eyes wide. Richie continued.

"Aye, it's a bonny spot. You'll be safe here with us and you'll soon be back home again, but it's a bit like being out in the country here. Even though you're only a couple of miles away from the city centre."

The lad continued to stare, as if in disbelief.

"Safe?" he asked, questioningly. "You really think so?"

Richie turned over the paper he was reading, glancing from Billy's incredulous face back to the page in front of him.

"Oh yeah, it's safe here. Everyone knows everybody else. Proper village it is. But they're all really friendly, Billy. There's nothing for you to stress about here."

He glanced at Sue who had briefed him very quickly about Billy's dash out of the house and up into the top of the tree. She had been at a loss as to what had triggered his flight. Just then he noticed another of Billy's fears on the top of the back of the page in his hand: water. As Billy dropped his head to continue eating,

Richie showed it quickly to Sue at the sink. She raised her eyes and took a sharp breath. Wiping her hands on a tea towel, she handed Richie his breakfast and the two of them sat at the table opposite Billy. He had his head down still and was now nervously slurping his tea.

"Billy…" she began, glancing at the back of the page Richie had given her, "when you dashed out of here this morning, was it the…?"

She paused, waiting to see Billy's reaction. Nothing. He slurped his tea, avoiding her eyes, staring over the rim of his mug to the table in front of him.

"Was it the river?" Richie asked gently.

Billy put his mug down carefully. He lay his knife and fork tidily together on his plate, just like his mam had always told him to do. Finally, he nodded his head.

"Yes? The river, Billy?" Sue asked.

Billy nodded. He kept his head down and mumbled, "It's right outside the window. It's so… deep…and fast, and green…" he added quietly. "I couldn't breathe for a minute," he told them, lifting his pale grey eyes to look at them both. "I just had to get away from it."

Sue reached across and placed a hand over his. She held it there for a minute.

She knew she couldn't belittle his fear by telling the lad he had come to stay in a local beauty spot, and that people travelled out of the city every day in the summer to stroll by the beautiful river, to fish, or to picnic and camp on the riverbank. The lad was terrified of water, and they had placed him in a house with the river Wear, right outside the front door! Idiots! What on earth had they been thinking of? Their incompetence amazed her. She'd be having serious words with Paul Costello and his team about this, she fumed. Richie was leaning in to talk to Billy across the table.

"Ah, right, the river. Well, I tell you what, Billy. It's high tide at the minute, so yes, I can see that it does look a bit fast and frightening, but very soon it'll all have drained away when the tide goes out. Then, you'll almost be able to walk straight across it to the other side."

Billy looked intently into Richie's face.

"Oh, it's not always that deep, then?" he asked, nervously twisting his fingers.

"No, no. Well, twice a day it is, but then twice a day the tide goes back out again. But you don't have to go in it, or too close to it, if it worries you so much."

Sue got up to start clearing the table. Her heart broke for this poor, frightened child. Here she was living in this beautiful spot on the river, and there was Billy, terrified of being here, and not seeing the beauty of it at all. In fact, it was only adding to his fears. And every time the boy glanced out of the window, he was reminded of it. She and her neighbours were so used to it, they set their clocks by the turning tide, knowing all the local visitors who walked along the water's edge, wishing they could linger a little longer. She sighed, but had an idea.

"I tell you what, Billy. Would you like it if we moved you out of the bedroom at the front and put you in the back bedroom instead?"

Richie raised an inquisitive eyebrow, but seemed impressed at the thought. He smiled encouragingly at Billy.

"That way," he began, "instead of seeing the river when you open your curtains, you'd be looking up towards the Monument instead."

Billy smiled shyly, trying to picture being able to see it at close quarters every day. He could see it from his windows at home in the city centre, but it was just a small object on a hill, far away from his flat. Here, when he was up the tree in the garden, he could make out small details on it and it seemed much bigger. Much more real to him.

"Yes, please," he breathed. "I'd love that. Thank you so much."

As his face went pink with joy, Sue thought her own heart would break. *What a simple solution,* she sighed to herself. *I wonder how long it will last, though?*

Billy and Richie spent a happy couple of hours moving things from one bedroom to the other. Not only were Billy's clothes and personal belongings shifted, they also decided between them to rearrange the furniture. The bed was tried in three different positions before leaving it where Billy could stare out of the window whilst he was lying down. Even though he couldn't actually see the Monument from this position, it somehow settled and reassured him just knowing it was there. Sue came in a few times to insist on Richie going to bed. He needed to sleep after his night shift at the car plant, but he argued that it was a hard thing to do when the sun was shining, the birds were singing and the rest of the world was getting up and going off to enjoy the day. After more nagging – *caring* she called it – Richie took himself into the large peaceful bedroom, overlooking the river, drew the curtains and went to bed.

Billy smiled as he heard him huffing and puffing about how unfair it was that he was missing out on such a glorious day. When next Billy popped up to the bathroom, he stood for a minute on the landing, smiling at the loud snores coming from the front of the house.

Sue and Billy took some tea and biscuits out onto the picnic bench in the back garden. Each took their sketch pad with them. Billy held his close to him, obsessively feeling the front cover and gazing nervously around as if for inspiration, or as if he might run off at the slightest moment. Sue watched his nervous grey eyes darting about, checking out the neighbouring houses, looking up and down the lane, and constantly returning to where he knew. Penshaw Hill and the Monument were in the near distance. The trees and the wood behind the hill tended to block the view of the Monument, but it was there, and a short walk to the end of the road revealed it in all its glory. Sue really wanted Billy to settle and feel more comfortable in her home.

"So, what's it like living in a flat in the city, Billy? I find it hard to imagine. What do you like about it?"

Billy paused, carefully folding the wrapper of his chocolate biscuit into a bow. He turned his head slightly away from Sue as if he was looking for his home.

After a pause he began. "It's so peaceful there."

She watched a small smile creep into his mouth and eyes.

"We're almost in the sky," he told her.

"How high up are you, do you know?" Sue asked intently. "I just can't imagine it, Billy. I rarely even go into town, let alone go up into a high-rise building."

"We're on the seventeenth floor," Billy told her. He laughed as Sue's eyes grew wide.

"Good God – you could get a nosebleed being so high!"

"No, it's amazing," Billy told her shyly. "When it thunders, sometimes, the lightning is below us. And the birds don't even get to fly so high as our windows. I can see the Monument from there and way across the city. I can see right into the Stadium of Light," he told her.

"You say that like it's a good thing!" she joked with him.

Billy grinned at her over the table.

"When they have a big rock concert in there, we can hear all of it and we don't have to pay. We can see the crowds going in and feel the excitement, but we don't have any of the mess and the worry."

"But, do you see many people up there, Billy, like friends and neighbours? You know, just to pass the time of day with?"

"Well, there's old Joe and his wife next door, but they don't come out much. And I see the cleaners in the lift sometimes. They're canny, but... well, I don't have friends. I like it just being me and Mam. It's best that way."

His face fell a little at the end of that statement, and Sue worried about him being isolated in the middle of a bustling city.

"Oh, neighbours and friends can be good for you, Billy. I'd be lost without mine," she told him happily.

"Really?" asked Billy. "Even the ones who leave dead mice in your garden?" he asked her bravely.

Sue looked puzzled for a minute.

"I heard you telling someone off for it this morning. That's a totally mad and weird thing for someone to do. See, these country folk must be a bit crazy if you ask me."

The penny dropped for Sue and she began to laugh. Billy frowned at her.

"Oh no, Billy, I'm not laughing *at* you. That was Fingle Brown I was talking to. He is a neighbour and I really do love him."

"What sort of a name is Fingle Brown?" asked Billy.

"Here," Sue began, "let me call him over to you. I think you two would get on fine. He's about your age, I should think."

Sue went to the back gate, leaned over it and called the crazy name out a couple of times. Billy could have died of embarrassment: he didn't think he was ready to meet the neighbours just yet. He was happy to just be with Sue and Richie. It felt safe with just the three of them. And really, what would he have in common with this person, other than being about the same age? He sighed sadly. At that moment a huge cat jumped over the gate and came slinking around Sue's legs.

"Here he is," she told Billy, bending down to stroke the cat affectionately. "This is Fingle Brown. He's the boss around here and he always gets his full title."

Billy hadn't been so close to a cat for years. Pets weren't allowed in the block of flats. There were one or two mangy ones seen sometimes in the town centre, wandering around the car parks trying to catch the heavyweight pigeons who waddled about, but Billy kept his distance. To him they were just… animals… other living things… and they had nothing at all to do with him or his life. He froze, staring intently at Fingle Brown, trying not to let the cat or Sue see how nervous he was. His knee jiggled, though, giving the game away and he subconsciously rubbed it to make it stop shaking. The movement of his hand drew the cat closer to him. It looked up at Billy with the most amazing golden eyes he had ever seen. He actually drew a sharp breath, so vivid and intelligent they seemed. The cat had lots of fluffy fur in all different shades. Some of it was brilliant white, but there were caramel flashes, black streaks, honey coloured patches and flashes of gold. Its tail was long and fluffy and both ears had little tufts on the edges, giving it an exotic appearance. The cat arched its back and purred and chirruped at Billy. He found himself mesmerised by it.

"See, he likes you. I knew he would. Fingle is a good judge of character." Sue smiled, stroking the cat confidently down the length of his back to the tip of his tail.

"He's on your wall," Billy told her, keeping his own hands on his sketch pad.

Sue gave him a quizzical look, not quite understanding.

"In the house. You've sketched him but you did it in black and white," Billy told her. The light of recognition shone in Sue's eyes.

"Aha," she told him. "You spotted him in there. Well done, Billy. I wanted to paint him properly, but I just haven't had time recently. You must have a good eye to recognise him from my sketches."

"Well, you couldn't miss him," Billy told her, gesturing to the cat. "And your work is fantastic." He said it warmly, making an obvious statement of truth. Fingle Brown, oblivious to the newcomer who didn't seem too interested in being a friend, sprawled out on the grass in the sunshine. He closed his golden eyes, twitched his giant fluffy tail and promptly fell asleep.

"Now's your chance," Billy told Sue, an eyebrow raised towards the cat.

"Well, I *was* going to clear out the pond, with you as my beautiful assistant…"

She began, smiling at Billy. He gazed at her, then down at her sketch book on the table between them.

"It's just… I'd really like to see you work. It would be…peaceful," he told her, looking up into the blue sky. Sue paused for only a second or two.

"OK, Billy. You're on. The pond can wait. And you're right, it's not often a beautiful subject presents itself and lies at your feet. We'll both have a go at Fingle Brown."

They shared a moment then, watching each other quietly opening their sketch pads, finding clear pages and selecting pencils from the small case Sue had brought out with her. They moved the coffee cups, sat back for a good look at the cat, selected their best angle and began to sketch. And it was peaceful, and calming, and for a few minutes the world, the river, and being away from his home in the clouds drifted away as Billy became immersed in his task. Then sweet, mystical music came to him, seemingly floating over the water and swirling softly in the air. *A host of Heavenly angels.* This sudden blast from the past from Primary School surprised him. Billy glanced at Sue; she was engrossed in her task and seemed oblivious. Closing his eyes and pausing for a second or two, Billy allowed the sound to wash over him. Wherever it came from, he was grateful. It felt *right* somehow.

Heads down, eyes occasionally glancing at the cat or across at each other's work, Billy and Sue spent a happy half hour. When the cat became bored and got up, shook himself and stalked off into his own garden in search of mice, Billy and Sue moved seamlessly into the shade to continue their work. They selected colours and continued their task, stopping once in a while to flex their fingers or to sharpen a pencil. For the first time in weeks, Billy had not worried, or become tearful, or fidgeted impatiently. He tried to find the words which would explain his feelings on that first sunny afternoon. He scratched his head and gazed in the direction of the Monument, seeing it only in his mind's eye. Safe. That's how he felt. Billy smiled and selected another pencil.

Chapter 9

Billy could sense, rather than feel, the blackness approaching him. He began to sweat and shake, breaking into a run but stumbling in his panic. The sand beneath his feet grew wetter and heavier, sucking him in. His legs turned to jelly. He cried out for his mam up on the cliff-top, but she was too far away and out of his reach. She couldn't hear him or help him. He looked back over his shoulder as the black wave bore down on him and engulfed him. It knocked him over and swamped him, stealing his breath and holding him down in its swirling, grinning grip. This time, it snaked out cold black arms and wrapped them around his legs, swirling up his body until they reached his neck. Billy tried to scream. He kicked and spluttered, still trying to escape its iron hold on him. He was drowning in this evil blackness. As he went down for the third time, with his legs held tight and his face twisting in terror and turmoil he heard a voice. In his last moments, Billy reached out a hand. Would the voice see it and grab him? The voice drifted closer to him again. Was this person on the beach, trying to get to him? Billy desperately tried to raise his head and open his eyes but the darkness swirled around him still, holding him, draining him of all life and hope. He felt another black wave rising above him to come crashing down, when a chink of light appeared somewhere close. Again, that voice, this time calling his name. Billy felt a glimmer of hope. Someone had seen and was coming to help get him out of there. But could they? It may already be too late. Was he already dead? The choke hold around his neck loosened slightly and suddenly, Billy was free. Cool calm hands were stroking his arms and shoulders, reassuring him. Was it an angel? Billy didn't dare open his eyes to look.

"Billy, come on, Billy, it's okay, it's me, Sue. You're safe, Billy. Sit up a minute."

Deliberately keeping her voice calm, and the curtains slightly open, Sue tried to coax Billy out of his nightmare. In the half-light before dawn she could see that the poor child was in a dreadful state, pale and sweating, his hair standing on end, and now his eyes were wide but staring sightlessly at her. He was gulping in air as if he'd been deep sea diving and had run out of oxygen. Billy's hands were clawing and clutching at the duvet, which had been wrapped tightly around his legs and shoulders. Sue sat carefully on the side of the bed and turned Billy's face to look at her, calmly untangling the sheet from where it had almost strangled him.

"Look, Billy, it's me. It's Sue. You're in my house and you're quite safe now. Can you hear me, Billy?"

The boy lowered his eyes a little, staring at his hands first, then touching his own neck and face. He looked lost, bewildered for a moment, but as Sue continued to talk quietly he seemed to realise where he was, coming slowly out of his panic as his shuddering breaths subsided. Sue handed Billy a glass of water from the bedside cabinet, and helped his shaky hands guide it to his lips. He sipped noisily three times, then handed the glass back to Sue before slumping back against his damp pillows.

"I thought I was dead," he told her flatly, in a muffled voice, as if he couldn't really form words properly yet. He sighed and clutched at the bedclothes again.

"Oh, Billy, it's just a bad dream. You're not dead, you're fine. Look, it's only ten past four. It's still night time, really. Do you think you could go back to sleep, or shall I make us a cup of tea?"

"Where's my mam?" Billy asked in a small voice, turning his head away from Sue to face the wall.

"She's at home, Billy, she's fast asleep," Sue told him quietly, speaking to him as if he was a toddler, trying not to rouse him too far from the sleep, which was obviously trying to claim him back. "But tomorrow she'll be going to the hospital. Then, very soon, she'll be well enough to come home and you can both be together again. In the meantime, she would want you to be happy and settled here, and to get lots of sleep. OK?"

The boy closed his eyes and nodded slowly. Sue waited on the bed for a few more minutes, checking that his breathing was returning to normal and some colour had returned to his cheeks. As she stood up to leave the room, Billy's quiet voice asked, "Will it come back and get me again?"

Sue turned back to him, clutching at the top of her nightie. *The poor child*, she thought. Moving to the window, she opened the curtain slightly so that a small streak of the promised pink dawn peeped into the bedroom. Outside, the air was soft and still, no breath of wind, with just an odd star or two twinkling in the pearlescent sky.

"No, Billy. It's gone, pet. Why don't you just lie there and think nice thoughts. Look, it's going to be a beautiful day when the sun finally wakes up properly. If you listen quietly, you'll hear that barn owl start hooting, and after him all the birds will wake up. You'll get the full chorus."

Sue gazed out of the window into the stillness and soft green of her back garden. Lights twinkled in the distance. *On the other side of the house*, she thought, *the tide should have turned and the river will be running deep and still, but I can't tell Billy that.*

"Can you see the Monument?" he asked her bravely, concealing a sob, or a hiccup.

"Not really, Billy. It's up there, though, behind those trees, at the top of the hill. And it can see you down here. It's waiting for you to run up there and hug one of those huge pillars." She gazed down at the boy and saw the glimmer of a smile light up the gloom in the room. Patting him on the shoulder, Sue whispered, "Night, Billy. Go back to sleep, pet. See you in the morning."

Then she slipped silently out and returned to her own bed.

*

The kitchen was warm and bright, the back door open to let the sunlight stream in, with the smell of toast and coffee in the air, tempting Billy to make his shy appearance at almost nine fifteen. Sue was standing against the sink texting on her mobile. She looked up and smiled brightly at Billy as he wandered sleepily in and slid into a chair at the table.

"Morning, Billy. Well, you look better than you did a few hours ago. Are you hungry?"

Sue poured some fresh orange juice into a glass and placed it before him. Billy nodded his head and smiled shyly at her.

"I don't normally eat breakfast," he told her. "Or, I just grab some crisps on the way to school."

He flashed a brief bright smile as Sue pretended to faint against the sink, grabbing the edge of it to stop herself from collapsing to the floor in shock.

"Crisps! For breakfast! Good God, lad. You might just as well pour a bottle of cooking oil down your throat, and chuck in a bowl full of salt to follow it. We've got to get you healthy." She playfully pinched his scrawny upper arm.

She was joking, wasn't she? Billy looked closely at her. He wasn't sure what time she had got up, but here she was, all smiley and glowing, looking clean and fresh and well-groomed first thing in the morning. Sue was so unlike his mam, he thought. Mam would be shuffling around in her old dressing gown with her hair like a bird's nest until at least eleven o'clock. Then he felt guilty and his heart hurt a bit because his mam was in so much pain and Sue wasn't. Sue did look like an athlete, though.

"Whilst you're here, Billy, my lad, you shall have a decent breakfast inside you. It's the one thing I insist on. You teenagers need to keep your strength up."

She opened a cupboard.

"Now, how about some cereal, for a start, then we'll decide on what else."

"OK, I'll try some of that," Billy told her, turning a range of boxes that were put onto the table in front of him. They all looked healthy and nourishing, and Billy instantly worried that he would feel sick if he tried to eat some this early. He wasn't used to this. Pouring out some cornflakes, he added milk and sugar, and started. And he loved it. They tasted refreshing, and he couldn't get enough of the crisp crunch in his mouth. Billy realised he was actually really hungry and tried to remember what his last proper meal had been.

Sue's mobile beeped a couple of times as she busied herself in the sunny kitchen, going into the fridge for bread, butter and bacon. It was Richie, she told Billy, preparing to come home off night shift.

"I'll get his breakfast organised as soon as you've had yours," she told Billy. "He won't be long. Just a huge shame he has to go to bed on a glorious day like this." Then she paused, looking into an empty basket. "Ah…"

"Something wrong?" asked Billy, looking at her puzzled face.

"Hmm." Sue was thoughtful. "I've run out of eggs. Not the full English for Richie this morning, then."

"Is there a shop? I could go and get some for you, if it's not too far."

Billy wanted to help. He really liked Sue and Richie, and it was time he stepped outside of this lovely house and garden, and saw a little more of this place he would be living in for some time yet. Sue shut the cupboard door and turned to him.

"Now that's a good idea, if you would, Billy." Her face relaxed and she seemed happy Billy had offered to help in this small way. Picking up an empty round basket she handed it to Billy and guided him to the back door.

"Out of the gate and turn left. The last house in the row. Just say I sent you."

Billy's face creased in concern as he looked at the basket in his hand.

"But… I'll need some money, won't I?" he asked her, puzzled.

Sue's eyes suddenly lit up in recognition.

"Ah, yes… well, no, not really," she began, then laughed again at Billy's puzzled expression. "It's not a shop, Billy. It's just my neighbour's house and he keeps chickens. I always get my eggs direct from him. Just say I sent you. It's Mr Dawson." She walked with Billy down the sunny garden path, opened the back gate and pointed to the end of the terrace to her left. "There you go. Thanks, Billy. Then when you're back, I'll crack on with your breakfast," she laughed. "Crack on. Eggs? Get it?" Still smiling to herself she left him to it and went back inside.

Billy stood for a moment and looked down the lane. It felt weird to be in this strangely quiet little place. He was glad he wasn't on the other side of the house, where the river was, but he liked this back lane. Walking slowly past the other houses, he looked up into the trees. It was remarkable, just how bright and colourful everything was here, after the harsh grey of the granite city centre. The trees waved softly above him, making gentle soothing sounds, and the greenery was almost painful to his city boy eyes. Birds were singing, and he closed his eyes for a second or two, letting the sunlight dappling through the trees dance across his face. He felt like he was in heaven for a minute.

Moving on, Billy came to the last house in the row. This one was bigger than the others, standing apart in its own large rambling garden. There was a fairly rickety wooden gate, which he pushed open with a squeak. He could still hear the heavenly music in the distance, and somehow it spurred him on to approach the house. Standing to one side of the house, was a large shed. It smelled of wood shavings and oil, and it looked as though many happy hours could be spent exploring it, if only he was brave enough to look inside. Billy paused – would he knock on the door, or go to the shed? He could hear chickens chirruping around somewhere and they'd hardly be in the house, would they? Clutching the basket closer to his chest, Billy approached the front door and knocked, gently and shyly. He was a bit worried about talking to this stranger, but Sue had put her trust in him. He stood back expectantly.

Suddenly, there was the sound of barking and scrabbling, and Billy's eyes prickled in fear as a huge black dog came hurtling out of the front door, knocking him flat in his surprise. Dropping the basket, Billy leapt up in terror as the dog chased after him, barking with delight at having caught a stranger at the door. Billy's legs trembled in fear as he leapt over the fence in one go, to lie panting in a shocked heap on the ground on the other side. The dog leapt up at the fence. It was laughing at him. Billy stood back and tried to look calmly at it. His heart was pounding in his chest, his ribs aching in shock and fear.

The dog sat back on the ground behind the gate and wagged its tail at Billy. It seemed happy to see him! Billy glanced over his shoulder to see if anyone had heard the noise and was coming to rescue him. Nope. Then, looking into the garden, he saw the fallen egg basket which he'd dropped in his panic to escape the mad mutt. Now what? He couldn't let Sue down. She was waiting for these eggs, and Richie had worked all night and needed his breakfast. Billy looked closely at the dog. It walked calmly to the gate and lifted its paw. It was trying to open the gate! Why? Did it want to come out and eat him?

Just then Billy heard the sound of footsteps. Phew. Someone was coming, but not from this house, from down the lane. They'd know what to do. His heart began to settle as he saw an older lady approaching. He smiled at her, and as she drew near, she laid a hand on his shoulder.

"It's all right, son, he gets everyone like that. It's just his joke. What you after?"

Billy smiled into her rather rough but friendly face and told her quietly, "Eggs."

He turned back towards the gate, expecting her to open it and take him in, but to his amazement, she suddenly bellowed right in his ear.

"Dagger! Dagger!"

Billy's heart leapt into his throat once more and he turned to run, ducking his head down and crouching his knees, in case a dagger should come whizzing past his head. Now what? Was someone going to start throwing knives at them? What sort of loony bin had he come to?

The woman gripped his shoulders, lifting him from his crouch and almost forced him through the gate. The dog, the least of his worries now, he suspected, simply turned and trotted off. Billy still had no idea where it had come from. The woman picked up the egg basket, handed it to Billy and pointed round the corner of the large shed.

"There you are, son. He'll be round there and can't hear you, silly old fool that he is. Off you go."

She turned away smiling and walked off, quite unconcerned about this person who might be flinging daggers this way. Right. Let's get brave and get this job done. The sooner he was out of this crazy place, the better. He took a deep shaky breath and stepped forward.

Now that he was in the garden properly, Billy could tell that it was quite a size. He could smell the river just off to his right and could still hear the chickens. The lovely music was still playing somewhere, a little louder now. Clutching the egg basket tightly, he rounded another corner, stepping carefully as chickens had suddenly appeared around his feet. He stopped to admire them in the speckled sunlight, scratching busily in the ground and pecking at dandelions, growing near the path. It was a happy, delightful little scene, and Billy relaxed as he stood patiently, watching them. It didn't last long, though.

An awful noise started up, making Billy's skin creep and the hair stand up on his arms. He had never heard a more devilish sound in his life, and it frightened the very breath out of him. He froze in fear once more. It was a deep wheezing, honking, braying sound, and Billy shrank back against the wall of the shed as an empty metal dustbin rolled clanking past his feet. This was followed very soon after by a rather large grey donkey, which simply pushed him out of the way and headed on towards the other side of the house as if Billy didn't exist. *That's it*, thought Billy. *Eggs or no eggs, I'm out of here. This place is like some old lunatic asylum.* But he found his legs wouldn't work, and he slid down the side of the shed, landing in a neat pile of donkey poo on the grass. As it soaked, damp and stinking into the seat of his trousers, Billy sat there and wanted to cry. The sun was hot on his face, and he felt like an idiot. Sue would think he couldn't get anything right, coming home empty-handed and looking like he'd filled his pants in fear of a donkey.

Suddenly, a huge shadow blotted out the sun. *OK*, thought Billy. *This is probably it. I'm really going to get it now.*

"Hello, son," said a deep voice. "What you doing down there, then?"

Huge hands with fingers the size of pork sausages reached down to grab Billy by the shoulders. Billy clenched his eyes shut against the frightening sight and started his usual litany, his teeth chattering in fear.

"One hundred, fifty-three, seventy, eighteen…"

Chapter 10

Billy felt himself lifted off the ground as if he weighed no more than a bag of sugar. He was still chanting and shaking with his eyes shut, when the giant spoke to him again.

"Hey, hey, it's all right. What happened to you, then, son? And where have you come from, eh?"

The voice was deep and warm and soft, like it had rumbled up from under the dark earth. After a minute, when the dagger didn't come flying, the donkey didn't trundle back and the dog didn't appear again from nowhere, Billy cautiously opened his eyes. The man was looking kindly at him, turning him in a concerned way, trying to brush some of the donkey poo and grass stains off Billy's trousers. Billy was embarrassed. He knew he must look like some kind of idiot, standing shaking and stinking in front of this stranger, in the man's own garden. He raised his eyes to the man's face.

"I'm Billy," he told him quietly. "I've come to get some eggs."

The man stood up to his full height then and looked Billy straight in the face. His eyes crinkled and his mouth stretched into a large friendly grin. Clapping one huge hand on Billy's thin shoulder, he said, "Ah, eggs, you must be the lad who's staying with Sue and Richie. She told me she had another little friend coming this summer."

"That's me," Billy told him, gazing up at him in awe.

This man was huge. He had dark hair, streaked with grey. It was fairly long and fluffy. His eyes were brown and twinkly, and his skin was lightly tanned and creased, possibly from being out in the sun and the fresh air all the time. He smelled of fresh air and wood shavings, plus something else. Maybe the river? His chest and shoulders were broad, and dark hair peeped through the open neck of his checked shirt. He had a bit of a belly, straining under a wide leather belt, but Billy couldn't help noticing his hands. They were huge and handsome, he thought. Tanned, with long fingers and looking as strong as an all-in wrestler he'd seen on the telly. There were fine dark hairs over the back of them, and he looked as though he could do a hell of a lot of damage to someone with them, if he wanted to. Luckily, he didn't seem to want to at this minute. He leaned forward and held one of the huge hands out to Billy in a friendly gesture.

"Dagger," he said, with a twinkle of those deep brown eyes.

"Sorry?" questioned Billy, a worried look creeping back onto his face again.

"Not from these parts are you, son? Dagger Dawson at your service. Any friend of Sue and Richie is a friend of mine."

"That... that's your name? Dagger?" stammered Billy, his face softening a little.

"Well, yes. That's my name. It's what people round here call me, any road. Always have. Ever since I was a little lad, younger than you."

Billy blinked up at him, then his eyes roamed the garden, warily.

"I got a bit of a shock when... and then the…"

"Ah, my two little mates surprised you, did they? Sorry, son. You should have been warned about them. They won't hurt you, honestly. Come with me."

He gently steered Billy towards the front of the house, where the donkey was happily grazing on the grass near the river. Billy instinctively held back.

"Don't be scared, son," Dagger told him. "If you're staying for a while you might as well get used to the locals. This is Dolly and she's probably a lot older than you are. And a right madam when she wants to be."

By now they were standing right alongside the donkey. Dagger was stroking and pulling on her long floppy grey ears. The donkey switched her tail and munched on, ignoring both of them. Billy was still unsure. He was standing right next to the river, too close to a rather large animal, with a giant at his side. Was he mad? Glancing up, he noticed the water was running smoothly downstream, and there were stones and reed beds very close. It wasn't too bad, actually. Not as threatening as he thought it would be. There were houses on the other side of the river, almost identical to the one he was staying in. He'd not even known they were there.

"Go on, Billy. Stroke her and say hello, then she'll be fine with you. She won't hurt you."

Billy tentatively reached up and touched the soft grey fur. It was warm and soft under his hand. Laying his palm flat on the donkey's shoulder, he could feel her strength and solidity, her muscles and sinews under her skin. She had a dark line running from her black mane to her tail, with a cross going down her shoulders. The donkey stopped eating and nodded her head up and down. She stamped one small neat black hoof.

"There you are, Dolly. A new friend for you. I told you she'd like you, didn't I?" Dagger told Billy with a smile and a reassuring pat on his back. "Well done, Billy. Now, for that other character."

Dagger led Billy away from the river, towards the house, keeping up the warm chatter about Dolly and leaving his large hand on Billy's shoulder. It felt heavy through Billy's shirt, but it also felt strangely comforting, walking along in the sun with this friendly giant. It was as if he was safe in his company. Approaching the house, up the garden path, Dagger stopped and called out, "Lennie? Get out here and meet my new mate."

The black dog appeared from nowhere again, in a flash, and Billy realised he had come through a hidden hole in the door itself.

"Woah!" he exclaimed, stepping back in shock. "How does he do that?"

The dog sprang forward and stood up to laugh in Billy's face, his paws on the boy's shoulders.

"Get down, Lennie," Dagger told him, and the dog instantly did as it was told, trying to sit on a wagging tale and grinning up at the pair of them.

"This is Lennie. Lennie Catflap," Dagger told Billy, fondly stroking the dog's glossy black head. "Say hello to Billy, Lennie."

The dog held out a paw. Dagger motioned with his head to Billy, who carefully took hold of the paw and shook it, formally.

"Lennie Catflap?" he asked, curiously.

"Well, it used to be a cat flap when he was a puppy. But as he grew bigger, I had to put a dog flap in the door. He broke two front doors trying to get out, before I got round to it. The name stuck. Everyone round here knows Lennie Catflap. Well, apart from the odd pizza delivery man, like. They're always good for a laugh."

Billy watched Dagger put his head back and chuckle at some far away memory. His face changed completely when he smiled, Billy thought. He looked almost like a boy again. Softer, charming and handsome.

"Now, about those eggs," Dagger told Billy, leading him towards another shed. Billy ambled after him, walking gingerly with his feet apart, like Charlie Chaplin, because the donkey poo on the seat of his pants was uncomfortable and was soaking through and starting to stick to his skin. Dagger opened a blistered and bent wooden door and popped inside. He was back out in a minute with ten speckled and muddy eggs held safely in his two big hands.

"I'll get the basket." Billy told him and hobbled towards the garden path where he had dropped it a few minutes ago. Dagger watched him go, smiling to himself. *Look at the state of this bairn*, he told himself, shaking his head. *I wonder what his story is. Ah, well. He's come to the right place and to the right people, too*, he thought. Billy returned, and he carefully placed the eggs into the warm wicker basket.

"There you are, Billy. Fresh this morning. They'll be gorgeous. Now, off you go. I can see someone who's in great need of a couple of those beauties."

Dagger nodded his head towards the gate where Richie was standing, watching the two of them with a big smile on his face.

"Morning, Dagger. Hiya, Billy. I see you've met some of the neighbours, then."

Billy was delighted to see Richie. He held the eggs out proudly to him.

"I've got your breakfast, Richie, look."

Richie looked at Billy, his stained trousers, rumpled hair, standing on end and a huge grin on his face.

"Have you met, Lennie Catflap, then?" Richie asked, opening the gate to let the lad join him in the sunny lane.

"Oh, boy, have I! I nearly died!" Billy told him animatedly, waddling alongside him back towards their house. "And Dolly, the donkey, as well... I even stroked her, and she didn't mind."

Richie looked back at the figure of Dagger, standing beside his dog. He raised his hand in salute to him.

"Cheers, Dagger. This is the most I've heard him say since he arrived. I think you've found a friend here."

Dagger waved back.

"No problem, Richie. He's had a bit of trial by fire, but he's survived OK. Any time he wants to come down and chat, he knows where I am."

Dagger started walking towards the river.

"And next time it won't be so frightening for him," he called back to Richie.

"We'll see," Richie called back, winking at his neighbour. "He hasn't met the geese, yet."

Dagger laughed as he watched the two figures making their way back up the sun lit, leafy lane: one waddling like a duck, the other with a gentle hand on his shoulder, guiding him home.

Chapter 11

"**P**lease, can you or Richie come with me to the hospital?"

Billy tried not to whine at Sue, who was washing the breakfast dishes at the sink. They had shared a wonderful warm and friendly breakfast together when he and Richie got in with the eggs. Sue had been shocked by the state – and the smell – of Billy's trousers and had sent him straight up to the shower, while she put a wash on in the kitchen. Richie had ruffled the lad's hair, telling him, "And don't use all of that Chanel shower stuff I bought for my beautiful wife, mind."

Billy paused at the door and looked back at him with a tint of pink creeping into his cheeks as Richie held his nose and made wafting gestures with his hands. He was smacked right on the side of the head with a wet dish cloth, thrown by Sue.

"Waah! She's too good a shot for me." He grinned at Billy.

"Years of practice, pet." Billy heard Sue laugh as he climbed upstairs to the shower.

When he came down, breakfast was ready – scrambled eggs on toast this time – and as he ate, Billy explained to Sue all about meeting Dagger and the animals. There was something about Sue that kept catching his eye, but as he ate and listened to Richie, telling them a story about someone getting locked in the toilet for two hours at work, it slipped his mind. Richie was tired, yawning by the end of his tale, and Sue insisted that he go to bed. He wanted to show Billy a particular bird's nest in the front garden, the river side of the house, but Sue shook her head at him.

"Later, Richie," she told him firmly. "It'll still be there when you wake up and Billy gets back."

Billy's head swung towards her.

"Back?" he enquired. "Where am I going?"

Sue collected the plates, and Billy got up to take their mugs to her at the sink. He stood beside her, smelling fresh and clean, with wide grey eyes, looking up into her face.

"The hospital, Billy. Have you forgotten? Your mam has her operation today."

Richie stood up to put things away in the cupboard, reaching past Billy as he told him.

"And she'll go into it a lot happier, if she sees your smiling little face before they put her to sleep."

Billy hung his head. He felt ashamed that he had hardly given his mam a thought since he arrived here two days ago. There was so much to do and see and, for once in his life, he felt more alert, awake, and more aware of himself, moving peacefully in the world. For once, he wasn't constantly on his guard, just waiting for something to go wrong or for someone to jump out at him and send him running in panic. His mam. In a cold, scary hospital and planning to go through that huge operation all on her own, while he was in this lovely place, in the sun, with new friends, not even thinking about her. Tears stung his eyes.

"It's OK, Billy. She'll be so much better, once it's done. She won't know herself." Sue could see the boy was getting upset, and thought he was worried about the operation and the pain and discomfort his mam was facing.

"And Paul will be with you the whole time, so you won't get lost, or have to go on buses by yourself, or anything," Richie told him, heading for the stairs and unbuttoning his shirt on the way. Billy sat back down at the table. Sue turned away from the sink to face him, sunlight flashing off her earrings as she studied his face.

"Go to bed, Richie. I'll explain to Billy."

Richie nodded, blew her a kiss and climbed the stairs. Sue came and sat down in front of Billy.

"I can't come with you, Billy. I have to go into work today. And Richie has to sleep, of course."

Billy looked confused.

"Work?" he asked. "I didn't know you had a job."

Sue smiled at him and ruffled his hair.

"Of course I have a job, Billy. I have to work, but I don't go in every day. What did you think I did with all my time, then?"

Billy smiled at her.

"I thought you were… you know…" He nodded at the passage wall. "An artist. A proper artist."

Sue grinned and sat back in her chair.

"Oh, bless you, Billy. I wish. I'm not that good, really."

Billy's eyes grew wide as he watched her opposite him, all bright and twinkling. She didn't know just how good she was! Her earrings were flashing at him again.

"No, I work up at the castle. I'm an Events Organiser," she told him. Billy's head came up.

"A castle? You work in a castle? Is it near here?"

"Well, yes. There are two castles near here, Billy, but I only work in one of them, mostly part time, or when special occasions come about, like Christmas, or weddings, or when the cricket is on. Things like that. I have to pop in today because I have a big wedding at the weekend. That's why Paul is coming to take you to see your mam. It's his job as well," she added. "Make him work for his money."

Billy was amazed. Not only did she live in this nice little place, where neighbours and their animals all had crazy names, and where you could nearly see the Monument, and where a river ran past your front door, but there were castles, too, and people could go in them. Wow. Some people had interesting lives, he thought. He looked keenly at her and realised what it was that had been catching his eye about Sue. Her earrings were silver chickens, with red jewels for their eyes. Billy opened his mouth to comment on them, but Sue began to speak. "So, come on, you. Teeth cleaned and get something decent on. Paul will be here in twenty minutes or so." She started to get up, but saw the look on Billy's face. "And don't worry. I'll be here when you get back. And you can tell me all about it. Why don't you pick your mam some flowers out of the garden and the lane? She'd love to see them when she wakes up."

Billy made his way up the stairs with a heavy heart. He wanted to see his mam, really, he did, but he was a bit scared about going away from here and back to the place where he was quite a different sort of boy. A place where he became grey, and silent, and introverted. Where things worried him and he couldn't look those things in the face. A place where nobody gave him any time, or spoke to him like he was just an ordinary boy – a colourful, friendly boy. They did that here and it was beginning to make a difference to him. He could feel it. He felt he was beginning to take shape here. Become, if not fully-formed, at least, like a half-built sandcastle. That thought brought him up short and he gasped. Was he still a sandcastle which could at any minute be washed away by the incoming tide, or jumped on by small, wilful welly boots? Billy shuddered and shook his head. Where on earth had *that* come from? He was aghast.

At the top of the stairs, he paused. He could hear Richie turning over and the bed creaking. The curtain at the small window, at the top of the stairs, was closed, but bright sunlight tried vainly to shine through. Billy knew that beyond that curtain, the river was running down to the sea, and his heart felt as cold as the greenish brown water.

*

Paul Costello's car was as disorganised and as messy as its owner, Billy thought, supressing a shudder as he climbed into the front passenger seat. He gingerly leaned into the back first, to place a bunch of freshly picked wild flowers on the back seat. Sue had wrapped them in tin foil and they lay there, bright and beautiful among the mess and clutter. Sitting in the front seat was difficult enough because it was piled with empty crisp packets, a Snickers wrapper, a woolly hat and, bizarrely, a wild, furry wig. Billy paused with one leg in the car. Should he just sit on the pile? Would it make any difference, if he did? Paul slumped heavily down into the driver's seat and looked at Billy across the mess.

"Just brush it all onto the floor, Billy. Come on, it'll be OK. In you get."

Billy did as he was told, but it didn't feel right, somehow. After only three days with Sue and Richie, he had got into the good habit of putting his things away and living in a tidy, peaceful environment. Even Dagger Dawson's yard had some air of normality about it, but this car… Billy brushed the clutter onto the floor in the footwell and sat down. He fastened his seat belt and wondered if it was being with Paul and away from Sue that was making him feel depressed, or whether it was being with Paul Costello, and the association with all his earlier fears and struggles, that was making his heart sink. He slumped down in the seat as Paul put the car into gear and moved away up the hill.

"So, you seem to be doing all right here, then, Billy."

Paul smiled at him, glancing sideways, as the car eased away. Billy couldn't help turning round to glance back at the little terrace of houses, where he had actually settled in quite well. He was struck once again by the neatness, the tidy colourful gardens, even the river, snaking its lazy way towards the coast. He looked back at Paul.

"S'alright, I suppose."

Billy didn't feel like he could open up to this man. He didn't really know why. He was friendly enough, always warm and offering some form of helpful advice. Billy thought, suddenly, about Dagger, his huge presence, and the joking twinkle in his eye. Now *there* was a man with whom Billy *was* comfortable and at ease. But why should that be? Dagger was a total stranger, really, and yet, Billy had warmed to him instantly.

They were turning off a huge roundabout and heading towards Sunderland now. Billy could see the Monument, standing stately and serene on its hill in the sunlight. His heart skipped a beat.

"Are we going close to it?" he asked Paul.

"What? Oh, the Monument? Yeah, we're going right past it, Billy. Then, not far from there, we'll be at the hospital. Bet you can't wait to see your mam. And I know she's desperate to see you before she goes into surgery."

Paul was babbling on about his mam, and Billy knew he should be paying attention and answering him, but as they drove past the green Penshaw hill with the Monument perched on the top, Billy was mesmerised. He gazed up at it, his mouth hanging open, eyes wide. It was spectacular, but there was something which drew him to it like a magnet. He could see people making their arduous way up the steep steps to the top, and some were already up there, scanning the incredible views and sitting on the highest ledges, taking photographs. Dogs were gambolling about, and Billy noticed a small herd of brown hairy cows, dotted among the dips and hollows of the hill. It was… magical! It tugged at his heart and called to him in a special way, but he wasn't sure why.

Billy's enjoyment of the beautiful scene was suddenly interrupted by an urgent buzzing sound. Paul slowed the car a little, searching in his pockets, giving Billy a better chance to take in the view of the local landmark. He gave an exasperated sigh.

"Billy, can you see it anywhere?"

Billy reluctantly turned his head away from the Monument, staring distractedly at Paul.

"What?" he asked him rudely, annoyed at being turned away from the sunny scene on the hill.

"That's my mobile buzzing," Paul told him. "I haven't seen it since last night. Are you sitting on it?"

With an exasperated shake of his head, Billy raised himself slightly off the seat and felt underneath him.

"No," he told Paul flatly.

"Well, it's still buzzing. It's in here somewhere. I have to find it."

Billy felt the funny sensation at his feet. Glancing down amongst all the rubbish he told Paul, "I think it's down here."

Leaning forward and straining against the seat belt, Billy scrabbled about in the rubbish. Discarding the mad fur wig, he found the mobile inside an empty crisp packet, but by then, of course, it had stopped buzzing. Billy held it up so that Paul could see it. It was sticky, and smelled of vinegar.

"Yours, I take it?" he asked, raising an eyebrow. Honestly, some people…

"Phew, there it is!" grinned Paul, trying to look at the phone, whilst managing to keep the smelly little car on the road. Just.

"Have a look for me, Billy," he told the boy. "I'll be in trouble, if the office has been trying to reach me. They know I'm taking you in to see your mam, though. But I haven't seen that thing for hours."

Billy scrolled through the phone. He had one of his own, somewhere, but he rarely used it. Why would he? He had no friends and rarely left the house.

"You've got seven missed calls and fourteen messages," he told Paul, trying to keep the accusatory tone out of his voice.

"Huh, most of them will be our lass," Paul sniffed. "I'll sort it, once we get to the hospital."

They drove on, but by now the Monument was behind them and Billy was upset that he hadn't seen as much of it as he'd liked. He would have loved to sit at the bottom and just gaze up at it in wonder. To absorb some of the power and big-ness of it.

The road wound on, becoming boring and grey as they approached the hospital. They drove past the cemetery, and Billy stared dully at the graves with their variously shaped headstones, many leaning forward drunkenly with age and the passage of time. It was a large and well-tended green space, a small oasis of calm in the middle of the busy hospital area, but Billy became deeply depressed at the sight of it. He should be going in to meet his mam in the hope of cheering her up so that she went into this big important operation feeling a bit happier about him being away from her for a while. He knew she was worried about him and about the operation, and the slow recovery after it. But Billy couldn't shake off a feeling of… what? Sadness? *No, despair,* he thought. But why? It was a good hospital, everyone said, and his mam needed to get well again. Later he would be back living with her and everything would be fine again. He should really be feeling happy about this day, but something was nagging away in his brain, like a mouse nibbling away at a nut, turning it over and over.

The car swept into the car park, and Paul jumped out, placing a parking permit on the screen inside, whilst at the same time scrolling through his phone. In his panic to find out what calls he'd missed, he dropped the phone and it fell apart on the gravelly ground.

"Damn!"

Billy supressed a smile, but bent down to pick all the bits up.

"What am I going to do now?" he asked Billy, raking his hair with his meaty hands.

"Well, stop panicking for a start," Billy told him. "I can fix it."

Transferring the slightly limp flowers into his other hand, Billy walked on, not really looking where he was going. Within a few minutes, the phone was back in one piece and working again, but they didn't have time to check the texts because they had to get in and find Mam.

Paul smiled wanly and steered Billy into the main building.

"Come on, son, we're a bit late. Let's go and find your mam's ward. We should catch her OK because her op isn't until this afternoon."

Together they walked along miles of green painted corridors, smelling of rubber and disinfectant. Occasionally they had to stand to one side, whilst a bed was wheeled past, and Billy felt sick at the sight of some poorly people with blood-soaked bandages being trundled along. Doctors and nurses bustled all around them, while cheerful porters whistled and spoke to each other, calling out along the corridors. It was an alien, weird world his mam had come into. No wonder she was worried, Billy thought.

They took a lift up to the fourth floor, with Billy trying hard not to stare at a lad not much older than himself in a wheelchair. The boy was wearing striped pyjamas and an SAFC dressing gown, and on his leg he had an ugly metal contraption, with bits of blood stained bandage still just visible under the dressing gown. The boy had a nurse with him, young and pretty.

"Ha, football injury, I bet," Paul said cheerfully, trying to make polite conversation to ease the tension of being in such a confined space with these strangers. The nurse turned quite pink and patted the boy on his shoulder.

"No. Actually I'm disabled and I'm just having some more operations to try to straighten my leg out a bit," he told Paul coldly, glancing at Billy as if to say "Really? Who is this joker?"

Billy dropped his head in horror so that he wouldn't have to face the embarrassment, and, luckily, the doors ping-ed open and they got out. As the doors slipped shut, he felt sure he heard the nurse sigh and say something to the boy in the wheelchair. The two of them sniggered and disappeared behind the closed lift door. Billy walked on blindly, not knowing where he was going, just praying the lad hadn't thought that Paul was his *dad*. Paul, however, seemed unconcerned. He steered Billy towards a desk, looking for a nurse to point him in the direction of Mrs Higson's bed. The flowers in Billy's hand had started to really droop and the smell was becoming a bit sickly in the confines of the ward. After a few minutes of waiting a large black lady arrived, looking harassed and carrying something covered in a cloth.

"Can I help?" she asked in a chocolate-warm voice, heavy with accent.

"Can you tell us where to find Mrs Higson?" asked Paul, one hand on Billy's shoulder.

Billy was beginning to feel quite sick. The ward was stuffy and smelled odd, a bit like sick and cough medicine all mixed up together. Outside, the sun was shining, but it didn't seem to help. If anything, it made Billy long to get back out into the fresh air. The ward nurse scanned a computer screen and gestured towards her right.

"That room down there," she told them, hurrying away with the strange-smelling covered bowl.

Paul and Billy squeaked off along the shiny corridor, gazing into side rooms as they passed. Billy was starting to tremble. These patients looked old and ill. Some were slumped down into their beds, some looked unconscious, hooked up to drips and bags of fluid. Others shuffled about with walking aids. Billy wanted to turn and run. How could he put his lovely mam through this? Was it too late to get her out of here and run back to their house in the clouds? He felt as if he was gulping in air like a goldfish.

They turned into a room with two beds in it: one was empty and stripped clean of bed linen; the other contained a little white haired old lady. She was sitting up in the bed, her hands clawing at the sheets, her eyes wide. Her scrawny neck and her brown face poking towards them made her look like a tortoise, Billy thought. Paul and he stopped by the empty bed.

"Who are you two after then?" rasped the old woman. Her voice was dry and cracked, like her skin.

"Mrs Higson," Paul told her. "I thought she was in here.

"Oh, her," she snapped, shrugging her shoulders. "Well, you're too late."

"What? What do you mean, too late?" Billy stammered. "I need to see her."

"You should have been here earlier then. She's gone. They wheeled her out of here first thing this morning, and she ain't coming back. Not that one, I'm telling you."

And the old woman flumped back onto her pillows and snapped her mad eyes shut, shaking her head.

Paul looked aghast at Billy.

"Gone? She can't have."

Billy took one look at the empty bed, flung the dead flowers on it then turned and ran out of that stinking, stifling ward as fast as his legs could carry him.

Chapter 12

Billy hurtled along corridors, crashing through swing doors and slipping on the shiny floors, his breath coming in ragged gasps, his eyes streaming with tears. Way behind him he could hear Paul's voice, yelling, telling him he'd sort it, but Billy dropped his head and ploughed on. Nursing staff dived out of his way, and a porter made a grab for him, but Billy was as slippery as an eel and desperate in his grief. He dodged them all, not knowing where he was going, not caring where he would end up. He just had to get out. As he ran he started chanting, "One hundred, fifty-three, seventy, eighteen…" But for once even his usual strange litany couldn't console him. Not this time. This was too big: too *final.*

Wiping his eyes on the back of his hands, and with his nose streaming, Billy skidded round a shining corridor and bumped straight into a ward assistant carrying a tray of teacups and glasses. He couldn't stop and slid straight into her, sending cups and glasses flying everywhere. He had no time to apologise, or look up into her startled face, but did his best to continue his mad escape from this hell hole. His foot landed in some spilled tea as he tried to stand up to race on and he felt himself flying and falling, sliding along the floor on his left shoulder, his head bumping off the floor and his legs whipping out behind him. Lights flashed above his head, doors opened and voices called out after him. Billy gradually lost impetus and slid to a stop, his nose almost touching the tiles, his hands scrabbling frantically to get up. He couldn't breathe, though, so he lay still on the floor, muttering to himself, crying and shaking, embarrassed. A door near the side of his head opened, a pair of black, very shiny, expensive shoes appeared next to his head, and a loud voice asked, "What on earth is going on out here?"

Figures gathered around him, hands reached down to help Billy up to his feet. He couldn't look at anyone. The pain was settling in now, his shoulder sore and aching, his hands burning, his face pink with fear and embarrassment. The man in the expensive shoes was also wearing an expensive suit. He lifted Billy's face to look at him, and when he next spoke it was with some kindness.

"Now, what have we here? What's happened to you, eh? Let me check you over, make sure there's no lasting damage."

"Oh, Mr Longman, don't you worry, I'll see to this young man and find out what on earth he's playing at."

A nurse had caught up with the group and had taken hold of Billy by the arm, a little roughly. She appeared to be angry and embarrassed in front of this man, but Billy couldn't work out why. After all, Billy was the one who was squirming, inside and out. Glancing up, he scanned the face of the man in the suit. 'Mr Longman' said the name on the door he was being led past into an office. *That's okay then*, Billy thought, *he's just an ordinary bloke, not an important doctor or something. I can soon get out of here.* But quickly, a thought flashed into his head. *And then what?* Where would he go? What would he do? How on earth could he find his way back to Sue and Richie? He dropped his head and sobbed again, as he was gently lowered into a chair in Mr Longman's office.

The man quietly found a tissue and handed it to Billy, waiting patiently and lifting the phone to make a quiet call to someone. His voice was smooth, educated and accent-less. He poured a glass of ice-cold water from a large machine in the corner, giving Billy enough time to compose himself a little. Moving to stand beside him, Mr Longman talked soothingly about how he'd heard a commotion and had come to see if he could help. He joked that he hadn't expected to find a body lying on the floor outside his door: usually his patients waited very calmly on the chairs at the end of the corridor, until they were called in to see him, but he was happy to help in any way. He gently moved the hair on Billy's scalp, making sure there were no bruises or cuts to his head. His hands felt warm and gentle as he manipulated Billy's left shoulder and arm, testing for pain or restricted movement. When he was satisfied that the boy was not really injured, he sat back down and looked enquiringly at him over his desk.

"So, young man. What's your name and where have you landed from?"

Billy could hear the smile in his voice.

"It's... B... Billy," he managed to stammer, jamming the damp tissue into his nose and sniffing deeply.

"Billy, okay then. What happened to you? Why are you so upset, Billy? Let's see if I can help you, eh?"

His kindness was too much. The floodgates opened again, tears streaming once again, the sobs making his shoulders heave. Mr Longman waited patiently and silently until the boy could speak.

"It's... my mam... She's ... I..." he gasped, closing his eyes tightly.

"Is your mam in this hospital, Billy? Is that it?" Mr Longman asked gently.

Billy nodded, balling up the tissue and reaching for another.

"Yes, well she was, but now she's... dead."

Mr Longman sat up then.

"I'm very sorry to hear that, Billy. Can you tell me what happened to her? Was she very ill?"

Billy looked at him then looked away, out of the window, towards the cemetery in the distance.

"She wasn't really that bad," he began. "At least, I didn't know she was that bad. She was just having an operation on her back. She was going to have it done this afternoon and I brought her flowers and everything, but when I found her bed it was empty and the old woman said she was dead! She told me my mam was never coming back."

Billy shuddered at the thought. His mind was racing. What was he going to do? Mr Longman had picked up a folder off the top of a pile and was flicking through it.

"An operation? On her back, you say?" he asked. Billy nodded sadly.

"What's your mam called?" Mr Longman asked gently.

"Carol." He sniffed, then looked at Mr Longman with tear-streaked sadness. "Carol Higson. And she shouldn't have died. It was only her back, not her heart or anything. I was too late."

Mr Longman sighed and closed the file. He smiled gently and got up to crouch down next to Billy.

"You're not really too late, Billy," he said.

Something in his voice made Billy look up at him quickly.

"What do you mean?" he asked. Why was this guy smiling at him like that?

"Your mam had her operation early, that's all. She had it first thing this morning, and now she's in the recovery room, waking up."

Billy's eyes widened, staring at him in sheer shock.

"But...but...that old woman said..." he stammered. Mr Longman continued to smile, standing up to his full height and reaching down to get Billy to stand up, too.

"How do you know that?" Billy asked, confused.

"Because she's my patient, Billy, and I performed her surgery. It went very well, too. Why don't I take you up to see her, eh? Then we'll get you sorted and get you home."

He walked Billy towards the office door and opened it into the corridor. The group of nurses and ward assistants on the other side jumped back hastily: they'd obviously been listening at the keyhole. They all looked nervous as Billy and Mr Longman walked out together and up towards the lift.

"Do you mean it?" asked the boy as he shuffled, sniffing, alongside the tall elegant figure of the surgeon. "Will she really be all right? She's really not dead?" Billy was trying so hard not to let his hope shine into his voice.

As the lift doors closed behind them, Mr Longman told him firmly, and cheerfully, "She'll be as good as new, Billy. Well, nearly as good as new. She'll have to recover, and you'll have to give her lots of time and patience, but she'll be fine. I promise."

Looking down at the tear-stained face and glowing smile of this thin little lad made his heart leap. *If only all his patients responded like this nice young man,* he thought, as they made their way up to Recovery.

Chapter 13

Billy was aware that his breath was still coming out in ragged little gasps as he trundled along endless corridors, up lifts and down stairs, alongside Mr Longman, as they went to find his mum. His shoulder had started to ache and he felt clumsy, hot and sweaty beside this tall, friendly, cleanly kind man. He noticed that the nurses stood back to let them pass and almost bowed their heads, as if he was in the company of royalty. *In fact, being with the Queen must feel a bit like this,* thought Billy. He wasn't sure he liked it, really. He was used to being invisible in his everyday life. Normally doors swung shut in his face – they weren't held open with this air of deference. It was just weird, but Mr Longman seemed to expect it and was very pleasant and polite to everyone he met. Finally, they swung through some more doors, having pressed a button and waited for it to open. Billy copied Mr Longman and used a hand sanitiser before shyly following him onto a quiet, subdued ward. The lights seemed dim here, and the nurses bustled about, speaking in hushed tones. They jumped to attention as Mr Longman appeared, smiling questioningly at him. Suddenly, a loud voice bellowed out.

"Billy! For God's sake, lad, where have you *been*? I've been frantic…"

Paul Costello lumbered into view from a side room; his hair was almost standing on end and his face was as white as a sheet. The nursing staff and Mr Longman turned as one, and each person present issued him with a sharp rebuke. "Sshhh!"

Paul, at least, had the conscience to blush. Billy almost smiled, watching the man's discomfort as his face turned from white to bright red. He held a clumsy hand up to his lips and bowed his head.

"Oh, sorry," he whispered. "Billy, are you okay? I didn't know how to find you. I thought you were lost," he told him in hushed whispers. "Look, your mam's here. She's OK, Billy."

He clasped Billy to his chest in a bear hug, almost lifting him clean off his feet. Billy's face was squashed into Paul's smelly jacket and he squirmed in agitation. Pushing himself away, he looked up at Paul and indicated to Mr Longman standing behind him. The surgeon stepped forward and introduced himself briefly.

"And who may you be?" he asked.

"Er… I'm his… care worker." He stumbled, releasing the hand he had been shaking. "I was looking after Billy and staying with him but, er, well, things got a bit out of hand, eh, Billy?"

He attempted a smile and a ruffle of Billy's hair. Billy shrugged him off and pulled a face.

"Yes. Quite," said Mr Longman. He was clearly unimpressed with Mr Costello and his 'care' of Billy. Stepping into a side office he took the two of them, and crouching down to look into his face, he began to explain to Billy, "Now, Billy, as I said, your mam has had her operation and she's going to be fine."

Paul Costello jumped in. "See. Just what I told you, Billy, didn't I …"

He was shut up by a curt glance from the surgeon and had the grace to blush again.

"Now, Billy," Mr Longman continued. "Your mam *is* going to be better, but I need you to know that today, when you see her, she will still look quite poorly. She may not be fully awake, or she may be feeling quite sick. She will have a drip in her arm and a bag of fluid at her side. Don't you worry about those things, though," he added, noticing a change in Billy's grey eyes and a frown starting to appear. "In a day or two, you'll see a huge change in her. Just be patient, eh?" He smiled warmly at Billy and stood up.

"See, Billy. Your mam's got to be a patient patient, and so have you, eh?"

Paul nudged Billy and winked at him, smiling hugely at his own pathetic joke. Billy just nodded, looking up to Mr Longman. "Please," he began nervously, rubbing his aching shoulder, "can I see her now?"

Mr Longman looked expectantly at the staff nurse, who nodded and beckoned to Billy to follow her. As he and Paul walked towards another Side Room, Mr Longman called quietly after him, "Remember, Billy, you know where I am if ever you want to talk to me."

Billy smiled gratefully at the surgeon, a proper smile which lit up his whole face. He waved his hand and hurried on after the staff nurse.

Nice little lad, thought Mr Longman, turning to leave. *Bless him.*

There was only one bed in this room, with lots of machines beeping and glowing in the dimmed light. Billy stood at the door and looked across at his mam in the bed; her face was very pale in contrast to her dark hair, which was spread out on the pillow behind her. She looked somehow very small in that huge metal bed, like a rag doll. It didn't seem to be his mam at all. He was used to her singing and laughing with him, shouting at him to get up and tidy his bedroom or go a message to the shops for her. *She shouldn't be lying so silently*, he thought, but then he remembered what Mr Longman had told him. It's only for a day or two, and then she'll be a bit better. Twisting his fingers nervously, he felt Paul's hand on his shoulder, guiding him towards the bedside.

"Come on, Billy," he told him quietly. "Say something to your mam to let her know you're here."

One of her hands was on the bedclothes, with a plastic tube coming out of it, attached to a bag of fluid, hanging on a pole. There was a trace of blood around the tube. Billy flinched. There was another bag of darker liquid hanging under the sheets, somewhere near his knees, and he was worried he'd knock into it and hurt his poor mam even more. It was all so strange and weird and like a nightmare. He wanted to cry, but he couldn't. He had to let his mam know he was here with her.

"Can she hear me, though?" he asked the nurse hovering near the foot of the bed, checking a clipboard with medical details on it.

"Oh yes, I think so, Billy. She might not be able to say much just yet, and she's feeling a bit sick, but yes, you can talk to her."

Billy took a deep breath and leaned in closer to his mam. He thought he could still smell anaesthetic on her. She didn't smell like his mam usually did, all sort of talcy and flowery.

"Mam, I'm here. Are you OK? Can you wake up, mam?"

He gently stroked her forearm with one finger. She felt very warm and solid, all of a sudden. He gazed at her face, watching as her closed eyes flickered, her long dark lashes fluttering on her cheek.

"Mam, I brought you some flowers from Sue's garden, but… well, I'm not sure where they are, but I'll get you some more, I promise."

His mam's eyes stayed shut, but she smiled then. Billy let out a stifled sob of relief. She really could hear him, then! *Quick*, he thought, *tell her something more!*

"It's nice at Sue's, Mam," he began, leaning in closer. "And you'll never guess – there's a donkey, and a dog that crashes through the front door, only he's really friendly, and there's a huge cat that I can draw, and Sue's ever such a good artist. And I changed my bedroom cos it was looking into the river and you know about me and the water and…"

"Woah, steady on, son," Paul told him gently, patting his back as if to slow him down a bit. "Don't tell her everything in one go. We'll be coming in again, when she's properly awake and able to talk back."

Billy stood up, staring at his mam's face. She was still pale, but now he could see a small change in her. She was in there, finding her way out of the deep sleep gradually, drifting slowly back to consciousness, but she knew Billy was right beside her. He felt her fingers wrap themselves around his wrist and hold him tightly. She smiled again and gave a small sigh.

The nurse checked her pulse and looked closely at the monitor beside the bed.

"I think that's enough for now, Billy," she told him, smoothing out the bedclothes. "She'll be asleep for most of the afternoon, probably until quite late this evening, but she knows you're here and you're OK."

Paul Costello stood up and walked Billy towards the door. The sun had gone in behind a cloud, and the room had become quite stuffy and claustrophobic. Billy suddenly needed to get out and get some air.

"Come on, son, let's get out of here. We'll come back another day, eh?"

The nurse followed them out. In the corridor, she told Billy, "You'll see a huge difference when you and your dad come back next time, Billy. You'll be a lot happier then."

Billy looked up at Paul and they both sort of squirmed at the nurse, but neither bothered with an explanation. Billy simply shrugged and turned to leave the ward, Paul following after him, thanking the staff as they went.

In the car park, the air felt fresher, but there was an odd green tinge to the sky. Billy sniffed the air like a dog, head up, the breeze ruffling his hair. He was glad to get out of that stifling environment and now he just felt exhausted. His knees were shaking and he wanted to lie down on the hot tarmac. The sun had gone, and he wanted to get back to Sue and Richie's house. He wanted to be away from this place, away from Paul, away from his mam even, with her drips and bags of fluid and her blood.

Paul opened the car doors, and they both stood back for a second or two, waiting for the hot air to flow out of the car and for some of the slightly cooler breeze to drift into it. Billy slumped back in the passenger seat and closed his eyes, willing Paul to say nothing, as they eased their way out of the hospital grounds and onto the road back to Fatfield. Paul seemed to sense exactly what Billy needed just then and remained quiet, for a change, concentrating on the traffic. Billy thought he felt – rather than heard – the deep rumble of faraway thunder and opened his eyes, as big fat raindrops splashed onto the windscreen in front of him. They were approaching the cemetery again. Billy stared into the cool greenery of the place: it was so peaceful in there, he thought, and yet… He shuddered. It had been years since he was inside that place. He remembered being there when he was little, standing at a graveside and holding tightly onto his mam's hand. Lots of other people were with them, all crying and upset. There was even somebody taking photographs, he remembered. A flash of lightning lit up the car, and the rain battered down more heavily now.

"I'm sorry that nurse thought I was your dad, Billy," Paul told him, turning the sidelights on and speeding up the windscreen wipers.

Billy turned his head and gazed at him. Had Paul been reading his mind? He looked past him, gazing sadly into the cemetery.

"Your dad would be so happy that you saw your mam today, and told her all about your new place," he told Billy quietly. "You did well. You had a big shock, then you came back and faced up to it. Well done, Billy."

The boy was staring into the trees in the cemetery now, watching them being lashed about by the wind and this small sudden storm. *It would be so much easier next visit,* Paul thought. *And I'll take all my calls and not lose my flaming mobile either,* he told himself, shaking his head and sighing. He thought he heard a small sigh from Billy just then, and the boy seemed to mutter quietly, "My dad. Yeah. Well done, Billy."

They drove on in silence, the only sound being the odd rumble of distant thunder and the swish of the tyres on the wet road.

Chapter 14

Sue was up early, getting ready for a day at work at the castle, following a disturbed night. Thunder had rumbled on and off and the rain had lashed down incessantly, bashing the gardens, trees and windows of her little house. At one point, she got out of bed and looked out of the bedroom window. The tide was in and the river was running deep and angry, the raindrops bouncing on the water, churning it up into angry little waves, which smacked against the riverbank. In the flashes of lightning, she glimpsed a solitary dog walker, hunched over, hurrying up Worm Hill; a sodden cyclist trundled his way over the bridge, causing spray to splash up behind his tyres. *Poor souls*, she thought, before tumbling back into bed. She lay quietly, listening to the storm and holding her breath, in case Billy was disturbed by it. All quiet inside the house, at least. Her mobile bleeped, and she reached out for it. *Richie*, she smiled, opening up the text. *Brill, eh?* he had asked. He loved a good storm. Sue imagined him having a toilet break and running to the big garage doors to stand and watch it. She smiled, put her mobile on the bedside drawers, and went back to sleep.

Now, in the early morning, she took her cup of tea and went out into the small front garden in her pyjamas. She stood on the wet grass in her bare feet, cradling her mug against her chest, and breathed in deeply. What a morning! The sun was shining, the birds were busy and singing loudly, and everything had that newly washed look and smell about it. It was still and peaceful, the sky a cloudless blue. The tide was going out, trickling away quietly, bubbling over stones, and a couple of little wading birds were padding about in the shallows, turning over the gravel in search of breakfast. Sue smiled as Fingle Brown slunk silently down the river bank through the reeds right next to them, also looking for breakfast. Further down the river, she heard the unmistakable bray of Dolly, the donkey. *Must be a quarter to eight*, Sue thought, looking at her watch. Yep, regular as clockwork, that one. She smiled, starting to plan her day ahead. She brushed some of the heavy silver raindrops off the ivy growing up the front of the house, picked some storm-blown leaves out of the bird bath, and went back inside the house, wiping her wet feet on the door mat on her way in. She straightened a couple of her pictures on the way into the kitchen. *I'll give Billy another half hour*, she thought, glancing up the stairs. *What a pity he can't come out onto the river side of the house and enjoy a wonderful start to the day like this*, she thought.

Sue went through the kitchen to her back garden. A couple of the plastic garden chairs had been blown over, and her sweet peas and pansies were a little worse for wear, leaning their heads forward heavily, as if tired, *or more likely drunk on too much rain water,* Sue thought. She'd need to tie them up a bit. Perhaps that would be a job for Billy? There were still huge puddles of water at the edge of the lawn, and a fat green frog jumped away from her towards the garden next door. There were small rivulets of gravel, which had been swept in by the rain from the back lane onto her path. *Billy could clear that, too*, she thought, turning to take in the delightful early morning smells of her wet garden. As she walked back into the house, two magpies chirruped at her and flew away. *Two for joy,* she thought. *That's good.*

Half an hour later, she was showered and dressed and making breakfast, singing quietly to the radio, when Billy wandered into the kitchen and sat at the table.

"Morning, Billy," she told him, putting down a glass of orange juice in front of him. The kitchen door onto the garden was open, and Billy was momentarily dazzled by the sunlight and warmth streaming in. Billy smiled and sipped at his juice, realising quite quickly that it wasn't only the sun causing the warmth in the kitchen. Sue presented him with a selection of cereal packets and a bowl, then sat opposite him.

"Have you remembered that I'm going into work today, Billy?" she asked, pouring herself some cornflakes.

Billy had his mouth full, but he nodded at her. Sue was relieved to see that he didn't seem too bothered about it.

"Richie will be in, but obviously, he has to sleep. I've asked Dagger if you could help him with some jobs down at his place. Is that OK with you, Billy?"

She watched his response carefully. He gazed back at her with his grey eyes, looked a little puzzled for a split second, then smiled shyly.

"Yeah, of course," he told her. He paused, his spoon in mid-air. "I like Dagger. He's a nice bloke."

Tucking into her own cornflakes, Sue leaned in a little closer and asked him, "How are you feeling about your visit to see your mam yesterday? I know it didn't go as well as we planned, but... well... you've seen her now. And you'll be back there again, soon."

Sue was actually livid with Paul Costello for getting it all so wrong. Fool! How could he have been so careless about his mobile? The guy was a liability sometimes. Then she felt a little guilty because she knew he had an awful lot on his plate, and over the years, she had found him to be quite good with the children in his care. She thought Billy looked a bit spooked by the thought of going back to the hospital again, so she reassured him.

"What if I go with you as well next time, Billy? Would that be OK?"

Billy's head shot up and he gave her a broad smile.

"Yeah – that would be great," he told her happily. The thought of having Sue with him made the whole prospect of another visit to that stinky, stuffy hospital bearable. And he could show Sue off to his mam, with her pretty face and her colourful hair, and her mad earrings. Fantastic.

Sue reached over and gave his arm a warm shake. She stood up and went into the corridor.

"Just got to put my face on, Billy," she told him. "Then I'll be off soon as Richie gets in."

Huh? Put her face on? Billy was surprised.

"You what?" he asked. "What's wrong with the face you've got on already?"

Sue popped her head back round the door, a wand of mascara in her hand.

"Good grief, Billy," she told him. "You don't think I'd go out without my make up on, do you? I wouldn't even put the bins out without my face on. Someone could see me!" she joked, going back to the mirror.

Billy sat back in his chair and smiled, shaking his head. She really hadn't a clue how pretty she was. He didn't think she needed anything on her face. "Well, I think you don't need any of that stuff," he told her.

Sue popped her head back out to smile at him, as the kitchen door opened and Richie wandered in. "I fully agree, Billy," he said, walking over to kiss Sue warmly. "You've got good taste, my lad. She's a beauty, with or without her face on."

Richie poured himself a cup of tea and sat at the table, too.

"Cracking storm last night, Billy. Did you see it? The lightning was amazing!"

Billy shook his head, watching Richie closely. He was still getting used to having a man about the house. He liked Richie's face, too. Hazel eyes, tanned face and short neat hair. He was all 'neat', actually, Billy thought. Not too big and bulky, but not small either. Cheerful, that's what Richie was. Billy couldn't imagine him shouting at anybody, ever.

"Never heard a thing," Billy told him, scooping up the last of his cornflakes.

"Honest?" Richie asked. "That's a shame. It was fantastic." He ruffled Billy's hair, then leaned in to tell him quietly. "Go on, son, drink the milk out of the bowl. I always do." He winked at Billy.

Sue's voice drifted in from the hallway. "If you're teaching that lad bad habits you'll be in big trouble, you."

Billy laughed at Richie, then quickly picked up the bowl and drank the last of the milk, wiping his mouth on his arm.

"Good lad, waste not, want not," Richie told him. "I do it each morning. Gets her every time."

*

After waving Sue off in her battered little car, Billy turned to walk down the leafy green lane towards Dagger's yard. He wasn't sure how he was feeling about today. The weather was gorgeous, for a change, and Sue had made sure he was happy with the arrangements for the day, but something was niggling away at his brain, keeping him on edge, worried without knowing the reason why. He presumed it was because of his mam, lying all alone and in pain in that hospital bed, and his fears that he had lost her. As he walked, he absent-mindedly pulled up long switches of grass and deseeded them, letting them whip through his fingers. *It was going to be a strange summer, that's for sure,* he thought. He wondered about what was happening right now in his house in the sky, up on the seventeenth floor. Dust would have settled and, in this warm weather, it would have become musty, without any breeze through a slightly opened window. And then he thought of all the windows below, in the town centre shops and offices, that would right now be reflecting the bright sunlight, flashing across the miles of city like Morse code. Billy liked to sit and stare for hours out of the living room window, watching and trying to make up coded messages, as cars flashed by over the bridge, and trains hurtled on towards Newcastle. Before he knew it, Billy had arrived at Dagger's gate.

He paused for a minute to look and listen. Should he just walk straight into the yard? Would it be better to call out to see if Dagger would come and welcome him in? Would that donkey and the dog be waiting to jump out at him, if he did just go through? Could donkeys jump?

All was peaceful. He could hear the faint clucking of chickens, pecking away just round behind the first shed. He thought he could hear a faint knocking sound, wood on wood possibly. Billy decided to go through and find Dagger for himself. Taking a deep breath, he pushed the gate open with a slight squeak and walked through. Turning to make sure it was properly shut behind him, Billy suddenly froze as two large paws landed on his shoulders and he felt hot doggy breath on the back of his neck. Lennie had made his usual shocking appearance, but this time he hadn't barked. Billy tried not to scream.

Half crouching, he managed to turn round and get hold of the dog's paws, fairly gently, just in case dogs didn't like their paws being touched. He realised he knew absolutely nothing about dogs, about how to speak to them or how to deal with them in any way. This one, Lennie, didn't seem to mind at all. He was looking into Billy's face with his mouth open and Billy got the distinct impression the dog was smiling at him. Its tail was wagging, and it was sort of hopping up and down as if it was delighted to see him. Billy managed to smile back at the dog.

"Err… hi, Lennie… can you… sit?" he asked it gently, then smiled happily, as the dog got straight down and did just that. It had obeyed him! Billy was thrilled in a small way that an animal, a creature he had only met once before, was willing to listen to him and to do as he asked. Wow. Nobody ever listened to him. Well, maybe Miss Dorwood did at school.

"So… Lennie… where's your dad, then? Where's Dagger?"

Billy raised an eyebrow, as he asked the question. He felt a bit foolish. It's the sort of conversation he would have with his mam, as if wanting to know what was for tea, but the dog seemed to listen and instantly jumped up, laughing again, and trotted off towards the back of the yard, stopping and turning once or twice to make sure Billy was following. He led Billy past the chickens, between two other sheds and to a larger one nearer the river. Billy stopped.

This was closer to the water than he had ever been before. He nervously scanned the scene in front of him. The tide was out, sunlight flashing off small pools and he could hear it trickling away. It seemed safe, innocuous even. Down here, near the water's edge, he could hear that lovely music playing again. He strained his ears, listening to it. The notes flowed and tinkled away, like the sound of the little streams in the river bed. Then he heard the sound of someone whistling along to the music. It was coming from the shed behind him. Stepping backwards, but with eyes downcast, so as not to stand in the piles of donkey droppings, Billy approached the shed.

It was newer than the other sheds in the yard, of a sort of honey-coloured tan. The large double doors were standing open, and the sound of whistling was stronger. He could hear sawing, and as he quietly approached the front door, he could smell wood shavings, varnish, and oils of some sort. It was quite tantalising to Billy, without him knowing why. Stepping closer, he made out the large shape of Dagger, bending over a piece of equipment, with a saw in his hand. He was watching closely as Dagger guided the saw through the wood, stopping his whistling to blow away some of the dust from the material. Billy watched the strong hands working away for a minute. Dagger had his sleeves rolled up, his dark curls were falling onto his forehead, a soft rag was stuffed into the pocket of his faded blue jeans. He had a look of pure contentment on his face. Stopping to blow some more dust off the wood, he spotted Billy, standing in the shade near the doors of the shed. A huge grin creased his large, handsome face.

"Morning, Billy. There you are. Come on in, then."

Lennie ran to Billy's side and back towards his owner, as if he too was giving Billy permission to enter this magical den. The dog sat down at Dagger's feet, thumping his tail wildly and looking towards Billy.

"Hi," Billy muttered, nervously stepping inside and looking around in awe. "Wow," he breathed, taking it all in.

Dagger allowed the lad to find his feet, watching in amusement as the boy got his bearings. He didn't want to interrupt the look of joy and amazement on Billy's face with inane chatter. The lad was obviously impressed, and Dagger wanted him to feel as at home here as he did himself.

Billy's mouth dropped open. His eyes were wide and his hands hung limply down at his side, as he gazed around the shed. It was much bigger than he had at first thought. As his eyes adjusted from walking into the shade from the sunshine outside, Billy could see it all. The tubs of sweet-smelling varnish; planks of freshly cut wood; boxes of off-cuts off wood; neat racks of tools, hanging up on the walls; rows and rows of old paint tins, containing nails and screws; brushes, leaning drunkenly up against the shelves, which contained carvings of wooden boats of every size and shape; and in the middle, resting amongst the rolls of wood chips and shavings, a large curious shape, all ribs and spines. It looked to Billy like a half-eaten fish.

"Welcome to my world of wood, Billy," Dagger told him with a smile, wiping his hands on the rag from his pocket. "Come on in and have a look around."

Billy did as he was bid, stepping inside. He moved round the shed quietly, touching things gently, inhaling the smells, stroking the shiny surface of the wood almost reverently. He moved to the shelves containing the boats and wooden yachts, all different, painted in glorious lifelike colours. One or two had blue sails, others were bigger ships, not boats. Some of them even had little people standing on their decks. He started counting and lost track after about eight. He gingerly put out a finger to touch the intricately carved lifebelt on one of the boats, then paused, looking questioningly at Dagger.

"Yes, son, go on. Of course you can touch it."

Billy was amazed. *Where had they all come from,* he wondered. Dagger appeared at his side, holding up a small red painted yacht with a white sail.

"So, what do you think of my work, then, Billy?"

Billy flashed a look up at the big man beside him. "You…you made these? All these boats?"

"I did," Dagger told him with quiet pride. "Yes, they're all my handiwork, Billy. This is where I spend most of my time. Keeps me out of trouble. And if any of the neighbours want anything mended, I can usually fix it for them."

Billy was lost for words. He stared at Dagger with shining eyes. "It's all amazing. I don't think I've ever been anywhere like this in my life."

He turned into the middle of the shed, staring at the strange shape of ribs in front of him. Placing one hand on the end of the rough wood, his curious expression spoke more than he could say.

"It's a boat, Billy. Or at least, it will be a boat, when it's finished. I could really use a hand with it, though. You up for that?"

Billy gazed at the odd shape in front of him, looked around the room once more in awe, then nodded, before realising that his hand was carelessly stroking the dog's silky smooth black head. He took his hand away and smiled up at Dagger.

"Yes please!"

"I thought you might say that. Right, but first, a cup of tea. Pull up a stool, then."

It was only then that Billy noticed the little camping stove in the corner, with a flat bottomed kettle bubbling away and an assortment of old mugs lined up. In next to no time, the two of them were sitting together at the doors of the shed, tea in hands, watching the tide turning and, for once, Billy didn't mind. Nothing could get him here. He was in Heaven.

Chapter 15

Sue put the phone down and sat opposite Billy, with a worried crease in her normally smooth brow. Billy paused, teacup in hand, staring wordlessly at her.

"It's OK, Billy," she told him, putting a hand out to touch his forearm reassuringly. "That was the hospital. Your mam has developed a bit of an infection in her wound and she's not very well, so we won't be going in to see her this afternoon as we'd planned."

Billy slowly lowered the cup. His lip trembled. He had been really looking forward to going to the hospital this time because Sue was going with him. He had been so happy about seeing his mam and being able to take charge of showing Sue where to park the car and leading her to the ward. It made him feel useful and a bit grown up, not like the trembling, tearful idiot he felt he had been when Paul took him.

Sue recognised his sadness. "Honestly, she's going to be OK, it's just that she needs some stronger antibiotics and she'll not feel too well today. But tomorrow, or the day after, we can go, just as soon as she picks up again."

Billy studied her face. Her blue eyes were shining. He trusted Sue to tell the truth and to not make the mistakes other adults had made with him in the past.

"So, I've got the day off, but I really need to get some jobs done. What about you, Billy? What will you do? Some drawing, perhaps? Or would you like to go out for a walk and maybe meet up with a few of the local people here? You haven't really been very far yet, you know."

Billy couldn't really tell Sue that he didn't want to meet other people. Other people worried him. They didn't understand him the way she and Richie did. He was happy in their cosy little cocoon with just the three of them. Even the river was losing its terrifying hold over him. He was getting used to it being there, bubbling away in the background, its gentle sounds quietly pervading his very being and mingling with the sunshine to soothe him. The nightmares were beginning to drift away, like the morning mist he knew wrapped around his beloved Monument like a blanket.

He nodded eagerly. "I'll do some drawing," he told her. "There's one I need to add a lot more detail to."

"Good lad. I've got some admin to do on the computer, but I'll be here if you need me."

Each of them got busy. Sue got her laptop out on the kitchen table, whilst Billy retrieved his precious sketch book from the safety of his bedroom. He sat at the table opposite Sue and slowly worked his way through the book, taking his time to study each page. He quickly became engrossed in his previous work, catching glimpses of the different moods he had been in, depending on the subject of each picture. The view of the Monkwearmouth Bridge, with its graceful green arch, was a good one, with soft flowing lines and no harsh edges. There was another good one of the windmill on Newcastle Road he had done one day when he had been out with his mam. He quite liked the lion statue from Mowbray Park, but it needed a little more doing to the trees in the background. Sue watched him closely as he turned the pages. She had not really pushed too harshly to study his work, as she knew better than most how private your own artwork was, how personal. It meant something to you. But from where she was sitting across from Billy, she could tell he had real talent.

Suddenly, Billy let out a quiet little gasp. He had stopped at a still life image of what appeared to Sue to be a bag or a backpack. It was leaning up against a wall, and next to it there was a pair of boots. But as she was looking at it from upside down, she couldn't be sure. Trying not to stare, Sue continued typing away on her computer. Billy's face had creased and sunken. His shoulders seemed to sag, and she could tell he was instantly deflated, like a birthday balloon slowly going down. She frowned, but decided not to say anything. Billy turned the pages before stopping at an image of a seagull. That's when he seemed to slowly come back into himself again.

In the hallway, the phone started ringing. Billy didn't seem to notice as Sue left her laptop to answer it. She chatted away for a couple of seconds, before coming back to the table.

"Billy, it's for you," she told him with a smile, sitting down at the table again.

He looked up from the seagull sketch, puzzlement in his eyes. "Huh? Me?"

"Yes, you. Go on."

As Billy walked into the hall, Sue reached over and turned back the pages of his sketchbook to the image that had so obviously had a negative effect on him. She now found it was a very good drawing, yet spotted instantly that it was darker and more aggressively drawn than the rest. It seemed to be an army issue backpack and a pair of boots. The camouflage was harshly drawn, but remarkably accurate. The straps of the bag looked worn and shabby, one strap hanging loosely, whilst the other was fastened up. The boots were caked in mud, and the laces hung like ribbons. But the background to this picture was dark and threatening, as if a big storm was brewing. It was an angry, aggressive picture. On the next page, there was yet another view of Billy's beloved Penshaw Monument, this one drawn as if from a long way off, like from his bedroom in the city, maybe. In contrast, this picture had a hazy sun and soft clouds in the background. It was a calmer, more serene image. Hearing Billy saying goodbye, she quickly turned back to the seagull drawing and put the sketchbook back in position.

Coming in with a small smile on his face, Billy sat back down. "That was Dagger," he told her.

Sue smiled back. "Ahh, yes, I thought it might be," she said with a grin.

Billy blushed. "He wants me to do a little job for him," he told her proudly. "Is it OK, if I do?"

"Yes, of course, Billy." She hesitated. "I love that picture of the seagull," she added. "You've got the look in its eye just right. It's a cheeky thing, isn't it?"

"It's a herring gull," he told her, pleased at her interest, turning the page so she could see more closely. Sue smiled and leaned forward. It really was very good. The bird was standing with a crisp packet in its beak.

"Those feathers are really hard to do well, Billy. But they look amazing. Why the crisp packet, though?"

Billy looked down at his work. "Well, in school, everyone hates the gulls," he said shyly. "And they're all terrified of them cos they're so big. Even the teachers. But I love them. I think they're really beautiful and clever. They're always tidying up in the yard after the kids."

Sue decided against asking about the backpack picture. It would save for another time. She'd have another opportunity soon enough.

"So, Dagger has a job for you? That's good. He doesn't trust a lot of people, you know, our Dagger."

"Why do you call him Dagger?" asked Billy. "He can't have been called that by his mam when he was little."

"Now that's something you'll have to ask him about," Sue told him. "And I'll be very interested to see what his answer is. *This* time," she said meaningfully, going back to her keyboard. Billy gave her a puzzled look and headed for the kitchen door.

"Take some sweets, Billy, and an apple with you." Sue gestured to the bowl by the kitchen door. Billy simply smiled, nodded and put a few crinkly wrapped mints into his pocket, stuffing a small sweet apple into the other. Quietly, he stepped out into the sunshine.

The big black dog, Lennie Catflap, was waiting in a sunny spot by the front gate. He wagged his tail and sat up with a grin, as Billy ambled towards Dagger's house. By now, Billy's initial fear of the animal had left him.

He stroked the dog's silky head. "Hey, Lennie. Where's your dad? Where's Dagger, then?"

Together, the two of them pushed through the gate and strolled past the sheds to the bigger boat shed. *I'm talking to a dog*, he thought to himself, and couldn't keep the smile from his face. Billy could hear Dagger whistling and sawing inside. He kept his eyes open, in case Dolly the donkey should suddenly come, shouldering her way past him, but there was no sign of her today. Stepping over the odd clucking chicken, Billy came to the door of the shed and stood for a minute, patiently waiting for Dagger to finish what he was doing and realise that he had arrived. It was soothing just standing there, surrounded by sunshine, smells and wood shavings at the cool entrance of the shed.

Lennie took the initiative and went inside to Dagger. The man looked up and smiled.

"Aha, Billy, my man! Come on in."

Billy didn't need telling twice, stepping forward happily and gazing all around.

"Hi, Dagger." He smiled and stoked Lennie's head. "What you doing?"

"I've just added another rib to this boat, Billy. It was a bit long so I've had some cutting and bending to do, but look at that. What do you think?"

Billy stepped forward.

"A rib?" he asked, puzzled.

"Ah yes, boats have ribs, just like we do, to hold everything together. And she'll have a heart, too, in the end, I hope. We've still got a few more ribs to put in before we can get on with other jobs, though."

Billy gazed at this big man, secretly delighted at his use of the word 'we'. He suddenly felt like he'd grown six inches. Here he was, working on a boat, being useful, and being trusted to do tricky jobs. He wasn't being a scaredy-cat-baby, frightened of his own shadows and the fears that menaced him, when he was least expecting them to come creeping up.

"Great. What do you want me to do, then?" he asked, stepping fully into the shed and feeling desperate to get his hands on the wood. *What tool would be best for this job*, he wondered. A saw, or a long-handled chisel? Maybe a heavy hammer? He looked up at Dagger, expectantly.

Dagger moved towards the bench at the back. Billy bristled in anticipation. Other boys did jobs with their dads, he knew that. He of course had always been denied that pleasure. Mam gave him odd jobs to do, like going to the shop for bread, or taking the rubbish out, or tidying his bedroom. But this, this was going to be a real manly job. Working with wood, building a boat with his best friend Dagger. Wow!

Dagger turned from the bench with a small parcel wrapped in brown packaging in his hand. He came to Billy and handed it over. Billy took it carefully, almost reverently, turning it over in his hands before attempting to unwrap it. Dagger quickly stopped him.

"Oh no, Billy, it's not for you. I need you to deliver it, please."

Billy looked up at him bleakly.

"Oh. Deliver it. It's not for me," he said quietly, his shoulders dropping a little.

"Please, Billy. It would save me a lot of time. It's for Frank. It's not far, and I thought the walk would do you good. Lads need to get out in the sunshine, you know."

"But… I don't know where Frank lives…" he began, but Dagger was going back to his saw and the ribs of the boat.

"Oh, don't you worry. Lennie will show you. It's the second house on the other side. Lennie's always over there. And it'll be a lovely, peaceful walk. You just ask for Frank, if you're not sure. Everybody knows Frank round here. Well, everybody knows *everybody* round here!" He laughed. "You'll find it OK with Lennie at your side. Off you go. I've said you'll be coming, so someone will look out for you."

Billy's face fell. He raised sad, wet eyes to Dagger.

"But… but… where do I go to find this house?" he stammered, feeling sad and unsure of himself. He wasn't ready for strangers, even though all the ones he'd met so far had been good and kind to him.

Dagger blew some wood shavings from his work.

"It's easy, Billy," he told him. "Left out the gate, left and left. Second house in. You'll see. It's easy. You can't get lost round here, son." And with that, he nodded at the door and went back to his wood. Billy turned sadly and trundled out, hearing the familiar whistling and sawing starting up again before he'd even left the garden.

Outside the gate, Billy paused, uncertain. He had been trusted with a job to do for Dagger, and that pleased him immensely, but on the other hand, he was stepping into unchartered waters. He didn't want to let his new friend down, yet… What to do? If he turned and went back in with the parcel, Dagger would think he was a coward and an idiot. The dog had stopped by him and was sitting at Billy's feet, with an expectant look on his face. Dagger had said Lennie would show him the way. And really, it was such a small place that if he really did get lost he could just turn round and find his way back here, couldn't he? He almost smiled to himself at the thought of leaving a little breadcrumb trail, like in Hansel and Gretel, just in case. Lennie yipped at him, an excited little bark and stood up. The dog jumped up at Billy, then moved on a few metres before stopping and turning back to him, almost pleading. He wants me to take him for a walk, thought Billy. More like the other way round, though. *I need Lennie to take* me *for a walk*. He stepped forward towards the dog, who yipped again with delight and trotted ahead. Billy gave a final look up the lane, towards Sue and Richie's house, then followed slowly. *Well,* he thought to himself, *it's a lovely day, and at least, I won't be alone. I've got company.*

For the first one hundred metres, under the trees dappled with sunshine, Billy was acutely aware of the river running alongside him on his left. He tried to ignore it, concentrating on the birds above his head, watching out for squirrels in the trees, stepping over puddles left by the storm the other night, and calling the dog back to his side. Anything, really, to avoid looking towards the river. Once or twice, the dog ran down to the water, trying to get as close to it as possible. Billy was terrified it would go in for a swim. His heart thumped so loudly in his chest, he thought Sue would hear it and come out to see if he was OK. His voice, when he called Lennie back, was tremulous and wobbly. *Breathe, breathe,* he told himself. *Nothing bad's going to happen; this dog knows exactly what he's doing; he's lived here for years.*

After a few minutes of walking, Billy began to think about his solo walks around the city centre. He wasn't at all uncomfortable there. He knew who the local characters were and which corners to avoid. He had his regular 'friends' who would look out for him and who always gave him a cheery wave. There was old Fred, the newspaper seller on the corner; Jackie Jansen, the homeless guy who stashed his stuff behind the big bins behind the flats; and Marley, the park keeper in Mowbray Park. Mrs Mack, who worked in the bakers on the main street, always saved apple turnovers for him. And not to forget, the Chinese lady who fed the ducks on the park pond. He was never afraid in the city centre, with its crowds and noise and smells; not like here. And here, he knew he was actually safer, simply because it was small and peaceful. But that was just it: he could continue to be a silent little nobody in the city centre. Nobody bothered him, other than to wave or to give him the odd treat. Here he might actually have to talk to people. And Billy wasn't sure he was ready for that, yet.

He wandered on, lost in thoughts about home, head down, following the path, when he suddenly stopped. Lennie had stopped dead in front of him, too, and was in a half-crouch, ears pricked forward, ready to jump on something or somebody. The dense green bushes on his right had started trembling. There followed the sound of a deep snort, and the bushes started thrashing about. Billy stood dead still, adrenaline coursing through his body and making him tremble more than the leaves. Should he set the dog on it, whatever 'it' was? How did you do that anyway? Should he simply scream and go running, like a baby, back the way he'd come? Frantically, he looked about him: there was no sign of any houses or buildings on this path. And he hadn't really been paying attention, anyway. Had he missed the left turn Dagger had told him about?

Clutching the small parcel tightly to his chest, Billy was aware that the bushes were now parting in the middle, a bit like Moses parting the Red Sea in the Bible story he had enjoyed so much when he was little. Something or somebody huge was charging through the greenery to get at him. Like the dog, Billy automatically dropped to a half-crouch, the parcel held out in front of him like a sword, waving about in his fear. That snort again, then Lennie jumped up excitedly and flung himself forward. Billy closed his eyes. Whoever had crashed through the bushes was now standing right in front of him. He could feel hot breath on his face. He was just about to scream, when he realised the breath smelled of grass. Huh? Lennie was once again yipping in excitement. Billy opened one eye, warily.

"Dolly!" he breathed out in relief. "What on earth are you doing down here? You, idiot! I nearly had a heart attack." He fondled one long grey ear as the donkey nuzzled warmly at his chest. Stepping around the big animal, he made to walk on. He felt like a fool and was still shaking; his knees were knocking together and he felt breathless, but he couldn't help a smile from forming on his face. What a thing.

The donkey clopped after him for a few steps, plodding alongside her friend Lennie. Billy was a bit bothered now. *She surely shouldn't be out here on her own?* He paused, looking for a field or a broken fence she had come through. Nothing. She seemed to just be wandering by herself. He knew that cars couldn't come along this river path, but he was still concerned. He stopped to talk to her and to give her some friendly advice.

"Now, Dolly, go home," he told her firmly.

The donkey simply nuzzled at his shirt again, pushing into him with her big hard head.

"No, Dolly. Go home, that way!" he told her, getting hold of her forelock as he'd seen Dagger do, and trying to turn her back. The donkey was, well, as stubborn as a mule. She stood her ground and butted him with her head. Aha. Billy remembered the apple and the sweets in his pocket.

"OK, Dolly. I'll give you one sweet, then off you go. OK? Deal?"

The donkey seemed to nod. Billy smiled as he reached into his pocket and unwrapped a mint. He held it on the flat palm of his hand, like he'd also seen Dagger do, and was thrilled when the donkey took it gently from him. She hadn't bitten him, and he hadn't dropped it. He felt stupidly pleased with himself, blushing at how good it felt to be in charge of this big, wild animal. Lennie had got bored and was sniffing around in the same bushes Dolly had just crashed through. Clutching the parcel tightly, Billy called to the dog, gave the donkey a friendly slap on her rump, called Lennie to him, and walked on. The sun was still shining, the birds were still up there above him, and he had almost forgotten about the river. And he had commanded not one, but two animals to do as he had asked – and they did! On he went, on his quest for his friend Dagger, swaggering ever so slightly.

He decided that he would have a sweet for himself. Slowing down he took another mint from his pocket and began to unwrap it. Lennie was still trotting about in front of him, stopping once in a while to check that Billy was still with him. It felt good. Billy was growing more confident by the minute. He could do this little job. It was just that he still hadn't come to a left turn, yet. The *river* was still on his left. He had no sooner put the sweet in his mouth, when he was punched hard from behind. Coughing slightly as the mint caught his breath, Billy spun round. Dolly was standing right behind him. Oh no. Now what?

"No!" he shouted at her. "Dolly, go home!"

He tried walking on a little faster, but she was easily able to keep up, nudging his pocket as he walked on. Billy slumped. What should he do? Take her home? She was obviously on a mission of her own. He stood beside the big grey beast, a frown creasing his face, wondering what on earth to do.

Suddenly, the sound of a bell on a bicycle made him jump. He grabbed hold of the donkey and tried to move her out of the way. She simply dug her four feet deeper into the rough track.

"Dolly, come *on*," he pleaded, trying to pull her to the side of the path before she caused an accident. The donkey sniffed his face closely, and Billy had a sudden thought. He took the mint out of his mouth and offered it to her, stepping backwards so she would have to move forward, if she wanted it. That worked.

The cyclist was an older chap in a checked shirt. He was wearing long shorts and had an old rucksack over one shoulder. He came up behind the trio of Billy, Lennie and Dolly, and stopped with a frown. "Hey. What are you doing with these two?" he asked, fairly roughly, Billy thought. "You're not nicking them, are you?"

He got off his bike and walked towards Billy in a menacing manner. Billy felt himself go red in the face, his knees started to shake and his tummy did summersaults inside him. Was he going to get a bashing from this big bloke? Tears started in his eyes, but he found his voice quickly.

"No mister, I'm not. Lennie is supposed to be showing me the way to Frank's house, and Dolly is just following me. I can't get rid of her," he wailed, almost crying in despair. This guy was going to be no help, he could tell. Fancy thinking he was stealing these animals. Why would anyone want to steal a mad dog and an even crazier donkey?

"Oh, they're friends of yours, are they?" The man stopped, moving forward to pat Dolly. Billy noticed his large fists had relaxed a bit.

"Yes. I'm doing a job for Dagger and I can't get rid of this stupid donkey."

The man turned suddenly, then, moving off to put one foot into the pedal and began to push away on his bike. He seemed to have relaxed now that he realised that this kid was on first-name terms with both Dagger and his animals. He wasn't some little tearaway from the city.

"I wouldn't worry about Dolly, lad," he told Billy. "She wanders everywhere down here by herself. Everyone knows that."

Billy stared dumbly at him, thinking, *but I'm not everyone.*

"Either just let her follow you, or ignore her. She'll be fine. She'll go home when it's tea time."

And with that he peddled off without a backward glance.

Billy sighed loudly, then he, Lennie and the donkey trundled on together. He should have asked the man if he'd missed the left-hand turn. That flaming river was still with him, but now he had these two new friends to keep an eye on, as well as deliver the stupid parcel to a complete stranger's house in a place he didn't know how to find. This job wasn't turning out to be as easy as he'd thought. Then he stopped in his tracks like a pantomime character, slapping his hands to his forehead. The parcel! Where was it?

Billy actually patted himself down, looking for it. When he realised it wasn't about his person somewhere, he turned on the two animals at his side. The man had gone, and there was no one else in sight.

"Now look what you made me do, you idiots!" he shouted.

They both grinned back at him, the donkey pawing at the ground and nodding her head, and Lennie sitting on his waggy bottom, smiling up at the angry boy. Billy pushed the donkey out of the way and frantically looked around. What would Dagger think? He couldn't get anything right, not even a simple little job for a good friend. Lennie went off sniffling around – for rabbits probably – and the stupid donkey started nibbling nonchalantly at the long grass at the side of the track. Billy flopped down beside her, hot, bothered and crying. He was worse than these dumb animals, that was for sure. How could he go back to Dagger now?

He allowed the tears to fall. Putting his head onto his knees, he sat in the grass and sobbed. The trees above him waved and whispered in the breeze. Even the birds had deserted him. He was all alone in this strange place, his poor mam was in hospital worse than when she went in, and he couldn't get anything right. He sobbed and shook in the dappled sunlight on the lonely riverside track.

The dog had stopped sniffing for rabbits and was back at his side. Billy couldn't be bothered with him. He longed to be back in his bedroom, in his house in the sky, far away from the worries in the world. He wanted his old life back, scary and lonely though that was. The dog put out a paw, but Billy shrugged him off. *Go away, stupid*, he thought. His eyes were blurred with all the crying. All of Billy's old worries streamed out of him, his nose was running and he sniffed sadly. The dog nudged him again, almost standing in his lap.

"Oh, Lennie, for God's sake…" Billy began, then stopped.

The dog was sitting down in front of him with the parcel in his mouth. Billy smiled, then giggled at the absurdity of the situation, then laughed out loud, holding onto the dog's neck and crying again. Only this time they were tears of joy, mixed with relief.

"And I had the nerve to call you a dumb animal," he told the dog, before kissing him on the top of his shiny black head and getting up to go on.

"Come on, Dolly, if you're coming, anyway," he told his other companion, standing up to continue his quest and getting another mint out of his pocket.

Chapter 16

Billy whistled an off-key tune as he walked on under the green canopy and smiled to himself. If anyone passed him on this mad journey, they would see a strange little group: a skinny, pale-faced kid, a large grey woolly donkey, and a sleek, shiny black dog, all ambling along together. Crazy! In actual fact, just around the corner they did pass a couple out walking their dog. The man smiled, and the lady wished Billy a cheery good morning, but nobody seemed to think they were an odd trio, at all. Next, a postman cycled by, stopping to say hello to Dolly and to give Lennie a biscuit from his pocket. He, too, greeted the animals by name and asked Billy if he was OK. He seemed relaxed and friendly as well, waving as he moved away on his bike. *Well, I suppose I'd be happy and relaxed, if I went to work on a bicycle and delivered to places like this*, thought Billy. He shook his head, thinking of the post being delivered in his block of flats: if the lifts were working, you got your mail through your letter box, but when they were out of order, the post was just dumped on a table in the entrance, and you had to get there quickly to make sure nobody had nicked whatever you were waiting for. Billy didn't think he'd even seen his postman since he was about six years old.

Billy was deep in thought, thinking about this, when he suddenly became aware of a huge building looming up in front of him, forming an ominous dark shadow. He stopped in his tracks, craning his head back to see what on earth it was. It was actually blocking out the sun, it was so big. Both animals took the opportunity to go, wandering off the track into the undergrowth. Billy stepped back to get a better view. Huh? Where had this sprung from? It was *huge*. He quickly strode forward, hoping to get to an angle where more of this shape would be revealed through the trees, and when he saw it in all its glory, Billy simply stood transfixed.

"Wow!"

The huge, graceful stone arches of the viaduct stretched before and above him, spanning the river and disappearing into the trees and the sky on either side. Billy's mouth hung open in a soft 'oh', and he felt dizzy, trying to get a good view of it. The incredibly high bridge seemed to spin a little in the sky above him, but Billy had to see more. Calling Dolly and Lennie to his side, he looked quickly up and down the path in both directions, then made up his mind. When he knew there was no one else around, he carefully lay the parcel on the ground and lay down on his back underneath the monolith. Now he could view it without hurting his neck and without getting so dizzy he would fall over.

It was incredible, massive and imposing! The river ceased to be for Billy, and he lay there, counting the arches, watching the birds fly in and under the highest spans, looking at the size of the blocks it was built on. Billy wondered how old it was, and why he didn't know it existed. This was amazing. It made his chest swell with pride or pain, he wasn't sure. He wanted to cry, just looking at it. People like himself had built this thing, he thought, yet here it was hidden away, deep in the river valley, where nobody knew such a thing of beauty existed. He was breathless, lying there peacefully on his back, staring up at its greatness. Wow. This is what the word 'awesome' must have been invented for. He wished he could tell his dad about this. He would tell his mam about it, of course, but Dad...? He would have loved this. He wondered if his dad even knew about this massive construction. Then he wanted to cry again, because he'd probably never know the answer.

"Aye, son. That's the best way to look at that viaduct. Used to do exactly the same thing when I was your age."

Billy suddenly shot up off the ground, clutching the parcel to his chest and making his head spin with the speed of the action. An old man, with a very wrinkled face and an equally elderly wrinkled dog, was coming along the river path. Billy blushed.

"No, no, son. Don't you mind me. If this is the first time you've seen it, I can imagine how it feels for you. It's brilliant, isn't it? Still makes me smile after all these years."

"It's...it's... just, wow," breathed Billy, smiling at the old man. The donkey and Lennie had come to sniff the elderly dog, curiously nudging at it with their noses.

"Lennie, Dolly, stop that. Come here," Billy told them sharply. He was still amazed when his new friends did as he told them.

"Oh, don't you worry about those two," the old man told him. "Old Ben here is as blind as a bat, and deaf, too. He won't mind them."

Billy took his eyes away from the animals and once again stared up at the huge edifice above him. "What is it, mister?" he asked the old man.

"That?" The old fella smiled. "That's the famous Vicky Viaduct, son."

"Huh? If it's that famous, how come I never knew about it?" Billy asked him.

The old man smiled and went on. "Victoria Viaduct, lad. It's even older than me and Ben, here."

"Wow," Billy breathed, still staring upwards. "How high is that? I bet it's higher than the Monument, even?"

The old man scratched at his whiskery chin. "You know, I'm not sure it is, son. Years since I've been up there. You'd have to climb up to see for yourself."

Billy's eyes nearly popped out of his head in shock.

"You can go up there?" he breathed in awe. "Actually go on it and over it?"

The old man shrugged his shoulders and got hold of his dog's collar.

"Well, you could at one time," he told Billy, then leaned in towards him conspiratorially. "Of course, there's always another way to find out," he said, nodding sagely.

Billy stared at him, willing him to give him some secret information on this amazing place he had discovered accidentally on his journey.

The old man put his finger to the side of his nose, half closed his eyes and whispered in Billy's ear. "*Google* it, son." Then he walked away, chuckling to himself, his old, blind and deaf dog plodding slowly after him.

It was only after Billy had walked properly under the viaduct and out the other side, that he thought he should have asked the old fella if he'd missed the left hand turn. Feeling brave now, he called after him. "Hey, mister. I need to get to Frank's house. Have I missed the left turn?"

The old man came back towards Billy, hand cupped round his ear, leaving the old dog standing mutely on the track.

"Frank's, you say? Left turn? Aye, lad, about fifty yards further on. You can't miss it."

He muttered something about it being big and green, but Billy didn't catch it under the rustle of the trees. Oh, well, not far now. Holding tightly onto the parcel, Billy called to his two companions and walked on, his head and his heart both feeling strangely lighter now.

Some moments later, Billy came upon a small terrace of houses on his right hand side. He had to climb over a wooden style to get to them, which the dog leaped across expertly. Together they wandered forward, Billy trying to spy into people's houses without actually appearing to be too nosy. He noticed quickly that these properties were actually very close to the river. Closer even than Sue's house, and Dagger's, come to that. They were all different sizes and shapes, with tidy gardens and neatly painted woodwork. Some of the doors were open, and he could hear a radio playing in the back garden of one of them, but there was no one about. Billy paused, one eye on the river, still on his left, when he heard that strange coughing, wheezing sound that he now recognised as Dolly's braying. Looking back, he saw the donkey standing anxiously on the other side of the wooden stile. Now what? He walked back to her.

"Right, Dolly, looks like this is where you and me part company. Off you go." He leaned over the stile and tried to push her back towards the tow path. The donkey stood her ground, sort of tensed her whole body, snorted and stamped her small hooves. She wasn't going to budge that easily. Billy looked down at Lennie.

"OK, looks like it's just you and me from here on in, Len. We'll just leave her here, eh?"

Together, boy and dog ambled back towards the houses, but they hadn't gone more than a metre or two when the donkey started making such a loud, wheezing racket that Billy ran back to her, before somebody called the police to them for disturbing the peace.

"Shhh, Dolly, shut up, will you? You know you can't get through here. Now, just go home. Go on. You're going to get me into a load of trouble."

The donkey nodded her grey head up and down, then started pawing at the stile with her hooves. Billy leaned over again, talking to her and stroking her face, in an attempt to calm her down. The worries were building up again, he realised, forming black clouds in what had just been the sunny landscape of his mind. His breathing was coming faster and he was starting to sweat.

Just then a woman appeared at his elbow. She was eating an apple. She took a huge bite out of the apple, gave the piece to Dolly to eat, then leaned over the side of the stile and lifted a catch, hidden in the brambles. To Billy's silent amazement, a gate opened swiftly, Dolly trotted through to his side, and the woman swung the gate back into position again. The dog watched, wagging his tail, as the donkey stopped further down to nibble daisies. Billy stood back as the woman took another bite of her apple and wandered back into the end house of the terrace, without saying a word to any of them.

"Right. Okay, then. On we go," he told his animal companions, walking on and shaking his head. *That woman must have thought he was totally thick*, he sighed to himself.

He walked on to the end of the terrace, and as he walked, he cautiously watched the river. The tide was still going out, he knew that now, but up ahead Billy thought he could see the left turn. Big and green, was what the old man had told him. Oh no. As he approached the turn, his heart began to thump loudly in his chest. This *was* the left turn, that was obvious. The dog and the donkey had reached it ahead of him, and both were standing waiting for Billy to catch up before turning left. Onto a bridge. A large, green bridge, *crossing the river*.

Billy caught them up and stood there shaking. The river was quite wide at this point, and he could see houses clearly on either side. There was even a little country pub a bit further down, but there was no one about at this time of day. Nobody who could help him, anyway. The bridge looked sturdy enough, but he knew he couldn't do it. He was shaking and sweating now, holding the parcel clutched tightly against his chest, like a safety belt. He tried to distract himself by looking further down the river. Boats had been moored, but were idling in the shallow waters of the turning tide, bobbing and rocking gently in the sun. A swan glided slowly by on the water, stopping to peck at the reeds near the other side.

"Oh, come on, Billy," he said out loud. "You can do this. For God's sake – it's a bridge. It's not going to collapse as soon as little you gets on it," Billy told himself sternly. He actually got as far as putting one foot onto the concrete walkway, but stepped back off again straight away, looking guiltily around to make sure no one could see what an idiot he was. He gave himself a shake and closed his eyes, willing himself to get on the bridge and walk over the river. He thought about Dagger, and what he would make of this ridiculous performance. He thought of the bloke Frank, on the other side, waiting for his parcel and wondering why it was all taking so long. He thought of the shameful laughter at having to turn around and going all the way back to Dagger's house to explain why he couldn't do a simple little thing like cross the bridge to somebody's house to deliver a parcel.

Lennie and Dolly had got bored now. They obviously both knew what was expected of them. Lennie got onto the bridge first and walked a few steps forward before stopping to wait for his friends to catch up. Dolly clattered clumsily up the three sloping steps and followed the dog. At that, Billy shut his eyes, took a deep breath and took a step behind them, following them onto the bridge. At first he simply counted each move of his foot. He could do it! *He was* doing it. He was crossing a bridge! He opened his eyes in delight when he was a third of the way across. But then, he felt the whole edifice begin to sway slightly, rocking with the weight of the three of them on it at the same time. Billy shrieked out loud, grabbed the side rails, then turned and hurtled back the way he had come. As he bounced off down the steps, shaking and sobbing, he looked back to see his friends happily continue on their way as if they hadn't a care in the world.

"Lennie! Stop, Lennie. *Sit*, Lennie!" wailed Billy, staring after his companions. They slowed down on the bridge, but didn't stop. Oh no. Now what? They would turn up at Frank's without him, then what?

Billy wiped the sweat and tears from his eyes. He was about to flop down onto the path to stop his legs from shaking, when he heard the sound of the most awful cackling and squawking. Looking back over his shoulder he saw a pack of geese, as big as the swan, wings stretched out and long necks lunging forward towards Billy. They were hissing angrily at him and flapping their wings. Aaarrghhh! Billy gazed wildly about for their owner. Nobody. The geese were out of their pen and were waddling quickly down the road straight for him. Without a second glance, Billy launched himself onto the bridge, running as fast as his legs could carry him. He passed the dog and the donkey well before they had even reached the steps on the other side, aware all the time of the bridge, bouncing up and down with every step, seeming like it would pitch him over the side and into the river. Flinging himself down the steps on the other side, Billy glanced back. Phew. The geese hadn't crossed the bridge after them. But he had! He sat on the ground on the other side of the river, sitting on the first step, and laughed and cried. He actually lay back, closed his eyes and shook in relief.

The dog and the donkey stood patiently behind him, simply gazing down at him, or looking up the river in the direction they had all just travelled. Billy smiled to himself at how much he had achieved in the last few minutes. He knew he hadn't really conquered his fears, but for a few rare minutes he had overcome them. It was a few doddery steps forward and he felt absurdly proud of himself. Now he wouldn't have to go back and tell Dagger that he couldn't do a simple job for him. He hadn't shied away from having a conversation with complete strangers he had met on the river path. He had discovered an amazing piece of architecture and might even be able to go up on it one day. He pictured himself in his mind, standing way up above the river, higher than the trees, maybe even higher than his precious Monument, king of all he surveyed. After this, he knew, anything was possible! Feeling the sun on his face and the solid foundation of the steps of the bridge under his back, hearing those mad geese in the distance cackling away, Billy actually chuckled out loud to himself.

"Oy, kid, move your arse!"

Huh? Billy opened one eye. A cyclist, wearing bright orange clothing and ridiculously tight shorts, was standing over him, peering down at Billy through fly-eye goggles, making the rider look like a demented alien. Billy sat up then and came face to face with at least fifteen of these creatures. And each one had an angry expression on his face. These were hardened, tough, sinewy cyclists, and Billy didn't fancy his chances with this lot. He jumped awkwardly to his feet.

"What's that bloody donkey doing on the bridge, anyway? Horses aren't allowed on it, you know."

One of the other riders was wiping his sweating brow; a couple of others chinked their bells agitatedly. In their bright colours, some with stripes, Billy thought they looked like a swarm of angry wasps. They were certainly unimpressed with Billy, Dolly and Len preventing them from getting on and crossing the bridge. A second rider pulled his bike closer to Billy, leaned forward and spat menacingly on the ground, near to where he was sitting.

"Get off the bridge, kid. Now. And get those bloody animals out of the way. You're holding up the traffic. Now move it, *before we move you!*"

As one, the gang of angry cyclists moved forwards towards Billy. He distinctly heard one at the back snigger, "Hope you can swim, kid."

Billy was up on his feet, grabbed at the donkey's bridle and managed to drag her down the two remaining steps with all of his might. Poor old Lennie stood on the bridge, looking bewildered at all the unfriendly faces, searching for one who would smile at him and make some time for him. His tail wasn't wagging as usual, and the dog was almost knocked to the ground as the angry crowd swarmed past Billy and the animals and buzzed over the bridge in a flashing, sweaty orange stream.

Billy stood by, embarrassed, hurt and upset. They had spoiled his momentous little victory. They were aggressive and nasty; how rude and impolite they all were.

"You don't even live here!" he shouted at their retreating backs as they hurtled on eastwards, towards the pub, leaving Billy burning with shame and humiliation. Getting hold of the donkey's halter, he led his little group away from the scene on the bridge, and padded slowly on towards the houses in the distance, his face burning and tears stinging his eyes. Billy shuddered. Was it just him, or had the sun gone in?

Chapter 17

There was more green space on the other side of the river, with benches where people could come and sit, and enjoy the peace and quiet. Billy thought it was a lovely spot, even with the river so close at hand. But, hey, he had got across the river in one piece, hadn't he? He hadn't fallen in, or got too close to it, and he still had Dagger's parcel. All right, the horrible cycling team had upset him, but he wasn't going to let them spoil his day and his achievements. He allowed the dog and the donkey a few minutes to have a wander and a sniff about, watching them fondly as he sniffed and shuddered at his own sense of embarrassment, taking the time to pull himself together again. *Yes,* he told himself, *the animals need to settle again before moving on…*

Walking on a few hundred metres, Billy thought that the river looked a bit different somehow, but he turned his mind away from it and concentrated on searching the path up ahead, where some more houses swung into view. The second one from the end, Dagger had told him. Watch Lennie – he'll take you straight to it. The dog was wandering everywhere, with his nose down to the ground, and didn't seem remotely interested in these houses. *Oh, well*, he thought, *maybe I'll go and knock anyway.* There was a tiny terrace of only four houses, each one tidy, clean and attractive. Billy stood for a minute, scanning the row of cottages: which end would be the second house, though? There were two ends to this terrace. Would it be number two, or number three? Should he just knock on them all and get it over with? Billy started to fret about this little dilemma, hopping from one foot to the other and passing the parcel between each hand. Dolly and Lennie wandered over to him and they, too, stood looking up at the cottages with him.

Just then, an older teenager came out from one of the houses, but Billy had already got himself into a state and didn't know what to do. The youth saw Billy standing awkwardly on the path and moved towards him, eyeing him with some suspicion. He was a lanky, spotty youth, with hair of an indiscriminate colour, standing straight on end. His over-large Adam's apple bobbed up and down in his pencil-thin neck. Billy stared at him warily.

"What's the matter, kid? What are you doing with those two?" he demanded, nodding his head towards the animals.

"Oh, they aren't mine," Billy managed to stammer.

"Well, I know that," the lad said flatly, staring Billy straight in the face and making a curious grunting, swallowing sound in his throat. "They're Dagger Dawson's, these two. What are you doing with them on this side?"

"Well, they just followed me. Are you Frank?" Billy asked quickly, trying not to look guilty or too panicky.

"You what? Frank? You want a slap? Do I look like Frank to you?" The lad almost spat this at Billy, standing up to square his shoulders at this weird little stranger, who was standing there, casing the joint, in front of his house. Cheeky little bugger!

"No, it's just… I'm looking for Frank's house. I've got to take this parcel there, from Dagger. He told me to…" Billy added lamely, showing the older boy the parcel. "And I don't know where it is."

The older boy smirked then, leaning in closer towards Billy, still making that curious swallowing, cawing noise. A bit like a demented crow, Billy thought.

"Give us that parcel, and I'll take it," he demanded, reaching out with one pale skinny hand, his eyes gleaming maliciously. Billy quickly stepped back.

"No," he told the lad, shaking his head and hugging the parcel closer to himself. "I've got to do it. It's my job. Dagger trusted me to deliver it."

The kid turned his head and spat a huge gob of mucus onto the grass at Billy's feet. As Billy shuddered and looked down at it, against his will, the boy suddenly grabbed the parcel from Billy's hand.

"Ah, but you don't know where you're taking it, or even who Frank is. I *do*. So I'll take it."

Billy wasn't having that. His new friend Dagger had trusted him with this job, and he wasn't going to let him down. His heart pounding, he reached forward and managed to get his fingers around the bottom end of the package, which the lad now had clutched to his front.

"Get off, you little squirt!" the youth demanded, pulling the parcel back towards himself and away from Billy's grasp, but Billy hung on tenaciously. He wasn't going to give in on this one. No chance. Stepping closer to the taller boy, Billy managed to stand on his foot and, although the lad winced in pain, he didn't let go. He did, however, lean forward in an attempt to get a tighter hold of the parcel. Billy thought it would rip in two, and started to tug harder, when suddenly his hands slipped off the end of the brown paper. The sudden release of tension allowed the package to fly upwards, hitting the taller youth smack in the face.

"Whaa…!" the youth wailed, dropped the parcel and put his hands up to his face, rocking forward in pain. Billy stood transfixed, watching as a trickle of bright scarlet blood dribbled from between his hands and onto the green grass at his feet. The tall stranger stood up and blundered about like a blind man, arms outstretched in front of him. Billy took a deep breath, grabbed the brown package off the grass and stood back, shaking, yet concerned about this horrible person, who was snivelling and spluttering in front of him.

"Right, you little maggot. I'm gonna kill you for this!"

Billy turned and ran, heading away from the little row of cottages and the angry, injured lad.

The river path left the little row of cottages behind and wound its way west along the other side of the river, back towards the awe-inspiring viaduct. Billy could see it ahead of him, much more clearly on this side of the river. He increased his pace, eager to pass underneath it once more, to feel its majesty towering protectively above him, glad to leave that awful incident behind. His two companions ambled along beside him, happy in his company, ears and tails twitching. Billy felt his breathing relax and return to normal in their company. He felt inordinately proud of them: his little team; his friends. He felt as if they had been through so much together and had bonded over shared experiences, even though they had only been on their quest for about forty minutes. Not ever having had friends of his own, this was a new feeling to Billy, and inside he glowed with secret pride and a sense of happiness, despite his run in with the angry youth. Passing once more beneath the viaduct, Billy traced the edges of the massive honey-coloured stones with his hands, head back, staring upwards and trying not to fall over the dog, or his feet.

Within a few minutes, the river on his left opened out and curved ahead of him. Billy could see he was now approaching more houses. Surely this was it? It felt like he'd been out of Dagger's house all morning, and was sure that with a normal person, or rather, a *local* person, this job would only have taken about five minutes. Oh well, at least he was nearly there, he felt sure. He felt it in his water, then smiled at himself because that's what his mam would have said. He couldn't wait to see his mam to tell her about all the new things he could do. She would be so proud of him.

The river was running the same way as him, he now realised. He was actually able to stop and look at it. Small logs and bits of gathered reeds and moss were matching his walking pace. When he had been on the other side of the bridge he realised that it was flowing his way. Now he had crossed over, it was *still* flowing his way. Did this mean the tide had turned? How would he now get back to Sue and Dagger? Would he still be safe? He could see the houses ahead of him, a row of quite a few, and to his mind they seemed familiar. But they couldn't be: he'd never been over here before. He'd never been to Fatfield before he'd landed at

Sue and Richie's place. In his head he was working out which house belonged to Dagger's mate Frank, when he heard a strangled cry near the water on his left. Billy paused and stood listening. He glanced back over his shoulder to make sure those vicious geese hadn't come after him, or that awful bleeding boy. Nothing. The donkey was plodding along slightly ahead, quite happily, obviously at home in her surroundings. The dog, however, had stopped and was scenting the air towards the river, ears pricked. Then Billy heard the sound again.

Lennie shot off across the grass towards the water. Billy called after him to stop, but the dog disappeared under the trees and bushes at the water's edge. Oh no. He'd have to follow. The houses were almost on top of him now, but at this time of day there was no one about. Yet, still, that voice called from down near the water. It sounded anxious. Lennie still hadn't reappeared, the donkey seemed happy enough nibbling daisies and Billy knew he simply had to go and see what was going on. It worried him, but he was still buoyed by his new-found confidence and what he had achieved already on this trip. Holding tightly onto Dagger's parcel, he crossed the grass and got as close as he could to the river, calling out to the dog as he went.

The sight that greeted him at the water's edge was shocking, to say the least. For someone with Billy's aversion to water, it made his hair stand on end. Lennie was pacing anxiously up and down a tiny sandy beach, where a pair of legs and feet, dressed in shorts and trainers, was sticking out of the water, back onto the grass. The body of this person was half in, half out of the river, lying on its front, arms reaching forward into the flow. The person was spluttering and coughing, hanging onto a branch that was floating by. Good grief, were they drowning? Billy had to do something, and quick. Despite his fear, he realised that nobody else was aware of this situation. He couldn't in all seriousness stand by and let this disaster happen. For a second or two, he closed his eyes, heart hammering away in his chest as if it would jump up and spill out of his mouth. The chanting started, coming from the back of his mind, deep in his stomach, to protect him in this moment of fear. "One hundred, fifty-three, seventy, eighteen…"

Instinct kicked in. Holding his breath and jumping down onto the sandy spit, Billy got hold of the feet and began pulling this person out of the river with all his might. Lennie thought this was a great game and leaped about, barking with delight. The coughing character slowly came back towards the bank, dragging the wood with them, whilst Billy dug his feet into the sand in order to keep a tighter hold and to add to his new-found power. It was coming closer to him, but it seemed to Billy that the head and torso of this person were sinking deeper into the river. Bravely, Billy stepped into the cool brown water, put his arms under the armpits of the person, and pulled backwards with all his might. Stepping backwards, Billy and the body flopped down onto the sand, struggling to breathe and shocked by what had just happened. Billy was bemused, but proud of his actions as he lay back, feeling the wetness of his trainers seeping up his legs. The sopping wet youngster sat up, breathing heavily and brushing dark hair from its face, one hand still on the log.

Billy flopped down beside the stranger, wiping his hands on his jeans and telling the dog to shut up. He was breathless and a bit shocked at what he had just done. The person sat back, pulled all the wet strands of hair from her face, then looked down at her shorts and T-shirt clinging wetly to her body. Then she turned round, gazed at Billy for a moment, then slapped him hard across the face.

"Ow!" he gasped, reeling from the power of the slap and the shock of the attack.

"What did you do that for?" each demanded of the other, in perfect unison.

A pair of angry blue eyes flashed at him, as the girl stood up from the sand and glared down at Billy, sitting wetly on the ground, feeling his sore red cheek with his hand.

"You grabbed my boobs, you pervert!" she yelled at him, hoicking her wet shorts a little higher.

"I didn't know you *had* boobs! I just saved you from drowning, you ungrateful little witch!" Billy roared back, surprising himself with his venom.

He jumped up to stand facing her, flexing his hands angrily by his side. This madwoman could have no idea what it had just cost him to step into the river, and here she was, having a go at him. Crazy!

"Drowning? It's only sixty centimetres deep, you idiot. And I can swim perfectly well, thank you." She looked down at Lennie then, by now sitting quietly near her feet and gazing up at her with a grin.

"And just what do you think you're doing with him?" she demanded, pointing to the dog.

"He's with me. He's my…" Billy was going to say 'he's my friend', but changed his mind at the last minute, adding, "…mine. He's mine."

The girl threw her wet hair back and gave him a contemptuous look, just as Dolly came crashing through the bushes to join them near the water.

"Is he, now?" she asked, raising one eyebrow. Then stepping back a metre from the water lapping at their feet, she called out across the river, not too loudly, "Dagger? Dagger!"

Billy was completely puzzled by now. What was she doing?

Suddenly, from across the water, he heard Dagger's voice float back to her.

"Hello. What you after?"

The girl twitched a look at Billy before calling back over.

"There's a daft lad here, with your Lennie and Dolly. He says you gave them to him. Is that right?"

Dagger's voice floated back and it contained a smile, which Billy could hear from over the river where he was standing with wet shoes and legs.

"Ha, does he say that, now? Aye, it's OK, pet. He's with me. Got a little surprise for you from me, Billy has. He's found you, then."

Billy was amazed. Dagger was right across the river, talking to them! Billy could even hear the laughter in his voice. Climbing backwards, up the bank a little, he looked across the short expanse of water, and there was Dagger, standing with his hands on his hips, a couple of his chickens pecking around his feet. What?

"Ah, there you are. Well done, Billy. I knew you could do it." Dagger laughed, waved and went back towards his boat shed.

Billy and the girl turned to face each other, glaring, eyes fierce, hands on soggy hips.

"So, you've got something for me from Dagger?" she demanded, glancing around them. Billy raised himself up to his full five feet.

"Actually, no, it's not for you – it's for Dagger's mate *Frank*," he told her defiantly, bending down to pick up the parcel from the spot on the grass, under the bush, where he'd left it to pull this little madam out of the river.

The girl couldn't hide the triumphant smile, which was twitching about her mouth. "*I'm* Frank!" she told him, holding her hand out for the parcel. Billy clutched it even tighter to his chest.

"Get away. You're a girl," he sneered. "You're not called Frank." He laughed scornfully.

The girl gave him a withering look, reached forward, and grabbed the parcel from Billy's grasp. She turned the brown wrapping over in her hands, before opening one end and peering inside.

"Oh, wow. I've been waiting for these." Then she stepped towards the water and called out again.

"Thanks, Dagger. These look great. Just what I needed."

Billy tried to grab the bag off her, and in doing so, the contents spilled onto the grass verge. The girl whipped around, glaring at him again.

"Watch it, you idiot," she hissed.

A set of small wood-carving tools spilled down onto the ground, shining in the sun and the wet grass. Billy crouched down to help her to pick them up. As one, both he and the girl reached for the largest wooden handle, each holding onto an end.

From across the water, Dagger's voice floated back to them, "No problem, Francesca. Now the race is on."

Billy, at least, had the good grace to blush then. Frank. Francesca. This was the mate of Dagger's. Oh oh.

He gulped, looking shyly up at the girl's wet face and hair.

"I'm sorry," he told her quietly. "I didn't know you were a girl."

Francesca gave him a cocky look as she bent down to pick up the log she had retrieved from the river. Billy felt the need to explain. She was right. He was an idiot and he knew nothing.

"I didn't know you were a girl, I didn't know you lived right over the water from me, and I didn't know that Dagger was just testing me in sending me to your house the long way round."

He turned and pointed to the little iron bridge at the end of her street, less than four hundred metres away from them both. "And I didn't know I could cross *that* bridge or walk straight over the river to get to you, cos I'm totally thick and such a fool."

He hung his head sadly: what on earth would she think of him.

"Let's start again, shall we?" she asked, a bit less fiercely now. In fact, when Billy raised his eyes to look into her face, he saw she was smiling at him quite kindly.

"Come on into mine, and we'll both get dried and have a drink. That OK with you, Billy?"

Billy managed a weak smile back.

"That's OK with me," he told her shyly.

Together, they bumbled slowly and wetly towards a house overlooking the Wear, slopping river water out of their shoes and trying to wring out their wet T-shirts and shorts. Billy felt like such an idiot in one way, slapping along wetly behind this confident, cocky girl called Frank, yet inside he was glowing because he, Billy Higson, terrified of his own shadow and particularly the water, had stepped into the river and pulled her out. Another notch on his belt, as his mam would say. He'd achieved so much since he set out from Dagger's shed less than an hour ago. He lifted his head to gaze up into the whispering green leaves above him and smiled secretly. No dark clouds hovering over him today, then. Well, not yet.

"Come on in, Billy, and I'll get you a towel."

Frank had arrived at the gate of her house and had turned away to show Billy where they were.

"Look, can you see? There's Sue and Richie's house over the water. I can almost see into their bedroom from here."

They both stopped to stare. The river was coming in faster now, closing over the empty space and the rock pools, which had been in front of them just a few minutes ago. How could he have not known about the street opposite? Billy shrugged, realising that he hadn't been in the front bedroom or the garden since he arrived a couple of days ago. That's why. He hadn't been able to face his fear. Now, however…

Billy turned to say something to Frank, but at that point the front door opened and a large older woman came rushing down the path towards them, waving a fluffy towel. "You blethering idiot, Francesca!"

The woman shouted, grabbing Frank by the arm and virtually hauling her over the gate, rather than through it. Her attractive face was flushed, and she was breathless with anger and indignation.

"What on earth did you think you were doing in that bloody river? Were you trying to kill yourself? You *stupid* girl! Get in the house, now."

Frank was dragged up the path away from Billy. She tried to argue her point all the way into the house, but the older lady wasn't listening. Billy recognised her: she was the one with the very loud voice, who had called Dagger out of his house, when he'd gone for the eggs for Sue. She'd made him jump then, and now she was making him jump and shake. What a big, scary woman.

"Nan, stop fussing. You know I was only…" Frank was trying to explain calmly, but her Nan was having none of it.

As the door slammed shut behind them, Billy could still hear the older woman nagging her. "You've been so ill, and here you go flinging yourself into freezing cold, dirty river water. Whatever were you trying to do? Now get into that shower…"

The voice tailed away to the sound of doors slamming and fresh accusations. Billy sighed deeply, looked up to where Fatfield bridge sat peacefully in the sun, and started to slop his wet way back to Sue's.

Chapter 18

"**T**uck in, Billy lad."

Richie sat opposite Billy at the table and gestured with his fork to the huge plate of food steaming in front of him. Billy sat down, picked up his knife and fork carefully, and examined his plate. He was still getting used to eating at regular times, and eating food which did not appear to come out of a packet or a box. Even the knife and fork were a novelty to Billy. He and his mam usually had something out of the freezer, or the chip shop on the corner. In fact, Billy realised, he hadn't even seen a chip or a hot dog since he'd arrived. Gone were the crisps and biscuits, replaced by fresh fruit, vegetables he helped to pick from the garden at the back of the house, and salads, scattered with snippings of herbs which grew fragrantly in pots by the front door. His plate was colourful, to say the least. Billy eyed it with some suspicion, moving bits of food around the plate as if expecting something unsavoury to leap out at him from behind the red peppers.

"Go on, Billy. Try it. It's very tasty, you know. My Sue's a good cook, when she has the time to experiment."

Richie shoved a large forkful into his mouth, tearing off a chunk of bread to dip into the sauce. It did smell nice, it was just all so new to Billy, this sitting at a table, with an adult, using a knife and fork, and eating home-cooked food.

"What is it?" he asked Richie, sniffing his food with some suspicion.

"Ratatouille," Richie told him, licking his lips with relish. "But don't worry: no rats were harmed in the making of this meal."

Billy's eyes and mouth opened wide, and Richie laughed out loud at his face, before handing him a hunk of bread.

"I'm only joking, Billy. Go on. Get stuck in. It's gorgeous."

Richie's appetite was infectious, so Billy scooped up a dainty portion and tried it. He closed his eyes for a minute, trying to block the image of rats and mice boiling away in a huge vat, being stirred by Sue wearing a pair of her manic earrings, this time soup ladles. He tested the texture on his tongue for a second before swallowing it, and yes, Richie was right. It was gorgeous. He could taste the tomatoes, the crunchy peppers and a hint of garlic and onion. Hungrily, he began shovelling more in, pulling off the bread and copying what Richie was doing in dipping it into the juices.

"So you had an exciting day, then?" Richie chatted comfortably from across the table. "I saw Dagger and he told me you'd met Frank."

Billy nodded; his mouth was too full to speak for a second. When he swallowed Billy replied, "And did he tell you he sent me the long way round to her house as well? I didn't know she lived right over the water. I didn't know I could have just crossed the bridge to get the parcel to her." The expression on Billy's face changed, from being one of pleasure at the taste of the food, to one of embarrassment, with a tinge of anger and incomprehension.

"Well, all I can say, Billy, is that if you'd been out on the river side of the house, you'd have probably seen Frank and her Nan over there. Yeah?" Richie paused in his eating, raised an eyebrow at Billy and gave him a gentle smile. "I know you hadn't, because you were so afraid of the water. Don't feel bad about Dagger's little trick. He did you a huge favour, really."

Billy's head was down and he was blushing. He raised sad eyes to Richie. "Really? I felt like such a fool," he said flatly. "I thought Dagger was my mate, but he was just taking the mick out of me."

He sat back into his chair, putting his knife and fork down gently, while the humiliation of the slap from Frank and the run-in with the cyclists, burned in his mind. Sitting opposite him, Richie realised he needed to say more because this lad was feeling a bit lost at this moment. He put his own fork down and leaned across the table a little, towards Billy. "Course he did, son. Look what you learned and achieved today: you now know your way around both sides of the river; you met more of the neighbours; you crossed the bridge; and you conquered your fear of the water. Well done, you. And well done to Dagger for sending you that way. The hard way." He winked at Billy and tore off some more bread.

"And..." he continued, pointing his knife at Billy. "You saved the life of a damsel in distress, on top of everything else. Now, would any of that have happened if you'd just walked over the bridge and knocked on the door of number twelve?"

Billy shrugged his shoulders and smiled. Put that way, it had been a good idea of Dagger's. He picked up his knife and fork again, and continued with his lunch.

"What is wrong with Frank?" he asked Richie. "I heard her Nan yelling at her for getting wet when she had been so ill."

Richie chewed and swallowed before explaining. "Ah, she's been off school ill for a couple of months. Had some sort of weird illness. That thing called... er... oh, I forget."

"What? Flu?" asked Billy.

Richie shook his head. "Nah, not flu. Worse than that." He was gazing into the middle distance, trying to remember the technical term for it.

"Worse than flu? Like…" Billy didn't even dare say the word. "You know… cancer?" This last word was mouthed at Richie across the table.

"Eh? No, Billy, not that! No, it was that, whatyamacall it – that *kissing disease*."

A kissing disease! And she'd accused Billy of grabbing her boobs! What sort of person was she? Billy was secretly horrified. Boy, you could get some people wrong. He shook his head at Richie in disbelief.

"Sue will tell you its real name, when she comes in," Richie told him, getting up to put his now wiped-clean plate into the sink. "Anyway, it's great that you two can spend some time together. I know Frank's been bored rigid, with everyone else still being at school."

He ran some water into the sink, turning back to the table to give Billy another wink. "Be nice for you to have someone of your own age around, eh?"

Billy gave him a weak smile, but inside he was thinking, *What? That stroppy mare, who accused me of grabbing her boobs and who gets diseases from kissing people? Nee chance!*

Richie continued telling him, as he busied about the kitchen, "Sue will be in a bit later from work, so why don't you go back to Dagger's and let him know how you got on with delivering his parcel, eh?"

Billy considered this for a moment. He had been wondering about the parcel, what it was for, and that comment from Dagger to Frank about "the race being on".

"Yeah, OK, I might just do that."

Putting his plate in the sink, he stepped into the back garden and set off down the path, glancing nervously to his left just occasionally, where the river was, deep and still, glinting under the amazing viaduct and gurgling and slopping under the little green bridge. He frowned at the thought of the angry cyclists, and hoped to himself that he wouldn't meet anyone as savage as them again very soon. He knew deep in his heart that people like them didn't belong in this peaceful place.

Dagger had his back to him in the wood shed, working away and whistling to himself happily, so he wasn't aware that Billy had come quietly in, until Billy suddenly appeared at his elbow. Glancing down swiftly, but not stopping his carving, he gave a mock jump of surprise. "Strewth, Billy, you drifted in there as quietly as a little ghost. You nearly gave me a heart attack, lad. You've got to be careful around an old guy like me, you know. The old ticker might give out with a shock like that."

He was smiling warmly down, though, but didn't stop working. Billy watched him carving away at another small boat. The shavings peeled away from the wood in a mesmerising way, scenting the air of the shed delicately and drifting down to the sunlit floor, like feathers. Dagger's large hands, freckled and strong, worked deftly, and he stopped once in a while to blow some of the dust away as he worked. Billy realised he was standing a bit too close to Dagger, leaning in against his right arm, but it felt nice, and right somehow: comforting, even. It gave Billy a warm glow, like a firefly was fluttering deep inside his chest.

"Can I help?" Billy asked, never taking his eyes off the job in Dagger's hands.

Dagger paused, looking intently at the boy. He had thought Billy might have been a bit upset at his trick in sending him over the river the long way, but he knew from Essie Bailey, Frank's Nan, that the delivery had been made, albeit with a bit of added drama at the end, with Frank going into the river, but that was nothing new. She was always in the river. Should have been a mermaid, that one, he thought to himself. He smiled at the way Billy was leaning into him. He was obviously forgiven. Canny bairn.

"Good idea. You see that bottle and that cloth on the side there?"

Billy moved slightly away from Dagger, eyes searching the cluttered workbench. He picked up a bottle and sniffed it. It smelled like honey and firewood on bonfire night, and a bit like cough medicine too, the nice stuff.

"Dab some of that oil onto the cloth, Billy, and run it over those other boats, the new ones I finished last week. See what happens."

Billy moved to the shelf on the other side, carefully took down a large, quite intricately carved boat and dabbed the rag against the bottle. Looking to Dagger to see that was OK, he gently stroked the cloth over the carving. Instantly, the boat began to shine and glisten as the wood came to life in his hands, becoming richer and darker in colour. Any small blemishes or scrapes in the carving seemed to sink into the boat itself and it appeared to glow in his hands with health and newness. Billy lifted his eyebrows and smiled up at Dagger. "Wow. Look at that. Isn't it gorgeous?"

"They all need a good coating of that oil, Billy, so if you've got the time...?" Dagger raised his eyebrows and nodded towards the workbench, quizzically.

There were at least ten different shaped boats, of all sizes and shapes, lined up along the shelves. Billy couldn't wait to get his hands on them. He worked slowly on the one in his hands, though, savouring the smell and the hypnotic rhythm of his job. It was heaven in this shed, he thought, standing here with his new mate, doing something as rewarding as this. Time slipped by slowly and peacefully, trickling past him like the tide going out behind the shed, with the chickens clucking about, and the odd honk of a goose down the river. The sun drifted into the shed through the open door, where dust motes floated and mingled with the odd bee that buzzed by, and back out again.

Dagger watched the boy out of the corner of his eye, for a moment. He was gone: engrossed in his job, a faraway look on his face, but it was a look that was more serene now, not the scared and stuttering stranger who had appeared from a pile of poo the other morning.

"Well done, for getting that parcel to Frank for me, Billy," he told the lad with a smile.

Billy paused in his oiling, then continued, glancing up at Dagger and returning the smile. "Why did you give her those little tools?" he asked, shyly. "It's a funny gift for a girl."

"Didn't she show you?" Dagger asked, blowing away more wood shavings. Billy shook his head, still engrossed in the stroking and polishing of the wooden boat. "I'm very surprised."

"Well, I *was* going into her house to get dried, but her Nan came out and had a hissy fit cos we were so wet."

"Ahh, of course," Dagger nodded sagely. "Essie Bailey got you. I thought I heard her dulcet tones across the water."

"She's very... loud, isn't she?" Billy asked, innocently, turning large grey eyes towards Dagger.

"Loud? She's got a gob on her like a foghorn, Billy. Should stand that woman at the end of Roker pier, that's what I think." Dagger smiled grimly, putting down his tools and wiping his hands on his jeans.

Billy looked over at him nonplussed. "What's a foghorn?" he asked.

Dagger turned to the lad in surprise, hands on his hips. "You, what? Call yourself a Mackem, Billy? You don't know what a foghorn is? Well, I never."

Billy simply shook his head back at Dagger, obviously waiting to be educated on this matter. Dagger sat down on an old chair and puffed out his cheeks.

"By, times are changing, Billy. When I was your age, on a foggy day in Sunderland, all you could hear was the foghorn, booming away in the mist. It was a big noise to warn the ships out at sea that they were getting close to the pier and the rocks. Bit like this. Listen."

Dagger cupped his hands around his mouth, and Billy watched in wonder as a huge booming noise came rumbling out of his chest, rolling out of his open mouth and drifted away out of the open shed door. Dagger repeated it a couple of times, with a pause between each. Then he sat back with a satisfied grin on his handsome face.

"That's what it sounded like, Billy, when I worked in the shipyards on the river. You don't hear it now, though, and haven't for years. It's a shame, mind. All done by computers now, I suppose."

Billy put down his oily rag and came to stand close to Dagger. Looking all around the inside of the shed, at the carvings and the skeleton of the half-finished boat, he asked, "So, you've always built boats, then? It's not just a hobby?"

Dagger stood up to switch on the kettle. Checking the old mugs and throwing out some cold tea, he told Billy, "Aye, Billy. I was a ship builder back in the days when Sunderland was the biggest and the best. We built the best ships in the world. Mind you, the Geordies always thought *theirs* were the best, but ours were always stronger, faster and built to last. Built with blood, sweat and tears, they were. But built with love and pride, too."

Billy considered this for a moment. He knew his city's history about ship building, his dad used to tell him about it. But it was alien and odd to Billy, growing up, as he did, in a city where cars were now the big deal. He could understand anyone being proud to say they'd built a *car,* but until today, helping Dagger in the shed, he hadn't given ships a thought. Oh yes, he'd seen them floating smoothly into the docks from his flat in the clouds, but in his life, they had always remained just hovering on the horizon. *Maybe that was the case for all of his generation,* he thought.

"Is Frank building ships as well, then?" he asked, returning to his original question.

Dagger poured boiling water into an old brown teapot.

"Now there's a question you can ask her when you next visit," he told Billy. "Just remind her that the race is on." He smiled over at Billy, who knew instantly that he would get no more on that subject. Billy looked over at Dagger's beautiful handiwork on the shelves.

"They're all different, aren't they, but they don't have names on. Shouldn't a ship always have a name?" he asked, genuinely interested.

"Come and have a cuppa, Billy, and I'll tell you the names of some of these boats I've made, and I'll tell you a bit about each one."

Billy hurriedly pulled up a stool and sat down next to Dagger's chair, gratefully accepting a chocolate biscuit and settling himself down happily. For the next half hour, Billy listened to Dagger's soft brown voice rolling over him like a gently breaking wave, telling him tales of the shipyards on the river Wear. He explained about the jobs he had done, the names of the ships he had worked on, told tales about some of the daft tricks the men played on each other whilst doing hard, noisy and sometimes dangerous jobs. Billy learned about the sense of camaraderie that existed in the yards, the satisfaction of watching a brand new ship roll down the slipway into the river, dragging all those massive chains behind it, the crowds who came to watch and cheer. Sitting with his fingers wrapped around his mug of tea, Billy was transfixed. What a life this man had known. What things he had seen. Somehow, though, it made him miss his dad all the more, and once in a while, he had to lower his eyes from Dagger's happy, animated face, as tears threatened to spill out and spoil the stories. His dad should have been sitting here, beside Dagger, as well, listening in, joining in once in a while with his own tall Army tales.

Billy sighed deeply, keeping his head down as a stray tear plopped onto the rag and mingled with the smooth oil on the glowing wood. Dagger rumbled on, standing up to smooth over the wooden skeleton of the large river boat he was constructing. And outside, unknown to Billy, the tide turned once more, taking away little bits of flotsam that had been held fast in the mud and the reeds, bobbing off on their journey to the mouth of the river and out into the vast North Sea.

Chapter 19

The next morning, before breakfast, Billy could hear Sue humming to herself in the little front garden overlooking the river. Glancing out of the small window in the corner of the stairs, he watched her for a while. She was picking up stray leaves, pulling out the odd weed and errant crisp packet that had landed in the bushes. Her dark hair glinted in the sunshine. Strangely, she didn't have any earrings in, Billy noted with a smile. She had bare feet, strong and tanned. Spotting the big cat, Fingle Brown, Sue leaned forward to talk to him, stroking him firmly and kissing the top of his proffered head. Billy thought she looked like a dancer, with graceful arms and her slim lithe body. His mind turned to his mam, still in that horrible, hot hospital bed, drips and blood bags surrounding her. She couldn't bend over like Sue. They didn't have a cat to stroke, and if Mam dropped something, either Billy had to pick it up or it stayed on the floor until he came in from school. Which was usually fine, apart from that one time it was a pancake that he came home to on Shrove Tuesday. His mam had flipped it and it had flown away from the pan and slid down the side of the fridge, leaving a sludgy trail all the way. By the time Billy came in, his mam had been in tears. She'd tried to pick it up herself, but the bending and stretching had been too much for her bad back, and she was sitting in a sad little heap in the living room, surrounded by damp balls of tissues. Billy smiled a sad smile at the memory. Tentatively, he opened the front door and stepped out into the garden with Sue.

She was standing in the wet grass in a patch of sunlight with her eyes closed and her face turned to the sun. Her floaty summer skirt moved slightly in the smallest of breezes. He thought he could hear that lovely music again. Surely, that was just inside his head? Birds were singing, a bus trundled slowly over Fatfield Bridge, and the cat gave a cheerful little chirruping sound, as Billy approached. Sue opened her eyes and smiled with delight to see him standing in the garden beside her. The garden which overlooked the river. Glancing at it, then back to Billy, she realised that the tide was out: shouldn't be too much of a problem for him, then, especially after the story about him going the long way round to Frank's yesterday.

"Well, good morning, Billy. Another glorious day, eh?"

Sue didn't move. She didn't want to give Billy a reason to go inside the house. She realised this was a huge step for him and she didn't want to put him off. The boy crouched to stroke Fingle, getting down to his level, his eyes lower than the view of the river. *Aha, very clever*, thought Sue, *you're not quite as brave as you are trying to be next to the water. But it's a start.*

"So, you think we could go and see my mam today?" he asked, looking anxiously up at Sue.

"I'm sure that would be OK, Billy. I'll have to ring the hospital first to see if she's a bit better, but I'm sure she'll be fine."

Billy stood up properly and smiled, then. Sue noticed the way his large grey eyes flicked towards the river occasionally, but he was still out there, in the garden with her, and was relaxing by the minute. He glanced across the water to the houses opposite, now that he knew where Frank lived, and looked questioningly back to Sue.

"Can you hear that?"

Sue wasn't sure if he meant the blackbird that was singing away in a nearby tree, or the piano music floating over the water.

"Gorgeous, isn't it, Billy? Just perfect on a morning like this."

Billy found a round, old tree trunk near the gate and sat down on it, his eyes closed in concentration. Sue watched him, feeling a wave of affection for this strange, quiet little lad bubbling up inside her. What a sweet child he was, behind all his fears.

"My mam would love it here," he said quietly, eyes still closed. Sue moved towards him, crouching again to stroke the cat.

"Well, when she's all better, you can bring her to visit us here. I'll cook a special meal and you can show her all around. That'd be good, yeah?"

Billy opened his eyes and smiled up at Sue. "Yeah!" He grinned, enthusiasm flashing across his face. "I could take her to meet my friend and show her all the wood carvings."

Sue stood looking at him, her hands in the pockets of her skirt.

"Frank would be very happy to meet your mam, I bet."

Billy squinted up at her, the morning sun flashing in his eyes. "Frank? Not her. I meant Dagger. You know, all those boats?"

In the background, over the river, the music stopped. Sue glanced downstream towards the boatsheds, where Dagger had his workshop.

"Ahh, *that* friend, Billy. Of course, Dagger. You and him are getting on really well, aren't you?"

Billy simply smiled and nodded. Pausing for a second, Sue was unsure how to ask her next question, but decided that she must, anyway. Coming to lean on the gate, with her back to the river, so that Billy's face was in profile she asked him, "I know your mam would love it here, Billy. Do you think it would be a place your dad would have liked, too, or was he a proper 'city type'?"

The boy seemed to still for a second or two, and Sue instantly regretted the question. Billy's dad had not been mentioned since his arrival. She knew from his notes that he had been a soldier and had died when Billy was very young, maybe only five or six years old. She didn't know if they ever talked about him as a family, or whether it was never up for discussion because it upset both Billy and his mam too much. In her opinion and experience that was never a good thing. Sue knew that a problem shared was definitely a problem halved. She and Richie had had enough 'lost kids' through their home and their hearts in the last few years and she understood how to bring them on, and out, of their troubles. She had never failed. It was why Paul Costello had brought Billy to them: no other carer had been considered Billy's best option.

Billy reached down and picked a dandelion, growing and glowing at his feet. He concentrated for a minute on pulling the petals off, one by one, and blowing them into the small garden. He didn't look up at Sue. He seemed to hold his breath for a minute, as if considering if he should answer the question or not, and at that moment, the music from over the river started again, drifting smoothly and peacefully on the breeze. He exhaled, blowing the dandelion petals into the air.

"Yes," he said finally. "My dad would have loved it here, too." Then he added quietly, "He loved the water."

Sue's eyebrows arched in surprise. Now, that was interesting. Billy's dad had loved the water, and yet, the child himself had been unable to even look out of the window at the river. She shook her head slightly and decided to probe a little further.

"Really? Was he a good swimmer?"

Careful, she told herself silently. Billy seemed engrossed in his petal- blowing but Sue could sense his mind working overtime.

"Yes. He was a brilliant swimmer," he told her quietly. "I used to watch him swimming in the sea, when I was little, and he used to take me to the swimming baths as well. My mam can't swim, though."

Sue digested this information for a second or two. *OK*, she thought, *let's try a little bit more, but I must tread very carefully here.*

"And what about you, Billy? Can you swim? Did your dad teach you?"

She turned to look him in the face then, judging his response. Billy closed his eyes and blew out a deep breath, sighing almost. He began to shake a little, very lightly at first, just a little tremor of his hands. He wanted to speak, she felt, was desperate to get something out, but he was being held back. Billy blew out his cheeks and stood up. His breath was beginning to come in shallow gasps. Oh no, a panic attack was coming, Sue was sure. She could see the warning signs. Putting a warm hand on his shoulder, Sue steered the boy towards the front door.

"It's OK, Billy. Let's go into the kitchen, and I'll get you some breakfast. Don't say anything else. Come on. You're fine with me."

As they got into the short passage leading to the kitchen, Billy paused by Sue's pictures on the wall. He stood stock still in front of the one of Penshaw Monument, gazing at it until his breathing slowed and became more normal. Sue waited patiently at his side until the lad settled. He turned his face towards her then, with a little more colour in his cheeks.

"He used to take me up there," he told her. "That's the place where I can see my dad. Right on the top of the Monument. That's where I've got to go."

*

Richie came in pale and weary from his night shift. Billy stood up as he came through the back door, moving his own breakfast things so that Richie could sit in the best seat at the table. His hair was sticking up on end, and he had dark rings under his eyes. Billy knew that he would tumble into bed and be snoring as soon as his head hit the pillow. It was sad to think of him sleeping through another lovely day, but Richie seemed used to it. He was quietly excited about the new model, which had rolled off the production line overnight.

"Gorgeous it is, Billy. Wait 'til you see it on the news tonight. Wouldn't mind one of them myself, actually. Purrs like a big pussy cat as well – what an engine!"

Richie sat down opposite Billy, but glanced over at Sue with a slightly puzzled expression. The lad seemed quiet and withdrawn this morning, despite having come out of his shell a bit over the last few days. Sue got up to go into the hall to make a phone call, shaking her head slightly at Richie, her eyes flashing in silent warning. *Oh oh, something's up*, Richie thought.

"So, what are you going to do today, Billy?"

He kept a close eye on Billy as he buttered some toast. His shoulders were drooping, and the lad had his head down. He had his sketch book in front of him and was smoothing it over with his hands, almost obsessively moving them over the cover, but making no attempt to open the book at all.

"You going to do some sketching, then? Lovely day for it."

Billy simply shrugged, not lifting his eyes to Richie. Putting his toast down, Richie reached out across the table and also smoothed out the cover of the sketch book.

"Mind if I take a look, Billy? Sue says you're really good."

The lad seemed to freeze for a second or two, then still without raising his head, he nodded slightly in answer to Richie's request. Richie gently slid the book towards him and began turning the pages. In the hall, he could hear Sue talking quietly on the phone. He took his time looking over the sketches, starting with the newer ones at the back first. Seeing the big cat, Fingle Brown, he exclaimed happily, "Aha – look at him, Billy. That's excellent. I can see all the textures of his fur and the different colours in him. Well done. He's amazing."

Richie continued turning the pages backwards. He stopped at the seagull with the crisp packet and laughed out loud. Billy actually lifted his head then, and looked at Richie quizzically.

"That's fantastic, that is, Billy. Look at his bright little eye. So realistic."

The boy half turned the book towards himself with a small smile, then turned it back towards Richie, who continued looking and commenting on the detail, the colours and the angles Billy had sketched his subjects from. Soon, he came to one of the Penshaw Monument, drawn with the sun coming up behind it, with a sky of purple, violet and indigo. The rays of the sun filtered out behind fluffy clouds. Richie paused for a moment, taking in the familiar sight, drawn with such obvious love and attention to detail.

"Wow," he breathed, sitting back in his chair to examine it closely. When he looked at Billy, he thought the lad was smiling sadly. "We must go up there one day very soon, Billy. Would you like that?"

He expected an animated reply from the lad, but looking at Billy's face, Richie registered some confusion there. Billy's eyes flicked out of the kitchen window to where he knew his beloved Monument stood, high on the distant hill, hidden by the trees at the bottom of the garden. He sighed and shrugged his shoulders. His response surprised Richie, who continued turning the pages of the sketch book backwards, until he stopped suddenly, feeling a sudden chill in the room as if a cloud had passed over the window. He had come to the drawing of the army boots and the rucksack. This drawing was so obviously different from the others, and Richie instantly picked up on the mood which emanated from it, flowing into the sunny kitchen and bringing with it dark corners and a sense of dread which spilled out and crashed back, like the ripples in a murky pond. Billy was quite still, sitting across the table from Richie. He had become statue-like, frozen, chilled, like alabaster.

Richie sat still for a few moments, studying this particular picture. He glanced at Billy who was now looking at him with a glint of defiance and challenge in his eyes. Those soft grey eyes, which could flash warmth and humour once in a while, were now flinty and hard. Richie took a deep breath and blew it out, puffing out his cheeks, his hands resting at the foot of the page.

"Now, *this* picture, Billy, is *quite* different."

Glancing quickly up at Billy to judge his reaction, and seeing nothing more than the challenging expression on the lad's face, Richie decided to press on.

"I mean, I love it, it's a powerful picture, Billy, but there's so much…" He struggled to say what he wanted to, without spooking the lad into another panic attack. "So much… *emotion* in here, Billy. And it's not a good emotion either. Were you very angry, Billy, when you did this picture?"

The boy dropped his challenging gaze and studied the picture, turning the page towards himself once more, but spending more time looking intently at it. When he turned it back to Richie, he almost whispered, "Angry. Yes. I was very angry. And I was very sad as well. But I had to do it."

Richie knew he had to play this one out carefully. He kept his voice steady, quiet and friendly, "I can see you were, Billy. That background is very dark and threatening. Is this picture about your dad, Billy? I know he was a soldier. Are these his things? His boots and Bergen?"

Billy nodded slowly, his eyes still on the picture.

"How old were you when he was killed, Billy? Can you tell me that, or is it too painful for you to talk about?"

Billy closed his eyes for a moment, then they flashed open. He reached out and closed the book, drawing it towards himself, protectively. At that moment, Sue put the phone down in the hall and came into the room, pausing at the door and looking expectantly at her husband, when she instantly picked up on the bleak mood.

Billy seemed unaware, at first, that she was even there. He was staring at Richie with sad eyes. "He wasn't *killed*, Richie. My dad, he… died."

Taking the book, Billy stood up and moved to put it in his bag, which was in the corner by the kitchen door. The sun really had gone in now, and clouds were building. Richie glanced at Sue and shook his head slightly, nodding over at Billy and making a wry movement with his mouth as if to say 'well, I tried'. Sue sat down at the table, raising her eyebrows at her husband.

She sighed deeply. "OK, Billy, come and sit down a moment, eh?"

Billy tied up the flap on his bag and sat down beside Sue. The room felt colder now that the sun had gone in. He could feel the tension. Only a few minutes ago, he had been laughing in the sun in the front garden with Sue, being all brave and confident, and now it felt like the earth had shifted all around him, and everything was changing shape. He watched Sue twisting her fingers and realised that, for once, she was anxious. That wasn't like Sue.

"I just spoke to the hospital, Billy. I'm afraid we won't be able to go in today to see your mam."

Billy's head flashed up, his eyes staring straight into Sue's sad face. She swallowed and continued, "Your mam has had another setback, Billy. She has to go back into surgery again today. It'll be another few days before we know anything."

She clasped Billy's hand in her own, then, smiling tremulously at him. "I'm sorry, Billy. They're doing everything they can."

Outside, at the front of the house, the tide was racing back in.

Chapter 20

Richie had gone to bed, Dagger had gone to town, Sue was doing some wedding preparation work on the laptop, and even Dolly and Lennie were nowhere to be seen, so Billy reluctantly found himself standing at Frank's gate. He paused, gazing up at the house for a while. His heart was heavy, and yet only a short while earlier he had woken feeling bright and slightly more confident than usual. He had been looking forward to taking Sue in to see his mam in hospital. He felt he had so much to share with her. His mam would be so happy for Billy, because for years she had worried about him, nagging him to see someone to get help for his many fears. Mam knew Billy wasn't good at opening up to people; she knew he was often bullied at school where the other kids found him weird and just gave up on him. And yet, here, on the riverside, of all places, Billy was gradually opening up, slowly at first. He felt a bit like a butterfly, unfurling its wings. He knew he was still wet and bedraggled, and that his new wings could tear at the slightest rough touch, but Billy had felt different this morning. But then… The memory of his sketchbook and the secrets it contained came whizzing back at him, punching him right in the stomach. Billy actually folded over into himself, leaning over the gate as he paused to catch his breath.

Suddenly, he stood up straight and listened. The music was floating back to him again. He closed his eyes and let it wash over him in gentle waves, feeling his breathing slow down and his face soften as he became lost in the sweeping sounds. He didn't recognise the tune, but he loved it. It felt to Billy like angels were gathering somewhere very near.

"Oy, you coming in, dozy boy, or are you going to stand there in a daydream all day or what?"

Billy's eyes snapped open with a start. Frank was hanging out of an upstairs window, laughing at him. The glorious music stopped as suddenly as it had started. Billy knew he was imagining it then.

"Come on in! I'm bored to tears in here," she told him, slamming shut the window.

Billy paused at the front door. These houses seemed a bit bigger than Sue and Richie's over the river. Their gardens were longer, and the row seemed well-spaced and roomier in general. As Frank opened the door and stood back to let Billy enter, the sun came back out, warming his back and guiding him forward. He glanced fearfully over his shoulder at Sue's house across the river: it was still there, sitting comfortingly in a small patch of sunlight behind the willow trees, near the water. Richie was asleep in the upstairs bedroom, and Billy could just make out the pattern on the closed curtains. He knew that further behind the house, up on its lofty hill, Penshaw Monument stood like a sentinel, watching him here in the distance, warming him with its solid presence, making him feel brave.

"Come on, Billy, get a move on. It'll be dark by the time you make your mind up and get in here."

Frank was down the passage towards the back of the house, beckoning Billy to follow her into the kitchen. She opened the fridge door and pointed to a chair at the table.

"Juice?" she asked good-naturedly.

Billy nodded and sat down, his eyes roaming the room, which was larger and of a more old-fashioned style than Sue's. But it was warm and welcoming, and Billy felt himself relax, the weight lifting from his shoulders, as Frank poured them a drink and handed him an old toffee tin.

"Try one of these, Billy. My Nan made them. Gorgeous, eh?"

The tin was full of fairy cakes in little frilly cases, complete with soft butter icing and little shiny metal beads on. He chose one carefully, peeling back the paper gently and taking a delicate little bite. Frank ripped the paper case off her cake and rammed the whole thing into her mouth, closing her eyes in ecstasy. Billy couldn't help but smile at the expression on her face.

"Go on, Billy. These are not cakes to be eaten like a vicar's wife. Get stuck in, son!"

She widened her eyes and reached for another cake. Billy looked down at the nibble he had taken out of his cake, then with a slow smile he popped the whole thing into his mouth, feeling the soft icing melt on his tongue. He, too, closed his eyes.

"Oh… wow…" he mumbled, spitting crumbs, then crunching on the little metal balls. "This is amazing."

Frank offered the tin and pushed his glass of juice forward towards him.

"Plenty more where that came from," she told him, peeling the wrap off another cake for herself.

"Should you really be eating all that sugar?" Billy asked her shyly.

Frank paused with the cake in the air, mid-bite.

"Aha," she said slowly. "Someone's been talking, haven't they?"

Billy felt his face flush slightly. He remembered the conversation he'd had with Richie about Frank being ill, that awful 'kissing disease', and also how her own Nan had shouted at her when she'd gone into the river to get that piece of wood out.

"Err, well, not really," Billy stuttered, picking up his glass to hide his embarrassment, and taking a big slurp.

Frank sat back and gazed at him from across the table.

"Oh, it's OK, Billy," she told him. "I know what people are like down here. It's a proper village. You can't even sneeze without everyone saying you've died. They mean well, but… it can get very annoying."

Billy looked at her. She seemed to be glowing with rude health to him. *In fact, she looks a hell of a lot healthier than I do*, he mused to himself. Her eyes were shining, deep blue, her cheeks had a healthy sun blush, and her very dark hair was thick and glossy. She was slim and athletic, taller than Billy, and he assumed, quite a bit older than himself. She was so relaxed and confident that Billy felt like a two-year-old beside her.

"Did you make these cakes?" he asked her, dragging his eyes away from her animated face.

"Me? Nah! My Nan did. She's a brilliant cook. She tries to feed me up cos I've been ill, so go on, Billy, eat as many as you want."

That nonplussed Billy for a moment. She was *admitting* that she'd been ill, had this awful thing? How could she catch something like that in a place like Fatfield? Billy hadn't even seen any other boys of her age, only that one spotty, weird one, with the Adam's apple, the day he'd met Frank. Surely, a girl like her wouldn't have kissed *him*? Yuk. He grimaced at the thought, and felt a stab of jealousy, too.

"What?" she asked him directly, her blue eyes boring into his face.

Billy tried not to look at her mouth. He swallowed hard. "What… what was wrong with you? Why aren't you in school? You look all right to me." He lowered his eyes then, playing with the crumbs on the table top.

Frank laughed and sat back in her chair.

"I'm fine, Billy. I think I should have been back at school two weeks ago, but the doctor says I still have to rest up. I'm sick as a chip of it. But I suppose I don't want to pass it on to anyone else." She sort of smirked at him then.

Billy gulped.

"You mean, you're still… what's it…contagious?" he stammered, getting to his feet.

Frank laughed out loud and swept up some of her own cake crumbs.

"Nah, don't be daft, Billy. I'm just winding you up. I'm fine now, really. Just, you have to be careful with *glandular fever*. It can come back again and leave you feeling rotten."

Billy became still and stared at her. Huh. That wasn't what Richie had said she had.

"Glandular... what?" he asked cautiously.

"Glandular fever, Billy," a voice said behind him. Turning, he saw Frank's Nan had appeared in the kitchen, carrying a large washing basket. He jumped to his feet. This was the same large, loud woman he's seen at Dagger's gate that first morning.

"Oh, hello, Mrs... er..."

"You sit down, pet," she told him, putting the basket down and opening the door to the washing machine. "Glandular fever is what she's had, Billy. And it can take a long time to recover from, that's why she's not at school for a while yet."

Billy glanced over at Frank who was casually licking stray crumbs off the table from her finger.

"Richie said she had something else. He told me she had a sort of disease..." he began.

Mrs Bailey stopped in her job and stood up straight, her hands on her hips. She was a big, handsome looking woman with the same wavy hair and piercing blue eyes as her granddaughter. She laughed at Billy's startled expression.

"I bet Richie Render told you our Frank had that 'kissing disease', eh?"

Billy's mouth dropped open in shock and embarrassment. He nodded dumbly at her.

"Ha, don't worry, Billy. Our Frank won't be kissing you, *or anybody else*, will you, Frank?"

Billy blushed deep red at that comment. He could feel the heat of it all down his neck and into his T-shirt. He wanted to die, right there.

Frank simply laughed.

"It used to be called that in the old days, Billy, because only teenagers got glandular fever. So it was called the kissing disease because they thought that's how it was passed on from one to the other. It doesn't really happen like that at all." Mrs Bailey poured washing powder into a little ball, threw it into the wash and slammed the door shut.

"So you don't have to worry, Billy. You're quite safe with me," Frank told him with a sly wink.

"Why don't you take Billy out and show him your birds, Frank?" Mrs Bailey asked, heading out of the kitchen. "The sun's out now."

Billy's head was up and his blush was receding. He loved birds. He stood up at the same time as Frank.

"Oh, yes, please," he told her happily.

"Come on, then. Follow me. They're out here."

Frank opened the door and stood aside so that Billy could go out ahead of her into the back garden. As he passed in front of her, she couldn't resist it: she pursed her lips and made loud kissing noises at the top of his head. Billy laughed and ducked out quickly into the sunshine.

*

Back across the water, Sue was on the phone with Paul Costello. She stood at her back door, absent-mindedly stroking the big cat Fingle Brown, who was making his mid-day rounds of the neighbours in search of a treat or two. Her pretty face was creased with worry lines.

"So, it sounds serious, then, Paul?"

She listened and nodded, chewing her bottom lip.

"Yes, of course, he's fine here with me. I thought we were making progress this morning, but then he started a small panic attack again. But Richie got out of him a most peculiar comment. Billy told Richie that his dad had died, that he wasn't *killed*. We just assumed he'd been killed in action, in Afghanistan or somewhere. We knew he'd been a soldier, but we weren't sure what regiment or anything. Do you know?"

Sue walked towards the passage where her art work hung and looked out across the water to Frank's house. She listened to the voice on the other end of the phone. It was as she suspected: Billy's notes weren't up to date. There were huge gaps where there should have been important details about the lad's life. Honestly. She sighed and tried another tack.

"He's pretty obsessed with the Penshaw Monument, Paul. I'm going to try to find out more and maybe get him up there one day soon. If it holds happy memories for him, maybe I'll get to the truth. He did say that he'd 'find his dad there'. That's my next step, but in the meantime I've unleashed my secret weapon on him."

She smiled and glanced over the rippling water to the row of houses opposite. She'd watched Billy go reluctantly into Essie Bailey's house. By now, he'd be pumped with sugar and other treats, and would be being perfectly distracted by someone closer to his own age.

"My weapon? Oh, a delightful character called Frank. Don't worry, Billy's in safe hands." Sue smiled into the phone. "You keep me informed how his mam is doing, and I'll report back on his progress."

She hung up then, straightened the picture of Penshaw Monument, then returned to her laptop.

*

"You hang on here a minute, Billy, and I'll bring my first bird out to you," Frank told him calmly, with a serious look on her face, before sliding behind the door of a shed and slipping in quickly, closing it behind herself. Billy stood in the yard and listened: he was expecting to hear tweeting and chirruping, if this was an aviary, but it was all completely quiet. Then, all of a sudden, that music started up again as he stood there in the sun. Billy was transfixed. It flooded through him and made him smile. And yet, he also wanted to cry. He could feel the music somewhere deep in his chest as if he'd eaten a fluffy cotton wool ball. He smiled to himself, heard the shed door creak, and opened his eyes to find Frank standing in front of him with her hands cupped together, holding something carefully close, as if it was very precious.

"Okay, Billy," she breathed quietly, "this is my very first bird. What do you think?"

Billy leaned forward carefully and slowly, as Frank gently opened her fingers. He looked closely, frowned, shook his head in disbelief, and glanced up into Frank's laughing blue eyes.

"It's a piece of wood," he told her, flatly.

"Ee, Billy. Come on, lad. It's better than that." Frank laughed out loud and looked shocked at his response. "Look again."

She handed the lump of wood to Billy, who took it gently from her, turning it over in his hands. Actually, the more closely he looked, the more he could see that it did look just like a little bird. It was rough and ready, but there was a definite shape about it. A small head, and a stubby tail on a fat little body.

"Is it a wren?" he asked, genuinely puzzled.

Frank grinned at him with delight. "Well done, Billy. It *is* a wren. I found the wood and made it myself. Cool, eh?"

Billy smiled shyly and shrugged at her.

"You made this?" he asked.

Frank smiled even more. "Yep. And there's more. I think I got a bit better with each one. Come and see."

She led Billy into the shed. It smelt a bit like Dagger's den, of wood and river water, but it was much smaller and tidier. There were only two shelves on the walls, a small window and a work table. Billy immediately spotted the little package he had delivered from Dagger's the day before, the shiny tools laid out on a soft bed of material. But his eyes returned to the shelves straight after taking in the interior. There were wooden birds everywhere. Some were quite tiny, but others were much bigger. He saw a rough carved owl in one corner, but Billy was drawn towards one of the biggest birds standing on a small plinth by itself. He gently stroked its head.

"Wow. A herring gull."

This bird was standing with its head arched back, the beak open and its wings outstretched. It looked exactly like the ones that used to land in the school yard.

"Did you make this as well?" he asked her, incredulously.

Frank glowed with pride. She moved towards the seagull, eyes shining.

"Yes, Billy. He was my last one. The little wren was the first one I did earlier this year, but I think I've got a bit better with each one. Do you agree?"

Smiling warmly at her, Billy moved along the shelves. The birds were arranged in all shapes and sizes, some polished and finished-off completely, others still with some work to do, some smoothing, polishing and oiling to be done. Billy smiled up at Frank, who met his eyes before moving along the shelf.

"Can you work out what sort of birds they are, Billy?"

She was testing him. What would happen, if he got them wrong? Would she fly off the handle and throw him out in disgust? Billy gulped. He didn't know her that well, but Frank didn't seem to be that sort of person. They'd already had a shared experience when he'd pulled her out of the river. And she was a good friend of Dagger's. And Sue knew and trusted her. So he would, too.

He gave a soft smile and moved to look more closely at her carvings, stroking the wood gently, and occasionally turning each bird, looking at the details.

"Okay," he began, hesitantly, glancing up at Frank. Her blue eyes looked back at him with interest, he noted, not challenge. That encouraged him to go on.

"I'd say this one is a coot." He raised an eyebrow quizzically, moving quickly on to the next wooden bird. "And this one is… I'd say it's a cormorant, but it needs some speckled detail in its wings."

Frank just gazed at him, smiling quietly to herself, her arms folded over her chest, as she walked slowly along the line of birds on the shelves in front of them.

"Now, this one is definitely a heron. I can tell by its long legs. But this little one I'm not so sure about. Until you add some colour or detail, it could be anything. Is that last one a puffin?" he asked genuinely interested, moving forward to look more closely.

Frank clapped him on the back, grinning happily at him.

"Billy, I'm really impressed! You do know your birds. And you're right. I'm not a proper carver, or an artist at all, so until I find someone to finish them off for me, I'm a bit stuck. And Dagger is winning the race."

Billy threw her a puzzled look. "What race? What's that all about, then? He said that to me, 'Tell Frank the race is on'."

Frank picked up a smaller bird and began to rub at its tail with some sandpaper.

"You know the little boats in his shed? The ones he's made? Well, he wants to match the number of boats he's made with the same number of birds I've made. But he won't tell me how many he's done. I think it's just a wind-up to stop me from being bored when I was poorly."

Billy sat down on a small wooden stool beside her. He seemed deep in thought for a minute. His eyes had a faraway look, but Frank noticed that the little worry line between his eyebrows had softened.

"You know what?" he began, picking up a warm wooden bird. "I've seen all his boats. They're amazing. He's got boats that were all made on the river Wear, here, and you've got all these little local birds, which you made on the river here…"

"Made of wood I fished out of the river myself," Frank interjected.

He grinned up at Frank. "Can I help you to add the details, the colours and the eyes and stuff like that? I'd love to do it," he added, his voice tailing away as he worried Frank would think it was a stupid idea. She gazed at him, her brow crinkling up and her eyes coming into bright blue focus.

"Would you, Billy?" she asked breathlessly. "Would you help me to finish off the birds? I know exactly how I want them to look."

Billy stood up, grinning happily.

"Yeah, 'course I would. I'm a bit bored here as well, and I'm not going back to school for a bit, so… yeah. Why not? And, I can tell you exactly how many boats are in Dagger's shed."

Frank's eyes grew wide. She looked at him expectantly, breathlessly. "So… How many, Billy? How many has Dagger made already?"

Billy's face fell. Try as he might, he couldn't remember the exact number, just the little details on the boats and the fact that some of them, like Frank's birds, needed finishing details.

"I…I, can't remember, Frank," he told her sadly, his head dropping down to his chest as he anxiously turned the little bird in his hand over and over. Frank leaned down to him and stilled his hand by putting her own over it. Billy looked up into her face.

"Tell you what, Bill," she told him conspiratorially. "I've got just the job for you."

Billy looked up at her quickly, smiling at the fact that, first of all, she had called him Bill – no one had *ever,* in his whole life, given him a nickname: he was *thrilled.* And secondly, Frank was obviously his friend now because she had a special job which she *trusted* him to do for her! His heart swelled with pride, for himself, and with gratitude to his new, brave and glamorous friend.

"A job? For me?" he asked her, trying to keep the tremor out of his voice. Frank looked pleased as punch as she leaned in towards him.

"Yes, Billy. You can be my spy."

Billy's eyes grew wide and his mouth dropped open. Wow. How dramatic was that? He hadn't been expecting that answer. A spy? That was like the most important thing anyone had ever said to him in his life! He was stunned, and happy, but a little worried about what being a spy might involve.

"Yes, Billy. You can sneak into Dagger's shed, count the boats he's made, and tell me how many more birds I have to carve to beat him. Yeah?"

Billy almost began to fizz with excitement. "Dagger's not in. We could go over there now and you could keep a look out, while I go in and do my job," he told her earnestly.

Frank almost leapt to her feet, grabbing Billy by the hand and dragging him out of the shed, back through the kitchen and towards the front door. "Woohoo. Come on, Billy. We've got work to do. Important work."

She flung open the front door and pulled him down the path behind her, heading towards the street and the riverside path. Stopping to fumble with the latch on the gate, she dropped Billy's hand, babbling away all the while, telling him how much fun they were going to have, how together they would beat Dagger and all his little Wearside boats. Billy smiled at her enthusiasm, glancing over the river to Sue's house and up and down the path in front of them, whilst carefully putting the little carved bird into his pocket. Suddenly, he tensed up and flung his arms around Frank, dragging her back into her garden with a sudden lurch. The two of them fell backwards, landing in a heap together on her garden path, as a pair of cyclists flashed past her gate without a backwards glance, swishing off down the road in a blur of orange and yellow.

"Are you all right?" Billy asked her breathlessly, hanging onto her for dear life, and frowning after the disappearing bikes. "Bloody idiots nearly knocked you out there, Frank!"

Frank sat on the ground in front of him, her breath coming in gasps, shaking like a leaf in shock and surprise.

"Phew. I'm fine. I didn't even see them coming. But there's just one thing. Can you do something for me, Billy?"

"Anything," he told her, watching as the cyclists sped off round the corner of the riverbend.

"Get your hands off my boobs, you perv."

Billy flung his hands off Frank's chest, put them into his hair, and dropped his head forward onto his own chest in horror. Oh no, not again!

Chapter 21

Frank chattered away excitedly beside Billy as they approached the bridge to cross the Wear back towards Dagger's house and shed. She had noticed that, as Billy drew closer to the iron fretwork of the bridge, he had suddenly gone quiet, throwing anxious glances towards the brown water on his left. As they reached the start of the footpath onto the bridge itself, Billy hesitated, turning back to look over his shoulder up the hill, behind the pub.

"What? What is it, Billy?"

Billy let out a sigh. The air was still and quiet, the day warm and the area peaceful, with no traffic or pedestrians about, yet a shadow seemed to cross Billy's face.

"You can't see the Monument from on this bridge, can you?" he asked her, shading his eyes from the sun and squinting up at her anxiously.

"Well, no, not really, Billy. It's hidden behind the trees, but it's up there all right. Come on, let's get going before Dagger gets back."

She started walking over the bridge, but stopped after a yard or two, when Billy didn't follow her. Turning back, she saw he was rooted to the spot, looking over the water, towards Sue's house. She retraced her steps to join him.

"Billy, you got over here to mine: come on, you can do it again."

"There was an old man who came over with me," he told her quietly. "He was telling me the story of the Lambton Worm. He said that's its hill, up there, behind the pub."

Aha, so that was how he had managed to get to her this morning, Frank thought. She knew about Billy's phobia of the water. She glanced up at the Worm Hill, noticing a couple of rabbits ambling about on the top, in the sunshine.

"That's the one, Billy. So, you had company on the way over. Now you've got me on the way back. Come on."

She took hold of his arm firmly, and gently led him forward, starting out over the bridge.

"So, this old guy was telling you the legend of the Worm," she began, leading Billy across. "I'll tell you one about those two swans down there."

Billy looked up at her and immediately glanced down at the water, where two swans were paddling about together, followed by a line of fluffy grey cygnets, in the shallows near Frank's house. He noticed that one of the parents was much bigger than the other.

Slowing down towards the middle of the bridge, Frank told him, "One of them got shot. They've been coming to the river for years, those two. Did you know that swans mate for life, Billy?"

He stopped and looked up at her. "I think I knew that," he said.

Frank casually leaned against the green railings of the bridge, pointing to the birds. Billy stopped beside her, waiting for her to continue her story.

"Well, a couple of years ago, some evil little get shot the cob – the male swan. He was quite badly injured. He nearly drowned. His wife was in a right state, she was totally panicking, squawking and flapping about."

Billy's eyes grew wide, looking up at Frank and listening intently.

"No," he breathed. "What happened?"

"We did what we always do, when there's a panic on the river," she told him. "We went for Dagger. He was able to paddle into the water 'cos the tide was out, and get the injured male out."

Billy was staring at the two swans, gliding serenely about on the still water below them. "But, I heard that swans can be really vicious," he said.

Frank blew some air out of her cheeks. "Oh, they are, Billy. But you know, only Dagger could have done it. I watched him that day. He spoke really quietly to the pen – that's the female – the whole time he was catching the injured male. I'm sure he can speak the language of any animal, that guy."

Billy smiled warmly up at her, thinking of how he'd thought the same, when he watched Dagger with Dolly and Lennie.

"He totally calmed her down, as he got to the poor damaged swan. He carried him back to his shed, and the female waddled off after him, hissing and squawking at anyone who came near. Dagger had quite a crowd by then. He was like the pied piper. Everyone had come out of their houses to see if they could help, but nobody dared get too close."

Billy was lost in the imagining of the scene, right here, down by the river, with his new friend being a hero. Frank smiled to herself, watching Billy's concerned face, and his mouth forming a silent 'wow' at the thought of Dagger's heroics.

"Go on. What happened next?" he asked, keen to hear more of the story.

"Well, he took the swan to his shed and kept it there. He managed to get the pellet out of its neck and he kept them both until the injured swan was well again." Frank paused, looking closely at Billy, standing in the middle of the

Fatfield bridge, leaning over the very water, he was so terrified of. She smiled to herself. Job nearly done.

"And then he wrote to the Queen," she told Billy with a laugh.

Billy looked up at her, smiling quizzically. "He did what?"

"Well, Dagger told me that all the swans in England are owned by the Queen, so he wrote to her and told her that he'd saved one for her and he was going to let it go back on the river, when it was better."

Billy frowned up at her. "That's mad," he replied. "That can't be right about the Queen owning all the swans, not up here, anyway. Maybe in London. That's just one of Dagger's stories, that is."

Frank put her chin on the bars of the bridge, leaning in close to Billy, as a bus trundled over behind them, heading up towards Worm Hill.

"No, it's right, Billy. I *Googled* it. She does own all the swans in the UK. And she wrote back to Dagger to thank him as well. He's still got the letter from Buckingham Palace."

"No! Wow." Billy's eyes were shining. "He must have been thrilled to get a letter from the Queen."

Frank laughed and turned to him. "Actually, Billy, he was well cheesed off."

"Huh? Why? He did an amazing thing and got a thank you letter from the Queen."

"He thought he was going to get a medal," Frank answered simply, with a smile. "Sir Dagger Dawson."

They both laughed then and made to walk on over the rest of the bridge, but Billy suddenly put his hand through the bars and caught a feather floating down towards the river.

"Wow, look at that, Frank," he told her, holding out a pure white feather in the palm of his hand.

Now it was Frank's turn to be impressed. She looked closely at the feather, then looked seriously into Billy's grey eyes.

"You've just had a visit, Billy. Keep that, it's special."

"A visit? You mean, from you?" he asked her, puzzled.

Frank laughed and walked on. "No, Billy, from an angel. A white feather is always a sign that an angel is near and is looking out for you. Come on."

Billy hung back, looking up at the sky above the bridge, and down at the swans on the water.

"Nah," he told her retreating back. "Must have been a seagull."

Without turning round, Frank replied, "Can you see any seagulls today, Billy? Or pigeons, for that matter?"

Billy gazed at the clear blue sky, up the green hill behind them, and down into the brown water, before raising his eyebrows, smiling to himself and running after Frank, clutching the feather tightly to his chest, his mind and heart bubbling fit to burst. What with the heavenly music he kept hearing, and now an angel feather, and a secret mission, what a day this was turning into.

Chapter 22

Watching nonchalantly, hands in pockets, as the bus trundled slowly up Worm Hill, away from them, two boys casually glanced over at the bridge, gave each other a nod, then quickly dashed commando-style to the small wall surrounding the pub. The smaller of the two stood up and stared at the two figures leaning out over the river, as his mate grabbed him and dragged him down to his level.

"Chick, man, they'll see you, you idiot. Get down!"

The boy crumpled down beside his friend, rubbing the knee he'd banged on the wall. "Ow, man, Baz, they didn't see me. They're looking down the river." Chick rubbed at his knee, scowling at his mate. "Do you think that's him? Is that the little toe-rag?"

Chick and Baz both popped their heads up over the wall. They could still make out the two figures of Frank and Billy, leaning on the rail of the bridge, looking downstream. Together they bobbed back down, a serious look on their faces.

"Got to be him, Chick," Baz said knowingly. "I've never seen him before. Mind you, he doesn't look as tall as Si said he was."

Little Chick popped back up for another look, before sliding back down to his mate again.

"I'd say he's not much bigger than me," he told Baz. "He certainly hasn't got the muscles that Si said this new kid had. Maybe it's not him, after all?"

Baz frowned, looking over the wall, as Frank and Billy slowly walked on across the bridge. "But that's defo Frank, and Si said this kid was looking for her, didn't he? Looks to me like they're going to that Sue's house now. You know, her who fosters kids?"

Kneeling up, with his chin on the wall, Chick watched the retreating backs as the two in the distance turned onto Sue's terrace.

"Aye, you're right, her house, or Dagger Dawson's."

Baz had his mobile out, scrolling through his contacts. The two boys were still crouched on the ground behind the wall, hidden from the bus stop and the prying eyes by the wheelie bins in the pub car park, but it didn't stop him from speaking to his mate on the phone in an exaggerated whisper.

"Si? Si… it's me, Baz. Me and Chick have just seen that kid with Frank. Yeah, *that* one! They just crossed the bridge. Me and Chick have them in our sights, and we're going to keep them under close observation until you get here. OK?"

Chick nodded at his mate, delighted to be of help and to be involved in the plan, his fluffy yellow hair floating about his head like a baby duck, shining in the warm sunshine.

Baz nodded into his mobile for a few seconds more, before telling his mate in a quiet, serious voice, "You take it easy, mate. You don't want to be doing any more damage to yourself than that little sod did to you. Get here, when you can. We've got them under surveillance. OK, over and out."

Suddenly, a huge shadow blocked out the sun. Standing behind them was the pub landlord, a big fella with a smelly bag of rubbish in his hands, opening the lid of the bin they were hiding behind.

"OK, Cagney and Lacey, get yourselves out of my car park and away home. You'll be up to no good, I expect. And why aren't you in school, anyway?"

The two boys jumped up, looking guilty, shuffling to their feet and mumbling together, "dentist" and "training day".

The landlord wasn't fooled. "Get away with yourselves before I get onto the school Board man. Go on, bugger off."

Throwing one more glance over the bridge, the two boys slouched out of the pub car park, still keeping low, just in case either Frank or her new best mate should turn around and spot them. Once away from the pub, the two of them crept over the small stretch of grass which took them down to the water's edge. From this lookout, they could see if Frank and the lad went into the front of Sue's house, but at the same time, they remained concealed behind some thick green plants. Sitting themselves comfortably on the riverbank, in the sun, they waited patiently for the arrival of their mate, safe in the knowledge that if either Frank or her sidekick came out of the terrace over the road, they would see them, follow them, and bring them to justice. That cheeky, aggressive little newcomer was going to get a taste of his own medicine.

*

Billy and Frank paused at Dagger's gate, listening quietly for any signs of life in the house or garden. The sun was warm on their backs, and they could hear the odd cluck of chickens as they pecked about, but all seemed peaceful. Neither could hear any knocking or sawing sounds coming from the shed, and Dagger's old green Land Rover wasn't parked in its usual spot. Frank smiled and gave Billy a nod as, together, they pushed open the gate. It creaked ever so slightly, and they were three steps in, when the sound of mad barking came from inside the house, followed swiftly by a black explosion bursting through the front door, eyes wild and teeth snapping. Billy trembled at the sight of Lennie flying through the flap in the door to greet them. As soon as the dog realised who the intruders were, he dropped to a crouch and started wiggling and laughing up at them, no longer the insane, vicious hound from hell he had appeared to be a second ago.

Frank laughed and crouched down to pet him. "It's OK, Billy. Lennie Catflap won't eat us, really, even though he looks as though he could."

Billy relaxed and laughed self-consciously. He still wasn't used to being greeted by *people* in a friendly way, let alone by animals who at first looked like they wanted to tear him apart, but who then greeted him with obvious recognition and affection. He gave the dog a gentle pat and together he and Frank made their way towards Dagger's woodshed. The donkey was nibbling grass down by the water's edge: she raised her head, snuffled softly in their direction, then continued eating without a care in the world. Billy gazed at her, thinking about the wonderful life this animal had here, with lots of love, no fear, and not a care in the world. He gave a small grimace, shrugged his shoulders and followed after Frank.

At the woodshed, they both paused again, looking around them to make sure Dagger wasn't going to jump out and frighten them, just for a laugh. Frank had told Billy Dagger wouldn't mind in the least if they went into his shed to check on the progress of the little boats, but it was much more fun to go in secretly and then surprise him by knowing exactly how many boats he had. And by being able to beat him, for once in her life.

"Dagger once challenged me to a race up Penshaw Hill, you know, Billy."

Billy looked sideways up at her. "Really? Did you accept the challenge?" he asked – a little tremulously, Frank thought. Odd.

"Yeah!" she told him with a grin. "Of course, I did. I mean, there was me, about twelve years old, at the time, and as fit as a butcher's dog. And there was Dagger, a big old, cuddly granddad of a bloke, aged about sixty-five. I couldn't refuse." She smiled at the memory.

"So, what did you win?" Billy asked.

"Win? Nee chance, Billy. He took off up that hill like a mountain goat. I was ahead of him, but I slipped and fell flat on my face. By the time I caught him up, he was dancing about on the Monument like Rocky, from the films."

"He beat you?" Billy was incredulous. "How?"

"Oh, he's not daft, Billy. Dagger had sneaked a look at my footwear before he even gave me the challenge. He knew my designer trainers wouldn't manage Penshaw Monument hill, but his heavy boots would. He's a sod." She grinned affectionately. "He might be old, but he's not daft."

They paused at the shed, Frank's hand on the door knob. They exchanged a look and gently pushed the door open. Lennie had already given up, now that there wasn't a burglar to savage, and was lying near the river, beside his friend Dolly, warming himself happily in the sun. The sunlight spilled into the gloomy interior, lighting up the shelves and the dusty windows, glinting off metal tools and warming up the smell of oils, paints and sawdust. Even the manure pile, not far from the door, smelled sweet.

Billy inhaled deeply, closing his eyes and smiling with delight. "Oohhh…" He breathed out.

"Wow…" breathed Frank, her eyes fixed on the little boats on the shelf. "Look at them, Billy. They're amazing," she exclaimed quietly, walking forward almost reverently towards the far side of the shed, to the workbench. Billy followed, still smiling, as Frank reached forward and picked up the first of the boats. Turning it over in her hands, she shook her head with pleasure, then bent forward to sniff at the carved wooden vessel. Billy laughed out loud.

"What?" she asked him defensively.

"Nothing," he told her. "I do that as well. Sniff everything, I mean."

They moved along the shelf, touching the boats, smoothing them with their fingers, looking at tiny details.

"He's got loads, hasn't he?" Frank asked, her brow creased in concentration. "Mind you, he's been doing this for years. Much longer than I have."

Billy stood back, his eyes moving along the shelf in front of him. "There's ten, I would say. And I'd also say they're nearly finished. He told me the other day that he has to add all the names to them, and paint in smaller details, like flag colours, lifeboats and stuff. He's so clever, isn't he?"

Billy's eyes were big and shining, bringing a smile to Frank's face, too. What a sweet little character he was turning into, she thought. Not at all the needy little geek she first thought he was.

"He's got names for them all?" she asked Billy.

"Yeah. He says they were all built on the Wear in Sunderland, all those years ago, so it shouldn't be too hard to find out what they'll all be called, should it? Bet he's got a list somewhere."

Frank gazed about the shed. "You're right, Billy. Let's have a look about, shall we? He'll be ages, yet, so we should be OK in here for a while. It's safe."

They split up then, moving to either side of the shed, gently opening drawers, and moving pots and cloths.

*

Back on the other side of the river, Baz and Chick had almost fallen asleep in the sun. Suddenly, the hoot of an owl drifted across the water to them. Neither one moved or said anything – they were so chilled out, lying flat on their backs, in the sun, on the grass behind the sweet smelling shrubs. The owl hooted again.

Chick opened one eye and nudged Baz, who was lying with his mouth open. Hoot, hoot, more urgently this time.

Chick sat up. "I thought owls only came out at night…" he began, as Baz suddenly sat upright, too, beside him. They still couldn't see clearly through the deep shrubs in front of them.

"Aye, you're right, Chick. Let's have a closer look."

As Chick reached forward to part the greenery with one hand, a loud voice yelled at them from the path behind them, "Oy! You two – FREEEZE!"

Obediently the two boys froze. Only their eyes moved, darting to one another, as their heads craned round to see who was shouting at them, and why. A postman was standing on the path, hands on hips, bag across his body, staring at them with angry amazement.

Baz mouthed to Chick, "What?"

Shrugging his shoulders, Chick shook his head back at his mate.

The postman put down his bag, walking towards the two boys carefully, arms reaching out in front of him.

"Barry O'Hara, how flamin' long have you lived on the bloody riverside? Do you know not, eh? Idiots. The two of you!"

The boys exchanged puzzled glances. Huh? Did this guy know what they were planning to do to that little weirdo new kid, then? Was he a mind reader? The postman had got closer to them, but now stood stock still, still reaching out to the boys in an attempt to keep them still.

"Take a look at them plants you're lying behind, eh? Recognise them?"

As Chick turned his head, he noticed Baz's hand stretching out to move the shrubbery so he could peer through it.

"NO! DON'T. MOVE," yelled the postman. Then slightly more calmly, he continued, "Whatever you do, do not touch those plants. Now. Step back slowly, so you don't slip under them. Gently. Move back."

Chick looked fearfully at the plants. What? Was there some creature lurking in there? A replica of the Lambton Worm? It had all happened right at this spot, but that was just a legend. Wasn't it? Glancing at Baz, he noticed he'd gone quite pale. Moving in slow motion, the two of them made it back to the path. Baz stood there, sweating and shaking. Chick, of course, was clueless.

"So what?" he asked, swaggering with mock bravado. "Were they Triffids? Were they going to walk up to us and eat us, like?"

The postman poked him in the side of the head with a bony finger. "Worse than that, thicko. They're giant Hogweed. Proper poisonous! One touch of them and you could have stripped the skin off your hand. Don't you know anything? That's what they should be teaching you local kids in school."

Both boys turned and looked fearfully at the spot where they had been sitting, so close to danger without realising it. Baz was trembling now as he looked back at the postie.

"Soz, mate. I never thought. Thanks for the warning. Phew, we had a lucky escape there."

He gazed down at the hand which had been reaching out to part the shrubs, then he turned and clipped Chick right round the ear.

"Ow! What was that for?" Chick yelled, holding onto his left ear with one hand.

"For not telling me to look out, you idiot. Honestly!" Baz told him, walking towards the bridge, towards the sound of the ever-hooting owl. Chick trundled after him, mumbling to himself about not even being from down here, anyway, rubbing his ear as he walked. The postman shook his head after them and went on his way. At the end of Sue's street, Si was lurking near the end of the bridge, waiting for his henchmen to join him, still making the mock owl hooting sound.

*

Frank and Billy had not been able to find the names of the boats. By now they were out in Dagger's garden, each eating an apple that they'd found in a basket on a bench, near the door. Billy took out the little wooden bird he'd brought from Frank's shed, turning it over in his hands. Frank looked down at it and pulled a face.

"What?" Billy asked her.

"Well, look at it, Billy. How can I ever compete with Dagger and his boats? It's rubbish."

Billy looked closely into her face. She seemed upset, glancing at him, then gazing out across the river. *She's actually embarrassed*, he thought.

"Frank," he told her gently. "Your birds are brilliant. This is your first one, you know. You got better as you went on."

Frank shrugged her shoulders, but continued to stare downstream. Billy continued, telling her earnestly, "Honestly. I guessed them all right, didn't I? Eh?"

Frank nodded mutely. Billy continued, "And anyway, I've seen Dagger's early boats, and they were rubbish." He crossed his fingers behind his back as he told her this.

Frank looked at him then. "Honestly?" she asked quietly.

"Honestly," he replied. "Dagger told me he put at least three in the bin before he got the hang of them," Billy lied. He knew it was wrong, just a little white lie. But he had never had a friend before – at least, certainly not one like Frank – and he wanted her to feel good about herself, not be embarrassed by her own handiwork. "Your work is great, Frank, and look how much younger you are than Dagger.

He's had yonks more practice than you. In fact, I think you should be showing your work to other people." He smiled warmly at the thought.

Frank smiled at him then, looking fondly towards Billy, her eyes shining with gratitude. Billy felt a rush of pleasure in her looking intently at him like that. There was a floaty feeling in his stomach, and he could hear that angel music again, drifting over the water.

He went on earnestly, "I think you should display all your birds on your side of the river, and get Dagger to display all his boats on this side of the river, then people could see how clever you *both* are." His face was glowing in the lightbulb moment.

Frank sat up straighter, pondering this idea. "What? Like... my very own *Art show*?" she asked, sitting back against the bench in the sun, as the idea settled into her, like a feather landing at her feet. She smiled slowly at Billy.

"Exactly that!" he told her, animatedly, warming to the theme. "Dagger's show on this side, and yours on your side. It would be fantastic. I'll help you with the finishing off, so I'll have a hand in it, too." He grinned at her, excitement bubbling up in his chest.

Frank gazed across the river, towards her own house. Standing up, she walked towards the water, where Dolly and Lennie were enjoying the peace and quiet of the day. She looked back over her shoulder at Billy, her blue eyes flashing in the sunlight. "But... how... and where could we display them, Billy? How would anyone see them outside?"

Billy joined her near the water. Looking up and down the river first, he tilted his head and looked up into the green canopy of the tree they were standing under.

"I know," he told her. "Up there. In the trees. You could put your carved birds up in the trees on your side of the river. Then Dagger could display his boats in the trees on this side of the river." He looked questioningly at Frank, waiting for the suggestion to sink in.

Frank closed her eyes briefly, imagining it, then she laughed out loud. "*And*... all the people doing the Fatfield walks would see them, if they did the river Wear circuit," she told him. "You know, the walk you did that day you found me in the river?"

"And saved your life!" He grinned at her. "Yeah, that would be amazing!"

They gazed at each other for a few minutes, imagining potential glory and great satisfaction in doing it, smiling warmly as the idea took hold. The music continued to float over the water, providing a classical backdrop for their fantasy world.

Dagger's gate creaked quietly, but ominously, as Si, Baz and Chick crept silently through.

Chapter 23

Billy and Frank wandered away from the bench near Dagger's door and walked towards the water. Frank was talking animatedly about their plans to display their carvings along the path on each side of the river, but she had half an eye on Billy as they drew closer. She knew of his fears and didn't want to spook him, but by pointing out tall trees over on her side and gesturing to the ones near Dagger's house, Billy seemed to be distracted from the deep brown water and appeared at ease. He stood at her side as she gazed across the stretch of the Wear.

"So you see, Billy, that first big ash, the one hanging over the water? Wouldn't that be brilliant for the first bird?"

Billy gazed over the water and back at her, nonplussed. "What? An ash?" he asked, frowning up at her. Frank spotted his confusion and smiled, putting him right, before he got even more embarrassed.

"An ash *tree*, Billy. The very tall ones with quite long leaves. See? The one stretching out over the river? There's quite a few of them down here."

Billy suddenly smiled in delight and recognition. "Ah, yes, an ash tree!" he exclaimed. "The squirrels like them, don't they?"

Frank patted him on the head, affectionately. "Very observant of you, Billy. Yes, they do. And look, there are some ash and a couple of willows near here for Dagger to start displaying his boats on this side." She gestured up and down the water's edge.

Simultaneously, they both looked up at the tree that they were almost standing under on the river bank. This one was solid and old, with gnarled branches stretching out like strong arms, reaching towards them. Billy gazed up into the dense green canopy, then squinted up at Frank. "But this one's not an ash? It's a…a…"

"Oak, Billy," she told him, before reaching forward and throwing her apple gowk over the river in a wide arc, watching as it hit the water near her house, with a soft plop. Billy laughed up at her, amazed. Not only did she seem to know all the names of trees, she had quite an aim as well. He was impressed.

"Wow, what a throw!" he told her.

Frank picked up a small stone from the grass at their feet and handed it to him.

"Go on, Billy. See if you can hit my apple gowk from here."

Billy looked unsurely at the river for a second or two, glanced nervously at Frank, then drew his arm back and threw with all his might. The stone landed not far from the bobbing apple, with a very satisfying 'splop'. Billy laughed quietly, took one final bite from his own apple then launched it into the river, where it landed just short of the other one. The two swans watched with interest, fluffing up their feathers, as their line of cygnets made their smooth way towards the bobbing apples with keen interest. Out of the corner of her eye, Frank allowed herself a small satisfied smile, watching Billy acting fairly calmly right next to the water. *He's getting there*, she thought.

*

The three figures made their silent entry through Dagger's gate and round towards the house, hidden, as they were, by the stable and the shed. They crouched along in single file, knees slightly bent, heads ducked down, but popping up once in a while to check for their enemy. Si was in the front, tall and gangly, Baz, stocky and mis-shapen was in the middle, followed by the small, slim Chick at the back, who stumbled and tripped along behind his friends because he couldn't see a thing, apart from Baz's bum, that is. Simon, at the front was the undoubted leader, making gestures and silently mouthing instructions to his team, keeping them in order, glaring at them through puffy, blackened eyes. When he whispered to them his voice sounded thick and nasal, because of the damage to his swollen, battered nose. An angry purple bruise lay across the bridge of it, clashing magnificently with his black and blue eyes.

"Keep down back there, and watch out for that dog," he told them over his shoulder. Baz and Chick both nodded, gazing around the garden.

"What about the fella that lives here?" Chick asked nervously. "I heard he's a big bloke. Don't want to get battered, mind, lads."

Si and Baz both looked back at him contemptuously. Gazing into Si's two black eyes was too much for Chick and he started to giggle and shake. Neither of the other two said anything: they continued to stare malevolently at him until he stopped.

"Sorry, Si," he mouthed, trying to look apologetic.

"S'not funny, you know. Bloody hurts," Si squeaked back at him.

Baz, in the middle, had taken a quick look over Si's head towards the river. He bobbed back down immediately, dragging Si down to his level and almost knocking him into the bushes alongside the smelly stable, in the process.

"Owww!" hissed Si, putting a hand up, protectively, over his face. "Watch it, man."

Baz felt immediately sorry for his mate. Reaching out, he patted him ineffectually on the shoulder, telling him in hushed tones, "Oops, soz, Si. But they're there. Over by the river. Frank and that kid. The vicious one."

All three boys raised themselves up slightly, to peer across the yard towards the water. They could just make out the sound of voices and could see the back of their enemies' heads, but they couldn't hear what was being said. Chick suddenly stood up, all defiant and angry.

"Right!" he announced, quite loudly and clearly.

Si and Baz grabbed him by an arm each and dragged him down to ground level. The chickens in the yard suddenly created a huge racket, clucking and running about in an attempt to get away from these uninvited guests.

"Chick, man, you flamin' idiot!" Si glowered at him, while Baz leant on him with his most impressive weight. "What are you doing? We need a plan. We can't just stroll over there."

"Yeah," Baz said, his fat face turning serious, his dark eyes crinkling into their folds. "I mean, that kid's dangerous. Just look what he did to our Si, here."

Si made his usual snorting gulp, but on this occasion, it sounded like pain and hurt pride to his mates.

Chick looked crestfallen. "Soz, mate," he told his friend, still resisting the urge to giggle at his bruises and smashed nose. Taking a big breath, he forced himself to be serious, but inside, he was thinking: really? That kid didn't look big enough to have attacked Si the way Si said he had. Overpowered him, too. Little maggot. Well, he was going to get what was coming to him.

"I think we should crawl forward from here, get as close as we can, then rush there and surprise them. What do you say, lads?"

"Deal," they both replied, getting closer down to the ground.

They started crawling forward together, sticking close, so that each one had the protection of the team should anything go wrong, but hey, they were commandos and they were going to get the guy who had hurt their mate. Excitement at the prospect of some action made them reckless, grinning together and puffing up their egos. At the front, Si was able to pick his way forward, carefully, avoiding sharp stones, or soft mud. Baz, in the middle, was slightly taller, so his big head was just above Si's back, which meant he couldn't really see much of where they were headed. Chick, at the back, had his nose jammed up against Baz's fat bum, and his hands were just taking pot luck at whatever lay underneath them. He grimaced and silently prayed that Baz hadn't had beans for breakfast, as he usually did. The sun beat down on them, the chickens clucked and moved out of their way, as the trio edged forward on their mission.

*

Frank and Billy had sat down in the sun, not far from the water's edge. They sat close together, chatting away about Billy's idea, enjoying the exciting intimacy of their joint venture. For Frank, it was an opportunity to actually achieve something out of her enforced time off school. Up until this point, it was only learning to carve the birds that had kept her sane. For Billy, it was a golden opportunity to overcome some of his fears. Who would have thought it? Last week, in school, he had been bullied mercilessly by those older kids, had been under the stage and up on the school roof, and yet here he was now, sitting in the sun, next to the *river*, with a stunning new friend – *a girl* friend, at that. Life was mad, but sometimes the madness was enjoyable, like today. He couldn't wait for Dagger to come home so he could explain his idea about putting his gorgeous wooden boats on display. Billy knew that he personally wouldn't have the courage to present their plan, but he certainly knew someone who could. *Frank could wrap Dagger right round her little finger*, he thought. Well, actually, he thought that Frank could wrap *anybody* round her little finger. He watched her blue eyes flashing as they reflected the sparkling water, her soft black hair shining in the sun, and his heart missed a beat. They watched the swans and cygnets floating idly on the river, as their skin turned warm and brown in the sun.

*

Baz stopped suddenly on their journey round the chicken coops, past the stable and towards the shed. They were still hidden behind dense greenery and bits of old boats and machinery. Si, completely unaware that his mate wasn't behind him, made his slow and steady way forward, issuing instructions in hushed tones.

"So listen, we sneak up on them, get as close as we can, find ourselves a piece of wood or something to batter that kid with, yeah? And… Baz? Baz, man!" Swearing softly under his breath Si gulped, snorted, turned around and shuffled his way back a few metres to where Baz and Chick were still some way behind, crouching near the stable.

"What the…" he began, his sore eyes beginning to water in the bright sunshine. "What are you doing, man?" he hissed.

Baz held up one fleshy finger. "Just had a thought, lads," he told them solemnly. "Is there any more of them flesh-eating plants in this garden?"

Chick had stopped grinning and had gone pale at the thought.

Si snorted at them both. "Don't be ridiculous," he hissed, getting up close to them, but all three peered very closely around themselves, nervously, anyway.

"What about them?" whispered Chick, pointing to the plants just on their left.

"Nah," said Si dismissively, the expert now. "Them's nettles. They're OK. They just make you itch for a bit. Right, come on, let's go get that little... get," he told them, nodding in the direction of the river. Together, they resumed their stalking.

Rounding the hen house, with half an eye on the nettles, Chick stopped. "Guys. *Guys!*" he hissed.

The other two stopped, looked over their shoulders and asked in unison, "What *now?*"

"Shouldn't we be wearing camouflage?"

"Look, this is flaming Fatfield, not Helmand Province. Just shut up and get on with it, will you," Si told him angrily, through quietly clenched teeth. Honestly. Some people! They moved forward again.

Baz followed Si faithfully, but his neck was starting to hurt, and as Si moved slightly to the left, Baz stayed on track, until he put his hand into something soft, warm and very smelly.

"Oh sh..." he began, forgetting to be quiet.

"Shhhh! Shut up, Baz, you idiot," warned Si. Behind him, Chick started giggling again. He hadn't had this much fun since he'd got kicked out of History last month.

Down by the river, Lennie had caught wind of something stirring near the chickens. It was interesting, rather than threatening. His ears picked up odd sounds, and his nose twitched at new smells in the garden. Standing up from his position in the sun, near Dolly, he moved quietly towards the hen house, watching with a puzzled expression and a tilt of his head, as the long grass swayed and moved. Trotting round behind, he came to a most peculiar sight. Someone was on the ground – his ground. Someone new and interesting. Lennie stuck his nose deeply into Chick's backside and inhaled loudly, trying to see if he recognised this newcomer. And at that point, the garden exploded into chaos.

Chick screamed like a girl and leapt into the air, as if he'd been shot from a cannon. Baz collapsed onto his face in shock and rolled into the nettles, leaving Si to grab a piece of wood for protection, and stumbled up to his feet as fast as his blinded eyes would allow. Chickens scattered in every direction, clucking madly, feathers flying, and Lennie set up a shocked, anxious barking. Dolly came running forward from the riverside, wheezing loudly, head down in full charge at whoever was upsetting her Lennie, as birds flew out of every corner of the garden in a cloudy explosion of sound and movement.

*

At the water's edge, Billy and Frank turned in unison at the screaming, babbling, clucking and frantic fury going on behind them. They glanced nervously at each other, standing rooted to the spot, until to their amazement, three lads came rolling out of the bushes towards them, swiftly followed by a very upset Lennie and a few cawing chickens. Si blundered about with a bit of branch in his hand, the fat middle one rolled on the grass, scratching at his legs with one brown-covered hand held away from his body, while the skinny little character at the back hopped up and down screaming like a three-year-old girl, whilst clutching his backside. Frank watched, shook her head and visibly relaxed.

"Lennie, it's all right. Stop barking, come to me. Come on, Lennie." She tried to calm the dog and get him to come to her, so she could make some sense of the madness going on all about her.

The three boys continued their wailing, shouting and screaming, until Frank yelled at the top of her lungs, "Right! Enough! Just FREEZE!"

And surprisingly, they did. Lennie continued to circle them, his hackles up, eyes wide and unsure, until Billy slapped his leg and quietly called the dog to his side. Lennie slinked over, wagging his tail comfortingly beside his new best friend, and sat down. Amidst all the noise and confusion, that little act of trust and friendship was not lost on Billy. Inside, he glowed. He felt a bit braver, and almost in control.

"What the hell are you three doing in Dagger's yard?" demanded Frank.

The three boys assessed the situation, looking nervously around them, and realising that they weren't going to be ripped apart, they cautiously lowered their hands and stopped their bawling. The fat one and the smaller skinny one merely shrugged and looked embarrassed but Si, the leader, held her gaze defiantly. Well, as well as he could with his battered face.

"What you doing with that piece of wood, Sid?" Frank asked, nodding to the branch in Si's hand.

"Do you know these three, Frank?" Billy asked quietly.

"Sadly I do, Billy," she replied. "Sid here, lives just down the river. The other two losers go to my school."

"It's Si, not Sid." He glowered at her, gulping and snorting in his usual manner.

Baz stepped forward, becoming braver now. "Yeah, Si," he told her. "As in... *Psycho*!" He sneered, pointing at Si with the hand covered in donkey poo.

Frank sighed and turned to Billy. "Spelling never was their strong point," she told him, then bending to his ear, she whispered. *"It's Sid, really – Sid, the snot gobbler."*

Billy's face lit up and he started laughing, just quietly. "And these two are Blockhead and Chick," she continued, gesturing to the others.

Billy could see why, and his smile turned into a grin.

"Er, I'm *Baz*, actually, Frank. As you well know. And he is Chick," he told her, still scratching his nettle stings and waving the poo-ey hand about.

Billy mouthed up at Frank, silently and with a shrug, "Chick?"

"Cos he's got fluffy yellow hair," Baz volunteered.

"And cos he runs like a girl," Frank informed Billy, as a matter of fact.

"And squeals like one an' all!" hissed Si through clenched teeth, shaking his fist at Chick.

"You still haven't told us why you're here, in the first place," Frank told them, subtly moving herself and Billy away from the river behind them and closer to the house.

"We've come to get that little freak, there," Si told her, gesturing to Billy with the branch in his hand.

"Really? Why would that be?" Frank asked, puzzled.

Big Baz stepped forward. "Because of what he did to Si, here. I mean, just look at him."

Frank and Billy looked more closely at Si's face. His two black eyes looked incredibly sore and his voice sounded even more thick and muffled than usual, underneath the bad bruise across his nose.

"Looks nasty," Frank told them, still edging herself and Billy away. "But what's Billy got to do with it?"

Baz stepped forward, angrily. "He bloody attacked him! He did that."

Frank and Billy exchanged amazed looks and were open-mouthed in disbelief.

"I've never even seen him before!" Billy said, looking up at Frank.

Si snorted, gulped and threw a shocked look at his mates who returned the look back, shaking their heads angrily.

"You cheeky little get! What a liar. You attacked me on the river bank the other day. You nearly broke my nose."

A light went on in Billy's head then, remembering the day he had taken the parcel to Frank, looking for directions. He flushed red, turning to face Frank, who was looking at him with one eyebrow raised quizzically.

"Billy..." she asked, in disbelief. "Did you really batter Sid... I mean, Si here and do all that damage? Little you, beating up a big ugly-looking bloke like Sid?"

"Oh... YOU!" Billy exclaimed. "I HAVE met you before. You tried to steal the parcel which Dagger gave me for Frank."

Si suddenly jumped forward, grabbing Billy by the neck of his T-shirt and trying to haul him off his feet. "Yeah," he began, nervously glancing towards his friends, before this little cretin told what really happened. Frank stepped forward and tried to get between them.

"I didn't hit him, Frank, honest. He tried to grab the parcel, and when I pulled it back, he hit himself in the face with it. That's the truth!"

Baz and Chick sniggered behind Si. He let go of Billy's T-shirt and turned towards them, threateningly. They instantly looked crestfallen and stopped grinning, trying to swagger and still look hard, which is difficult when your hand is covered in donkey poo, and your legs are itchy and blistered. Only Chick seemed to have escaped any form of injury.

Frank saw a movement out of the corner of her eye, behind the three amigos, close to the water's edge. She nudged Billy, and he, too, peeked in that direction. Together they glanced around them, trying not to give the game away to their would-be assailants.

Baz was trying to fling the muck of his hand and was scratching his shin with the other. Chick had half an eye on Lennie, in case he should stick his nose where it really didn't belong again, and Si was busy snorting and gulping.

"So anyway, we're gonna fill him in, aren't we, lads?" he asked with a swagger.

"Why? Because you picked on someone much smaller than you, and you hit yourself in the face in the process?" Frank laughed. "Dream on, losers."

Si suddenly reached forward and pulled something out of Billy's pocket. It was the little wooden bird, which he had carried from Frank's shed – he'd completely forgotten he still had it.

"And what's this you've got, eh?" sneered Si, happy to be in control of a situation again that had been in danger of slipping away from him. "Some little piece of treasure?" Turning it over in his hand, he held it up towards his mates for their disapproval. "What's this supposed to be, then?"

Barry Blockhead moved a little closer to look at the bird, his eyes crinkling into his fat face. Taking it from Si's hands, he, too, examined it closely. Frank blushed and reached out for it.

Billy wanted to grab it back for her, becoming distressed at her obvious embarrassment, but Baz held it out of his reach.

"Looks like a carved wooden…" he began slowly, but Billy shouted at him.

"Bird. It's a bird! Give it back, now!"

Baz swung towards his mates, holding the little bird aloft. "Bird?" he asked, mocking Billy, and Frank, with her furious expression. "It looks more like a carved *turd* to me!" he exclaimed. His mates howled in delight at his feeble joke and the other two's obvious discomfort. "Ah, look, lads, they're upset. You know there's only one place for this, don't you?" he sneered at them, holding the little carved creature up in the sunlight. "Yes, with me. It's mine, actually," Frank told him angrily.

The three boys laughed viciously together, then whooped and cheered as Baz flung the carving over the back of his head, where it landed in the middle of the river, with a splash.

"Aye, well, all turds end up in the sea in the end, don't they?" He smirked, not even glancing back to the water. The other two cheered and slapped their hands in a high five. Billy and Frank were shocked and angry, but Frank felt that if she over-reacted now, their chance of escape might be scuppered because she could see what their assailants couldn't.

The two adult swans were emerging out of the river behind Si, Baz and Chick. Disturbed by all the noise and confusion in Dagger's yard, and ready to defend their cygnets, they came waddling and hissing, up out of the water, necks stretched out, wings held out at an angle. They meant business. The boys, however, hadn't seen or heard them until it was too late, intent as they were on dealing with this cheeky little sod, who was calling their mate a liar.

Frank nudged Billy again and said in a loud voice, "The oak tree, Billy! Run!"

The two of them broke away from the three lads, dashed straight past them and were up in the safety of the branches of the oak tree before the screams began below them. From their vantage point, they watched, enthralled at the sight of the dumbos on the ground, frantically trying to escape from the swans' vicious attack. Baz was covered in poo and couldn't climb anything, being too fat, anyway. Si's long skinny legs took him to the roof of the hen house, and in all the confusion, Dolly charged again and knocked Chick straight into the pile of manure, head first, where the male swan nipped him on the ear and bum, before waddling back to the river with a satisfied cluck, calling to his pen and cygnets on the way. The oak tree at the river's edge shook as Billy and Frank laughed like drains. Chick lay on his back in the manure heap, slightly out of breath, trying to not breathe too deeply of the noxious smell, when, suddenly, the sun went in. A huge figure blocked the light as a large meaty hand reached down and physically hauled him up, holding him off the ground by the scruff of his collar.

"You, get out of the nettles, you flamin' idiot; you – get off my shed; and you, you little dung beetle, explain to me what the hell is going on in my garden!"

All three boys visibly quaked in their shoes, stumbling and slipping from their places of supposed safety, wiping their hands and rubbing at sore limbs.

From the oak tree, Frank sang out in a cheerful voice, "Morning, Dagger! Can you just hang on to these three for a minute? We're coming down."

Chapter 24

"**S**o, Dagger Dawson to the rescue, eh?" said Richie, sipping on a mug of tea in Sue's bright kitchen. Sue herself was crouching at Billy's feet, inspecting a sore-looking graze on his knee, a piece of cotton wool in her hand. Frank sat at the other side of the table to Billy, her eyes shining with excitement as she told their tale. Both she and Billy had retreated to Sue's, after Dagger had given the three boys a right telling off, sending them on their way along the river bank to where Si's house was. He would have given them a thick ear, but Chick already had one where the male swan had nipped him. They could hear them muttering and complaining as they made their limping way along the path towards the bridge down the river, where, no doubt, they would gather in Simon's house to nurse their hurt pride and their various bruises and scrapes.

"They were blaming Billy for attacking that stupid Sid-the..." she began, before pausing, looking at the three faces in front of her, and continuing, "I mean, Simon. Billy didn't attack anyone. They were just looking for trouble."

Richie poured the remains of his tea down the sink and turned the tap on. "Sounds to me like they got it as well," he said with a smile. "I mean, apart from Dagger, those swans can be pretty scary! I wouldn't go near them."

"Well, they've got their babies, and you know how protective they can be at this time of year." Sue dabbed on some stinky ointment and stood up, as Billy rolled his trouser leg back down. "And anyway, why weren't the three of them in school? Everyone else is, apart from you two, and you've both got good reason to be at home."

Billy smiled at the word "home". It was actually beginning to really feel like home now. In fact, in some ways it was better, because here he had company, excitement and something to challenge him all the time. He was overcoming some of his fears and was learning to stand up for himself a bit more. Normally, he would have been the first one to cut and run when faced with bullies.

But then he looked around the bright, warm kitchen and felt really bad about his mam, still in hospital, still poorly, still unable to get any pleasure from knowing how well her Billy was doing. His face dropped a little and his shoulders sagged.

"Well, Billy and I aren't going to even think about those three losers anymore, are we, Billy?" Frank looked at Billy's face – he'd suddenly gone very quiet, and it was like the sun had gone behind a cloud.

"Billy?" she asked gently.

Sue gazed at him. She knew. The black mood could come from nowhere, could strike at any time, and from her experiences with teenagers like Billy, she understood that it could hit hardest following some fun and laughter. She screwed the top back on the ointment and gently tugged at the leg of his jeans.

"So, Billy, I understand you lot are going to put on a little Art display?"

Billy raised damp grey eyes to her face and struggled to hold back the tears, hiding his embarrassment as he reached down to adjust the leg of his jeans.

Frank had read the change in mood, too. Glancing sharply at both Sue and Richie, she stated loudly, "Bet our birds are way better than Dagger's boats, eh, Billy?"

Billy simply nodded and looked disconsolately out of the kitchen window into the sunny, bright back garden. *He's looking for the Monument,* thought Sue. *He's looking for his usual source of reassurance.*

After a second or two, Billy said quietly, "He threw my little bird into the river. That one was special."

Frank was sitting close to Billy and reached her hand across the table to him, holding his fingers gently in her own. "Oh, don't you worry about that, Billy," she told him firmly. "I've got just the one for you, one you haven't even seen, yet, 'cos it's in my bedroom."

Billy's eyes came back into focus, looking at her questioningly, one eyebrow raised. "Honestly? You've got some more? You're not just saying that, are you?"

Frank was glad at his reaction. He was looking more like the real Billy, the one who could actually see some fun in what had happened to them in Dagger's garden that morning; the one who, she knew, had some fire in his belly to help her with their quest; the one who made her feel a bit like that female swan, protecting her cygnets.

"'Course I have. And you and me, we've got some painting and finishing off to do if we're to get them finished and make them better than Dagger's collections of boats."

Richie grabbed a biscuit from the tin and got a smacked hand off Sue. "Well, I know Dagger's carvings are something special, and he's had years of practice, so you two had better get a wiggle on. When are you hoping to have them finished and up on display, then?"

Frank and Billy exchanged puzzled looks.

"Actually, I hadn't thought of the timescale," Frank admitted. Billy simply shrugged his shoulders and looked blank.

Sue took the biscuit tin and put it in a high cupboard, as Richie reached for it again.

"Well, school breaks up for the summer in two weeks' time, so why don't you set that as your completion date? I don't mean to display them – that may take some time – but if they're all ready, it would be a good time to begin planning getting them out on display."

She handed her husband an apple from the bowl by the kitchen door, which he took from her with a scowl.

"And by then, you'll have had a good look at where to put them and how to secure them so no little..." he paused, looking at the two youngsters. "...Little *thieves* can nick all your beautiful hard work."

Billy smiled at Frank, watching her mind racing as she thought and planned.

"Two weeks..." she mused. Then they grinned at each other. Frank grabbed Billy by the hand, dragging him suddenly to the back door.

"Grab your paints, Billy," she told him firmly, nodding at his sketch book and bag, containing his colours and art equipment. "We've got work to do!"

The two of them left the kitchen like whirlwinds, dashing off down the garden path, laughing and talking excitedly.

"See you in a couple of weeks' time," Richie joked, calling after them, then he smiled, biting deeply into his apple.

*

Battered, bruised and bloody, Si, Baz and Chick were crammed into Si's tiny bathroom, sweating and swearing, vowing revenge of the highest order on those who had blighted them. In the sink and on the floor, was the evidence of their physical injuries – bits of cotton wool, soggy clumps of toilet roll, strands of sticking plaster, and clumps of mud and grass. Si was holding his hand under a running tap, looking at himself in the mirror through black and purple eyes; Chick sat on the edge of the bath with a cold, wet flannel clamped to his left ear, as manure dripped from his once yellow hair onto his tee shirt; Baz perched on the edge of the toilet, warily, his trousers round his ankles, his legs covered in angry red blotches and grazes, as he dabbed at them ineffectively with ointment. The whole room smelled like a combination of a barnyard and a vet's surgery. Nobody said a word. The atmosphere was thick. And angry.

Si turned the tap off and turned to his depressed friends. "You do realise this is war, eh, lads?"

Baz and Chick looked up at their friend with a mixture of hurt pride and expectancy.

"I don't know who to be most angry with. That little maggoty kid, Dagger Dawson, Flamin' Frank…"

"…Or those stinkin' swans," interjected Chick, still holding the ear that had been viciously nipped by one of them. The other two gave him a withering look.

Sighing deeply, Baz said, "Yeah, all of them. But what are we gonna do? How do we get them all back after this?"

Si turned away from the mirror, holding up an injured forefinger, which gave him an added air of commanding presence. It was his bathroom, after all. And it was his beef with that newcomer kid. Si had to stop himself from grinding his teeth in temper. "Right. We need a new plan of attack, guys."

His friends sat up then, looking, as usual, to their leader for guidance.

"Okay," began Baz, slowly. "What you got in mind, mate?"

Si blew on his injured finger, then winced in pain. "Well it's really hard to launch a new plan of action, when you've got such a painful injury to deal with, but I'll do my best."

Chick was shaking his head, still trying to take some of the pain out of his nipped ear, and trying to dislodge the mud and manure from his hair.

"Chick, man – stop fidgeting and listen, will yer?" Si told him angrily.

"It's only a spelk, Si," Chick told him, pointing at the injured finger. "I've got a sore ear and an even worse nip on me bum. Now *that's* painful!" He grimaced, edging up off the bath a little.

"Right. That lot down the road are in for a load of trouble from us. They've really done it this time."

Baz chimed in, "And you know what? I've really gone off Frank, an' all. She's not as fit as I thought she was, sticking up for that cheeky little brat like that."

Si glanced at him. "Aye, you're right there, mate. Her nose is sort of…wonky."

Baz shook his head and shrugged his shoulders at his injured friend. Poor bugger, he was looking worse by the minute, what with those eyes of his. And a *spelk*, too. Ouch.

"I think her eyes are too close together. Never seen it until now. And you know what they say about that, eh?"

Chick nodded and smiled, but still wasn't listening properly out of his throbbing left ear.

"So we're gonna get that mangy little dog she's hanging around with, and sort him out good and proper." Si gulped and snorted – he was back in charge, happy to have some revenge to take his mind off his war wounds. They all paused for a minute or two, gazing from one to the other, as the silence ticked by and birds sang in the garden, beyond the window.

Suddenly, Baz raised a finger. It looked for a second that he was mimicking Si, who bristled slightly, but then Baz spoke and his intention became clear. "Right, listen. That kid isn't from round here, is he? The little mongrel."

Chick looked up, the flannel still pressed to his ear. "So?" he asked.

"Well, think about it. If we nab him on the road, we can hide him away somewhere and really do him in. He won't know where he is to get help." His eyes flashed.

Si snorted and stood up straighter, looking off into the middle distance. "You might have something there, Baz," he said. "He is like a little stray: nobody loves or wants him. We could keep him as long as we wanted."

He tried to wink at Baz, but it hurt too much and his eyes streamed again. Chick looked up at his mates, thrilled that they seemed to be coming up with a plan. "We could even ask for a ransom!" he declared brightly. "After what he did, it's the least we can do. I mean, it's all his fault, isn't it?"

His two friends were delighted with this plan – cash in hand for taking a maggoty little mongrel off the streets, and giving him a taste of his own medicine. Oh yes!

"Right, lads. We're on. Let's talk tactics," said Si. He gave each a high five – difficult as it was with the spelk in his finger – but miss-hit Chick's hand because of it, sending the lad sliding backwards into the bath, where he banged the back of his head on the tap.

"Ow, watch it, man, Si," Chick moaned.

*

In Frank's garden, all the little carved birds sat in the sun in a row along the back wall. Billy smiled fondly at them, while Frank gazed on more critically. Some of them looked, for all the world, as if they were about to take off, whilst others had their heads angled up to the sun and the trees above them.

Head to one side, hands on hips, Frank began, "They're a bit…"

"They're amazing," they said in unison, before squinting up at each other and grinning.

"Ee, I dunno, Billy," Frank said, rubbing the back of her neck, where the sun was starting to burn her. "Out here, in the daylight, they look really… well…" She paused, shaking her head, then sighing deeply. "…They're amateurish," she continued. "I can't put these out on display."

Billy jumped in front of her, forcing her to look into his face, not at the birds. "Frank, are you daft? These birds are gorgeous. Trust me. All they need is finishing off, some little touches."

Frank dragged her gaze from the flock on the wall to his face. She still didn't look convinced.

"This time tomorrow, you'll see a huge difference. Honestly. Dagger had better look out."

Frank smiled at her friend's enthusiasm.

"Yeah. There's a new kid on the block!" Billy grinned. "Now, where shall we set out all our stuff? In the shed, or out here, in the sunshine?"

Frank considered this for a moment, looking from the birds to the sheltered table, under the honeysuckle hedge. "Out here," she told him. "And I'll start by getting the supplies ready." She moved towards the kitchen door.

"Frank, my bag is here, beside the wall. It's all in here."

Frank turned back and called over her shoulder, but continued walking.

"Ah, but you haven't got crisps, cake, fizzy drinks, sweets, chewy, have you?" She laughed and entered the kitchen. As Billy took out all they needed from his bag and arranged it on the table, he could hear her banging cupboard doors and clattering about inside, singing a song, loudly, "Two little birds, sat by my window, and they told me I don't need to worry…"

*

Over the river, Sue was talking on the phone to Paul Costello, a concerned look on her face. Richie was asleep upstairs, after his night shift, and she didn't want to disturb him, but she felt she needed to confide in someone.

"OK, Paul. I don't know what to say, just yet. Do you think she's going to be OK? It's a huge worry. What on earth could have gone wrong? I'll have a think about how to put this new development to Billy. He needs to know."

She drew a tired hand across her brow and turned to look through the open door, towards Frank's house over the water. The river ran deep and brown, and peaceful, yet she was in turmoil. What a worry. She'd have to have a think about how to phrase this so as not to panic Billy, especially as he was settling in so well. Lord, life was never straightforward.

*

Billy had painted in two pairs of bright eyes onto a pair of the birds, and was busy adding tiny details to their wings. Frank watched him, fascinated. He was lost in his work, his tongue sticking out as he concentrated. Just then, her Nan Essie appeared behind them, reaching over the table to take away some plates and glasses.

"Well, Billy, look what you've done!" she declared with a grin. "I would never believe that those little touches could make such a difference. Those eyes look proper real now."

Billy put his brush down and smiled gratefully. "I told Frank – they will look amazing. And look at the one she's just finished." He reached forward and turned a small bird towards her. It was still glistening with flashes of green and yellow paint.

"Well, look at that. It's a mallard. I'd have recognised it anywhere." She smiled and ruffled Frank's curly black hair.

Frank swung round to her Nan, amazed. "Nan! It *is* a mallard! Well done, you."

Billy grinned at both of them and continued mixing paint to make a soft grey. "See, told you," he told Frank, smugly. "They are all going to be amazing."

Essie Bailey smiled warmly and returned to the house. Billy and Frank worked on quietly for a while, dabbing into small pots of paint and swishing their brushes into clean water. The birds in the trees above them seemed quite fascinated by the quiet activity going on at the table, hopping around on the wall and at their feet, pecking at crumbs, scattered on the ground beneath the two youngsters. Billy sat back to admire the carvings, turning the birds this way and that into the sunlight. Each was already on a little carved plinth, so painting them was easy. In the quiet of the sunny garden, the heavenly music started up again. Billy closed his eyes and let the notes flood over him, soothing out any wrinkles and worries he may have been hiding in his heart. His mind drifted with the music, until after a moment he opened his eyes and looked at Frank. She was lost in her work, too, adding wing flashes to a small pied wagtail.

"Where's you mam?" he asked her, suddenly. Until that point, he hadn't given Frank's family a thought. In his mind, Frank just lived over the water with her Nan, but she must have a mam and dad. Surely?

Frank lifted her brilliant blue eyes to him and flashed a smile, then continued with her job. "In Africa, with my dad," she told Billy, as she blew away a speck of dust from the carving.

"Africa? What are they doing there?" Billy asked, confused.

Frank also sat back and admired her painting, moving the wagtail into a patch of sunlight on the table. "They work there. Well, at the moment they do. They work for a children's charity, Billy. So they go where they are needed most. Usually, when there's been a natural disaster, like an earthquake or something."

Billy nodded at her, mouthing a silent 'wow'.

"When did you last see them, then?"

Frank had to think, doing a quick calculation in her mind and squinting up at the sky. "Oh, about three weeks ago," she told him. "They ring when they can, and sometimes *Skype* me so I know they're safe. They didn't want to go this time because I'd been so poorly, but I'm so used to being down here with my Nan… And they know I'm safe and getting better all the time."

Billy was enthralled. He just assumed that Frank lived here, across the water, all the time.

"So, where's your house, then?" he asked.

Frank reached for more paint, adding highlights to the bird's eye, the way Billy had shown her. "Just up the hill," she told him. "Five minutes away."

Billy was amazed. This was another thing they had in common. Not just the art and the carvings, and their appreciation of and friendship with Dagger. Her mam was also far away, and maybe unsafe, too.

"Aren't you scared for them?" he asked.

Frank put her brush down and picked up a biscuit. "Sometimes, I am," she said. "If they're in a war zone. But they are helping after the famine, so they're pretty safe, at the moment. And they've always done this job, so it's not new to me."

"So, you don't have any brothers or sisters, then?"

Frank reached into the back pocket of her jeans and brought out her mobile. "Yes, Billy," she began, opening up the images and holding the phone open for him to look at. "I've got one brother, Sam, but he's away at university, in York. He'll be home soon, for the summer, but he's got a job which he is finishing off first."

Billy looked at Sam, closely. There was no mistaking him as Frank's brother. He was tall, had the same curly dark hair and incredible smile. He looked relaxed and confident, safe in the knowledge that he was his own man, and nobody would ever push him around. Billy could tell that Sam was both brave and breezy. His expression said it all, as he stood with his arms wrapped protectively around his little sister.

"Have you got anyone, Billy?" Frank asked. Her head was down again, as she was adding very tiny dark stripes to the bird on the table, in front of her. She asked the question quite innocently, in a matter-of-fact way. Billy knew she was just being friendly – not nosey, like some people could be.

He took a deep breath, wondering how it might sound to her ears. "Just my mam," he said, reaching out to dab his brush in water.

Without stopping or looking up, Frank continued, "Tell me about her, then, Billy. Do you look like her? What's she like? As a person, I mean."

Billy found himself smiling as he kept his head down and concentrated on the job in front of him.

"She's quite small, and very slim, and she has hair the colour of a field mouse."

Frank lifted her eyes to him and smiled encouragingly, then continued working.

That gave Billy a little confidence so he continued. "She loves dogs, but we can't have one in the flat. We used to have one when…" he paused for a moment, but Frank didn't flicker from the job in front of her. "When I was younger," he continued, carefully.

"She'd love Lennie, then, do you think?" she asked, glancing at him, then straight into the paint pots, selecting another colour.

Billy grinned, thinking of the dog wandering freely about Dagger's garden and the riverside. "Yeah!" he said, smiling to himself. "And the donkey as well, but she'd be scared of those flamin' geese, just like me."

"Ah – she's not into birds like we are, then?" Frank asked.

This pleased Billy, being paired up with Frank like that – his cool, new friend. "She quite likes little birds, but she doesn't really get to see them that much, being stuck in the flat since her back got bad. She loves chickens, though. She says her granddad used to keep them in the back garden, when she was little. One day, she says, we might have some of our own."

Thinking about a possible future with his mam, with chickens and a dog, gave Billy a funny feeling in his tummy, like bees battering away at a window, trying to get in. It was a wonderful dream, but only a dream. His mam was still so poorly. She had a hell of a lot of getting better to do before they could think of moving, or pets, or anything.

"My dad's allergic to birds," Frank continued the conversation. "He can't breathe around them, so he stays away from Dagger's chickens."

Billy smiled at the thought of Dagger, as he and Frank sat surrounded by birds, albeit wooden ones.

Frank read his mind. "That's why I do this, I suppose. So my dad can see how beautiful they are." She grinned, waving a hand over the assorted species on the table in front of them.

"My dad was allergic to horses…" Billy froze, hand and paintbrush in mid-air. The words were out before he had even the time to stop the thought forming. He blushed, but Frank didn't even flicker. She continued concentrating hard on her wagtail.

"Just as well you live up in those flats, then!" She smiled, working away, head down.

"My dad didn't live in the sky with us," he told her, quietly, placing the bird closer to the others and reaching for a new one. Frank held her breath, but continued working.

"We used to have a house and a garden, when I was little. It was not far from the beach as well," Billy continued, rubbing away at the new bird with an oily cloth. "We knew all our neighbours and I had a friend in the street. We had a budgie, I think, as well."

Frank looked at him then, and smiled. She nodded at Billy to continue and resumed her own work.

"My dad was away a lot, of course, but when he was home it was…" Billy sat back in his seat and closed his eyes. The heavenly music seemed to give him strength. "It was magical," he said, before adding quietly, "we were so happy together."

Frank worried, then, that Billy would spiral into the sudden depression which she'd seen happen to him a few times already, but he suddenly opened his eyes, smiled at her, and reached for his glass of juice on the table.

Frank reached for more paint, adding highlights to the bird's eye. She was happy that she'd gleaned just a nugget of information from Billy about his dad, but instinct told her not to push her luck, or he would clam up and be wary of saying any more next time they were together. "I think we'd better make an inventory of these birds, Billy, so we can see if we have enough. What do you think?"

Billy put his brush down and looked confused. "A what?" he asked.

"An inventory, Billy." Frank smiled at him. "A list; we need to know if we have enough birds to match Dagger's boats. Let's stop for a while and do a head count."

As the two of them happily started sorting the birds, putting them into finished, still-to-complete and not-good-enough groups, the peace and quiet of the day was disturbed by a large truck pulling up at Frank's gate. The sound of a vehicle reversing sent the garden birds soaring away, rough male voices could be heard calling, and the heavenly music simply drifted off into the sky, following the birds. Essie Bailey appeared in the front garden after a minute or two and came to report back.

"Noisy buggers," she told the two youngsters. "Workmen. Come to dig up the drains leading into the river again, no doubt. They tell you nothing these days, flaming council."

Billy and Frank had to go through the front garden to go back over the river to check on Dagger and his boats, breathing in the heat and fumes of the big truck and avoiding the workmen, who were off-loading equipment. In the far distance, Penshaw Monument stood high up on the hill, in the sunshine. Billy walked happily beside his friend, safe in the knowledge that it was still there, still watching over him, still in his heart. He smiled to himself, thinking about the last time he'd actually gone up the hill and touched the cold stone, gazing out from the summit, mesmerised by the view. Him and his dad. Happy days.

Chapter 25

Chick was meandering along the river path on his way to meet up with the lads at Si's house, cheerfully chomping away at a huge packet of beefy crisps. He liked it down here. Even though he lived a couple of miles away, he had spent many a happy hour with his mate by the river, messing about at the water's edge and getting into bits of bother. He knew the area well. The people in Fatfield all knew each other and were pretty all right, really. They looked out for one another. In his street, everybody got up early, went to work, came home, and shut their doors on the outside world. His new estate was posh, compared to Si's cosy little cramped home; his street, with its neat lawns, mock Georgian windows and double garages, was much sought after, but Chick liked it down near the river. Dipping a hand into the packet, he gazed about him, up into the towering trees, at the viaduct as he passed under it, at the swans on the river, and winced, automatically rubbing his still swollen ear. He felt the anger, bubbling up inside him like poison, threatening to spill up into his mouth and out. He clenched his fist, remembering the plan to get back at that stupid kid who had caused all the trouble. Whilst thinking angrily and chewing aggressively, he bit the inside of his cheek. Ow! Something else to get that little sod for now!

Ahead of him, on the path, and just round the river bend, Lennie was on a wander – nose down, trailing a rabbit into the long grass. He spotted it hiding and twitching under a bush, pretending to freeze and not look at him, but it was fooling nobody. Lennie's face was happy, his eyes alert and bright, long ears pricked up, as he pushed his nose into the undergrowth and let out a cheerful woof. The rabbit bounded off, bobbing its bottom and flashing its white tail, as it disappeared down a hole. Realising the game was over, the dog padded on his way. A few metres further on, another delightful smell wafted towards him on the river breeze. He stood still, head cocked to one side, nose twitching, deep in puzzled thought. This was unusual, to sense something that smelled like his dinner out here, on the path, far away from Dagger's yard and his bowl. He trotted on in search of this delightful and enticing new thing.

Chick had stuffed the crisp packet into his pocket and was intent on trying to hit a log in the river with stones he had picked up on the path. They plopped close, but missed each time he tried. The fourth time he tried, aiming steadily and staring hard at the log, he launched the stone and scored a direct hit. Yes! He punched the air in delight. *Wish the lads had been here to see me do that*, he thought. But they probably wouldn't believe him – they'd think he was lying, just bigging himself up to get into their good books. Because Chick and his whole family were quite small and slight in stature, Si and Baz somehow believed he wasn't very clever or good at anything. And yet, he could run faster than the two of them, was good at Maths, *and* scored higher in spelling tests. He knew the difference between affluence and effluence, for example.

Smiling to himself, he stood on the path, absently watching the water, then nearly shot up in the air in shock, when a cold wet nose stuck itself into his pocket and inhaled deeply. Not that bloody dog again!

Leaping backwards and shooing the dog away, Chick clutched at his heart. What was wrong with the stupid thing? It grinned at him, wagging its tail gently, head tilted to one side.

"Bugger off, dog," he told Lennie, sharply. The dog simply walked closer to him and sat down at his feet, waiting expectantly. Chick looked around him to see if Dagger or the kid was coming down the path to find the dog. Nobody. The river drifted by, and the trees whispered over his head.

"I said, get lost, you mongrel," Chick stated loudly – and aggressively, he thought. He'd show it who was the boss, this stupid animal which had given their game away and got them into so much trouble. He put a foot out to nudge the dog out of his way. Not kick it, mind; he wasn't that cruel.

The idiot dog stood up and woofed quietly at him, nudging his pocket again. Chick was pressed back up against the grassy bank, now, where nettles and gorse grew. He wasn't going to be intimidated by this stupid creature. And then a thought struck him: if only he had a way of getting hold of it and leading it back to Si's house, he could start the whole ransom process...

This sudden thought excited him. His heart beat faster as the idea took hold. This was his chance! He would show the lads just what he was made of. They would have to see him as being their equal, if he was able to get hold of the dog and take it to them. They had already decided that his plan was brilliant, hadn't they? And here was the very dog, sitting staring at him, grinning in a friendly way. But how could he get it to the other side of the river? It had no collar on and the tide was in, so it wasn't like he could just walk across. If he led it back to the bridge, it would just run off home.

Lennie had decided that enough was enough. He knew that this lad had about his person something yummy to eat. He could smell it. He was used to people giving him treats, and this lad was holding out against him. Leaping up, he put both of his front paws onto Chick's slim shoulders and pushed him further back into the bank, breathing hot doggy breath into his face. Chick screamed like a girl and flung his hands back up over his head, protecting his sore ear. The scream caused more pain in his bitten cheek. He clutched at the grass in the bank, behind his head, and a huge chunk of it came away in his hands. Dry soil and clumps of moss and weeds spilled onto Chick's blond hair. Urgh – there might be beetles and worms in it! He screamed again. The dog thrust its nose deep into Chick's pocket and pulled out the crisp packet.

Phew! So *that* was what it was after! It wasn't trying to eat *me,* Chick thought with relief. He bent forward, shaking the soil out of his hair, and was trying to grab the crisps back off Lennie, when he realised that something was amiss with the grassy bank in front of him. Giving the dog a crisp, then telling it to sit and wait patiently, Chick moved more of the undergrowth, clawing clumsily at it with his small, pale hands. Hidden behind the weeds and wild flowers, was a door, built into the bank. It was quite small, coming only up to his waist, and was made of rusting metal. Huh? Chick scratched his head in wonder, dislodging more soil and a spider, but he was too puzzled to freak out about it.

Curiosity got the better of him. He gave the dog another crisp, got hold of the heavy metal handle, and pulled with all his might – which wasn't a lot, it had to be said. The door gave way with a loud, heavy metal groan, and Chick was left facing the deep, dark entrance to an old tunnel. It must have been hidden for years in that undergrowth, as flies buzzed around it and a dank, damp smell drifted out of the gloomy interior.

"Woah…" Chick breathed, looking more closely inside. "I'm not going in there," he said to himself out loud, but quietly. Behind him, Lennie woofed again, holding a paw up, pleading for another crisp. Chick grinned maliciously. Taking a big, crunchy beefy crisp out of the packet, he squatted in front of the dog. *But I know someone who is*, he thought with glee.

"Here, boy, here, Lennie. Come to Chick."

*

Sue reached a hand across the table, towards Billy, and gave him a gentle, reassuring shake. The time had come and she'd been dreading it. Billy was making excellent progress here, with her and Richie. He'd settled, eaten her out of house and home, was sleeping through the night, now, and had stopped that mad mumbling of numbers, which had puzzled everyone who had heard it. But sadly, his mam wasn't making progress: in fact, she had slipped worryingly backwards following the operation on her spine. She'd had to be isolated, and there was talk of transferring her to a hospital in Newcastle, if she didn't pick up soon.

The lad sat numbly in front of her. His face seemed pale, and his grey eyes seemed even bigger than usual, giving him the appearance of a cartoon character. He's such a pretty lad, Sue thought distractedly. He'd caught the sun, whilst out and about with Frank, and there was a soft dusting of new freckles over his nose, adding to his sweet air of vulnerability. His hand, on the table in front of her, twitched nervously, his fingers making clawing movements.

"Do you understand what it all means, Billy?" Sue asked gently.

The boy nodded, silently. He swallowed once or twice. Sue tried again. "So, this infection will put her progress back a bit. They've put her into an isolation ward, and they're trying her on a different set of tablets to bring it under control. It just means we can't go and see her for a while, that's all."

Billy rubbed at his nose with his hand. His eyes were smarting, and he felt a bit breathless and dizzy. He gulped once or twice. "Is she going to die?" he asked Sue, quietly.

He couldn't bear to lose his mam, especially after what had happened to his dad. Couldn't bear the thought of never returning to their house in the sky, never seeing her flipping pancakes, or feel her dripping cold water onto his head to get him up for school.

He knew the numbers were bubbling up inside him, could feel them spiralling upwards. There was nothing he could do to prevent them from spilling out of his mouth. Head down, he gasped for breath.

"Seventy, one hundred, fifty-three…" he breathed quietly, his fingers twitching, eyes closed. *Oh no*, thought Sue. *I spoke too soon. Here we go, a panic attack starting.* But suddenly, Billy got up and ran into the back garden. Sue tried to walk calmly after him, keeping him in sight as he got to the gate. By the time she reached him, he was panting a bit, his face was flushed, and he was half way up the tree again. Sue knew that he wasn't going to bolt. From her position, she watched calmly as Billy expertly climbed the tree. The numbers continued until he reached the upper branches, then it all went quiet.

Shading her eyes, Sue stared up through the leafy green canopy and watched Billy closely. She felt he was safe; the branches were sturdy and there was very little wind. Billy had his eyes closed and was holding on tightly, but his head was faced away from the house in the direction of the Monument in the distance. As she gazed upwards, she saw the boy's shoulders relax, his face grow still, his breathing become steadier. *What was it with that Monument and this lad*, she wondered again. He wouldn't talk about it with her – maybe Frank could prise it out of him. Or Dagger.

After a minute or two, the tree began to tremble slightly and Billy's trainers appeared at her shoulder height. He landed lightly at her feet and stood before Sue, head down, shoulders slumped. Sue reached out and gently lifted his chin so she could look into his eyes. "OK now, Billy?"

Billy nodded mutely, then mumbled, "Sorry, Sue."

She pulled him to her and gave him a light hug, rubbing his shoulders, affectionately. "S'alright, Billy. Don't mention it. And no, your mam is *not* going to die, Billy. It's just a setback. It's a worry, but she'll be OK."

Ruffling his hair, as they turned back to the house, she asked him gently, "So, The Monument worked its magic on you, did it, Billy?"

Billy's large grey eyes flashed directly at her. His face went red and his eyebrows lifted as if a guilty secret had been discovered, but looking at Sue's soft open face he smiled back, shyly. "Yeah, it did, actually. Always does."

Sue kept one hand on his shoulder, guiding him back into the bright kitchen. "Will you tell me how it does that for you, Billy? One day, I mean. Not now. Not today."

Billy gazed from Sue's face to the back gate in the direction of Penshaw Hill, then back at her. He smiled sadly. "One day, Sue. Yeah."

*

Dagger stood in his sunny riverside garden, wondering where his little mate had got to. He'd explained that he would be out all morning, made sure he had everything he needed for an hour or two, and left him snoozing peacefully in the sun, beside the hen house and chicken run. *Odd*, he thought. But then Dagger remembered seeing a few new baby rabbits on the riverside path as he'd driven out of the yard earlier. That would be enough to entice Lennie out. That dog couldn't resist the lure of a young rabbit. Dagger smiled at the thought. He'd never seen the dog hurt anything – he was a friendly and kind soul, with a lot of love inside of him. He liked to just sniff them out, then lie down and bark gently at them, tail wagging fondly, as if asking them to play and be his friend.

The sun was warm on the back of his neck. Dagger rubbed at it with a large freckled hand, and glanced over the water where some movement had caught his eye. One or two workmen were digging up the path outside of Essie Bailey's house. *Ha, she'll love that*, he thought. *She'd be out there, busybodying about them, getting in their way, stopping them from doing their job properly, telling them how to do their job properly*, he thought… *Hmm, new faces on the riverbank might be enough to entice Lennie over there to investigate.*

As he watched, the lady herself appeared at her front gate, chattering away non-stop, tea tray in hand. Dagger smiled to himself: it'll be cakes and biscuits next, followed by bacon butties. Actually, now that he came to think of it, he could smell them from his side of the water. His mouth watered. It had been a long time since breakfast. Lifting his head and turning towards the water, he called across cheerfully, "Ho, Essie Bailey. You'll make those lads fat. Let them get on with their work, will you?"

A few heads turned towards him, and one of the workmen raised his mug in a happy salute to Dagger, over the water. Behind them, Essie Bailey stepped forward and bellowed at the top of her lungs, "You mind your own business, Dagger Dawson! They're doing a good job over here on these drains!"

Dagger grinned as the lads on her side jumped back in alarm at the volume she'd produced. They were, obviously, not aware of how the sound travelled over the water, and Essie's foghorn voice had been a shock to them. They weren't to know, of course, that she reserved that voice purely for him.

Dagger waved good-naturedly to Essie. "Aye, Essie – with one of your blessed bacon sarnies in them, they'll be able to work even better," he called back, only slightly projecting his deep rich voice.

"Well, if they're that good, there's one here for you, an' all!" she bellowed back.

Dagger blew her a kiss from his side. "Thank you kindly, me lady," he told her, bowing gallantly from the waist. "Don't suppose you've got Lennie Catflap over there, eating one with those lads, have you?"

"Nah – not seen him this morning!" she yelled back. "But come on over, and I'm sure he'll turn up for bacon as well!"

Dagger waved and made for his gate and the path to the bridge. *Aye, so will half of Fatfield after that announcement,* he thought to himself with a smile, shaking his curly dark head.

Five minutes and a cup of tea later, Dagger was slightly worried that nobody had seen Lennie for some time. He had been known to wander off on his own for a whole morning, but he usually appeared from one of his usual haunts when he heard Dagger's van pull up. The workmen were hard at it, but had promised to let somebody know if they saw him. Essie stated that the dog would be holed up in somebody's house.

"I've never known an animal have so many friends. Stop worrying!" she shouted at Dagger, standing only four feet away from him.

Billy, sitting on the wall beside Frank, was fascinated by the body language going on between the two adults. It had gradually dawned on him that the two of them had a deep understanding of each other, but at first, you would have thought they didn't even like each other very much. They would stand quite close together, Essie's eyes followed Dagger everywhere, and he had a gentle, jokey way of addressing her. It was just the yelling at Dagger he didn't get.

Turning to Frank, after another ear- bashing aimed at his friend, Billy whispered, "Why does she do that?"

Frank just smiled back at him. "She's always spoken to him like that, leastways, as long as I've been alive." She shrugged. "My Nan thinks Dagger's deaf."

Billy was astounded. His eyebrows shut up and his eyes grew wide. "Deaf?" he asked, puzzled. "Dagger Dawson can hear a fly fart at fifty metres. Well, that's what he told me, anyway. And I believe him."

Frank laughed, watching the two adults standing together on the riverside path, gazing towards the viaduct, looking for the dog. "Well, you and I know he's not deaf, Billy. It's just that for years, he wound her up that he couldn't hear her, in an attempt to get some peace from her nattering away at him. And as the years went on, she got louder and louder, and he, of course, thought it was really funny. She only shouts when she's talking to him, and of course, she thinks that all those years of working in the shipyards made him deaf. She doesn't know it's a lifestyle choice and a wind up – he only answers her when he wants to. *We* all know that; Nan doesn't, though."

Billy was a bit bemused. He gazed at the adults and back to Frank. "Is that not a bit… you know… cruel?" he asked.

"Nah. It's just a habit now, Billy. Dagger says he will own up. One day. Just not yet. He's having too much fun with her. It's gone on for years."

Billy started to laugh. Frank watched fondly as his eyes closed and a huge smile lit up his face. He tilted his face up to the sun and chuckled loudly. His happiness made the giggles inside of Frank bubble up and out, until the two were chuckling helplessly.

"I think you should buy her one of those old ear trumpet things for Christmas," he told Frank.

"Or I'll get Dagger a megaphone," she responded. "Can you just see the two of them, doing battle over the water, when all he wants is a cup of tea."

Dagger heard his name and glanced fondly at the two youngsters. How wonderful to see that lad looking so relaxed, happy and animated, he thought. But as he watched, a strange thing happened. The two kids were standing near the gate, when a local jogger appeared on the riverside path, chugging along with a spaniel, trotting at his side. The jogger was carrying a big, heavy, army-style rucksack and was wearing a maroon T-shirt with a regimental logo on it. Dagger knew this lad well. As he approached the group, Dagger called out to him, "All right, Nick? How's your dad?"

The runner didn't even break his stride: he glanced up at Dagger and the gathered group, flashed a huge grin and called back, "On top of the world, Dagger. I'll tell him you asked after him."

He ran on, giving a cheerful wave. Dagger cupped his hands round his mouth to answer his retreating back. "And tell him, he still owes me that pint!"

When Dagger turned back to the group, they were all smiling fondly after the running man and his dog, but Billy had gone as white as a sheet. His face, which had previously been a picture of happy contentment, was now pale and tearful. He seemed tense and very upset, all of a sudden. *What on earth…* thought Dagger. *Very interesting…*

Dagger glanced down river after the jogger, Nick. Maybe it was the sea fret rolling up the river towards the bridge that had unnerved Billy.

Frank wasn't looking at Billy's face, though. She jumped down off the wall, dragging him with her to talk to her grandmother. "Tell you what, Nan. Why don't Billy and I go and look for Len? Then you two can settle. What do you think, Billy?"

Billy was keen to help in any way. He was happy to be included, to be thought of as the sort of reliable person who *could* be invited to do this important thing. He gulped, trying to dislodge the thoughts that were creeping into his mind. His head swam a bit with this new responsibility. Nothing like this had ever happened to him before. He stood up straighter, nodding his head in agreement with Frank, trying to focus on this important new thing he had to do. He would not burst into tears here.

"What good kids you are," Essie told her. "It'll settle his mind," she added, gesturing to Dagger, who was whistling over the water, looking keenly towards his yard.

"OK. Billy, you search the other side – Dagger's side – and I'll do my side. That'll speed things up."

Frank gave him a gentle steer in the direction of the bridge. Billy was instantly deflated: he'd wanted to search with Frank. He drew strength and courage just from being with her, he realised, but knew that she was putting her faith and trust in him to do this job by himself. He couldn't let her down. Or himself down, for that matter.

"OK," he gulped, walking off towards the bridge, trying to appear confident and jaunty, with the gratitude of Dagger and Essie easing him on his way.

"Just shout out if you find him," Frank called after him. Not turning round, Billy gave a wave of one hand, trying to look cool and in control, but he was still trembling.

Chapter 26

Si looked at the mobile in his hand. Baz was sitting in the sun, in Si's garden, his back against the wall, head down, playing on something *really important*, if the look on his face was anything to go by. Si was fascinated by Baz's tongue. It was sticking out of his mouth, and Si suspected that when the character on the screen went round a corner and fell off the cliff, his tongue seemed to do the same, flashing around his lips in an effort to keep up with the speed of Baz's fingers and thumbs.

"Chick says he's got something big to tell us," Si told his mate, scrolling through his own screen.

Baz ignored him, head down, lost in his own entertainment.

"He says we've got to go and meet him on the river path on the other side. Baz. Baz, man!" He kicked Baz, who dropped his mobile in alarm and jumped up angrily to reach for it on the grass.

"Ha'way, man, Si. What's the matter with you? I was on the final level," he groaned, head in hands. "I've never got that far before…"

Si smirked happily at his mate's dejection. "Chick says he's got big news for us. We have to go and meet him."

Baz frowned, settling back onto the lawn. "Tell him to get over here. We've got far more important things to do." He wiped the screen of his mobile on his jeans and tried to start the game again, still not looking at Si.

"Yeah, you're right. It's probably another piece of gold he's found by the river."

Baz chuckled, remembering the last incident, when Chick had been ecstatic and convinced that his find was going to make them all rich. He hadn't even had the grace to feel ashamed when it turned out to be a lump of old metal, which had fallen off the back of the bin man's lorry. Si texted Chick back, then actually raised his head from his own screen, remembering.

"And remember when that old lamp was washed up on the beach? He was convinced it was Ming Dynasty. Just as well we stopped him going on The

Antiques Roadshow with it, eh?" Baz laughed, shaking his head. "You'd think the "made in Taiwan" stamp would have been a dead give-away, wouldn't you?"

Si's phone bleeped again. Looking at the screen, he declared, "It's him again. He says we've *got* to go over to the other side. Says he can't leave this find and we have to take his word for it. Says, this time, it's *proper* massive."

"And no doubt we're going to be rich, again...?"

Si nodded, putting his mobile in the pocket of his jeans. "Yep. Come on, we might as well."

The two boys lumbered out of the garden, heading towards the bridge at Coxgreen, stepping widely to the side of the geese who hissed and cackled malevolently at them. The boys hissed and cackled back, then lost their confidence and legged it at top speed as the leader of the goose pack took umbrage and flew at them in a mad temper. Once they got through the gate and the stile, they slowed down to enjoy their riverside walk in the sun.

"I tell you what," began Si, opening a packet of chewy mints. "It had better be good this time. If I miss Loose Women because of that loony, he'll be in big trouble... What?" he asked, looking askance at Baz's face. "It's the best thing on telly, mate. Don't pretend you never watch it either. It was you who told me about that report on the woman whose false boobs exploded on a plane last week, and you said..."

Their voices faded and echoed up under the arches of the viaduct in the distance. The geese settled down near the bridge to hassle the cyclists who might chance by, and the swans floated idly up the river, towards Fatfield.

*

Chick paced the river path, nervously, checking his mobile every thirty seconds, his breath coming in ragged gasps. He couldn't decide if he was elated or terrified, but boy, what a rush! His plan was coming together. It had been his idea to get the dog and hold him for ransom, and here it was – inside a tunnel, which Chick didn't even know existed until a few minutes ago. Phew! He did have a slight pang of conscience that the animal was holed up in the dark, under the hill, but he had spent a minute or two at the heavy metal door, shushing its whining, telling it to sit and calm down. He told Len, through the undergrowth, that he wouldn't be in there for too long, then he'd get him out and take him for a nice long walk: to Si's house, ha! At one point, a jogger had run past and had eyed Chick suspiciously, watching out of the side of his eyes at this lad who appeared to be talking to the trees. *Ee well, takes all sorts,* he'd decided, and run on.

Come on, guys! Where are you? Chick was dancing up and down, anxiously. He couldn't wait to show off what he'd done. Hadn't Si and Baz agreed that his plan to get this dog was a really excellent plan? And here he was. Now they just had to hide it at Si's house for a while and get that skanky kid to fork out a load of cash to get it safely released. They wouldn't hurt it, would they? Chick stopped pacing to consider this possibility. He shook his head. No, they weren't *cruel,* exactly, his mates: thick, a bit dim, but not cruel… Well, he knew *he* wouldn't hurt the dumb dog. Oh, do come on! He stopped dancing up and down to listen, straining his ears to decipher the sounds of voices, which might be approaching, from those of the birds and the swaying of the trees. *Aha. Is this the lads coming?*

*

Across the water, Frank was walking slowly, her eyes probing the hillside and the undergrowth, just in case Lennie had got caught up in some netting or discarded fishing wire, or something. He was too big to fit down a rabbit hole, she knew, and although he loved the water, he wouldn't just jump in. He had to be chasing a ball or a stick. He was so used to the river and the creatures which lived on and around it, that they weren't exciting to him like they were to visiting dogs, which often ended up in trouble. Occasionally, she called his name, then turned back to glance back up the river, towards her house, where she could see the workmen outside. It was a puzzle, definitely, but she wasn't too bothered, yet. *He'd come home soon enough*, she thought. Maybe Billy was having more luck on the other side. She looked out over the stretch of water, but couldn't see his fair head. *Must be in the back lane*, she thought.

*

Billy was idling down the lane, behind Sue's house. One or two cars were parked up, and he spotted old Mr Shannon who lived further up, but when asked, he said he hadn't seen Lennie for a while. All was quiet. Billy stuck his head into Sue's kitchen. She was sitting, working on her laptop, and barely glanced up when he appeared. Briefly, he asked if Len had been in the garden or the house in the last hour, and when Sue told him no, he informed her he was on a mission and wouldn't be out for too long. As the door closed gently behind him, Sue smiled to herself and continued her task. What a canny bairn he was.

In the garden, Billy smiled gently to himself. *I'm so lucky to have Sue*, he thought. *Isn't she great, sitting there, wearing little fishing boats in her ears.*

At Dagger's gate, Billy stopped again. He called gently and whistled as best he could, but there was no woof or waggy approach in answer. Dolly raised her head from her grazing and whinnied softly at him, before resuming her eating. *Well, Billy thought, she doesn't seem bothered. Len's not here.*

Walking on down the river path, another jogger slipped silently past Billy. This one was older and more grizzled than the last one, the one outside Essie

Bailey's house. That guy had freaked Billy out, and he worried massively that he would meet him and his spaniel, coming up this side of the river towards him. He didn't think he could cope. He felt the numbers bubbling up inside him, and he put his head down, staring at the stones on the path, counting them, the birds on the water, the trees on the other side, anything to repress his fears. *Get a grip, Billy, get a grip*, he breathed, gasping softly. Just do your job. It's important. It's for your friends. His breathing slowed eventually, and he was able to concentrate on trying to find Lennie. He sighed. Close thing. His head came up. Could he hear voices up ahead? He was passing under the wondrous viaduct and sound travelled easily here, and over the water, too. He'd ask the next person if they had seen a friendly black dog, wandering out by himself.

*

"And about time, an' all!" declared Chick, as his two mates ambled up the river path towards him. "Don't break the speed limit, will yer?" He looked pointedly at his watch. As they got closer, he could see that Si's black eyes were turning a mottled shade of purple and he was still holding his sore finger with an outsized bandage on it. Baz was shuffling along, with his hands in his pockets, walking with his toes turned out, in his usual fashion, a bit like that old silent movie guy – the one with the baggy trousers and the big shoes. Honestly. Didn't they know how important this moment was? How much their lives could change from this moment on, and all because he, Chick, was a genius?

"We've only been five minutes. What's the emergency, anyway?" Si demanded.

"Five minutes!" declared Chick, facing up to his friends. "I could have flown here quicker."

"Aye, you could that, little Chick," stated Baz, fondly rubbing Chick's fluffy yellow hair.

"Oy, watch it. Mind me bad ear." Chick winced, ducking his head out of the way. Why everyone was fascinated by his hair was beyond him. It was really annoying sometimes, especially when he had such impressive news to share.

"So, come on, then," began Si. "What's the big deal?"

"You'll never guess what I've got," Chick said, standing up proudly, his shoulders back, a smug grin on his impish face.

Si and Baz gazed at each other, delaying their mate's obvious pride in telling them.

"Head lice?" asked Si.

Baz wiped his hand on his jeans and grimaced. "Another thick ear?"

Si smiled.

Chick was positively bouncing. "I…" began Chick, swaying importantly, "… I have got him." And he nodded his head towards the undergrowth. His friends looked into the green bushes, smiled at each other, and bent down to have a closer look.

Baz reached a meaty hand in, grabbed something and turned to his friends with his eyes wide, his hands cupped. "He has, an' all, Si. Look!"

Si leaned in to look at the cupped hands. Si flashed them open in Si's face, declaring, "A leprechaun! Chick found a leprechaun. Look at him go!"

They both stared up unto the sky, laughing loudly. Chick wasn't impressed. The sun had gone in, and an odd mist was creeping up above the water. He just wanted to get on with his cunning plan. "No, you idiots. I really have found him. Don't you remember the plan? The ransom? The one we hatched, after that little mongrel got us into so much bother with Dagger Dawson?"

A light dawned in Si's eyes. "What? You mean... you got that little rat?" He looked around him, up and down the path, shivering slightly.

"No, you haven't, Chick. It's another of your fantasies, isn't it?" Baz told him, shaking his head.

"Ah, that's where you're wrong. I *have* got him, and he's locked up, while we decide what to do with him. While we decide how much to charge for his release, I mean. We're going to be rich, boys!"

Chick moved back a bit, standing closer to the cliff face. Si and Baz weren't convinced.

"So, come on, then, big clever lad. You're telling us that, all by yourself, you've managed to get that little runt and keep him somewhere safe, tied up, until we can decide how much we want for him?"

Chick nodded in delight. It was so good to hear it being said out loud, and just wait until they see *where* he was, he thought. He raised a hand and parted the straggly bushes and weeds with a flourish, as if he was parting the Dead Sea.

"Ta da!" he sang, cheerfully.

"I'll *ta da* you, you idiot..." began Baz, but Si raised a hand. He tilted his head to one side, deep in thought. No, it couldn't be... could it? Stepping towards the cliff face, he looked down at his delighted little mate.

"I don't believe it," he stated quietly, parting the weeds in the crumbly wall. "Chick, I think you've found..."

And yes, he had. Si's fist banged on the partly-revealed heavy metal door in the cliff face. He turned to face his mates, incredulous.

"What?" Baz began. "What is it?"

Si was dragging more and more weeds and straggly growth from over the door. "He's only gone and found one of the historical tunnels that have been down here for years!" declared Si in astonishment. "Chick, mate, people have been looking for these tunnels for yonks!"

Now it was Baz's turn to look impressed. He stepped forward.

"Woah…" he breathed, eyes wide, then turning to Chick, he asked, "And is this where he is? Your victim? In a tunnel, down by the river?"

Chick swelled with pride, his eyes shining. "Yep. Got him, the little sod. He's in there all right." He beamed.

Si and Baz looked at their friend in awe.

"Honest?" Si asked.

"And he didn't even put up a fight?" asked Baz. "Wow."

"It's easy, when you know how," stated a proud Chick.

Together they stepped away from the tunnel entrance, still closed behind the heavy old door. They looked furtively up and down the river path, making sure no one was coming.

"Right, what we'll do is get him out, and drag him along to my house. We can force him into the old wood shed, out the back. Nobody ever goes in there."

"Yeah," nodded Baz, sagely. "Only the spiders. And as there's three of us, he probably won't put up much of a fight. But just to be sure, lads…"

He nodded to his mates to arm themselves, and each had a quick shufty-round, until they all held a branch or a large stone. Then, together, they moved towards the old door, hidden in the cliff. Si grabbed the rusted handle, his stick held in the air above his head.

"OK, guys. After three…"

"He's very quiet in there," whispered Baz. "You sure he's really in here, Chick? I mean, if this is a wind-up…"

"No, he's in there all right. He was eating some crisps."

Si and Baz exchanged a look, then Si leaned into the door handle. He gritted his teeth; well, they all did: this was a momentous occasion.

"One, two, THREE!"

The door creaked and groaned achingly, years of dust and old mortar breaking free and falling out onto their hands. It smelled rank in there. Baz actually held his battered nose. Poor little bugger, he thought. How long has he been holed up in here? That Chick must have some guts after all!

The three boys jumped back as if they'd been electrocuted, their weapons held aloft. For a split second nothing happened. Exchanging worried looks, all three approached the chasm cautiously.

What if the kid was dead?

He might have suffocated!

He'd better still be in there… They kept their thoughts to themselves for fear of looking soft.

Suddenly, Si screamed. Something large and furry pushed past him and out onto the riverside path. Baz tried to climb up the cliff face in his terror whilst Chick attempted to rugby tackle the escaping Lennie.

"No!" he wailed, as the dog shook himself and trotted off towards Coxgreen. "You flaming idiots. Now look what you've done. You've let him go. We'll never get rich now."

Turning slowly, breathing angrily, he faced the wrath of his two mates who were standing there red-faced, steam almost coming out of their mouths and ears.

"It was the *dog*. It was the bloody dog, not the kid! You moron, Chick."

"Can you not get anything right?" demanded Baz, rubbing soil and muck out of his eyes. And at that very moment, the sun went behind a cloud, the mist rolled up the river, and Billy appeared from round the bend.

∗

Dagger was pretending not to be worried. Lennie had a bit of wanderlust about him, and as everybody in the area knew him, and considered themselves his friends, he was relatively safe. The dog rarely ventured far from the riverside path, stopping at the gates of his favourite people for a stroke and a biscuit. He was a lovable, calm and good-natured dog, who had never been in a fight with anyone, the sort of dog who was comfortable in his own skin, who loved his neighbours, but who was a homebody, too. Dagger could feel the love and pride for his little mate bubbling up in him: he would walk himself up to Fatfield Bridge and see if his pal wasn't hanging around on Worm Hill with a friend. He set off, wishing he'd actually put a jumper on that morning because that sea fret was rolling up the river, and it was a bit chilly. Mind you, it could be gone in an instant, too.

At the corner of the bridge Dagger paused, hands on hips, his brown eyes searching up and down the hill behind the pub and across to the other side of the water. Nope, nothing. He sighed and dropped his head. A voice from outside the pub called over the road to him.

"Hi-aye, Dagger. You'll not earn much standing there, marrer! How you doin'?"

Dagger looked over and grinned at his mate, stepping behind a bus to cross over the road. Sitting at one of the tables, with a pint in his hand, was a slight, fair haired, freckled man, with a big grin on his face. Dagger was happy to see him.

"Hello, Bob. Haven't seen you for a while. How you doing?" He sat down beside his friend and declined the offer of a drink. "I'm just looking for my dog, Bob. You haven't seen him trot up this way, have you?"

"What? Your Lennie? Nah, mate. I've been here for about half an hour and he hasn't come by. And you know he'd stop for a chat, if he saw me here. Are you worried?"

Dagger's brow crinkled, and his brown eyes tried to look nonchalant, but Bob knew him better than that.

"Well..." Dagger began.

"He'll be fine, your Lennie. Probably just chasing after a bit of tasty lady, if you know what I mean, mate." Bob winked at Dagger.

"Nah – he's too much like his old dad, that boy." Dagger grinned back. "The days of tasty ladies are long gone, Bob!"

Bob took a swig of his pint and spluttered a bit, wiping his hand across his mouth. "You what? Not what I heard, mate!" He winked again.

Dagger sat down opposite his old friend. "'Funny, I should bump into you, Bob. I've just seen your Nick out on a run with his dog. Backpack on, and everything. He going away again soon?"

Bob grimaced and looked down into his pint. "Aye, Dagger. His unit is going to be deployed again in about a month's time. Not sure where, yet. Just hope it's not bloody Afghanistan again, this time."

Dagger made conciliatory noises and gazed into his friend's face.

"Do you think your Nick could do something for me, before he goes, like? If he's not too busy?"

Bob finished his pint and leaned across the table.

"For you, mate – anything. But it'll cost you."

Dagger grinned and stood up. "Another pint, marrer?"

Bob sat back and smiled serenely. "Make it two, mate – you still owe me one from Easter Sunday!"

Dagger laughed, ducking his head into the doorway of the pub.

*

Billy's mouth had gone dry, yet his tummy had the collywobbles and fizzy liquid was sloshing about in there. His head was swimming a bit, and his breathing was shallow and gasping. His arms were pinned to his body by a vice-like grip on each side of him. Two leering henchman had him held tight, the stupid little fluffy one with a girl's name, and the big thick idiot that lumbered about like a clown. The other one – the one who called himself Psycho – was standing in front of him, leaning close to Billy's face so that Billy could smell his hot, rancid breath. He shut his eyes tight and turned his head away.

"So, you little maggot. We've got you. Now we need to decide what to do with you. What do you think, lads?" Si sneered, turning in triumph to look at his posse, who sneered and cheered back at him.

Chick was positively bouncing up and down with excitement, until Si gave him the death stare, too, which said 'cool it, kid, before I give you a slap as well'. Chick stopped bouncing and tried his best to look as menacing as his mates, which was hard to do when you were only six-stone, wringing wet, had fluffy yellow hair and one thick ear.

"Chuck him in the river," snarled Baz, nodding his head over his shoulder, noting with delight that Billy's eyes flashed open in fear.

"No, maybe later. We need the ransom money first, don't we?" Chick stated, glaring at his friends: really, who was in charge here?

"Aye, you're right, Chick. We do. But we haven't decided how much we're gonna ask for, yet."

Si pursed his lips and looked thoughtfully up and down the river. The sea fret had a curious effect on sound now, muffling everything, and even the trees above took on a sinister shape as the leaves dripped damply down onto the four youths.

"The log shed?" enquired Baz.

Billy was trying to make sense of what was happening. Surely, they would just rough him up a bit, then go on their lumbering way to brag about it to their friends, assuming they had any. What was this talk of log sheds and ransoms? What were they on about? He wanted Frank, or even better Dagger, to come along the path to help him, but he knew they were both on the opposite side of the river, searching for Lennie. His arms hurt. Why were there never any cyclists when you needed one? He thought of his mam, all of a sudden. She wouldn't stand for this. She'd wade in and kick their fat backsides. But then the thought of her caused tears to well up, his poor mam and her hopeless situation, and he didn't want to cry in front of these morons. Oh no, they'd love that.

In an attempt to stop the tears, Billy began to struggle, using his feet to lash out at Si, who was standing right in front of him and was the closest. He managed to get a couple of kicks to the shin, before one foot made contact a bit higher up, between his legs. The weight of the lunge made the three of them stumble back and, for a split second, the boys watched in awe as Simon's head came up in shock, then the pain set in, and he lumbered forward, falling towards them like a tree. He hit the ground and rolled around, grasping at his crown jewels and wailing in agony. Next to him, Billy felt Baz and Chick gulp and gasp in shock, but still they held him tight.

Chick let go of Billy and rushed to help his friend. Sadly, Baz hung on tight – Billy could feel his thin arms bruising in the grip. Chick crouched down beside his stricken mate.

"Si, Si, are you OK? Have you got any ice?"

Baz looked at Chick in disbelief. "Ice? Chick, man, it's July and we're on the riverside. Where the hell are we going to get some ice from?"

Chick looked along the river to where he knew the pub was, shook his head, looked around himself, then appeared to have a brainwave. Spotting something caught in a bush, he grabbed it and made a clumsy dash down towards the river. Si was crying now, proper hot tears which matched the pain of his injury. In two minutes, Chick was back, clutching what looked like a large crisp packet. Lying Si gently on his back, with Baz and Billy watching in wonder, Chick poured cold, dirty river water all down the front of Si's trousers, completely soaking his crotch area. Si gasped even more and attempted to sit up in disbelief.

"Wha…? What the …? Chick, you maniac!"

Baz couldn't help himself. He burst out laughing. Even Billy managed a wry smile. Si managed to get to his feet and lumber about on the path, still holding onto his now wet and throbbing privates. With one long arm he attempted to thump Chick in the head, but succeeded in only clouting him on his already swollen ear, making the spelk in his sore finger throb, too.

Chick howled in protest. "Ow, man, Si – I was only trying to help!"

Si's eyes were red and smarting now, he looked as though he had wet himself, and Baz was cackling like a demented hen. Billy wondered if this might be a good time to make a break for it, but Baz was onto him and held him even tighter.

Stepping forward, Baz decided to take control. Chick was useless, and Si was in no position to make any decisions now, so someone had to man up before this situation got out of control. Dragging Billy towards the cliff face, Baz nodded to Chick, who simply looked vacant.

"Right. We need some thinking time. Chick, get over here and open this up." He nodded towards the place in the undergrowth where the metal door was hidden. "Come on, get a move on. We can come back for him later, when we have decided what to do, and when Si is feeling up to it."

Chick darted forward, glancing worriedly at Billy. Billy wondered what on earth they were talking about. Now what? Then, to his utter horror, a door appeared in the face of the cliff – an old rusty metal door – and behind it a gaping, dark hole, with spider webs and a thick, clotting smell of decay oozing out of it. A tunnel! No, no, no, no, no…

Si managed to stumble forward once he realised what his mates were up to. He fully agreed with Baz and had a plan to help. As far as Si was concerned, this little maggot could rot in there forever. No one would ever find him. As Baz bundled the screaming, kicking and howling kid inside the tunnel, the other two leaned against the door to prevent Billy from pushing his way out. Si rolled a huge stone across the entrance, then, still on his knees, he built up a bank of soil and rubble in front of the door, before hiding it with more undergrowth.

The three youths stood back, listening to the anguished, but muffled, howls of the kid inside the tunnel. Then they gave each other an exhausted high five, before lumbering away back along the chilly, damp river path – Si walking like John Wayne – listening as the cries became fainter, until they could no longer hear the kid at all.

Chapter 27

Frank had walked as far as stupid Si-the-Psycho's house along the river, but there was no sign of Lennie. In fact, the whole river area was as quiet as a grave. *Probably, this sea fret, rolling up from the coast, had put people off going out,* she thought. She knew it would clear as quickly as it rolled in, and had the same belief in Lennie strolling home very shortly. Well, she'd done her bit. She would now go back and catch up with Dagger and Billy to see if either of them had had any luck. Turning round, she put her hands in her pockets and whistled tunelessly as she walked. All very odd, though, she thought.

There was no sign of Billy on the other side of the river. Frank called his name out once or twice, as well as Lennie's, but when there was no reply or sign of either of them, she gave up and headed for home. She could see the workmen in their yellow jackets, still digging away outside her Nan's house. The river was running deep and smooth, and looked as though the tide had just turned. She shivered slightly as cold water dripped from the trees, down the back of her neck. She was anxious to get in and make some progress with all of her little birds, and Billy was turning into an excellent assistant. She'd show that Dagger a thing or two. She smiled at the thought of him: his boats were amazing, but between herself and Billy, she was certain he had met his match.

*

Dagger was heading home in the opposite direction. He, too, had his eyes on the workmen outside Essie Bailey's house, but his mind was far away. He was glad he'd bumped into Bob, happy that his mate might be able to do some digging for him, but he was still a bit worried that his dog hadn't come home. Trudging on, he hoped that either Billy or Frank had had more luck than himself. Hmm, very puzzling…

*

Inside the tunnel, Billy was lying flat on his back with his eyes scrunched shut, desperately trying to breathe. He had fought, scratching at the walls and heavy door in the pitch darkness. He had scrabbled at the damp earth, until his fingertips bled; he had shoved and pushed with all his might against the solid metal, and screamed and bellowed, until he was hoarse. His eyes and his throat hurt, and he truly thought he was going to die this time.

"One hundred, fifty-three, seventy, eighteen times six foot six."

His breath shuddered out of his body. He had no idea where he was or how he would ever escape. Last time, a teacher had come to his recue, but who knew he was in this tomb, this time? He hadn't even realised that this place existed. He tried again to calm his breathing, trying the other version of his mantra.

"Thirty, sixteen, twenty-one, two metres."

It didn't help. He could feel the utter panic rising in him like a tide. He screamed out again, hoarsely, into the unrelenting darkness. He recognised that he would die of a panic attack, if he couldn't get in control, so he started again. Taking a deep gulp of stale air, he whispered the words out through clenched teeth, "One hundred, fifty-three, seventy…"

In his mind, he pictured where he was, what had happened only moments ago, on the river path. He tried to imagine the trees and the river, the cyclists trundling past, the dog walkers and the postman, but each time one picture came into view, it slipped away again to be swallowed up by this terrifying damp darkness. He tried to bring to mind his Monument, knowing as he did that it *always* worked, *always* calmed him. He fought desperately to see himself standing right on the top of the hill, gazing out to sea, or looking down to Durham city, with its cathedral tower in the distance. He tried to envisage his tower block in the centre of Sunderland, but although the images came into view, they quickly wobbled and wavered, slipping away from him. Billy sobbed in despair. His eyes were full of tears and soil. He reached into a pocket, looking for a hanky, anything, to try to calm himself. This couldn't be how he would die. Could it?

In the pitch blackness, Billy found a tissue and put it to his face, trying to wipe some of the dirt and the fear from his vision. He felt his eyes clear a little, which helped. Opening them, they weren't quite so gritty, but he was still entombed. His vision cleared a tiny bit; he could see dark, brick-lined walls, with bits of root growing through. He must be getting used to the dark, he thought to himself with another shudder. Straining his ears, he listened for the sound of voices passing along the river way. Nothing. He was completely alone.

Surely, those three would come back for him? Billy kicked his feet at the heavy door once more, but it was no good. It didn't budge an inch. He was feeling exhausted – all that fighting, screaming and clawing had really taken it out of him. What if he ran out of air? He lay back in the dark and let the tears come.

Where was his Monument when he needed it most? It had never let him down in the past.

Suddenly, something soft tickled his face. Billy froze. What was it? A spider? No! Not that, on top of everything else that was happening to him. Please don't let this place be full of creepy crawlies, too! What if there were rats in here? He'd seen the odd one slip into the river of an evening, when he was out with Frank. *Please, God, not rats,* he begged. Putting his hand to his face, he suddenly realised that what was tickling him was a feather. Huh? A feather? In here, of all places? Trying to think more clearly, he remembered what Frank had said to him about feathers, when he'd found one on Fatfield Bridge.

"You've had a visit, Billy. An angel is near."

Billy let out a sob. An angel? He needed a whole heavenly host, not just one! But the thought of the white feather he'd found gave him a tiny glimmer of comfort. He'd laughed at Frank's face on the bridge, when the feather floated down from a clear blue sky, and now here it was, entombed in this tunnel with him. Billy suddenly felt a little calmer. *It must be because I've thought of Frank*, he decided. *She'll come looking for me*, he told himself. The feather unfurled softly on his cheek, like a kiss. Maybe there was someone in here with him, he thought. It wouldn't be the first time, after all, would it? He thought of his mam's soft voice, telling him gently that it was going to be all right. And then, out of nowhere, his dad's face appeared before him. He was smiling down at Billy, his blue eyes alive and sparkling. His face was serene, and calm. Billy felt his own face, and his fear, relax a little – he was not quite so afraid anymore – and tried to focus on the feather, not on his fear. His dad reached out and smoothed some of the dusty soil off Billy's brow, moving his fringe back with soft, warm hands, just like he used to do when Billy was a toddler. He was telling Billy to relax, to breathe, to have trust… Help would come, he was saying.

"Please, God," Billy began, saying it out loud. "Let my dad be right. Let someone come and find me, before it's too late."

He squeezed his eyes tightly shut, tried to breathe more calmly, and attempted to picture, once more, that faithful image of himself standing at the top of Penshaw Hill in the sunshine, with the big, solid Monument behind him, steady and permanent. And this time, he could see it more clearly. And in the picture, he felt the sun on his back and a warm, strong hand holding his.

*

Frank met Dagger at her gate. She had asked the workmen if Lennie had come back, but they shook their heads and continued digging.

"Where's Billy?" Dagger asked. "Has he not seen or heard anything, either?"

Frank shook her head and raised her shoulders. "It's odd, Dagger, but I haven't seen anything from him."

Dagger looked across the water to Billy's house. He smiled and shook his head. "You know what?" he began, turning to Frank. "I bet the two of them are having a cup of tea and a biscuit at Sue's, and they've completely forgotten about us."

Frank folded her arms, also gazing over the river. "Shall we go and look? I bet they're working in your woodshed."

Together, the two of them started walking up towards the bridge, but one of the workmen put down his spade and called them back. "Don't know if it's any use to you two, but we thought we heard a fight going on somewhere along the river. I don't think it was on this side, mind. It's hard to tell the way sound carries down here, isn't it?"

Dagger and Frank exchanged looks. A fight? Down here? That didn't seem right.

"OK, cheers, mate. I'll check it out," Dagger told him with a frown, as he steered Frank gently up towards Fatfield Bridge.

*

Si and his posse – henchman, amigos, call them what you will – were standing at the open door to his woodshed, in the back garden. It was a gloomy, dusty sort of place, full of old buckets, empty bottles, gardening equipment and old paint tins, as well as wood. Nobody had really been in it for years. You could tell that the most human contact it had had recently was when one of the family opened the door and simply threw an item in. It was a jumbled mess, and cramped with it.

Si made his usual gulping, snorting sound, which Baz took as a sign of approval. "Yeah, Si, it's a bit of a mess, but we can chain that kid in here, no problem. Look, there's even a hook on the back wall for it."

Si leaned in questioningly, squinting his bashed black and blue eyes to get a better look at the hook. Baz pushed him forward, into the doorway, but Si held on tight to the door frame, hurting his injured finger in the process.

"Ow, man, Baz, what you playin' at?" he demanded, stepping back into his mate, who was too close behind him. Baz winced too, as Si clashed with his nettle-stung legs.

Chick neatly side-stepped the two bigger lads, asking them in disbelief, "What's the matter, now? Why won't you go in the shed, Si?"

Si snorted in mock disgust. "Phuh! Me, not go in me own shed? Don't be stupid, man. I was just being a gentleman – letting Baz have a good look first."

Baz had gone a bit pale in the face and was showing a genuine reluctance to take his mate up on his offer. Shaking his head, he told them, "Nah, not me. I'm not going in there first."

All three exchanged flashing looks, only their wide eyes showing any movement. They each waited for one of the others to make a move.

Si gulped again. "And what's wrong with my shed, may I ask?" he demanded, pompously.

Baz scuffed his feet and scratched at his itchy injuries. "Might be spiders in there." He sniffed quietly. All three boys had a quick look, then ducked their heads straight back out.

"Or woodlice." Chick shuddered.

"Thought I saw a mouse in there the other day," Si admitted. All three stepped away from the open door. They paused, looking from one to another, expectantly.

"But... but... So what?" demanded Chick, incredulously. "Really? Is that a problem?"

Baz swayed and swaggered on his turned-out toes. "Could be, like, for that kid!" He grinned. "And just what he deserves, an 'all."

"Aye," stated Si. "We could put food in through the window, and blacken the glass. No one ever comes out here. It'll give us a chance to decide how much money we want to release him, and who's going to cough up for him."

They all grinned at this idea, seeing pound signs forming in front of their eyes. Lots of them.

"I could get that new Xbox I've been after..." Baz grinned.

"And that new iPhone." Si laughed back, punching his mate on the arm, then wincing, when the spelk took yet another knock. Thoughts of filling their pockets with the sort of cash that was ordinarily out of their reach made them giddy, and they spent a happy few minutes dreaming of frittering it all away on the sort of rubbish that would make their lives complete.

Chick suddenly held up a finger. He looked at Si's bandaged digit and quickly put it down again. "Just one thing, lads," he began. "Err, isn't that kid an orphan, or summat?"

Si and Baz looked pointedly at him.

"I mean, isn't that why he's here, in the first place? Just wondering, like, who's going to be coughing up for him to be released? Does anybody care about that kid?"

Baz folded his arms in thought, Chick raised his eyebrows, and Si gulped in disgust.

*

"He was here, a while back."

Sue was talking to Dagger and Frank at the kitchen door. "He said Lennie hadn't come home and you were all out looking for him, but that was some time ago."

Dagger was trying his best to look normal, and cheerful, but Sue had known him too long. There were worry lines in his brow, where normally his face was smooth and handsome. She felt the first wave of concern roll around her tummy.

Frank looked from one adult face to the other. "Oh, they'll both be fine. I think they're in Dagger's shed right now, getting clues about how many of the little boats are ready."

She took hold of Dagger's arm and dragged him down the garden path. He kept looking back at Sue with an unreadable expression on his face.

"Call me, when you find him. Them, I mean," she told her neighbour, firmly. Dagger waved back in response. Sue pulled her cardigan more closely around her chest. She felt chilled, all of a sudden. *Must be the sea fret*, she thought, closing the kitchen door.

Frank and Dagger had a cursory check around his garden and shed, but it was immediately obvious that nobody was there. Dolly wandered over and whinnied softly, nuzzling into her owner's large freckled hands.

"Where's our Billy and your little mate Lennie, then, Dolly?" he asked her, stroking her soft, warm fur. The donkey whoofled and snuffled back.

"Well, you're not much use to me, are you missus?" he told her, before she returned to her favourite spot, near the water, to graze. He and Frank left the garden, latching the big gate behind themselves, and continued down the river path, making for the viaduct. Frank kept half an eye across the water, on her side, in case she should spot one of them ambling homewards. Once in a while, Dagger whistled softly, searching the path and the undergrowth, which sloped down to the water on one side, and up towards the banked cliff sides on the other. Nothing.

Passing under the viaduct, a minute or two later, Frank suddenly grabbed Dagger's sleeve. She stopped in her tracks and pointed up ahead. "Look, Dagger."

Up ahead of them, on the path, Lennie was trotting towards them, head down. Dagger's face broke into a large grin, and Frank let out a huge sigh of relief.

"Lennie!" he called. The dog lifted his head, and trotted forward in delight, head down, wagging his tail. Frank was convinced the dog was smiling at the two of them.

Dagger crouched down, roughly stroking and patting his little friend. "I've been so worried about you. Where've you been, eh?"

Frank crouched down beside him. "And where's Billy, eh, boy? Have you seen Billy?"

The dog appeared to light up at the sound of Billy's name. He turned back the way he had come and trotted along, pausing once in a while to look back at Frank and Dagger as if to say, 'Well, come on, then'.

Dagger watched his dog, a puzzled frown on his face. "Billy must be along this way somewhere, then," he told Frank, eyes searching ahead of the two of them. "Come on, let's see if we can see him."

"Yeah," she said, tagging along after him. "But isn't it odd that the two of them aren't together? I find that very strange."

Their voices echoed and bounced around, underneath the viaduct, as they trundled on together.

After only a minute or two, Lennie suddenly disappeared, snuffling into the undergrowth. Dagger and Frank continued on the riverside path, chatting amiably now that Lennie had turned up. Some of the heat was off: if the dog was safe, Billy wouldn't be far away or in any other trouble, either, they reasoned. After all, this was Fatfield riverside, hardly the Bronx or Beirut.

Dagger looked back over his shoulder and continued walking on, whistling to his dog as he did so. When Lennie did not respond by bounding after them, the two of them stopped, Frank calling to his pet again. Frank glanced up at Dagger with a puzzled expression.

"Do you think there's some dog in heat around here, Dagger? He's being very odd today is Len."

Dagger frowned. He knew his pet better than anyone in the world. He was a good and well-trained dog, happy to obey his owner, usually. This was odd, him disappearing like this. Dagger walked back a few paces to where Lennie had slipped away. As he approached some straggly bushes, the dog appeared on the path in front of them again, but this time he sat down and held up one paw.

"Oh, do you think he's stood on something sharp?" asked Frank, crouching down beside him.

"What's wrong, Len?" Dagger asked, bending over to look at the proffered paw. "Have you picked up a thorn, eh?"

Lennie woofed up at the two of them, then darted back into the bushes. Frank and Dagger exchanged a look, as Dagger whistled for him to come back out and join them on the path again.

"Well, that's odd. That paw seems fine to me." Dagger scratched his head. What was he playing at? As they watched, Lennie came back out from behind the bushes and repeated the whole scenario again: paw up, head cocked to one side, and a little bark at his owner and friend.

Frank smiled. "Daft dog," she told him, starting to walk away.

Dagger, however, was curious. He moved towards the dog as, once again, Lennie dived behind the bush. Frank sighed and followed them. Dagger stopped and looked at the ground around him, a frown on his darkly handsome face, hands on his hips, deep in thought. Frank glanced up and down the river path, then quickly across the water to the other side of the river. Nobody about, all was quiet and peaceful. Dagger crouched down onto the sandy path. Lennie looked at him expectantly.

"Frank…" he began. "You know, the workmen said they'd heard a fight going on? What do you think? Look around you, here."

Frank stopped gazing about and concentrated. Actually, now that she was focused, there were signs of a scuffle on the path. Bits of broken branches were lying at odd angles, stones had been kicked over, there were signs of water being spilled and litter, where normally the path was smooth and slightly dusty. Even the undergrowth seemed 'messier' than was usual for here – some old branches and roots exposed, and new growth torn down.

She looked at Dagger. "You'd make a wonderful red Indian chief," she told him with a grin.

Dagger straightened up, glancing up at the embankment in front of him. *Funny*, he thought. *Something's odd and new here.* And he knew these paths like the back of his hand, having been walking down them every day for forty years or more. As he parted the bushes to see what the dog was so intent on, he noted some large white stones, which had been pushed up against the soil and the mossy undergrowth. One side of the stones glowed white, whilst the other side looked as though they had been hidden in the ground for years, before being disturbed. And very recently, Dagger judged. Standing up straight, Dagger looked directly at the embankment at about waist height, and then it dawned on him. His eyebrows shot up, he let out a low whistle and began moving more of the shrubbery.

Frank watched, fascinated. "Dagger," she began, then her face, too, lit up as she realised that her neighbour had found what appeared to be a door, built into the side of the hill. What?

"What on earth…?" she began, staring up and down the old door, noting the stones heaped at the bottom of it and the earth banked in front of it.

"Well, I never," stated Dagger, standing back to look more closely at his find. "One of the tunnels! After all these years. I thought they had gone forever."

Frank was amazed. Who knew this was here? She'd lived here all her life and knew nothing of it.

"A tunnel? Where does it go? Why is there a tunnel here, of all places?" she asked.

"There's a few of them, Frank, but I didn't think I'd ever see one. There used to be old quarries round here, in the last century, and they used the tunnels to get all the sandstone down to the river to load onto the barges. Well, I never!" He grinned. But then, his grin faded. He looked with concern at Frank.

"Wow," she breathed, then noted the change in Dagger's expression. "What…?" she began.

Dagger put the flat of one hand against the rusting, heavy door. He was sure he felt it vibrate ever so slightly. His expression became dark, angry looking. "Quick, Frank," he said. "Help me get this thing open. I have an awful feeling about it."

The two of them began moving rocks out of the way and trying to dislodge the built-up earth from the base of the door. Even Lennie joined in, digging with huge, waggy enthusiasm, enjoying the game. After a minute or two, Dagger took hold of the heavy old door and pulled with all his impressive might. The door creaked and groaned, reluctantly inching forward slowly, until dank, cool air drifted out as a hole appeared, only thirty centimetres wide or so.

Dagger peered inside, squinting into the gloom. Reaching a hand behind him, he snapped at Frank, "Mobile, Frank, quickly."

She handed it over, watching nervously as Dagger held it inside the old tunnel. She could see the faint green light. For some reason, she felt sick to her stomach. Dagger's face looked like that of a madman, peering into the gloomy interior, lit by the eerie green glow.

"Billy!" he called, dragging the door further open, heaving with his considerable weight. His face looked ashen, his craggy laughter lines creased in anguish.

"Oh, God – Billy!"

Chapter 28

Frank shivered and stepped back. Billy? Billy was trapped in this hell-hole, which she didn't even know existed? How could that be? And look at Dagger's face: he was frantic. He had gone as white as a sheet and looked like a madman. Was Billy seriously hurt, or worse? Was Billy dead? Frank clutched at her heart and felt faint. Her head was spinning and she felt like she was going to pass out, but Dagger and Billy needed her now. Dropping to the ground on her knees, Frank began to pull away at the stones and the earth, which was preventing the door from opening more easily, to allow Dagger to release poor Billy. Her breath was coming in erratic sobs.

After a minute or two of frantic scrabbling, pushing and pulling, Dagger entered the tunnel, his voice echoing inside, floating out of the open door in muffled, yet soothing, tones. Frank sat back on the ground and tried to calm her breathing. She wanted to cry out to Dagger, to follow him inside the gaping dark maw of the entrance, but instinct, and some fear, made her wait her turn out in the fresh air, so as not to impede Billy's rescue in any way. It was a tight squeeze for Dagger, being such a big man, but after a minute or two, his back appeared in the entrance, dragging something out of the tunnel.

Frank jumped up, realising in an instant that it was Billy's feet, in his trainers, which Dagger was hauling out. Dagger had cobwebs and chalky dust in his hair and on his face, as he backed out of the tunnel. His expression was bleak, and grim. By the time Billy's pale face appeared, Frank was crying hot tears of worry. Was her little mate dead? He certainly looked it. Crouching down beside him, Frank wiped away some of the grime and sweat from his brow. Dagger held up one of Billy's hands, bloodied and battered, earth and blood encrusted round his torn fingernails. The poor little lad had been trying to dig his way out. He must have been scared for his life in there, he thought. Which bastard was responsible for this? He felt for a pulse: it was there, but weak and fluttery.

"Frank, ring for an ambulance," he told her, trying to stay calm, but fighting back an immense rage which was starting to boil inside him.

Frank raised her head from Billy's chest to look at her neighbour. "Who would do this, Dagger?" she asked. "Who would lock little Billy in there? It's cruel. He's nearly dead!" she wailed, a sob breaking from her aching throat.

"Just get an ambulance here, pet – quickly, now."

Dagger set to rubbing Billy's pale face and hands, whilst Frank was busy on the mobile, trying to stay calm to give the instructions, but obviously struggling. *Poor little lass*, he thought. *When I find out who's behind this…*

"Come on, Billy. Come on, son. It's all right. You're out now. You're safe. Come on, Billy. Please."

Dagger was almost pleading with the lad on the ground in front of him, smoothing his hair, shaking his chest, trying to force his love into the stricken child. Billy's head was lolling to one side, but Dagger felt that some colour was coming back to his cheeks.

Frank put her mobile in her back pocket and came to crouch beside Dagger. "They're coming," she told him, patting Billy softly on his cheek.

Suddenly, Billy's eyes flashed open, his mouth gaped as he struggled for air and he began fighting like a madman. His large grey eyes were bulging, his matted hair standing on end as he began to lash out. He caught Dagger right in the eye and kicked out at Frank, sending her sprawling into the bushes on her back where she bashed her head against one of the dislodged rocks. Dagger rubbed at his stinging eye and reached out blindly to try to calm the lad with one hand.

"Billy, Billy, son, it's OK. Look, it's just us. Just me and Frank. You're all right now. Come on, Billy."

He tried to coax the lad into calming down, so he could wrap him up in a warm bear hug to comfort him, but the boy was in a complete blind panic. Slight as he was, he had the strength of ten men. Billy didn't know who he was or where he was; he just knew he was no longer entombed.

He started scrambling up through the undergrowth above the tunnel, making his way up the side of the steep embankment, rather than make his way back along the river path in the mist to the safety of Sue's warm kitchen. Billy was screaming now, raging like a rabid dog, tearing at roots and bushes in a mad attempt at freedom. He had no idea of what he was doing. He was simply fleeing for his life and for his sanity. His voice was like that of a wild bear, guttural, roaring. He was away up the side of the hill, scrambling and fighting, desperate to put some distance between him and that all-consuming hell hole.

On the ground beneath him, he had a vague idea that someone was calling his name. Or was the sound coming from above him? He couldn't tell. Maybe it was inside his head. He couldn't breathe properly, he couldn't see or think straight, and he couldn't stop. He had to escape!

Down on the riverside path, Dagger rubbed his stinging eye as he helped Frank to her feet. She was a bit sore, but not badly hurt. She was whimpering a bit – in shock, he thought.

"Well, he looks as though he's not too badly injured, Frank," Dagger told her, watching as the lad made his frantic getaway up through the embankment. "But we've got to get him back. He could end up anywhere."

Frank raised her watery blue eyes to Dagger. To his mind, she looked pale and very young, and lost.

"That's just it, though, Dagger," she whispered to him. "I think I know exactly where he's going. And why."

She craned her head back, looking towards the viaduct with a bleakly worried expression. Dagger followed her gaze, noting the abject fear in her face and voice.

"The viaduct? No."

Dagger shook his head in disbelief as Frank suddenly took off after Billy, taking a more subtle and well-trodden path up the side of the hill, away from the river. Looking back over her shoulder, Frank forced down a hiccup of fear. For a big bloke, Dagger Dawson could still move fast.

*

Completely oblivious, and uncaring, the three boys were holed up in Si's cramped and faintly smelly bedroom, plotting their revenge on the brat they were so proud to have captured and to have put in a safe place until they were all agreed on a satisfactory outcome. Si was lolling about on his bed, his long legs and gangly arms held out at funny angles, still trying to protect the finger with the spelk in it. And, of course, the other tender parts of his anatomy that had taken a bashing today.

Si's injuries were becoming a bit of an obsession, Chick thought. Almost like war wounds. And they weren't half as bad as his own sore ear, which was still hot and throbbing. Although, remembering the delivery of the kick to his mate's privates did make Chick want to faint at the mere thought of it. Baz was on a tiny stool, near Si's homework desk – not that any homework had been done on it since year four. It was now covered with well-worn and partly broken small figures, holding weapons, with huge heads and arms, bits of battle dress falling off, creatures lying around drunkenly with vacant expressions, some of which still had heads attached to their bodies. Baz had his trousers rolled up to the knees. His lower legs were still bright red, but now there were tiny bits of toilet roll randomly stuck all over his lower limbs, attached by Calamine lotion. He looked like a fat frog, waiting to leap into a pond, Chick mused, sitting on the floor, squashed up against the bedroom door. He knew his place, even though by rights, Chick truly believed that catching the kid was all his idea and none of it would have happened without his brilliance.

Sid made his usual grunting snort and looked down at his friends. "So, we're all agreed on the plan, then. Yes?"

"Defo," nodded Baz, sagely.

"I'm in," agreed Chick.

Si laid his head back on the pillow and raked at his hair with his hands. "Finally!" he stated, a suggestion of exasperation creeping into his voice, as he sat up. "So, we send a note to that Frank, asking for £1000 in used notes..." he began.

"Demanding." Baz held up a fat finger, looked at it, dropped it again, and continued. "*Demanding* £1000. She's dealing with proper hard lads, here. We don't ask nicely, now, do we?"

Chick chuckled near the door. "Nah, or *she'll* get the next pasting, eh?" He giggled maliciously, rubbing his hands together with glee.

Si snorted on the bed. "Er, remind me, Chick: who exactly *did* get the last pasting, eh?" Drawing his knees up self-consciously and pointing at his mates with his spelky finger, Si cocked one eyebrow and continued. "She has to leave the money in a brown envelope by this time, tomorrow evening, or we'll tell her she'll never see the kid again. Right, lads?"

The other two cackled with delight, sat back and thought about the plan for a minute or two in wonder, until Chick raised his hand.

"What?" demanded Si.

"Well, if we only ask for £1000, that's only....about £300 quid each, isn't it?" Chick told him.

There was a minute's silence, as each of them tried to do the maths in his own head, Si counting on his injured fingers. They all looked at each other, blankly.

"Oh, ha'way, man, I need more than £300 measly quid for what we've been through," complained Baz.

"Aye, that's true," agreed Chick. "I mean, that new game I'm after costs nearly that by itself."

Si was desperately thinking of what the money would buy them each, and he had to agree they were right. "OK then, how much do we demand? £2,000? More?"

Baz sat forward, and the stool he was sitting on made a loud squeaking noise as his trousers strained around his fat thighs.

"Fwoar, man, Baz. Give over," Si told him, reaching out to give him a slap. "I've got to sleep in here, you know."

Chick held his hand over his nose and mumbled something.

"What?" they both demanded in unison.

"Three thousand!" he declared from behind his hand, his eyes bulging.

Baz shook a fist at Chick, who was making noises from behind his hand, wafting the air with the other.

"It was me *trousers,* man, Chick!" he declared. "I wouldn't fart in a mate's bedroom. What do you take me for, some kind of chav? Honestly." Baz was affronted.

The other two pondered this figure for a minute, their eyes searching each other's faces for agreement. Now *that* was enough money for each of them.

Si sat up on his bed. "Three thousand," he mused, dreaming of what a difference the money would make to his life. The friends he could impress, the feisty females who would come flocking to his door…

"Yeah, right," Baz sneered. "Where's that lass going to get that amount of money from, eh?"

"Well, I know for a fact she had a paper round last year," Chick told them, pompously.

Si threw a shoe at him, which bounced off Chick's damaged ear, causing a further outbreak of stifled howling. "I bet her Nan has got money stashed away. And that Dagger always has cash lying around from all the jobs he does for people," he informed the two of them. "But maybe we should give them a bit more time to get it together…" He paused, a worried expression on his face.

Baz stood up defiantly. "I don't believe you two," he said in disgust. "*Where will she get the money from? Shall we give her some more time?*" he mimicked, putting on a girly voice. "Ha'way, man, lads – we're criminal masterminds here, not babysitters! Who cares where she gets the money from, or how long it takes? Just get her telt and let's get some cash and get this over with, before I lose the will to live!"

Si and Chick had the grace to look slightly mollified. Si shuffled off the bed.

"Aye, Baz, you're right. Soon as she gives us the money, we'll let the kid out of the tunnel, and we can go on a spending spree. Let's get to it. Now, who has her mobile number?"

The other two exchanged confused glances.

"What do you want Frank's mobile number for?" Chick asked, puzzled.

Si sighed and threw his head back in mock disgust.

"Ee, come on, man. Keep up at the back, eh? So we can get the ransom demand to her. Right, thicko? Did you think we were just going to roll up and knock on her door, like?"

Baz folded his arms and looked down on little Chick, shaking his head in amazement.

"Just as well one of us has brains, eh, Chick?"

Baz pondered for a minute then his face lit up as he leaned into his friends, his trousers making the ominous squeaking sound again. He raised a warning eyebrow in Chick's direction. "I've got it, lads." He paused for effect. The other two leaned in towards him, expectantly.

Baz puffed himself up on his little stool. "We'll use my mam's old mobile – that way no one will recognise the number. Then, we'll tell Frank to place the money in an envelope, and put it in that burnt out tree, just along the riverside there. Yeah?" His eyes glowed with pride, as he watched for a reaction from his two mates.

They in turn puffed out their cheeks, gave a fist pump and sat back in delight. Si snorted.

"Woah… Baz… what an idea. There's a little hill behind that tree where we can sit and watch, and make sure she comes along by herself." Chick was jiggling on the floor in delight.

"We'll warn her she *has* to come by herself, otherwise the kid won't get released at all. Then when the coast's clear we can nip in, grab the money and get outta there. Oh yes!"

Chick crawled across the floor to give his mate a high five, but on the way he knelt on a broken metal figure that imbedded itself into his knee, causing more howling in horror and much hilarity from his friends. Oh yes, life was looking good, Si thought.

*

Billy had only one thought in his head as he forced his way upwards. He wasn't planning a route, was simply carving a way up the embankment in blind terror. His breath was coming in straggly bursts, his hands were scratched and torn, his knees were bashed and battered, but some deep instinct drove him on. He was sweating yet clammy, dimly aware of the cold mist which was clearing slightly above him. A dark shadow loomed up ahead but this one was tempting him on, not driving him away like the tunnel. In his head the chanting proved a silent mantra, calming him just enough to not slide back down the slippery slope to the river as he focused on the familiar numbers.

"One hundred, fifty-three, seventy, eighteen…"

Again and again, gasping for breath, pushing upwards towards the light. Freedom and safety was up there. Somewhere below him he felt that he was being followed. Not his three tormentors, surely? Glancing behind he could not see them, but he was aware that someone was climbing steadily. He could hear them crashing through the trees and bushes. Billy forged on. He *had* to get up there. Had to.

Dagger and Frank paused for breath and to get a better foothold. He held out a strong hand to pull Frank a little closer, gazing up through the mist to the noises up above. His heart was pounding, not from being out of breath, more from fear at what might happen next. He was terrified for that little lad and what could happen to him in this flight to freedom. He and Frank had both called out to Billy to stop, to wait for them, but it was no good. He didn't think the lad could even hear them. Dagger was frantic now, feeling that Frank was right: Billy was heading up to the viaduct, fifty metres high, straddling the river Wear in its majesty. Please God, he prayed silently: don't let that bairn get close to the edge. Please don't let him jump off in his terror. The fall alone would kill him, never mind hitting the water at that speed. Or worse still, the riverside path underneath. He stretched his long legs out and made a huge effort to gain on the child.

Frank was making good progress but she too was by now in a blind terror. In her mind, she had visions of Billy running to the edge of the towering viaduct and slipping over the side. She was trying to remember if there was a safety rail, but couldn't picture it. She was sure there wasn't one. It was possible to walk across from the Washington side to Penshaw, following the track that trains had used in the past, but most locals treated the viaduct with great respect and never took risks up there. It was simply too high, too terrifying for most people. She'd seen many go up for a look, only to panic and turn back, chickening out. Please, God, she prayed, keep Billy safe up there, just until me and Dagger can get close to him. Please.

Following Dagger's broad shoulders and back, Frank felt they were nearing the top of the viaduct. She hadn't been up there in a long time, but she remembered the top of it quite clearly in her mind – loose shale and stones on the top path over the river, old stone walls and bushes, and just a thin metal rail at the sides. In the past, she'd heard the local stories of drunks who had fallen off, trying to cross the viaduct in the dark, and of course, the sad characters who had used the one hundred and seventy foot high bridge as their final spot on this earth, before dropping into the water below like a stone.

Frank shuddered. She couldn't lose Billy like that.

Her foot suddenly slipped in her hurry to reach the top, and she started sliding back down the embankment. Her mind was in such a jumble that, at first, she didn't even realise what was happening, but as she slid further back on her bottom, she tried grabbing at branches as they whipped her face. Frank became aware of a sharp pain in her ankle as she twisted to try to save herself. Oh no, not now! She came to a sudden stop against the trunk of a tree and gasped as the breath was knocked out of her. Now she was even further behind Billy. She'd never get to him in time!

She sat in a soggy, scraped heap of pain against the tree and sobbed, her head down, trying not to picture what was happening on the top of the viaduct.

Suddenly, a big figure loomed over her and Dagger's rough hands gently guided her up into a standing position. "Are you OK, pet? Have you hurt yourself?" He brushed her hair out of her eyes and looked into her face, concern creasing his brow.

Frank winced as she tried to stand on her left foot, biting her lip in pain, but she was determined. She would *crawl* up that hill to get to Billy, even if her leg was broken! Gritting her teeth, she shook her head, smiled up at Dagger, then taking his hand, the two of them ploughed on. It slowed them a little, but in a minute or two, they reached the summit and fell onto the path which led across the viaduct, over the river. They were in the bushes, pushing them out of their way, when they heard a loud splash from the river below. Stunned, they stopped and gazed at each other in horror.

"Noooo…" wailed Frank, clasping Dagger's hand more tightly.

He in turn closed his eyes for a minute and appeared to be praying silently. When he opened them he leaned closely into Frank, forcing her to gaze deeply into his dark eyes. "Right, Frank, now listen to me."

Frank's own eyes filled with tears and opened wide in horror and despair. She started to tremble. Dagger pulled her closer to him.

"OK, now, it's going to be all right, pet, but I think you should stay here and let me look along the viaduct. Right?"

Parting the last of the bushes, Dagger stepped onto the top of Victoria Viaduct, his legs feeling like jelly, his chest pounding, his eyes misted with worry. Surely, that lad hadn't gone over? He stepped forward and walked on a metre or two to where he felt Billy would have reached the top path.

Behind him, Frank's knees gave out and she sank to the ground, sobbing and clutching her knees. *Please, God, let him find Billy up here, and not floating face down in the river below,* she begged.

Dagger paused for a second, scanning the bridge ahead of him. It was calm and peaceful. The breeze up here was clearing the sea fret, and the air was eerily silent. The trees waved slightly below him, and all around there was the sound of birds. But no sign of Billy. A sob escaped Dagger, as he wiped his bleary eyes. No, no, he can't have gone over. Just then, he heard another splash from down below. Moving forward across the top of the viaduct, Dagger could just make out the dark shape of a figure right at the edge, near the flimsy rail. The figure appeared to be sitting down, with its feet hanging over the edge of the viaduct. Dear God; a hundred and seventy feet in the air, and there was Billy, dangling over the side of this ancient monument. Dagger stopped in his tracks for a split second, then carefully walked forward. He didn't want to scare the lad into falling off the top. He started to whistle nonchalantly, putting his hands into his pockets to stop them from shaking. He was about five metres away, when the lad looked up and spotted him. Then, from behind Dagger, came an anguished scream.

"Billy – No!"

Turning sharply, Dagger spotted Frank lurching along the viaduct path, towards Billy, abject terror on her face. As she approached, Dagger kept half an eye on the boy and reached out to grab the girl as she tried to dash past him to get to her friend.

"Oh no, you don't, Frank," he told her firmly, holding her close to his body. "We don't want to panic him into making any mistakes, do we?"

He glanced over at Billy, who had turned his head towards the noise and who was now watching them with a curiously blank expression. Dagger noticed the boy appeared to be talking to himself. As they watched, Billy picked up a rather large stone from the path and dropped it over the rail, watching intently as it tumbled down to hit the river with a subtle splash. Dagger gave Frank a stern look, made a gesture with his hands to tell her to stay clear, then walked up to stand beside Billy. He admitted to himself that he was actually feeling a bit wobbly after all his exertions and worry.

"Alright, Billy?" he asked, casually, standing as close as he dared without freaking the boy out into any sudden movement. "What you doing up here then?"

Dagger noticed that Billy's legs were, indeed, dangling over the side, but that his arms were resting on the top of the rail that acted as a barrier. The lad stopped mumbling, gulped once or twice, looked up at Penshaw Monument in the distance, then glanced back at Dagger.

"It's not as high as the Monument," he told Dagger in a small voice. "I thought it would be higher. Do you know how high it is?"

Dagger, too, glanced at the Monument, then back at Frank. The girl seemed to be encouraging him to chat to Billy, nodding her head and gesturing down at her friend. Dagger moved closer and sat clumsily down beside the lad, so that his own legs hung out over the river as well.

"Phew, that's better," he breathed, shuffling close so he could grab the boy if he needed to. "I'm a bit puffed out after that climb, Billy. I haven't been up here in years."

Billy gazed up at Dagger, and his face seemed to register a little more of what was going on around him. He peered into Dagger's friendly face.

"I've never been here before," he told the man, sitting beside him now. "But I came up 'cos I thought I would be higher than the Monument. Do you know how high up we are?" Billy looked up the river towards the church steeple in the distance, up at the clouds that were drifting in, and down at the river, which was beginning to reappear, now that the sea fret was blowing away.

Dagger, too, picked up a stone and dropped it over the side, waiting for the splash, before telling Billy, "It's all of one hundred and seventy feet high, Billy. I couldn't tell you what that is in metres, mind."

Frank silently came and sat down on the other side of Billy, so the three of them were close together, three pairs of legs and feet dangling over the side. Glancing at her with a brief smile, Billy turned back to Dagger.

"Fifty two metres," he told him.

Dagger was impressed, smiling at Billy and leaning into him in delight. "By lad, that was quick. I see you're good at maths, then."

Gratified to see the lad's shy smile, Frank asked him, "And do you know how high Penshaw Monument is, Billy?"

Billy looked at it in the distance. "Oh yes, that's easy," he told her, never taking his eyes off it. "It's seventy feet high – that's twenty one metres."

Frank and Dagger exchanged puzzled glances across the top of Billy's head. Dagger cleared his throat. "Now that's pretty impressive, too, Billy. But… do you think we could talk about what drove you up here, in the first place, eh?"

Frank leaned in close to her friend, so that their shoulders were touching. She slipped one arm behind him, giving him a reassuring cuddle.

"We just want to know who did that to you, Billy. Who locked you in…" she faltered, "…down there." She indicated the river path with a tilt of her head, her blue eyes never leaving his pale face. "Please tell us, if you can. We can help."

Billy glanced at both of his friends in turn. This was new to him. *Two* friends who wanted to help, who wanted to make the world a better place for *him* – lonely, little, sad Billy Higson. He was amazed. Taking a further glance at his beloved Monument, he felt he could do it. He *could* tell. Maybe not right now, maybe not today even. But soon, very soon.

Chapter 29

Sue sat at Frank's feet, wrapping a tight bandage on the girl's ankle, as she listened to their tale. They were all gathered in Sue's kitchen, cups of sweet tea were passed around – one laced with a strong whiskey for Dagger, "for the shock" – biscuits issued, and a chewy stick given to Lennie, one of the heroes of the day. Billy sat near her at the table; she kept looking up at him, noting that he was getting a little colour back in his cheeks, finally. When the three of them had come crashing through her door, Sue had nearly fainted in shock at the sight of bedraggled and battered little Billy. Before asking any questions, she had hauled him up to the bathroom to wash some of the blood and muck off him so she could inspect his injuries, carefully. Prising his hair back, she checked his head for bumps and bruises, then concentrated on adding ointment to his grazed hands. She had ordered Dagger to get the kettle on and take a seat, so that she could get to the bottom of this shocking event. She recognised that the three of them seemed to have suffered in some adventure, and she needed to know which one of them was going to get the hairdryer treatment from her first. Sue was shaking in anger as the story unfolded. Each of the three added their own comments and observations, as the tale of terror came out.

"I'm going to kill them!" she declared, her eyes flashing, mirroring the sun sparkling off her earrings, mouth set in a thin angry line. "Why would they do this to Billy? Why? For God's sake, they don't even know him."

Billy sipped from his cup of tea, trying not to let Sue see the effect her anger was having on him. It had been a long time since he's been surrounded by such love and comfort. In fact, he couldn't remember a time when he had faced such compassion and *care*. *Well,* he thought, *just that once… so many years ago.* He wished that he'd had Sue, Dagger and Frank in his life then. He would be a very different boy now, if they had been.

"I didn't even realise that one of the tunnels was so close at hand," Dagger was telling Sue. "I'll have to get on to the council to get it properly sealed up, before someone really does come a cropper in there." The whiskey and the tea were warming him through now, and his hands had stopped shaking, but he still kept them wrapped tightly around his mug. Frank sipped her hot tea, too, her eyes wandering from Billy's face to Dagger's – calming down a bit now – to Sue, crouched at her feet on the floor, getting madder by the minute.

"If we hadn't found Lennie, Billy might still be in there now," she said, gazing fondly at the dog in the corner, scratching himself without a care in the world.

Sue stood up and patted the dog.

"It's true, Sue," Frank added. "He wouldn't leave the embankment, where Billy was locked in. He knew what was wrong and where Billy was."

The dog realised he was being talked about and grinned, wagging his tale and woofing up at the plate of biscuits on the table.

Sue turned suddenly. "Right, I'm going to ring the Police," she declared.

The other three raised their eyebrows at one another, before Dagger reached out a hand to stop her. "Now, hang on a minute, pet." He noticed Billy had gone quite pale and was looking anxious again, all of a sudden.

Sue turned to her neighbour questioningly, then she, too, noticed Billy's reaction.

"I mean, what can the Police do, eh?" he asked gently. "They'll say it was a schoolboy prank and nobody actually got hurt." He raised his hands as if in self-defence, as Sue gestured to Billy's broken finger nails and scratched skin. Dagger nodded at her. "I know, I know, but let's see if we can sort this just between ourselves, eh?"

They all looked at Billy, who swallowed hard and gently nodded back at his friends in agreement. His sense of panic was subsiding somewhat.

Frank faced them all with fierce determination. "Oh. Yes. Please," she declared viciously. "Just let me get my hands on those three losers. I'll make mincemeat of them all."

Sue stood up and went to open a cupboard. Taking out a frying pan, she said, "Right. I know just the thing to take away some of our shock and worry, and give us some brain power to help to formulate a plan of revenge."

Looking from one puzzled face to another, she asked with a smile, "Who wants a bacon sandwich?"

*

Si, Baz and Chick were delighted with their work. The ransom demand – well, *text* – was ready. It had taken six attempts to get the wording right, arguing, as they had been, about how to spell the word ransom, the final amount demanded, the instructions as to where to leave the money, and who would be in charge of picking it up from the dead tree by the river. Si was a bit concerned because the tree where the money would be deposited was fairly close to his house, on his side of the river, but the other two had told him that that was to their advantage: no one would suspect them of being behind it because, as Chick told them pompously, you didn't "defecate on your own doorstep". And no one had ever seen them with that kid, only the stupid dog, and he was a safe bet to keep his mouth shut. And, who knew that one of the old quarry tunnels had opened up, eh? They had sealed that lad in good and proper, so nobody would have a clue where he was. They would all go to retrieve the cash when Frank turned up with the envelope. They would get there early enough, so that they could be well-hidden and nobody would be any the wiser. Ha. Sorted!

"So…" began Si, standing up with his mam's old mobile phone in his hand. "Who's going to press 'enter' and get this sent?"

Baz looked squarely at Chick, daring him to reach out to grab the phone off Si. This little kid was getting a bit too big for his boots. And anyway, Baz was a bit worried about actually pressing the 'enter' key. That made the whole thing seem real to him. Up until then, it had seemed like a lark, a daft laugh. But now, things were hotting up. The law was about to be broken, and for all his swagger and sway, Baz had always been too much of a coward to get into any kind of real bother. Well, his mam would knack him, if she found out he was mixed up in this *espionage*. I mean, his mam had nearly killed him for nicking a bottle of milk off old Tommy Wilson's doorstep some time ago. He'd been grounded for a month! She might only be five feet two wringing wet, his mam, but having brought up three strapping lads by herself, and run three jobs to do it, she was certainly no push-over. Baz was scared of his mam – not that the lads ever knew that, of course.

"No, Si," he said, getting to his feet to stand near his mate. "That privilege is all yours. You're in charge." He glanced down at Chick and gave him a stern look.

Si gave one of his famous gulps, snorted, and sent the text to Frank. Then he quickly dropped the phone onto his bed, as if it was a hot scone, and all three stood around, watching it warily, nervously. Nothing happened. Chick walked carefully towards the bed, eyeing the mobile suspiciously, as if it was a bomb which might go off at any minute. A silence had fallen.

"Maybe she's got her phone on charge," he told the lads, quietly.

"What if she doesn't recognise the number and doesn't read the text?" Baz asked his mates.

Si also looked down at the mobile, peering at it with a nervous twitch. "You did give me the right number, didn't you, Baz?"

Baz was immediately affronted. "Of course, you moron. Maybe you typed it in wrong."

Now Si was upset. "Me? Don't be stupid. I'm not six years old, you know. I know how to type a new number in, you idiot."

Chick took charge. Reaching down, he grabbed the phone, and went back through the contacts list and recently sent texts.

"Right, Baz. Read out that number again. It should end in… 6561," he told Baz, still staring at the tiny screen in his hands.

Baz went back through his own mobile contacts list. He found Frank's number from that embarrassing time he'd invited her to go to the Kite Festival with him. His face burned at the memory. "See, here it is. 6516." He waved his phone at Chick, who gazed down at the old one in his hands.

"No. It's 6561," he told them firmly.

Si reached forward and grabbed the phone out of Chick's hand. "Here, give me that!" he told them, exasperated. Scanning through the numbers, he paused, shook his head and asked, "Right. What text did you finally send?"

The other two looked at their friend's face and reminded him. "You mean, the text *you* sent, Si…"

Si read the message again, then flung the mobile back down on the bed in disgust. "Oh, for crying out loud… I don't believe this!" He began tearing at his hair with his hands, the snorting and gulping going into overdrive. "It's only gone to Father Andrew, at St Michael's Church, hasn't it?" he wailed at them in disbelief.

"You what?" asked Baz, incredulous. "You mean, the text, demanding £3000 in ransom for that shitty little kid has gone to a *Catholic Priest*? The text, telling him to put the money in an old envelope and hide it in the dead tree on the riverside, near the viaduct?"

"Or he'll never see that kid ever again? THAT text?" asked a shocked Chick.

Si slumped onto the bed and groaned. "Oh, my God," he wailed, shaking his head.

Baz came to him in shock, trying to retrieve something out of the situation. "OK, look, we'll text the priest back and say… it was … a school project!" he beamed, trying to lift the gloom which had descended.

Chick was determined to milk the situation for all it was worth. "I mean, really: who has the mobile number of a *Catholic Priest* in their contacts list?" he demanded sarcastically, staring hard at Si. "Was it just underneath *Pope Francis*, like?"

Si blushed. "Well, me mam, of course! It just said 'Fra…' on the list, and I thought… It's her old phone," he tailed off lamely.

Chick grabbed the mobile and quickly resent the message, this time checking against the proper number so that it went to Frank, not the local butcher or the bloke who delivers pies to the shop up the hill. *Honestly*, he thought, *call yourselves Masters of Menace, or what.*

"Right. *Now* it's gone to Frank. Let's just wait and see what happens, shall we? Now, you Si, get back on to that priest and put him off the scent." It felt good to be back in charge again, Chick thought, glaring at the other two.

Si immediately gulped, snorted, and started texting. Baz looked a bit concerned. Si glanced up from his texting, noticed Baz looking uncomfortable and asked, "What now?"

Baz shrugged and started mumbling. "Just doesn't seem right, that's all," he began, shuffling about with his head down.

"What doesn't? Don't tell me you're backing out of the ransom plan?" Si demanded.

Chick's head snapped up. It was *his* master plan, after all.

Baz was bumbling on. "No, I mean, lying to a priest. It just doesn't seem…"

A trainer bounced off his ear, at that point, and Baz wailed in defeat.

*

Back at Sue's, everyone had decided that as no harm had been done, and they'd got Billy back safely, probably the best thing for them all would be to take their minds off the awful event, and the time was just about right to finish off the birds and boats, and get them out on display. This thought cheered them all up. Billy's face actually looked colourful and animated, as he and Frank gently ribbed Dagger about who had the most, and which of the carvings would be the best.

Sue was relieved to see that normal service was being resumed. She was a bit worried about Frank's ankle, and hoped that the excitement and stress of the day wouldn't put her recovery from glandular fever back a bit. As for Billy, well, he was a bit of a dark horse, and she felt sure that he would definitely slide back in the progress he'd made. She would just have to watch out for it starting up in him and do her best to bring him back to normality again. She was placing the cups in the sink, and Dagger was throwing crumbs from the table out of the back door, when Frank's mobile pinged.

Dagger was calling out to someone in the garden. "They're not for you, Fingle Brown, and neither are the birds. Now hop it." Turning back into the bright kitchen, he caught sight of Frank's face. She was staring at her mobile in disbelief. Everyone stood still and looked at her expectantly.

She glanced up at them all. "Oh, you really won't believe this," she stated, her eyes wide. Sue moved to her side: Billy froze.

"It's only a flaming ransom note!"

Dagger gave a wry smile. "A what?" he asked gently, with good humour.

Frank waved the phone around so they could all see. "A ransom text, demanding I put…" She glanced down at the message. "… 'three thousand pounds for the safe return of that scummy kid. Put it in an envelope, and put the envelope in the dead tree, beside the river, near the viaduct. Or else you'll never see that lad again'." She looked at each of her friends in shock, then back at the mobile again. "'And get it there by six pm this evening. Or else'!" she added, her shoulders slumping.

Dagger blew out his cheeks, while Sue started laughing. Billy just stared blankly at them all.

"Did they sign it? Has a name come up with the number?" Sue asked, looking at the phone more closely.

"Just a number, and one I don't recognise," Frank told her.

"Well, we can guess who's behind it then, can't we? Cheeky little gets. I'll three-thousand-quid them!" Dagger was getting angry again, his fists clenching.

Frank shook her head. "The flaming idiots have obviously no idea that we've already got Billy back, then, eh?" she asked, cheerfully. "They must think he's still locked in there."

Sue, Dagger and even Billy smiled then, looking from one face to the other, happily. Frank rubbed her hands together cheerfully.

"Game on, then, I think, yeah? OK, guys. What shall I text back?"

*

All was still silent in Si's bedroom. He was still sprawled on his bed, Baz was squatting on the small stool at the homework table, and Chick was sitting on the floor with his back to the bedroom door. Si was trying to peel the now fairly mucky bandage back, so that he could inspect the spelk in his finger, wincing occasionally as it snagged. Baz was idly scratching at the nettle stings on his leg, while Chick rubbed at his sore ear. Baz suddenly started to whistle tunelessly, but his mates stopped their scratching and peeling and gave him a withering look, so he shut up again, quickly. They all glanced at the mobile, lying silently and sullenly on the bed beside Si, then resumed their introverted inspections. The sun was coming out again, and the gloomy atmosphere in the room was lifting slightly. Baz suddenly stopped scratching, raised his head and glanced around the room. His mates ignored him.

"I spy with my little…" he began, but clamped up as soon as he saw the trainer being picked up by Si, who waved it threateningly in his direction.

"Moron," stated Chick.

"No, I was going to say, 'beginning with P actually'," Baz told him with annoyance.

Si looked hard at him. "I can think of something beginning with P right in front of me," he told Baz, arching an eyebrow. Just then the mobile on the bed pinged into life. All three boys jumped, startled, and glanced anxiously at each other.

Chick leapt up. "Get it, then. Answer it!"

For a split second nobody moved, then each boy gave an exasperated sigh and lunged for the mobile on the bed. Si got to it first, the other two fighting each other off, pushing and shoving in the small confines of the bedroom.

"Give over, you two. You're like a couple of kids," he sneered, then stared hard at the phone. Baz jiggled up and down, uncomfortably. Chick giggled nervously.

"Come on, then. Is it her? Is it that Frank?" Chick's eyes widened. "Or is it that priest, Fr. Andrew?"

The other two obviously hadn't thought of that, and eyed Chick back in shocked surprise, glancing at each other first, then back at the phone.

"Open the text, then – find out," Chick urged.

Si pressed a few buttons, and the small screen sprang into life. He stared down at it, concentrating hard, his forehead knitting his brows together, then he looked up at the boys and blew his cheeks out in surprise. His eyes were wide, his mouth hanging open.

"What?" Baz demanded. "Is it her?"

Si closed his eyes for a second or two, adding to the drama of the situation, and thrilling at being in control of this momentous occasion. "It is, lads. *And…*" He paused for effect. The other two leaned in towards him, eyes and mouths gaping. "…They've only gone and gone for it!" he told them, triumphantly.

Baz and Chick stared first at Si, then at each other, then back at Si, who snorted in delight, before the three of them started leaping about the bedroom, screaming, belly-bumping each other, crashing into the fixtures and fittings, and giving each other high fives.

When they had all calmed down a bit, Baz grabbed the phone to inspect the text message.

Chick jiggled and giggled in delight, his fluffy yellow hair flopping about. "Read it out, Baz, quick, come on!" he squealed.

Baz took a second to scroll through the message, his mouth forming the words as he read it silently to himself first, then he sat on the small stool and coughed to clear his throat. He, too, was making the most of the drama of this moment.

"Right. It says, 'After some careful consideration, I have decided to agree to your demands, so that my best friend Billy is returned to me unharmed. I will put the money in the tree as you asked. But I warn you, if I don't get that boy back in one piece, you and your friends will suffer the consequences. Your lives will never be the same again'."

Baz glanced up at the other two. Si puffed out his cheeks and sat back on the bed heavily.

"She sounds a bit cheesed off, doesn't she?" he asked quietly.

Baz shuffled on his stool. "What do you think she means by that?" He looked worried now. Were all his fears coming true, about the law being broken?

Chick started jumping around again. "Give over, you absolute *girls*," he shouted. "This time tomorrow, we'll be rich. RICH! Now, come on, start planning."

*

Billy and Frank were, by now, in Frank's shed, sorting out the best birds for display. One or two needed some tiny details added, the odd bit of paint or varnish, but they were satisfied that the final selection of eight was more than enough to get started. They worked together companionably, laughing at the ransom note, planning ahead, busy with their respective tasks. After they left Sue's kitchen over the river, they had all piled into Dagger's shed, and he very gamely showed them some of his carved boats. Billy had marvelled at them, at their detail and craftsmanship, admiring the names Dagger had painted on, like Sygna, Daydawn, Happy Dragon. Dagger had explained that these were the names of ships built in the A&P yards on the Wear in times past, that they were part of a rich history of the life of the river and the city, and should be kept forever as a memorial to all who worked and sailed on them. Sue, Frank and Billy were actually in awe of what Dagger had produced. Really, there *was* no competition: he would win, hands down. Yet, they were happy with their birds and were starting to get excited at the prospect of displaying them.

"I tell you what, Dagger," Frank began. "I'm glad my birds are across the water and not next to your boats. These are amazing!"

She was quite stunned by her friend's creativity and skill. Dagger was positively glowing, relishing the warmth and affection, looking forward to getting them out on display now. Together, they had decided that they would place the carvings in the trees, just high enough so that passers-by on the river path could see them, but slightly too high to be touched or damaged. They would space them about fifty metres apart so that the trail didn't stretch too far along the riverside. Sue had said that she would print and laminate some notices so that visitors could see what the little display was all about, giving some of the history of the boats and some background detail on the sort of birds that use the river and which were in the trail. All four of them were so buoyed up and keen to get started that the memory of Billy being locked in the tunnel began to fade. But not fade so far away that it was erased from memory. They had a plan. Oh yes, they had a plan for those boys.

Chapter 30

Billy and Frank sat in her shed, sorting and completing the final flock of birds which would go on display along her side of the riverside walk. The sun was shining again, there was that heavenly music playing quietly somewhere in the background, the tide was out, and bees buzzed happily in the lavender under the window. Billy gave a little sigh, then paused and turned the carved wooden shelduck he was polishing. Frank glanced at him, but continued adding flecks of gold paint to the eye of the blue tit she was completing. She smiled to herself, watching her friend as he became more relaxed into the job with every dab of polish. Billy's face had settled, the frown lines had disappeared, his colour had come back, and his whole countenance had lifted with every detail he added to the birds. Frank felt that with each bird he attended to, a little bit more of Billy was being released from the prison he held inside himself. She had a sudden instinctive feeling that if Billy had arrived just a few weeks earlier than he did, and had become involved in the carving and creating of the wooden birds, somehow, he would have healed a little quicker. She smiled quietly at him, watching his tongue poke out as he concentrated hard. He was lost in the moment, in the job, and he was happy.

Billy finished his bird and sat back, watching Frank working for a minute. He watched the way she held the brush and made delicate little dabs of paint into the speckled eye of the bird in front of her, just as he had shown her to do. He watched her perfect rosebud lips twisting slightly as she turned the bird to have a closer look. Her dark curly hair flopped forward, once or twice, and she flicked it back out of the way with a toss of her head, her blue eyes flashing in annoyance at the interruption. She was tanned and lithe: no one would know she had been so poorly, but at least she had company now, and she was getting stronger by the day. His heart swelled with something, just sitting there close to her, his friend. Was it pride? Or something else? Billy couldn't tell. He just knew that, for once, for the first time in a long time, he felt happy, safe and fulfilled. He didn't want that feeling to ever fly away and leave him again.

"Frank, can I use your loo, please?" He put his polishing cloth down and sat back waiting for her answer.

"'Course you can, Billy. Up the stairs and along the landing."

She didn't even look up from her job, just carried on with the great focus he'd come to expect from her. Billy got up, walked past her and somehow resisted the temptation to give her soft curly hair an affectionate rub. What an idiot he was turning into! He went through the kitchen and walked up the stairs, much wider than Sue's and with ornate carved rails. Frank's house was bigger generally, with lots more windows and a large wide landing.

At the top, he paused: the landing led off in two directions. Which way would he go? The music was swelling much louder up here. He could almost see the notes floating up in the air in front of his face. Billy walked along the landing to his left. He stopped outside a door, which was slightly open. He felt that the room was almost vibrating with the wonderful sound. Putting a hand on the door to test his theory, Billy was slightly startled when the door swung open a little. He stepped back in awe and embarrassment. There, in the room in front of him, was Essie Bailey, sitting at a large piano and playing away, with her eyes closed. Billy watched her, entranced. Her large pale hands flew across the keys, her feet pushed at peddles at the base, and her whole body looked relaxed, yet very much in control, as she swayed slightly to the music. Her eyes remained closed for a few more moments and her face had a beatific expression. Her hair swung loose down her back, and she was obviously in heaven.

Suddenly, Essie's eyes flew open to see Billy standing entranced at her door, watching her closely. Without missing a beat, she smiled and winked at him, nodding at the boy to come in and sit awhile. Billy slowly drifted forward, into the room. He felt as if he was moving under water, floating along in a big glassy bubble. The music swelled and swayed, rolling and booming like waves on a beach one minute, then trickling quieter like the river, slipping over stones, in the next moment. Without even realising what he was doing, Billy sat down softly on a stool and watched until Essie brought the piece to an end. She closed her eyes and stilled her hands, waiting until the very last note echoed out of the room and along the landing. Billy's mouth was open, his eyes wide. He almost expected the final note to be found floating somewhere in front of his face. Strangely, he felt like crying. Essie opened her own eyes, closed the lid of the piano and turned towards Billy with a smile on her face.

"I didn't know…" Billy began, shaking his head at her, but with large eyes which never left her face. "I didn't know it was you. I thought it was…"

Essie's face broke into a bigger, softer smile. The music had had an amazing effect on her, too, it seemed. Billy was used to her yelling at Dagger, at Frank, busying about all the time with washing baskets, or carrying shopping into the house, flapping dusters or washing windows. He had never seen her so composed, so quiet, so content. It was as if she had a golden aura all around her. She was sitting near the window, overlooking the river, and dappled sunlight shone in, making her glow.

"Did you think it was a record, Billy?" she asked softly.

Now it was Billy's turn to smile. His eyes seemed to come back into focus as he told her, "No. I thought it was angel music. Honest. I didn't know you could do that."

Essie put back her head and laughed, sweetly. "Angel music, Billy? Bless you. Well, I never."

Billy, still sitting on the stool near her feet, his hands clasped in front of him, continued – he wasn't embarrassed: he needed her to know. "You know, I've come here, to the river, to this lovely place, where the people just accept me for what I am. It's been…" he paused, thinking deeply. "It's been…wonderful. I think you've all saved my life. And when I heard the music, sometimes in Sue's garden even, I really thought it had come from angels. I don't really believe in angels, but Frank said…" he paused, putting one hand into his pocket. Yes, the feather was still there. It would always be with him, from now on.

Suddenly, a voice spoke in the doorway. "Frank said he'd had a visit when he found the feather on the bridge. See, Billy, I told you angels were true." Frank came into the room and budged Billy along the footstool, so she could sit beside him. She looked deeply into his eyes and nodded towards her grandmother. "It was angel music, Billy. An angel was playing it. My Nan." She grinned at the two of them.

Essie stood up and arched her back, glancing out of the window to the river at the foot of her gate. "And when the air is still, the sound does float right across the water, Billy. I sometimes think they can hear me right up the top of Worm Hill."

Billy stood up, too. "You're so good at it," he said. "What was that you were playing?"

Frank joined him and lifted the piano lid, tinkering with some of the notes. Essie opened the window, took a deep breath and turned to tell him. "It's a piece by Debussy, Billy, and it's called La Mer. Which means…" She looked askance at Frank, who stopped tinkering and looked up.

"Which means 'the sea' in French."

Billy smiled brightly.

"It sounded just like water! Can you play as well, Frank?"

Essie snorted.

"Her? I tried to teach her, Billy, but she can't sit still for long enough to learn. But I bet *you* could learn."

She winked at him and began to move towards the bedroom door. Billy's heart swelled with pride.

"And I bet you could teach me," he told her with a grin.

Frank sighed and grabbed him by the arm. "Come on, you, we've got work to do."

She pushed him gently towards the door, winking at her Nan as they went, thinking to herself – *just look at his happy little face. He's positively glowing!*

*

Dagger and Sue had their minds on other things. Dagger's boats were ready because he had built his collection over the years. They were already lined up on the shelf in his workshop. He'd just never thought about putting them on display somewhere: he'd only ever given a couple away. Once to an old friend who was fascinated by the River Wear shipping industry, and once he donated one to the Antiquarians for a talk on the history of the shipyards, but mostly they were just a hobby to him. Kept him out of trouble, Essie Bailey would say. He was so happy that young Francesca had spent some time learning a new skill and showing such an interest in carving, too. He knew she wouldn't go for boats as well – that was his own thing – but she loved her birds and wildlife, so she had accepted the challenge, readily. Kept her off her mobile and games console, too, and gave her a massive sense of satisfaction in creating something out of a block of wood. And she was good. He smiled at the thought of the way she had adopted that little lad Billy, knowing that, although the boy was quiet and had problems, Dagger had never met anyone yet who could resist her charms. He could see that Frank could set Billy free, too, like the birds she carved. Canny bairn.

Sue, sitting opposite him in the woodshed, was busy cutting and sorting paper. She stopped occasionally to check the measurements, making sure each pile was the same size. Her cheeks were still a bit pink, and Dagger knew that, although she chatted amiably as she worked, she was still absolutely livid about what those lads had done to her poor little Billy. She was like a tigress, Dagger thought, protecting one of her own. She'd been ready to go down to Si's house and kick his front door in, almost crying hot tears of anger and frustration, but Dagger had eventually managed to calm her down. Once they had sent Billy and Frank back over the water to sort and finish the collection of birds, she and Dagger had talked calmly and had come up with a plan of sorts, one that didn't involve any violence. He took her mind off her temper by discussing the written explanation she was creating, for the signs to go up with the birds and boats on the riverside walks. Together, they had decided on images, logos and the wording they would add, so that walkers would understand something of the display and know why wooden boats and birds had suddenly appeared in the trees.

"Mind, if I see him, that Si, I'm still going to kick his backside," she grumbled to Dagger, lining the sheets of card up in the guillotine. "And I'll tell Richie to catch his dad in the club at the weekend. He'll sort him out, the ugly little weasel."

Dagger sat back and watched her fondly. She was a local hero, looking after all the little waifs and strays who came her way. So sad and strange that she'd never had her own, though. She'd have made a smashing mam.

"Oh, I have a feeling that it'll all get sorted out soon enough. Remember, they don't know we've got Billy back. I can't wait to see their faces, when they see him behind us this evening. Should be a laugh. Make sure you have a camera ready."

He stood up to go into the house.

"Right, that looks about ready to me, Sue. I've got a nice, big old brown envelope and some string somewhere, just to make it look the part."

He ambled off across the yard, shooing Dolly out of the way and talking cheerfully to Lennie, who was sitting by his back door.

Sue smiled to herself. Yes, it would be fun to see their faces and hear their explanations… But she was still going to kick their arses.

*

"Shall we go incognito?" asked Chick.

Baz looked at him as if he was mad, shrugging his shoulders in disbelief. "No, we're not going anywhere other than the dead tree by the river, at six o'clock tonight, idiot. Have you forgotten or what?"

Si snorted, gave him a withering look, implying that Chick was the thick one.

Chick shook his head. "No, I meant… Oh, never mind. Are we going in disguise, then?"

The other two then had the grace to look surprised. They obviously thought they were just going to roll up, collect the cash and head to town to start spending. It really wouldn't be as easy as that, Chick knew. Honestly, he should be the leader of this motley crew. Baz stared at Chick in a very unnerving way, his lower lip hanging down like an ape.

"What are you saying, Chick? That they might catch us and lock us up if they see who we are?"

Si was rocking back and forward on his heels, snorting and swallowing in disdain. "Nah, we'll be well-hidden man, *and* they didn't have our names or numbers because we used me mam's old mobile phone. They won't know it's us. Will they?" he asked, hesitantly. He obviously hadn't thought it through properly. The three boys looked anxiously from one to the other, puzzlement with a hint of fear showing on their faces.

After a moment or two of silent thought, Baz lifted up a finger, his face brightening. "Actually…" he began. Baz liked the word 'actually'; he thought it added a certain gravitas to any situation. And this one needed an 'actually'. The other two looked at him expectantly. "We could all swap clothes." He smiled encouragingly at his mates. "That would confuse anyone who spotted us."

Only their eyes moved, silently measuring each other up and down, noting the height difference of Si, at nearly six feet tall and wafer thin, Baz who was shaped like a dumpling – even his feet were fat – and little Chick, all five feet of him, and sinewy as a snake.

"Nah." Si shook his head.

"Thickwit." Chick was withering.

Si held up his spelky finger. "We could all wear hats, though. That might put people off the scent. Have you got a hat, Chick?"

Chick was instantly affronted. "Why do you ask me first, like? What is it about me that says I need a hat first?"

His mates looked at Chick's fluffy yellow hair, moving softly in the breeze, and stifled a giggle. Baz nearly felt sorry for him.

"Actually, I think it's not a bad idea. I bet we've all got a hat somewhere at home. Yeah?" he asked, brightly.

The three of them nodded in agreement, thinking about an assortment of headwear to put on for this momentous occasion – the collecting of their hard-won ransom money.

Si was back in charge. "Right, lads, hats it is. Nothing too flashy, mind, so you don't stand out in a crowd. Maybe something we can bin straight after we've collected the cash. Agreed?"

The boys gave a group high five, Si wincing as he bashed his bad finger, but boy, was it going to be worth it. Roll on six o'clock tonight!

*

"So, we're agreed on the final flock, are we, Billy?"

Frank had lined up the birds on the wall in the back garden. She and Billy had stood back silently for a minute or two, staring, examining them, casting a critical eye over the collection. The carved birds sat underneath the overhanging blackthorn bush, lightly oiled and polished, glowing in the dappled sunlight. Frank's arms were folded across her chest; Billy was standing squarely, his hands on his hips. Neither spoke for a moment or two. Above them, real birds chattered and skipped about in the trees.

Billy puffed out his cheeks, blowing air out slowly, as he turned to look at Frank. "They're absolutely amazing, Frank," he told her quietly. "You should be so proud of them."

Frank glanced sharply at him. "Me?"

"Yes, you," Billy confirmed. "You made these. You started them long before I got here."

He smiled at her warmly, but Frank continued, moving to his side. "But you showed me how to finish them off and bring them to life, Billy. I mean, just look at their eyes now."

She picked up one bird, a brightly painted kingfisher, turning its face towards her friend. "I actually expect this one to fly away any minute," she told him, proudly. "I couldn't have done it without you, Billy."

Billy's face was glowing. Frank noticed that the earlier shock had left him – he was so absorbed in his work with the birds and their quest to display them – and he seemed older, somehow, calmer, less likely to fly off himself now.

He lifted his large grey eyes to her blue ones and asked, "So, when are we going to get them up into the trees?"

Frank thought for a minute. She led Billy through the house to the front garden and, together, they stood at her gate, watching the tide trickling out towards the sea. She gazed up at the bridge first, then to the trees, and finally, back to Billy. She had decided. "Right, Billy. Tomorrow morning. Yes?"

Billy also gazed at the water: funny how it didn't bother him anymore. In fact, it was soothing and calming to him now, he realised with a small shock. He looked across the water to where he knew Penshaw Monument stood on its hill behind the trees. He closed his eyes for a moment, letting the sun play across his face. Frank watched him and instinctively knew where his mind had taken him. After a second or two, he turned to his friend and flashed a smile.

"Tomorrow, yes. Let's get started. Let's do it."

Frank frowned briefly, telling Billy, "But, of course, tonight we have to sort out those morons from down the river. We'll deal with them first, then, when that's out of the way, you and me can get busy with the birds. But I want you to promise me something, Billy."

Frank turned her crystal blue eyes on him, shielding them from the sun with her hand. Billy nodded at her, and Frank took a deep breath. "Will you come up to the top of Penshaw Monument with me, Billy, just as soon as we've put the birds on display? Will you do that? Just you and me?"

Billy closed his eyes for a moment, breathing calmly and deeply. Frank was just beginning to think she'd gone too far with her request, when he opened his eyes and turned to her.

"Yes, Frank. I'll do that for you. I'll come to the top of the Monument."

Frank put one arm around her friend's shoulders and hugged him warmly.

"Brilliant, Billy. That's a date." She grinned at him.

*

As they left Si's front gate, the adrenalin was surging through the three teenagers. Si's snorting had gone into overdrive, Chick was bouncing about on the balls of his feet like an untrained puppy, and Baz had gone peculiarly quiet, muttering and mumbling to himself, and shaking with nerves. It was only five o'clock, but the boys wanted to get into position in plenty of time, just in case Frank also had ideas about beating them to it to the tree, or worse, bringing a posse with her to lead an attack to scupper their plans. It was a beautiful, still evening. The sun still shone, bees buzzed about the bushes, growing by the river, and very few people were out and about on the riverside. The tide had come back in, and the water ran deep and still, only the odd heron screeching at them from the reeds on the opposite bank. Si was wearing a too-big baseball cap, which sort of sat on the top of his ears, making them stick out at a funny angle to his head. It flopped down over the front of his forehead, though, hiding a lot of his face and eyes. He couldn't really see through it and his fringe, so he believed he was safe from closer inspection. Chick had found a multi-coloured rasta hat, made of thick wool, occasionally adorned with cannabis leaves knitted into the pattern. He'd nicked it off his big brother, who had hidden it from their mam, at the back of his wardrobe. It sat squarely over his bright blond hair, hiding it completely. Baz was wearing a very plain, black woollen hat, folded up over his forehead.

Si gazed at Chick's multi-coloured adornment, warily. "Err, it's not exactly subtle, Chick, is it? I mean, you don't exactly blend into the bushes, do you?"

Chick was ready for them. "Ah, but…" he began. "Has anyone ever seen me wearing this before? *And*, will they ever see this hat again, lads? NO, I tell you. 'Cos as soon as we've got the money, this hat is going in the river."

Baz, in his very boring black beanie, nodded in appreciation. "Good idea that, Chick. This time tomorrow that hat will be in Belgium."

His two mates looked at him and shook their heads. Chick opened his mouth.

"Do you not mean…" he began, but Si silenced him by raising a hand and giving Chick a stern look.

"Just leave it, Chick," he said, shaking his head. "Baz was chucked out of Geography when we did the British Isles. Come on, let's get a move on. We need to get into position and get settled in quickly and quietly."

Together, they started walking west along the river bank, towards the dead tree, about half a mile away. The nerves were getting to Chick now as well. For some reason, they were walking in single file, with Chick in his usual position at the back. He noticed that each of the other two had developed a curious gait, their knees bent, heads down, shoulders up. He tried to do the same but stumbled into Baz's bulky backside. Baz, in turn, paused, tutted loudly, gave Chick a withering look, then continued moving forward. After a minute, Chick was overcome with the urge to start whistling. At the front, Si stopped in his tracks, causing the other two to bump into the back of him.

"If that's the *Mission Impossible* theme tune, I'm gonna knack you, Chick. Give over, man – we're supposed to be quiet, you know."

Chick stopped whistling, coughed once or twice, and fell back into step behind his mates. In no time at all, they reached the dead tree.

This stretch of the riverbank was fairly secluded: there were no buildings and not even much of a man-made path. It was deeply overgrown around the tree, which stood back from the footpath on a small hillock, surrounded by spiky brambles and blackthorn bushes. The tree itself was ancient and crumbling, though it was well anchored into the ground. At the front of the gnarled old trunk, within the deeply grooved bark, there was a deep recess. In the past, somebody had lit a match and thrown it in, leaving behind a black cavernous mouth, gaping towards the river. At night, owls sat in its branches, spiders made massive webs in it, and a whole world of wildlife lived among the twisted, snaking, bare branches. Surrounded as it was by towering, healthy trees, the dead tree lurked malevolently in the shadows, seeming to glare down on innocent passers-by with an open, screaming mouth. Stopping in front of it, the three boys glanced furtively up and down the path, then as the coast seemed clear they dived through the undergrowth to get into a huddle behind the broad trunk.

It was a bit of a squash. Si, being tall and thin, and the leader of the pack, got into position right in the middle of the trunk, quite hidden from the front. Chick, being small and wiry, managed to slot alongside him, but Baz, being built like a bear, was edged out to one side. Si turned his head to look at the group, giving a quick inspection to make sure all were safely in place. There was money riding on this, after all. He sighed deeply.

"Baz, man, I can see your fat backside sticking out. Breathe in, can't you?" He hissed at his mate in an exaggerated stage whisper.

Baz was immediately affronted. "It's him, Chick, taking up all the space." Baz shoved Chick to the side with a shoulder barge, sending Chick and Si sliding out of the other side of the trunk into full view.

"Oy! Give over, will you!"

Si was getting angry. "Look, shove up together and be quick about it. Frank might be along here any minute with our money, and if she sees your fat arse hanging out, she'll be away and we'll end up skint." He snorted and glared at the other two.

They dutifully got back behind the trunk, although they couldn't resist the odd push and shove at each other. For a few moments, all was silent as the three of them huddled in the shadows, listening to the sounds of nature all around. Only their eyes moved; they even tried to breathe silently, staying as still as they could. Si tried to calm his nerves by focusing on a caterpillar being eaten by a legion of ants, while Baz took to counting daisies in the grass around them. But Chick was jiggling about, wiggling his shoulders and hips.

Si gave him a dig. "Chick, man, what's the matter? Have you got ants in your pants, or summat?" He looked down fiercely at his mate.

Chick looked up at the other two. "I need a wee, now," he told them quietly. They both exhaled noisily, blowing out their cheeks in exasperation.

"No, you don't," Baz told him firmly. "It's just nerves, that's all."

Chick was just about to reply, when Si grabbed him by the face, clamping a large sweaty hand over his mouth. Baz looked at him in surprise as Si nodded silently in the direction of the path.

"Sshhh. Someone's coming. Get ready," he mouthed, pulling his cap further down over his face.

They froze. Someone was, indeed, coming along the river path from the direction of the bridge, and that someone stopped right in front of the dead tree. Each boy held his breath, pulling their headgear further down over their face, trying to sneak a look at the feet they could see that had paused in front of the tree. Female feet. There was the sound of huffing and puffing coming from the front of the trunk. Chick gazed up at Baz to find himself confronted by a head hidden in a full face balaclava. Only a pair of slitty eyes glinted back at him, with just a gash of a cruel mouth. Having only seen Baz wearing a black beanie, the shock was too much for Chick. He screamed like a girl and jumped sideways to avoid this monstrous creature. All three boys then rolled out from behind the tree in shock, sliding down onto the path to land wheezing, right at the feet of the startled female. She, in turn, shrieked in alarm, then swung a mighty left hook, which landed right on the side of Baz's head.

"Baz – what the bloody hell are you doing behind there?!"

The three boys leapt to their feet, shaking and shocked.

"Mam!" shouted Baz from behind his balaclava. Chick fell over the two shopping bags she had placed at her feet whilst she stopped to catch her breath. Si grabbed a tin of baked beans, just before it rolled off the path into the river.

"You flaming idiots," she muttered, grabbing the tin from Si's hands, ungraciously. "You nearly gave me a heart attack. What do you think you're playing at?" she demanded.

The boys glared at each other, Si casting a furtive glance at his watch.

"We're just playing, Mrs O'Hara," Chick announced, eyes darting to his friends. "Sorry, we thought you were …"

"…Danny."

"…Jacob."

"…Kieron," they all announced in unison, giving each other a sharp dig in the ribs and glaring at each other for giving the wrong names.

Mrs O'Hara was unimpressed. Pulling the balaclava from her son's fat face, she gave him a quick crack over the top of his head, grabbed her shopping bags and marched on her way, muttering back over her shoulder.

"I want you in for your tea at seven o'clock, mind, our Barry. Right?"

Si and Chick snorted and smirked.

"Yes, Mam," answered Baz, twisting the balaclava in his hands. Together, the three boys watched her round the bend on the river bank, then Si shoved them all back behind the tree.

"Get in there quick and not another sound!" he demanded. "It's twenty to six now. Frank could be here any flamin' minute."

With much shoving, pushing and silent recrimination, the three of them took up their positions and prepared to earn their fortunes.

Chapter 31

For once in her life, Frank was actually feeling rather nervous. Angry as she still was at the three dimwits who had locked her best little buddy in that terrifying tunnel, some of her seething indignation had simmered down, leaving her feeling quietly determined to get her own back on them. Billy watched her pacing up and down, furtively checking the time on her mobile every thirty seconds or so. He sat at her Nan's kitchen table, hands clasped nervously in front of himself. He, too, had the collywobbles and had already run up to the bathroom a couple of times in the last fifteen minutes. He looked closely at Frank's face: her eyes looked dark and dangerous in the subdued light of the evening kitchen. He thought she looked older, taller and slimmer than she had that lunchtime, when they had been sitting quietly and peacefully together, finishing off the birds. Despite her light tan, her face seemed pale, and her mouth set determinedly. She stopped pacing, picked up a large brown envelope off the table in front of Billy and squared her shoulders, staring defiantly down to him.

"Right, Billy. I think this is time enough."

Billy leaped to his feet and followed her down the passage to the front door.

Turning to him as she opened it, Frank told him firmly, "Now, you stay in here until it's your time, Billy. They mustn't see you. One of them could easily be watching from over the water, in those bushes."

Holding the packet close to her chest, she gave him a smile and a nod, then stepped out onto the path and headed for the gate. Billy reluctantly closed the front door behind her, then ran upstairs as fast as he could. Sneaking into the front bedroom, he crawled up to the window and watched from his knees as Frank disappeared down the path to the left, heading towards the dead tree and his three tormentors.

Billy realised he was shaking with nerves. The memory of what those three had done to him was still in his head, smouldering away, threatening to reignite like a bonfire, causing acrid black smoke to billow out and engulf his little world. To calm himself, he gazed at the river, idling deeply green and glistening near the front gate. A couple of moorhens bobbed past and a seagull swooped low, but other than an old lady walking her dog on the other side, all was peaceful and gentle in the early evening sun. Billy closed his eyes and counted to thirty, then opened them to look again. His breathing was better, less shallow now. He could see Sue's house just over the water and knew that behind it, somewhere up the hill, was his beloved Monument.

The thought of the Monument made his heart skip a beat. He had promised Frank that he would go up to the top with her tomorrow. It made him shake with wonder, just the thought of it, but if he was going to go up with anyone, it would be Frank. After all, she was the one who had opened up his world. All of his new friends down on the riverside had given Billy hope, and something he hadn't felt for years – a sense of purpose and pleasure. Mesmerised by the water, he realised that for a little while now, he had begun to think and respond to it just like a normal boy of his age. His fear had faded, slipped away like the tide. It dawned on him that now he had things to look forward to and targets to try to achieve. Sometimes, now, he realised, he was actually *happy!* And that felt weird, and wonderful. Glancing up across the river, Billy noticed a splash. It was time. Double checking that there wasn't one of the boys watching, he got up, went downstairs, and quietly made his way down to the path.

*

Behind the tree, Si's leg had gone into a painful cramp. He bent down to rub at his calf and bashed heads with Baz, who was squashed in beside him. His still swollen nose ached even more, and tears formed behind his bruised eyes, but Baz and Chick were glaring at him to not make a sound. They had abandoned the headgear and were now desperate for some action and some cash. Where was that girl? Chick exhaled loudly, Baz threw his head back and breathed deeply, and Si snorted, when suddenly they heard a branch snap. All three froze. Si nodded to little Chick on the outside, and he dutifully slid down to the ground to peer out from behind the bushes. He popped straight back up and nodded fiercely at his mates. It was her. This was it.

Only their eyes moved as they held their breath, waiting for the sound of something sliding into the front of the tree trunk. A minute passed. Nothing. A bird suddenly took off from the branches above them, making the three of them jump in shock, but still no sound of movement from the front of the tree.

The tension was too much for Baz. Staring straight into Si's black and blue eyes he mouthed, "Is she there? Has she put the money in?"

In reply Si simply raised his shoulders and looked back questioningly. Now it was Chick's turn to demand answers.

"Has she done it, do you think?" he mimed at his mates. Both simply shrugged.

"Now what?" mimed Baz. Si was just about to mime back, when Frank's voice floated out from the front of the tree.

"I know you three are in there," she stated, clearly and calmly, her voice breaking through the bushes. The boys' eyes darted from one to the other. Si held up a hand to stop the other two from doing anything rash. The voice came again.

"If you want your money, you'd better get out here now, because I'm not putting this much in here and walking off."

Slowly, awkwardly, trying to look both hard and in control, but actually feeling nervous and foolish, the boys edged out from behind the tree. They gathered on the river path in a line in front of Frank. She was standing there, seemingly as mad as hell, holding a large brown envelope tightly against her body, her blue eyes flashing from each of them in turn, a slight sneer on her lips. Baz thought she looked like a warrior princess; Chick thought she looked like she could eat the three of them no problem; and Baz thought she looked like something out of a Hollywood movie. The boys attempted to adopt a classic, careless pose – Chick with one hand on his hip, although one leg twitched with nerves, Baz with his arms folded tightly across his chest, and Si with his hands clenched at his sides like a gunslinger – but they felt they just looked feeble compared to this magnificent creature. For a second or two, nobody spoke. Only their eyes moved as they nervously assessed the situation.

Si snorted and took charge. "OK, you're here. Now hand it over."

He nodded towards the envelope, then, just for effect, spat on the ground at Frank's feet. She wrinkled her nose in disgust. That made her mind up: she would milk this for all it was worth.

"No chance," she told them firmly, glaring back at the three numpties in front of her. "I need proof that Billy is OK first," she told them, stepping backwards on the path a little, as if heading back to her Nan's house.

This freaked Baz out a bit. "Of course he's all right. What do you think we are, like?" he demanded, panicking a little.

Si was in charge here, though. He flashed an angry look at Baz, warning him to shut up and let him take the lead. "That little weasel is quite safe. He can't come to any harm where he is. Isn't that right, lads?"

He cast a quick look at his mates on either side of him. Chick sniggered, and then realised he looked a bit like a girl, holding one hand on his hip like he was doing, so he, too, crossed his arms in front of his chest and swayed back on his heels, smiling broadly. He was enjoying this.

"Yeah," Chick crowed. "That little mole is shut up tight in his hole."

He beamed at his mates, who sniggered back in delight at his feeble pun.

Not to be outdone, Baz joined in as well. "Ha ha – he'll not ferret his way out of there in a hurry."

And the three of them gave each other a high five in triumph. Frank glowered at them, but knew she had to hold her temper and not be tempted to punch them in their stupid, fat mouths. She had to remain calm. She had to play for time. She kept one eye on the river, one ear cocked for tell-tale sounds.

"OK, if that's how you want to play it. You won't be getting any of this, then." Reaching into the envelope, she raised some of the cash and flicked the top notes casually in their direction. Walking backwards, away from the boys, she tantalisingly gave them a sneak preview of the money inside the envelope, flicking and rippling the colourful notes, before stuffing them back into the brown cover. Then she gave them the finger and turned on her heel, making her way back in the direction she had come from. Smirking to herself, she silently counted in her head. One, two, three...

"Right, OK, just stop right there."

Si was looking at the boys with a worried expression. They hadn't bargained on Frank being so cool and in control. They had naively thought she would just hand the money over and they'd be out of there, on their way into Sunderland, to spend it quickly. How dare she put conditions on their hard-won cash? Who did she think she was? Now what? Still walking slowly backwards, Frank turned around.

"Look, just stop. Stand still and let's get this over with, shall we?" Baz was taking charge now. Stupid snot-gobbling Si was going to lose this, if they weren't careful.

Chick was looking nervously about the riverside path. "Guys. What if someone comes? We'll be stuffed, then. We'll get nothing."

Si looked quickly around, assessed the situation and quietly told his little mate, "Right, Chick. Go back there a few metres and whistle if anyone comes." He was back in charge. Stalking towards Frank, he told her menacingly, "That kid is fine. You'll just have to take our word for it, won't you?" Then licking his lips lasciviously, he asked her, "What's he to you, anyway? Are you going to marry that little spelk?"

Chick thought this was hysterical. "Spelk," he interjected, pointing to Si's bandaged hand. Then he saw the glint in his mate's eye and shut up quickly. Baz stepped in, giving Chick a derogatory glance.

"Soon as you hand that money over, you can see your mate. We'll let him go. In fact," he continued with renewed authority, "we'll send Chick, here, to get him. Just so you know there's no funny business going on."

Si thought this was a stroke of genius but wasn't about to show Baz that. Chick, on the other hand, looked vastly worried. He had images of him releasing a screaming Tasmanian devil from a hole in the ground, fists flying, teeth gnashing, and him all by himself. Frank was stalling, playing for time.

"How do I know that he won't just run off to his mammy for his tea?" she asked sarcastically.

"Because he wants his cash. We all do," Baz told her calmly, glancing at each of his friends in turn. They nodded in his direction. Now it was Frank's turn to be worried. She had to play this just right, just as planned. Almost imperceptibly, she kept moving backwards, back towards her Nan's house. Without realising it the boys moved to keep up with her.

"So…" she began. "Do we just hang around here, until Billy turns up in one piece, then? Cos there's no way you three are getting a penny of this money, until I see him with my own eyes."

Si was getting mad now. Who the hell did she think she was, calling the shots and trying to spoil their fun? Chick was still hovering behind him, unsure of whether to run and release the kid. Baz was huffing and puffing angrily at his side, throwing accusing looks in Si's direction as if to say, 'Come on, lad, get a flaming grip here'. And this stupid lass looked like she might just bolt for it any minute with all that cash. Desperation forced him into a decision. Holding up his bandaged hand he called back to Chick, "Right. Enough. Let's do this and do it quickly. Chick, run back to…" he glanced back at his little mate, "… *that place* and get that brat out and here as quick as you can. And make sure you drag him here, if you have to. We'll just wait here. OK?"

All three stared hard at Chick, who gulped loudly, nodded his head, then started stumbling and mumbling on his way round the river bend out of sight. When he was sure he was gone, Si and Baz turned back to Frank, menacingly. They took a step towards her in unison. Frank glowered at them, held forward the envelope, then smiled and stuck it down the front of her T-shirt. She grinned back at them and folded her arms over her chest, standing stock-still, glaring back defiantly. Inwardly Baz groaned: this was just ridiculous. Frank glanced ostentatiously at her watch.

"Shops'll be shutting soon, guys. You'd better hope your mate is a quick runner."

Si was livid. He tried to adopt a casual stance, hands in pockets, scuffing his feet on the dirt track.

"Don't you worry – he'll be here soon enough. We can wait."

His foot, however, gave the game away, twitching as it was. His eyes kept darting about, and watering, so that he had to take his hand out of his pocket to wipe away the treacherous tears, which threatened to show him up. At his side, Baz was desperate for some action. He picked up a stone off the path, walked menacingly towards Frank, then at the last minute, he launched it over her head, above the bushes, past the trees and into the river, where it landed with a splosh. Grinning into her face, she actually flinched, flashing her eyes at him, but stood her ground defiantly.

Minutes passed. The trees swayed and sighed above their heads. A heron croaked and crashed off up river, a fish popped up and plopped down again in the water leaving a circle of ripples behind. Nobody spoke. Time seemed to stand still.

"Where's that flamin' kid, Chick?" Baz demanded after a while. He had started pacing up and down restlessly, eyes scanning the river and the path. Frank watched him under hooded lids, scrutinising his body language. This one was ready to explode at any minute. She had to be careful to not get caught out by him. Si was back in charge, however.

Turning to his angry friend, he told him firmly, "Just calm down, Baz. He'll be here. We just have to be patient and trust in Chick."

Now it was Frank's turn to worry, but she didn't dare pace about, in case the envelope slipped out of her T-shirt. She could feel the sweat trickling down the packet against her skin. She was silently praying that the others were in place.

Another minute passed. Soon it was too much for Baz. "Where is that bloody kid?!" he demanded angrily.

At that minute, there was movement from round the bend. Someone was coming. Si and Baz grinned at each other in delight. There were raised voices coming along the river path and one of them was Chick's. Yes. He's done it. He'd got the kid. Bloody marvellous! Now, for some action. And some cash!

Glaring triumphantly towards Frank, Si moved forward, until Baz's voice stopped him in his tracks.

"Oh for… what the hell…?"

The three of them turned as Chick appeared from round the bend on the path. He was twisting and turning, his feet were barely touching the ground because he was being held in a vice-like grip by the scruff of his neck by the huge and very angry Dagger Dawson. Alongside of Dagger, Sue strode purposefully, eyes ablaze, mouth set. Boy, did they mean action. Baz jumped close to Si, and the two exchanged worried glances. No kid, though.

"Look what we found, Frank!" Dagger declared, flinging Chick forward to his mates with such force that he landed at their feet in a heap. Chick slowly staggered up, rubbing his sore neck. Si shook his head and blew out through his cheeks. Clipping Chick over the back of the head, he told him angrily, "Chick, man, you were supposed to be keeping a watch out. Why didn't you tell us these two were coming?" he hissed.

Chick whimpered back at him, "Because they came out of the flaming river, didn't they. They crept up on me from a bloody boat on the water. S'not my fault."

Frank heaved a sigh of relief and silently thanked God. Help had arrived, but things were not over, yet. Dagger was standing squarely over the three lads. His face was dark with temper and he was just itching for a fight, but he knew he had to take his time. Sue stood to one side, fully prepared to grab the first yob who tried to dash past her. Oh no; they were ready for this: justice would be served, one way or another. Grabbing Baz by the ear, she growled, "Where's Billy?"

Si jumped forward to protect his mate, but Dagger grabbed him in an arm lock, twisting his bandaged spelky hand behind his back, viciously. How he wanted to clatter this kid! Si yelled out in pain.

"He's safe, honest, he's safe. Ow, man, let go, you're hurting me!"

Frank stepped forward now, drawing the envelope out of her T-shirt. "You promised me you'd bring him here. You're not getting this, until I see Billy. Now, for the last time, before I chuck this money in the river, WHERE IS BILLY?"

Chick was bubbling, Si was weeping real tears from his blackened eyes, and Baz was hopping about nervously, from one foot to the other, when behind them they heard a voice.

"Billy's here, actually."

The three boys stared at Billy, uncomprehendingly. Huh? What? How was that kid here? He was supposed to be locked in the tunnel on the other side of the river bank. He was supposed to be a snivelling, snotty wreck. And here he was, as large as life, looking clean, calm and very cheerful under the circumstances.

Billy stood triumphantly in front of them all. Smiling from Frank to Sue, to Dagger, he asked mildly, "Is there a problem, here?"

Si launched a kick at Baz, who in turn clipped Chick across the head, each one responding with an outraged, "Ow!" Then the recriminations started. The peace of the riverside was disturbed by yelling, kicking accusations. The three teenagers rolled around on the ground, kicking, spitting, flinging fists, pulling hair, punching and slapping. Frank, Billy, Dagger and Sue watched in a bemused fashion, as the other three tore into each other like a nest of vipers. After a minute or two, in which time the three on the ground had obviously forgotten all about the money, Dagger stepped forward and took Billy by the shoulder. Smiling warmly at him he gazed down at the lad. "I think our work here is done, don't you, Billy?"

Billy grinned back. Sue walked towards her friends, stepping round the tumbling trio on the ground.

"Anyone fancy an ice cream back at Essie's?" she asked cheerfully as the four of them smirked at the other three, still rolling around in the dust, before moving back to Frank's Nan's house, chatting amiably about what flavour they all would choose. When their voices had disappeared round the bend in the path, the other three stopped fighting and sat up, one by one, arranging torn T-shirts, wiping their faces and licking their bruised knuckles. Suddenly, the light dawned in Si's face.

"The money!" he shouted.

All three leaped to their feet and took off after the other four. Keeping their distance, they watched in disbelief and delight as Frank took the large envelope out of her T-shirt and, with a jovial comment to Billy, she threw it into the bushes next to the river. The boys hesitated, then dived behind a tree. Watching as the others went into Essie Bailey's house, Si turned to his bloodied band of brothers. "Did you see that? They threw it away!" He was completely aghast, shocked to the core.

"Whoa… that's mad, that is," breathed Baz through a thick lip.

Chick wasn't convinced, however. "Summat not right here, lads. I'm not sure…" he began, but Si was already up and on his feet, heading towards the undergrowth with a crouching, lumbering gait.

"Si, wait. Perhaps we should…" Baz called after him in a stage whisper.

The front door to Essie Bailey's house was still open. It could be a trap. Si was determined, however. Still crouching, he hissed back, "You two cowards can stay there if you want," he told them angrily. "But I'm going to get that cash. You saw it. There's real money in there, and it's got my name on it. And…" he hissed at them. "…If I get it, I'm keeping it. All of it!"

Without another word, Si almost crawled to the bushes near the river. He couldn't see the envelope, but he had a good idea of where it had landed. Pushing the long stalks of the plants away, he nosed his way through, seeking the package like a sniffer dog. Behind him, he heard a loud male voice shouting.

"Nooo! Stupid kid. Stand still and don't move. You flamin' idiot, no!"

Si froze and stood up. Were they talking to him? Looking over his shoulder he noticed the other four standing at the Baileys' gate, their mouths open in shock and horror, eyes wide. What now? He glanced at Baz and Chick, who were now also at the gate, looking worriedly in his direction. Dagger Dawson moved forwards, his hands out in front of him, placating Si in the bushes, warning him to put his hands up above his head. What? Was he going to *shoot* him? Si frowned back at the group by the gate. Frank was shaking her head. She cupped her hands round her mouth to call out to him.

"Si, stand still! Don't move. You flaming idiot. You're in the giant hogweed."

It was then that his hands, arms and legs started to blister and burn.

Chapter 32

Overnight, it belted down. Thunder rumbled and tumbled above the close-knit community, the river swelled menacingly, then retreated, lightning flashed and fizzed, trees shook and swayed, and Billy slept right through it, safe in his back room in Sue's house. Sue, worried by Billy's last reaction to a storm, had crept out of her own bed, quietly opened the door to his bedroom and peeped in. In the early morning dawn light, she could see Billy lying flat on his back, head resting comfortably to one side, his mouth slightly open, breathing deeply and peacefully. Smiling gently at his child-like innocence, Sue padded silently back to her own room, flinching as a huge fork of lightning lit up the top landing, then running swiftly to leap into bed beside Richie, as the next thunder clap rolled over the house, shaking it to its roots. Her husband reached out an arm protectively, asking her sleepily as she snuggled deeper, "OK?"

"Sleeping like a baby," she told him, then sighed and tried to go back to sleep.

*

Across the river, Essie Bailey was also disturbed by the storm. She had looked out of her own bedroom window to check on the state of the river Wear. It looked worryingly deep and dangerous, lapping very close to the path and threatening to spill into gates and front gardens. In her lifetime, it had never actually come into the houses, being a tidal stretch, but Essie still worried. A huge flash of lightening lit up the whole scene, leaving her eyes sparking with pinpoints of white light. Crossing herself quickly, and taking a deep breath, she ran around the house, opening windows and taking the phone off the hook. She unplugged the television and stood quaking for a minute in the darkened hallway. She'd heard all the old wives' tales about getting struck by lightning, about it getting into your house down the phone lines or television aerial, and although Frank always laughed at her for it, she wasn't taking any chances. The next rolling thunderbolt sent her whimpering and scurrying back to the safety of her bed, where she dived in and pulled the duvet over her head.

*

Dagger was out in it. He loved a good thunderstorm at the best of times, and although it was nearly three o'clock in the morning, he wanted to check his creatures. He'd pulled on some old trousers and boots, and was out checking the chickens first. The hen house was locked up tight and there were some reassuring clucks and coos coming from inside – nothing too anxious or demented – he was happy to hear. Something was banging away in the garden, though. Moving away from the poultry, he headed towards Dolly's stable. The top half of the stable door had come loose and was swinging wildly in the wind. Dagger peered inside at his beloved donkey. She was at the back of the stable, as far away from the door as possible. Her head swung his way, and she whinnied gently, stamping her small hooves when she heard her master. Dagger spoke softly to her, raindrops dripping from his curls, and switched on a nightlight on the wall near the stable door. As the small light grew, Dolly stopped her agitated shuffling. Dagger firmly shut the top door, double-checking the sliding bolt was in position. He glanced quickly at the deep dark water of the river, noticing that Essie's light was on as well. He smiled, knowing what she would be doing over in her house. What a woman, he thought to himself. Hurrying back into the dry hall, he stopped to speak to Lennie on his bed under the stairs. The dog looked up at him with a worried expression, his tail thumping the ground, his head ducked down.

"It's OK, Len," Dagger told him, stroking the sleek black head. "It'll soon be over. Go to sleep, there's a good lad."

Making his way upstairs, he rubbed at his soaking hair and shoulders with an old towel. He was at his bedroom door and ready for his bed, when he heard the frightened whimper from his dog again. Looking over the top of the bannister Dagger called down to him, "Len, it's all right. It can't hurt you, daft lad. Go to sleep."

The dog huffed softly in reply. Dagger made to get into bed. He had one foot in, but couldn't do it. Going back to the top landing, he called out, "OK, come on, then, if it's the only way either of us will get any sleep tonight."

Before he even had time to pull the bedclothes up, Lennie Catflap was on his bed and curled up in a ball at Dagger's feet, sighing majestically.

*

Sue was in her riverside garden with a cup of coffee, looking for storm damage, the next morning. As far as she could tell, all was fairly normal. The reeds by the river were bent and bashed, a couple of branches had come down, but everything looked brand new and freshly washed in the golden sunlight. The colour of the trees and grass was staggering after the rain, and raindrops glistened from flowers and hedges, turning cobwebs into diamond necklaces. And the smells from the riverside and wet garden were simply magnificent! Inhaling deeply, she closed her eyes, then sipped her coffee, as some of Essie's morning music drifted across the water.

*

Some time later, Frank wandered into her Nan's front bedroom to see how the land lay after the storm. She, too, had slept through it. Billy had texted her to say he'd even had a lie-in and would be over 'in a bit'. This made Frank happy. After the events of the last couple of days, she thought he might have slipped back into his stressed worrying, unable to settle or concentrate on anything. And yet, here he was, sleeping through that huge storm and last evening cheerfully discussing how fate was getting its own back on that stupid Sid-the- not-gobbler for his treatment of the poor lad. They had watched Si being driven off to hospital, wrapped in wet bandages, the blisters swelling up and threatening to burst all over his chest, arms and legs. *What an idiot*, she thought, staring deeply into the thin water, as the river made its way to the sea. Surely, he'd lived here for long enough to have more respect for the dangerous giant hogweed which grew next to the water. She *almost* felt guilty for having thrown the fake money into the plants, but after a moment's thought she shook her head and wised up. Really, she thought: did Si *honestly* believe it had been *real money?* She and Sue had made it and printed it, but she knew it would just be absorbed into the mud by the river, especially after the storm. There'd be none of it left. The blisters, however, would hang around for months… Ouch.

Shutting her Nan's bedroom window, she wandered down to the shed in the backyard. The yard and garden were still quite soggy after the rain. Unlocking the door, she went into the shed and stood for a moment on the threshold, just inhaling the comforting smells of wood, oil and paint. She remembered that she had promised Billy that she would take him up to the top of Penshaw Monument today. She began to feel a bit shaky about the responsibility of the trip; her tummy was fluttering; she wondered if Billy would back out of it at the last minute. Frank knew that in his head, the trip, like the Monument itself, was massive. *It was like a talisman to him*, she thought. She often caught him gazing wistfully up towards it when they were down near the river. She thought back to when Billy had been released from that terrible underground tunnel, how he had rushed up to the top of the viaduct in a dreadful state of blind panic, but when she and Dagger got there, he was sitting quite calmly, breathing in the view of the Monument over the trees. She suspected that was as close as he'd ever come to it lately and couldn't understand his reluctance to climb the hill to the top. I mean, it *was* just a hill after all – a hill with a beautiful, grand monument at the top of it. Wasn't it?

Taking her mobile out, she texted Billy over the water, 'Get up, you – we have things to do today J', then she set to tidying, moving, polishing and sorting all her favourite little carved birds, the ones she and Billy had decided would be going up on display. Today. The thought almost thrilled her! She was really looking forward to actually doing something with them, rather than just have them hanging around in the shed, to grow dust and spider webs.

*

Dagger laid out his assorted boats on the wall in front of him. Standing with his hands on his hips, sleeves rolled up, he had to admit he was proud of them. They had just the right amount of detail, not so much as to be fussy or over-dressed, and each had its own unique character, he liked to think. Very much like the hard men of Sunderland, who had grafted away for years on the banks of the Wear, turning out vessels which ruled the world and took a little bit of their hearts and their pride with each and every sailing. They had carved the very essence of themselves into each gangplank and gunwale, every rowlock and rudder. He wasn't really going into competition with that little lass over the water, with her birds. He was paying homage to his history and that of his beloved river: his heritage. But it had helped Francesca to keep her mind off her illness, and that great little lad Billy had been a bonus, too. Dagger was impressed with the way that lad was coming on. He could now look you in the eye when talking to you, asked questions about Dagger's work and memories, and under Sue and Frank's care, he seemed to be getting there. There was still just the bairn's constant fascination and fear of the Monument to get round. Dagger thought they were getting closer to the truth, though – especially if the news he had heard last night was anything to go by. His drinking buddy Bob had come good, ringing Dagger with some very interesting, yet disturbing, information. Now Dagger just had to decide what to do with it, how to handle it for the best, without sending Billy into a tailspin, once again.

*

Frank was growing impatient. Where was Billy? They were going up the Monument today, and what a day it was for it. The views from the top were amazing any day, but now, after the storm, and while the other local teenagers were still at school, it would be perfect up there. She couldn't wait to drag Billy to the top of the hill and show him their kingdom. Imagining the view in her head, she suddenly wondered why she might have to *drag* Billy up Penshaw Monument: she did recognise his reluctance to get too close, despite his obvious longing for the building. He talked about it, she believed he dreamed about it, and she knew he drew it regularly – she'd seen his sketchbook. And yet… Frank had a deep suspicion that Billy might actually be reluctant to face the Monument with her today. But she was determined to try.

Running down to the front gate, she scanned the riverside path to see if her friend was on his way. A friendly cyclist trundled past, giving her a cheery wave as he did so. A local, she thought. They were always nice and had a smile on their faces. Well, really, she mused: who wouldn't have a smile on their face pootling along here in the sunshine? There was no sign of the workmen, just their barriers and some spare equipment standing lopsidedly near the trees at the water's edge. There was also no sign of Billy. Sighing deeply, she returned to the front door to call in to her Nan, telling her she was going out with Billy. Grabbing some cash and her mobile, she turned right at the gate and headed towards the bridge.

Billy was sitting in the back garden, going through his sketchbook. It was quiet, and there was a calmness to the scene that could usually be found just after a storm. Bees buzzed around the lavender, near the back gate, a blackbird sang lustily above his head, and the gentle swish and hum of Sue's washing machine almost lulled him into a trance. Billy turned the pages in a dream-like state. He wasn't really that keen on his earlier sketches: they had a hard-edged darkness to them, an anger which Billy felt in the pit of his stomach. He found the one of the army backpack with the boots standing by. It was good – but that was not the reason it took his breath away. The little details were almost painful to him now: the scuffed boots, which had always been polished to within an inch of their life; the faded straps; the pocket, bulging at one side of the Bergen. Billy touched the pocket on the paper, imagining the items that were stuffed carelessly in there, anything from a baccy tin, a tiny jar of fiery Jack, to a crumpled handkerchief. The sob instantly rose in his throat. Turning the page quickly and rubbing at his eyes, Billy soon came to the drawing of the Herring Gull with the crisp packet. He smiled at this one, remembering how the same gull used to come and land on the same spot on the school roof every day, just waiting for scraps from lunchtime. Billy had got as close to it as he could, so that he could study its magnificence in detail. And the huge bird was cheeky and confident enough to let him, especially since it had come to associate Billy with tasty bits of school flapjack, tossed carelessly closer and closer to the boy's calm and quiet frame. Billy laid his head back against the wall and closed his eyes, trying to stop a flood of memories from sweeping in, flushing everything else out of his head.

The gate creaked. Billy was immersed in both the pleasure and pain of scenes that flashed into his head. Some were tormenting him, teasing him, challenging his reserve, but others were soft, beautiful and calming. Just for a second, he allowed them to trickle in.

"And there he is – sunbathing! I might have known."

Billy opened one eye to squint towards the sun. Frank was standing with her hands on her hips, smiling at him. She was only pretending to be annoyed. Coming to sit beside him on the step, Frank instantly gauged Billy's mood. She felt confusion and a touch of sadness welling from him, as she slumped down beside him.

"Hell of a storm, Billy. Can't believe you slept through it. Did Sue drug you or something?" She laughed, taking the sketchbook from him and idly turning the pages. She laughed at the picture of the gull, commented on one he had started of Worm Hill from Fatfield Bridge, then stopped when she came to one of Penshaw Monument. Billy glanced at it, then turned away. Frank was prepared for some kind of negative response from him. She'd got to know him quite well quite quickly.

"So, Billy. How are you feeling? Are you OK to do this?"

At that point, Sue stuck her head out of the open kitchen door. "Hi, Frank. Do what? What do you two have planned for today?" Sue knew she was going to have to take Billy up to the hospital any day now to visit his mam. She had the feeling that Billy's mind wasn't where it should be, and she was worried herself by Billy's seemingly lack of emotion about his mam. Sue felt that she needed to get the two of them together again very soon, before any damage was done to their relationship.

Frank and Billy jumped up to talk to her, although she did notice that Billy was much slower and less enthusiastic than Frank.

"Me and Billy are going up to the top of the Monument today, Sue. Isn't that right, Billy?"

Frank was bright-eyed and flushed with excitement. Billy, however, looked down at his feet and scuffed them about on the path. He nodded his head, dumbly. Ah, thought Sue. Maybe not… Glancing from Frank's face to Billy's, Sue tried to find a good reason for them to stay and think about this for just a bit longer. The washing machine behind her began that irritating bleeping it does, when the cycle has finished. Holding up a finger, she dashed inside to turn it off, and as she glanced up, she thought the expression on Billy's face was one of blatant fear and pleading. Coming back out, Sue looked directly at the two teenagers.

"I'm not sure that's such a good idea, Frank…" she began. Instantly, Billy raised his large wet grey eyes to her as if in silent relief. It was Frank's turn to protest now.

"No, we'll be fine, won't we, Bill? I mean, he'll have me with him, and it'll be quiet up there, and the sun's shining…"

"And the grass will be soaking wet after the storm, and the place will be a quagmire. You could break you neck going up there today, kids. Well, a leg at least," she suggested firmly, folding her arms. "Look. Why don't you give it one more day? Eh? This sun will dry the hill out and it'll be safer tomorrow. It will still be quiet up there, too. What do you think?"

Frank blew out through her cheeks, glanced at Billy, then back at Sue. She was disappointed, but then she knew, deep down, that Sue was probably right.

Billy finally spoke up. "Yes, tomorrow. We'll go tomorrow. It will be better, then."

Frank gave a frustrated sigh. "Oh, okay, then. So, Billy, now what? We had plans and now we're stuck."

Billy smiled gratefully at Sue, then grabbed Frank by the arm, tugging her towards the back gate.

"We've got all those birds to get up into the trees by the river. If we ever want to beat Dagger at his game, that is. Which one are we putting up first?"

Frank grinned at him in delight. Oh yes, action stations! "The swallow of summer," she told him proudly, heading away from Sue and back towards the bridge. Sue gave Billy a smile of encouragement. Thanks, he mouthed at her shyly.

*

Baz and Chick were on the late bus to school, gazing malevolently into the gurgling brown water of the river Wear, as they crossed Fatfield Bridge. It looked so calm and peaceful, they mused. The water was deep and brown after the heavy rain, a bloke on a bike slowly cycled by, waving at someone he knew, a jogger and his dog ran steadily along the riverside path. A peaceful, almost bucolic scene – although, only Chick knew the meaning of that word. No one could have any idea of the dangers the riverside posed to unsuspecting teenagers, simply out to have a good time and improve themselves. Baz tutted to himself and shook his head. Last night, they had gone to visit Si, after he'd been released from A&E, and had been shocked by the state he was in. OK, he was never the prettiest of specimens, was he, but, strewth… He now looked even more like an elongated gargoyle than ever. Chick sighed loudly alongside of him, also looking down the river path.

"Poor Si." Chick pulled and scratched at his battered ear. He felt huge relief that it hadn't been himself who had waded into the deadly plants to try to retrieve the money that stupid, gormless Frank had thrown in, then immediately felt guilty.

"Aye, poor Si. He looks like he's been boiled in oil, doesn't he?" Baz asked with some awe.

"He does." Chick nodded, opening a packet of cheese and onion crisps – his favourite breakfast. "Or like he joined a leper colony, poor bugger."

"And to think he was worried about having a spelk," Baz agreed, helping himself to a crisp with one huge meaty hand. For some reason, this observation got to them and their shoulders started to shake. After a second, they were both rolling around the back seat of the bus in helpless mirth, gasping for breath, eyes streaming, slapping their thighs in delight. As the bus reached the far side of the bridge, they caught a glimpse of Frank and Billy making their way up from Sue's house. That stopped their hilarity in its tracks. They spun their heads round, eagerly following the younger kids' progress until the bus rounded a corner and they were lost from their sight.

Staring grimly straight ahead, Baz decided, "We've got to put our thinking caps on, Chick, and get those two sorted, once and for all."

Chick stuffed his crisps back into his pocket. "Dead right, mate. We've got to get revenge now, for our mate Si." Baz thumped one large fist into the back of the seat in front of them, causing a small blonde girl with freckles, sitting in front of them, to give them the finger and an angry glare.

"Aye. Business! Poor bugger," he added, swallowing back another giggle.

*

Billy and Frank spent a blissful day together, finishing off the birds, polishing them up with oil, till they glistened and gleamed in the sunshine, just like real birds after a dip in the river or a bird bath. They hunted out the cable ties they would need to secure the birds to the branches, and drilled holes into the base of the small plinths each bird stood on. Dagger was doing something similar with his boats, they knew, and they wanted to get a head start on him. He had teased them earlier that he knew exactly which order he would be positioning his ships in the trees, starting with one of the earlier ones built on the Wear and ending with the last one. Beginning with "Sygna", he had chanted the names at the two youngsters, ending with "Superflex", the last ferry, launched in 1988 when his beloved yard had finally closed its doors and lain silent, a sleeping elderly giant closing its eyes and dying. The kids had seemed puzzled at the mood this brought about in their beautiful, big friend Dagger, but had cheered him up by chanting back at him the names of their birds – Grey wagtail, shelduck, swallow, kingfisher, heron, barn owl, curlew and cormorant. Then they took off, back over to Frank's workshop to get on with their work, a tangible air of excitement shimmering all around them.

They were counting out the cable ties on the table in the workshop, when Essie Bailey popped her head around the door. "Frank, where were you? I was shouting for you. Your dad was on the phone earlier. He wanted to talk to you," There was an element of reproach in her voice. Frank stopped counting and looked up at her Nan, crestfallen.

"Oh, Nan," she began. "I didn't know he was going to call. Is he OK? Do they know when they're coming home? Is he going to ring back?" Her eyes were large and luminous. *She's really upset*, Billy thought, as he watched his friend's shoulders sag.

"He's going to try to ring back later tonight," Essie told her. "It was a bad line, and I couldn't hear him properly. But they're both fine and send their love. You can talk to him and your mam later." Closing the door quietly she returned to the main house.

Frank seemed to have frozen. She had stopped counting and seemed quite distracted, moving her hands from one item to another, absentmindedly. Her mouth was held in a tight, thin line.

"It's OK, Frank," Billy told her. "You'll speak to them later, like your Nan said." He picked up a cloth and started rubbing away at the shelduck, rubbing its eye which shone like a gemstone. Frank slumped down onto a small cracket stool in the corner, her hair falling over her face in dark tumbling curls.

"I know," she mumbled. "It's just... I missed their last call as well, and when I did speak to them about three weeks ago, the line went dead and we were cut off. I miss them so much, you know?"

Billy gazed at her, completely still. She had gone very quiet and subdued. So had he. In the tense silence that followed, Frank raised her eyes and stared at Billy, standing in front of her with his head down, almost manically polishing one of the birds, but totally unaware of where he was or what he was doing. Frank jumped to her feet and went to him.

"God, Billy. I'm *so* sorry," she told him, putting one arm around his shoulder and leaning in towards him. "Here's me going on about missing a phone call from my dad, when you miss yours every day!" She rested her head on top of his in an attempt to console him. She wasn't embarrassed by their physical closeness, she just needed to undo some of the pain she felt she had so clumsily caused. "It must hurt so much," she almost whispered to him.

Billy didn't flinch or pull away from her. He allowed himself to be comforted by Frank, just for a minute. Then he raised his head and stood back from her.

"S'alright, Frank. Honest. You get used to it, in the end. At first, it's like you can't breathe, all day, then the pain comes in crashing waves, then eventually it's like the tide has gone out and there's just this huge empty space left behind. At some point the tide turns, but you're not really aware that it's coming back again. It comes in little waves, trickling in. But I never forget - you can still drown in them."

He gave a huge sigh and sort of shuddered, but quickly he began sorting the cable ties again. Frank exhaled deeply: she had never heard Billy discuss his grief, ever. In fact, she'd never heard Billy string so many sentences together at one time! Ruffling his hair, she told him affectionately, "Ee, Billy. We'll have you spouting forth on Speaker's Corner before long. Well, I never."

Billy laughed gently, and together they worked on through the afternoon.

Chapter 33

B y early evening, in the summer, the riverside had sprung to life. People were out walking their dogs after a hard shift at work, strolling along the river path in dappled shade, sleeves rolled up, jackets casually slung over one shoulder. Little children rode cycles and scooters, racing ahead of parents, stopping occasionally to launch sticks and stones into the water. The odd fisherman lounged on the banks waiting for the tide to come fully back in, lying back on the grassy banks with bottles of water, or beer. Joggers took full advantage of the slightly cooler air and even the cyclists, who raced through in pairs, minded their manners.

Frank had quickly recovered from her disappointment at missing yet another call from her parents. She knew her reaction had caused some pain to Billy and had gone out of her way to take her mind of it. The birds were all arranged and ready, and by about seven pm, when the riverside was settling down for the evening, she and Billy were positively hopping about, desperate to make a start. They had run over to Dagger's yard during one tea break and he had jokingly blocked the door with one big foot, keeping them out and telling them to get a shift on and get some work done over on their own side. They begged and pleaded with him to have a look at his collection, so he had tantalisingly picked up one beautiful carved specimen and waved it at them through the crack in the door.

"H'away, man, Dagger!" Frank teased him. "We need to see more than that. We don't think you're ready to put your collection on display," she told him, grinning at Billy as she spoke.

Billy piped up after her, "We're ready, Dagger. In fact, we're going to go over there now and get our first bird up in the tree. So there!"

Dagger opened the door a few more centimetres and peeped out at them with one crinkly brown eye.

"Get away. You kids don't fool me. You're not ready to start, yet – not tonight at any rate. You're winding me up."

Frank and Billy laughed at him, backing off and waving cheekily at the crack in the workshop door.

"Get your binoculars ready, Dagger," Billy mocked, but kindly.

"He won't need his bins, Billy. He'll see exactly what we're up to. And he can hear every word we say tonight. That is, unless he's still busy carving boats..." she added. "See you soon, Dagger."

And the two of them hurried straight back up the path and over the bridge. Dagger smiled fondly and shook his head. They really were keen, those two. But, he wondered, how were they going to get the birds up into the trees and secure them there?

*

Frank had borrowed a set of extending ladders from one of her neighbours, who trusted her enough to lend her them without asking why she needed them. She was a lovely, sensible girl, and it made the neighbour happy to see her out and about with a friend, when she had been so poorly for the last few months. The ladders would be returned safely. Now she and Billy were gathered by the foot of a tree on the riverside, keeping a close eye out for very rare road traffic or anything which could put them off their task. The swallow lay at their feet in the long grass, eyeing up the daisies, so it seemed. Frank tentatively rested the ladder against a branch then gave it a good tug to make sure it was safely in place.

"OK, Billy. You hold tight onto the base here to keep me steady, then hand the bird up, when I get into position."

Billy put one hand on her strong brown arm, so that Frank took her eyes off the upper branches and looked into his calm grey eyes.

"Actually, Frank, don't you think I should go up first?" he asked, but the question was quite firm. Frank bristled at him, taking one foot off the bottom rung.

"You? Why? Because you're a *boy* and I'm just a *weak little girl*?" she demanded, blue eyes flashing.

Billy wasn't giving in to her. He remained calm and didn't bite back.

"No, because it was *my* idea to make the competition with Dagger and put the birds on display in the first place," he told her with some dignity, standing as tall as he was able to do, and returning her glare. Frank stood down and faced him. She folded her arms across her chest and tilted her head to one side.

"Yes, Billy, but they are *my* birds, and *my* trees, and *my* neighbour's ladders so..." she tailed off, raising her eyebrows at him. Billy was not to be outdone.

"*And*... without my help they would still be just lumps of wood." He quickly realised his error here and rushed on. "Very beautiful bits of carvings, actually, Frank, but I helped you to finish them off and bring them to life. Yes?" He cocked his own head back at her, his eyebrows raised. "And you hurt your ankle the other night, so..."

Frank blew out her cheeks. "Okay: toss you for it. Heads, you go up first, tails I do. Agree?" And she fished in her jeans pocket for a coin.

About one hundred metres away, down the path towards the viaduct, Baz and Chick had spotted Frank and Billy standing in a huddle, near the water's edge. As soon as they had heard Frank's voice, floating on the evening air, they had dived behind a bush – checking its safety first, just in case. They peered through the greenery, ears straining to see what the other two were up to. Baz was the first to speak, whispering to Chick, "Shall we push them in the river?" His eyes flashed at his mate in excitement.

Chick gazed up and down the river, assessing the situation. "Nah, mate, the tide's going out. It's just thick mud."

"That's fine by me!" hissed Baz, rubbing his hands in glee. "Can you see what they're doing, anyway? By the time we get close, they'll have moved on and have left the water, anyway. Let's just watch for a minute."

Crouching behind the bush, they heard the unmistakeable sounds of a ladder going up into a tree, followed by the ring of footsteps ascending, plus animated chatter from both Frank and Billy. One of them was up the tree, doing something. Frank seemed to be on the ground giving instructions. After a few more minutes, during which time Baz got cramp in his left leg and Chick decided he needed a wee, both Frank and Billy appeared to be up the tree. Baz looked quizzically at Chick and they both stood up.

"Right, they're both up there. Let's rush them."

They had just darted out of the bush when a truck trundled towards them on the road, heading for the farm behind them, down the track. They dived back behind the bush again.

"Damn!" Baz stated. "Just as we were getting close to them as well."

Crouching back down, they raised their heads fractionally above the bush, then dropped back again.

"Right, whatever they're up to, they've moved on. They're coming a bit closer now. Shhh."

Baz and Chick listened rather than saw, hearing the sound of the ladder being dropped, then moved, and voices coming closer. Frank was telling Billy that it had been much easier than they had thought, whatever 'it' was, that is. Chick heard, but simply shrugged his shoulders at his mate. Baz mouthed, "eh?" at Chick, and Chick mouthed back, "clueless, mate," and shrugged back at him. But he was beginning to realise that if the pattern were to be repeated, both Frank and Billy would end up in a tree, for some reason, and then he and Baz could get them. He began to grin. "Watch and learn, Glasshopper." He breathed quietly. "Watch and learn."

Over the river, Dagger didn't need to see too much to know that within about fifteen minutes the two youngsters had their first bird in the first tree. He distinctly heard a triumphant "Yes!" followed by delighted giggles across the water. *Well I never,* he thought, shaking his head gently and scanning the bank on the other side. They really did mean business. *Better get my act together.* But his tummy was rumbling, and there were animals to be fed and cleaned out. His first ship would go up in the morning – let the two bairns have all the glory. He just hoped they were safe on that flaming ladder.

*

On the other side of the river, Baz and Chick stayed well-hidden, even when the jogger and his dog ran back on his return journey and the dog stopped for a lengthy sniff at their bush and a wee, just missing Baz's foot. Baz wrinkled his nose in disgust, whilst Chick shook in silent mirth, his blond hair flopping about his face. Once the jogger was on his way, and Frank and Chick were once again behind a tree, Baz cautiously stood up, though he remained at a half crouch.

"Right, Chick. If they go up that tree, we're going to nick their ladder and leg it. OK?"

Chick was delighted, falling into a fit of giggles, instantly. Giving each other a high five, they began to slink out from behind the bush. Just as they did, another van rolled into view, causing them to return to their original positions.

"This is ridiculous!" hissed Baz. "You get no traffic down here for weeks on end, and now it's flamin' rush hour!"

Chick had had an idea, though. Waiting until Frank and Billy were deeply involved in whatever it was they were doing down at the water's edge, he slipped out, ran up the road a short way, and grabbed a barrier that the workmen had left leaning against a wall. Placing it across the road, just out of sight from the tree, he lolloped back to Baz in the bush. Sliding in beside his mate, he glared in triumph.

Baz was impressed. "Whoah, man, Chick. Awesome move, dude."

Chick was thrilled at the recognition. "It even says 'road closed' on it, so we'll be quite safe. No more interruptions. And if a van does come along, it'll have to pull onto the jetty and hang on for a bit. Now, let's just wait for them two to get up that tree."

It didn't take long. If Frank and Billy were aware of Chick moving the barrier onto the road, they didn't register it. Engrossed in their job as they were, they would have simply assumed it was a workman, tidying away. They'd been busy in the street for a couple of weeks, so any sound of equipment being moved meant nothing to them.

For the second tree, Frank was going up first, while Billy held the ladder at the bottom. The first bird, in a large ash tree, looked amazing. It had been a bit fiddly, tying it onto the branch securely, and Frank had insisted in joining Billy on the branch to make sure he'd done the job properly, but they were both delighted with the result. They had climbed down and stood back on the road to make sure they could see the bird – the swallow – sitting on the branch. It was just the right size to catch the eye of passers-by. Now, it was the turn of the beautiful coloured shelduck, and Frank was already on a strong branch, with the bird tucked under one arm. Billy was impressed at her speed of climbing, and her bravery, generally. *She ran up that tree like a squirrel*, he thought, grinning to himself at the bottom.

On the branch, near the water's edge, but not hanging over it, Frank looked over the water towards Dagger's house. The door to his workshop was open, but she couldn't see him. Dolly was grazing by the river, and some hens pecked about. Frank straddled the branch, assessing the best place to secure her bird. She thought back to when she had first started this wood carving, after Dagger had encouraged her. She'd loved doing it, but realised now that, until Billy came along, she'd actually been quite lonely. She turned to say something to Billy and found herself wobbling precariously on the branch, which swayed dangerously. Billy was instantly up the ladder to see that she was okay.

"Phew, watch it, Frank. You nearly came off there!" he gasped, his large eyes alert to the danger.

"Oh, stop fussing, Billy. I'm fine. This is a big, strong tree. Hold that a minute, will you?" She handed him a cable tie and positioned the bird. She felt a bit like a bird herself up there, among the swishing leaves, dappling in the evening sun. Billy stood on a high rung of the ladder at her side, watching carefully.

Suddenly, something flew past their heads. They both glanced up, but thinking it was a bird they had startled, they ignored it and continued on with their job. In a few minutes, Frank had the bird safely tied onto the branch and she called Billy onto it to join her.

"It's great up here, isn't it, Bill?" she sighed and looked around herself from their perch in the sycamore tree. The river was almost out, and there were a few ducks and gulls plodging about in the mud flats, turning over stones, looking for insects at the water's edge. There was a fresh, damp smell. Then, something else whizzed past their heads and landed with a soft splop in the mud, about four feet from the water. Billy and Frank stared at each other and looked down. A large stone hit the tree trunk next to Billy's head.

"What the…?" began Billy, automatically ducking his head.

Frank glanced down over her shoulder. "On no, not you two morons again!" she declared angrily.

Billy followed her line of sight: Fat Baz and his stupid, fluffy little mate Chick were standing on the path, throwing stones at them.

"Can you two get a life and bugger off?" he called down to them, ducking again, as one just missed his ear. The two loonies on the ground simply cackled with glee and chucked a couple more stones – badly, it seems, as they all ended up in the river.

Frank and Billy began to fume at them. How typical of those two idiots to come and spoil their fun on this gorgeous sunny evening, just when the two friends were getting so much pleasure and satisfaction from a job done well. Frank had worked so hard to reach this point, and Billy was livid at the interruption. He was angry that he had nothing to hurl back at them, other than swear words and insults. Just then, one of them – the fat, lumbering one – ran to the base of the tree and took the ladder away.

"Oy, you, Baz!" Frank shouted after him, getting red in the face with frustration. "Bring that back now, you flamin' fool. It's not even mine!"

Baz and Chick stood in the road, each holding one end of the ladder, looking up at the two, stuck in the tree. Chick wiggled his bum at them, and Baz gave them the finger.

Chick started the chant in a cracked sing-song voice, "Frank and Billy sitting in a tree, K I S S I N G…" Then Baz launched into a version of the Birdie Song, clucking and moving his elbows in and out like chicken wings.

Frank wobbled again on her branch in anger and agitation, but Billy reached out and grabbed her. The branch swayed sideways, and Billy began to turn pale in fear. "Frank," he hissed, looking nervously at the branch they were both sitting on. "I think it's going to snap. We have to get down." He began to shuffle back towards the trunk and some other branches.

Frank was still waving her fist down at the two on the road. "I'm gonna knack you two for this, you scummy little weasels…"

Baz and Chick laughed at her, pulling faces and turning round to shake their backsides up at her and Billy, obviously impotent to hurt them, stuck up the tree. Baz was just about to call something up to them, when he glanced down the road towards Frank's house and stopped in his tracks. He grabbed at Chick, and together they launched themselves off the road and into the bushes.

Frank looked at Billy in puzzlement, before they, too, glanced down at the road. They watched in horror and disbelief as about fifteen of the angry cyclists, heads down, visors glaring in the evening sun, legs pedalling like mad, headed straight for the barrier Chick had put across the road.

Frank called out a warning, but it went unheard. At the last minute, the lead cyclist spotted the barrier, too late, and swerved to his right, onto the slipway which led down to the water. All four teenagers watched in horror, as fifteen cyclists and their bikes, worth thousands of pounds, all followed the leader into the river in a splashing, screaming, swearing, tangle of metal, spokes and mud. Some of them sank about half a metre; at least four of them went head first over the handlebars into the stinking green mud; three skidded to a stop and fell off before rolling down to join their teammates in a screaming, slippy scrum. The air turned blue.

Up in the tree, Billy and Frank watched, helpless. It was probably just as well they were stuck up there and couldn't get down to help. Baz and Chick slowly popped their heads out from behind the bush, saw the absolute muddy mayhem they had caused, and quickly turned and legged it up the bank, through the undergrowth, putting as much space between them and the screaming, angry horde as possible. In his shock and dismay, up in the tree, Billy began his old chanting again.

"One hundred, fifty, thirty, eighteen…" His eyes were shut tight, he couldn't look at the anger and despair going on below him, as the cyclists flailed and floundered about in the mud.

Frank glanced at poor, nervously chanting Billy, looked back down at the stinking pile of goo and twisted metal, and began to giggle. It was all just too much for her. She started to laugh properly, out loud, then became breathless in her absolute delight at the scene unfolding in the river. She howled in glee, pointing to the bikers and gasping at Billy, who actually opened his eyes and stopped counting. He wished he hadn't, though. As Billy stared at the scene unfolding in the brown water, the end of the branch where Frank was sitting opposite him swayed out towards the river. Billy grabbed at an upper branch, and Frank stopped laughing just as the branch snapped. Her eyes opened wide in disbelief, then she plummeted down to the ground below, landing just alongside the bikers. Billy heard something snap and crack, and instinctively knew it wasn't another branch.

Chapter 34

The repercussions rippled up and down the riverside community for days afterwards, discussed over garden gates with cups of coffee, frowned about in the pub on the corner. A child had been seriously hurt, not to mention the cost in dignity, fair play and finance to the cyclists, whose most treasured possessions had been virtually destroyed. Equipment belonging to the council had been tampered with, so the workmen were in trouble as well, and a pair of ladders, belonging to a local householder, had been damaged. Luckily, they could be easily repaired. Not so young Francesca Bailey's ankle, which was badly broken. And that little lad, who was staying with Sue and Richie Render, seemed to be suffering from the trauma of it all. He'd gone very quiet, retreating back into his shell, seemingly undoing all the good that his time in the riverside community had done for him. Billy was once again a small, pale, scared child, and that canny lass Sue was beside herself with distress for him.

Sliding a sausage sandwich, oozing tomato sauce, over the table to him, Sue spoke gently to Billy.

"Look, pet, you weren't to blame. You know that, don't you? What you were doing was having a good time, peacefully minding your own business and bringing something lovely to the riverside walk. You weren't to know that those two idiots would cause such trouble."

Billy took the sandwich, but simply played with the corners of it, opening and closing the slices of bread. He still felt sick, and in his head, he could still hear the snap of Frank's ankle bone, hitting the path, and her tears of pain as she gasped in agony afterwards. At first, the cyclists had been too busy trying to get themselves and their expensive machines out of the river mud, but gradually it dawned on them that the girl was hurt, and that it had had nothing to do with her what had happened to them. She'd been up a tree for some reason, and hadn't been involved in what had gone on. The little lad with her was frantic, whilst an ambulance was called, shaking, muttering and mumbling, until some big bloke from over the water came to his rescue.

That was three days ago. Now Billy was trying to get his head and heart round being by himself on the riverside, and it felt strange. His happy little bubble had burst as Frank was driven away in the ambulance. The sun seemed to go in and the light was harsh and unreal; the street seemed to have a hard, threatening edge now and was no longer warm and comforting; even the river was malevolent again. Billy's shoulders slumped, and Sue sensed his despair. She had spoken to Billy's care worker, Paul Costello, but both had agreed that, despite the shock and upset, Billy was still better off in the small community by the river, rather than being moved on yet again to different foster carers. She was hugely relieved about that. Sue knew instinctively that the truth was still to be discovered from Billy, the reason for his fears and torment had yet to come out.

They had been close to finding it out the other night, she felt. Dagger had rung to say he had some news about Billy, and Sue worried at the tone of his voice. However, she felt that Frank was getting closer and closer to the truth. She'd watched the two teenagers going cheerfully about their business of displaying the birds in the trees over the water. She had heard them chatting away cheerfully as they worked, and felt that the girl was doing an excellent job of bringing Billy out into the open about his past life. Sue realised it was risky, the two of them climbing like that, but she also knew you had to allow them to find their own way and learn from any mistakes they might make. No one had understood that those mistakes may end up with a broken ankle, though. In the ambulance, Frank had cried in pain and anguish, more about not being able to go up the Monument with Billy than the physical damage she had experienced.

"So, what shall we do today, Billy?" Sue asked gently. Billy still toyed with his food, avoiding her eyes and shrugging his shoulders. "We could go to the hospital, kill two birds with one stone…?" Billy shook his head quickly and took a gulp of breath. Sue smiled ruefully at him. The lad was obviously blaming himself for the accident, somehow, and couldn't face up to his part in it by visiting Frank. She was determined not to give up: this lad was going to do something constructive today, come hell or high water.

"Well, we could go for a ride out, take our sketch books?" she suggested. At this, Billy looked up at her quickly. Aha, a glimmer of hope there, she realised. Billy sat back then and took a bite out of his sandwich.

"Yeah, that would be good," he told her through a mouthful.

"Brilliant." Sue smiled back at him. "What do you fancy drawing today, then, Billy? We could go down to Durham, if you want."

Billy took another bite. "I fancy trying to draw a building, or a bridge," he mused, relaxing.

Sue stood up, happy that they were planning something to take his mind off his troubles. Putting her own plate in the sink, she told him, "Or, we could go to the beach? There wouldn't be too many people out because…"

Billy had suddenly frozen, large eyes bulging at her. Sue noticed his hands shaking all of a sudden.

"Billy? What is it?"

Billy gulped and stood up to back away from Sue, shaking his head. *The beach?* That must have been the trigger. She felt that the counting would start up at any second. Quickly, she ploughed on, "Okay, *not* the beach, Billy. Let's go down to Durham. We can have a picnic and watch the tourists in the canoes."

Billy's shoulders settled again and the fear left his face. He glanced over her shoulder, out of the window, towards the back garden, staring off into the middle distance.

"Me and Frank were going up the Monument today," he said quietly, with a little gasp. He looked so crestfallen that Sue's heart went out to him. She felt that time stood still in her kitchen for a minute, floating around the two of them like a bubble, which could burst open at any minute.

"Well…" she began tentatively. "We could do that. You and me, Billy. I'd go up with you."

Billy turned his luminous pale eyes to her – in hope or despair, she wondered? Sue rushed on, but gently. The lad obviously was ready to climb that steep hill, and if Frank couldn't be with him as planned, she was the next best person, she decided.

"We could sit and draw at the top, Billy. Or, just sit, maybe talk. I could take a picnic. We could see if Lennie wants to come up with us as well," she added, knowing the comfort the dog provided Billy, now that his only other friend Frank was laid up.

Billy stared wistfully at Sue. He loved what she was trying to do for him, and other than Frank, or maybe Dagger, there was no one else he would trust to go to the top of that hill with him. He really wanted this: he needed it, he knew, deep in his heart. But… could he? Should he? Maybe it was now or never. Lovely Sue, so beautiful and supportive, standing there with her silver feather earrings flashing at him in the sunlight. It was the thought of the feather that spurred him on. He remembered finding it in his pocket; the comfort it brought him inside the tunnel; the way it gave him strength. He gulped and nodded, twisting his fingers.

"Let's do it, Sue. Let's go up the Monument today."

*

Billy found himself moving around Sue's house as if he were in a dream. His movements were slow, deliberate. He found his sketchbook, carefully selected some pencils and crayons, placed them into his backpack with shaking hands. His heart and stomach were fluttering, battering away inside him, like moths at a window. Sue watched him, as she busied herself in the kitchen, putting together a picnic. She glanced at the lad out of the corner of her eye, not distracting him with idle chat, just allowing the idea to settle into him. He was obviously preparing himself for something. She could see his hands shaking slightly, could tell by the way his eyes darted around the room and kept returning to the window, for comfort or confirmation, she wasn't sure. She felt that Billy was holding his breath at times, forgetting to breathe.

The back door opened, and a loud, cheery voice called out.

"Anybody home?" Dagger sang cheerfully. Billy stopped at the sound of his voice and smiled up at Sue. His eyebrows were raised in question.

"In here, Dagger," Sue called to him, perching on the edge of the settee. Dagger's handsome dark head appeared round the kitchen door. He took in the mood in an instant, glancing quickly from Billy to Sue, then stepped into the living room and sat opposite Sue.

"Aha, are you two going off out somewhere, then?" he asked, nodding at the bag in Billy's hands and the picnic items Sue was holding. He thought Billy was looking a little bit shell-shocked, large eyes blinking in his pale face.

"Why don't you tell Dagger what we're going to do today, Billy?" she told him, gently.

Billy gave Dagger a watery smile, hugging his bag closer to himself as if for protection. He gulped a couple of times before answering. Dagger waited patiently, smiling at the lad, understanding how rattled the bairn had been since Frank's accident.

"We're going up the Monument," he told Dagger shyly. "Me and Sue – we're going to climb up to see the Monument."

Dagger raised his eyebrows at the two of them, quizzically. "By, lad, what a day to do that. It'll be just perfect up there today."

Billy opened his mouth to say more, but Dagger cut in, giving Sue a knowing look.

"I wish I could come up with you, but you know what they say – three's a crowd, an' all that." But seeing the lad's disappointment, he carried on. "I'd love to be up there with you two, but I have to go into town. Summat's come up." He looked pointedly at Sue and waved his mobile in her direction. She gave him a comical look, then nodded back at him.

"We wondered if we could take Lennie with us?" she asked Dagger, who grinned back in reply.

"Yeah, 'course you can, pet. He'll love that. He can be my representative, if you like. Seeing as I can't make it," he added. "What time are you planning on going?"

Sue glanced at Billy, then told him. "Well, we're going to walk all the way there, up the hill, have a picnic at the top, then walk all the way back again. So, we'll set off soon."

Dagger appeared to be making some mental calculations, glancing at his watch then up and out into the middle distance. He seemed lost in thought for a minute.

"Right..." he began, then seemed to snap into action, standing up abruptly and decisively. Billy stood up, too.

"Me and Frank were going to go up there together today," he told Dagger sadly. "But obviously she won't be climbing *anything* for a while, so me and Sue can do it. *Can't we, Sue?*" The lad seemed to be pleading with her.

Sue stood next to him and put her arm around his slim shoulders. "'Course we can, Billy. I know it won't be perfect, like if Frank had been with you. But me and Lennie can be the next best thing, eh?"

Billy smiled up into her face and settled into the hug, gratefully. Dagger was looking at Sue with a glint in his eye, she thought. Stepping back out into the kitchen, he told her, "Perfect. Just...perfect. Lennie's sunbathing near the river. Give him a whistle and he'll come along quite happily. I'll... see you all later." He opened the back door then popped his head back into the room. "Have a great day. Got to go, see you later." He winked at them before hurrying out into the sunshine. Sue gave Billy a puzzled look and shook her head.

"Weirdo," she told him, and Billy smiled happily back at her.

*

It was a long but enjoyable walk from the riverside and Sue's house up to Penshaw Monument. They went the back way, ambling along country lanes, passing horses and riders, the odd cyclist, talking companionably together. At first, Billy seemed rather apprehensive, Sue thought. He kept glancing up towards the hill, shading his eyes against the sun. She noticed how he often rested one hand on Lennie's collar, more as you would touch a talisman than to keep the dog in check. As they drew closer to the fields at the back of the Monument, Billy paused on the track and stared up at the dark shape glowering before them.

"I've never come up the back way," he told Sue quietly. "I only ever climbed the hill from the front." It seemed to Sue that a shadow passed over his eyes.

"Well, from our neck of the woods this is a more direct route, Billy. Plus it's quieter to approach the hill this way. Less of a shock, maybe," she added, and when Billy glanced at her quickly, she continued. "All those steps and that steep hill can be a bit daunting," she explained. "This way, we'll climb up through the woods and come out right behind the Monument. It'll be lovely. Trust me."

Billy grinned at her, licking his lips and wiping a trace of sweat from his brow.

"Okay, then. I'll be ready for a drink and that picnic when we get up there. It's a long way."

Sue patted his shoulder as they walked steadily on. "But so worth it, Billy. When you get to the top, you'll see how far we've walked."

Billy plodded on beside her. "You can see the whole world from up there," he told her quietly.

Their breath came in shallow gasps as they made their way up through the trees, at the back of the Monument hill. A couple of times Billy's foot slipped on damp leaves and Sue had to reach down to haul him back up again. Lennie was in his element, running around, chasing the odd rabbit or squirrel, yapping happily and wagging his tail. The dog occasionally paused and waited for his friends to catch up, grinning, his tongue lolling. He knew where he was going and was anxious to get to the top, too. Coming to a thin rickety fence, Sue paused, one hand on Billy's shoulder. She looked deep into his eyes, catching her breath. The Monument loomed up ahead of them, brooding, dark and slightly sinister from this angle. Billy felt his knees trembling and wasn't sure if that was from the long walk and climb they had made.

"OK, now, Billy? You ready?" Sue asked him. Billy could only nod mutely. He didn't trust himself to speak. He wished Frank was beside him to offer words of advice and comfort, or just to tell him to man up and stop being a wuss. Sue was opening a small gate, built into a wooden stile.

"Right. Come on, then, Billy. We're here."

She took hold of Billy's hand and almost dragged him out, along a short path, up a slight rise and there it was – Penshaw Monument, in all its glory, standing strong and proud, boldly basking in the warm sunshine. The sky above it was a magnificent blue, in contrast to the dark pillars. The green hill tumbled away at the front of the building, leading down to the fields, main road and the park opposite where the lakes shimmered in the midday heat. Turning his head, Billy gazed at the city of Sunderland on his left, spotting the tall tower block which was his home. He could see the parks, church steeples, the football stadium, Monkwearmouth Bridge, and the river, snaking through to the sea. He let out a sob and walked forwards, the better to try to take in this magnificent view. Lennie stepped in alongside of him, nudging the boy's hand with his wet nose. Sue followed at a short distance, not wanting to interrupt.

After a few minutes of staring silently, and sniffing a few times, Billy turned back and took in the Monument itself, tilting his head back and gazing upwards. He stared intently at the pillars, the heavy stonework, the size of the base, and finally climbed the wooden steps and wandered about inside the edifice, silently taking in its size and sense of grandeur. Sue watched patiently, sitting down, with her legs dangling over the front of the base, as Billy put out his hands to feel the pillars. *He's almost caressing them*, she thought. And just look at his face. He seemed to be glowing, but tears were streaming down his cheeks, and he let them fall unchecked. Eventually, he turned to Sue, smiling tremulously.

"It's just…" He tried to speak, gulped a few more times, then attempted to clear his mind and his heart. "It's just like it always was, Sue," he told her. Wiping his face with his hands, he came to her and sat down beside her. "I'd nearly forgotten what it felt like to be up here," he told Sue, gratefully accepting a small bottle of water she was handing to him. Unscrewing the top, he continued to gaze into the distance, towards the sea and his former home. Billy took a swig of the drink, then seemed to settle into himself, sighing deeply.

"OK, Billy?" Sue had sort of expected the tears. She knew that in this boy's head and heart the Monument represented something far bigger than simply a local landmark. She took out a sandwich and unwrapped it for him. If he could tell her, then great. If not, at least she felt he might get some sort of closure from being here. She wished fervently, not for the first time, that Frank had been able to join them. As if reading her mind, Billy turned to her.

"Frank would have loved this, wouldn't she?" he asked sadly.

"She would, indeed, Billy. But you know, as soon as she's able to walk again, you two can come up here by yourselves. It's not going anywhere, after all."

Billy took a bite of the sandwich. "I know," he nodded sadly. "It's just going to take ages for her ankle to get better. And by the time that happens, I might be back at home again." He glanced towards his tower block and chewed thoughtfully. Tears were springing up again, and he swallowed them down with the bread, wiping his eyes with a free hand.

To take his mind off missing Frank, Sue began pointing out local landmarks. "Look, Billy, you can see Durham Cathedral right over there, in the distance. And just take a look at the new bridge on the Wear!"

Billy gazed in that direction. "Wow…" he breathed.

"And look, there's lots of horseboxes at the riding school. There must be a gymkhana going on."

They ate in companionable silence for a minute or two, watching other visitors climbing the hill, cars coming and going, picking people up and dropping them off. Seagulls swooped overhead, calling out to share their lunch. The sun shone on them, warming their face and hands.

"Look." Billy pointed down to the gate at the foot of the hill, where it joined the road. "Another horsebox. Do you think we should tell him that this isn't the riding school?"

Sue followed his gaze. "There's probably no room left to park it, Billy. Unless it's going into the farm, or the garden centre, of course," she added. Together, they munched on, idly watching the movement at the foot of the hill. There was something familiar about the horsebox, and the driver, when he got out to unload, but at this great height no features were clear. Billy continued chatting to Sue, telling her about life in the tower block, and comparing the differences with living on the riverside at Fatfield. Sue was just telling him about her childhood on the street there, when Billy suddenly stood up, grabbing her hand to do the same.

"Dagger," he said, unexpectedly.

"Oh, yes, he was always there, Billy. Always up to something, even when I was little. Honestly, I could write a book about that…" But Billy cut her off, shaking her hand and pointing down the hill, to the road at the bottom.

"No, Sue, look. Dagger. It's Dagger… and…" He squinted his eyes against the glare of the sun."

Sue wiped her sunglasses on her T-shirt and put them back on again. She, too, gazed down the hill, past the grazing cows and the visitors climbing the steps, to the horsebox which was definitely unloading…

"Huh? Dagger… and Dolly, his donkey…?" She turned to Billy, questioningly.

"And if I'm not mistaken, *Frank*. Frank, riding on Dolly the donkey!" he told her triumphantly, grinning away like a Cheshire cat, before throwing his sandwich to the gulls and haring off down the steep hill, towards his friends.

"Billy! Be careful!" Sue called after him in delight and disbelief. "You might…"

"Break a leg?" Billy called back over his shoulder, laughing as he slithered and skidded his way down to greet his friends.

Chapter 35

By the time Billy had skidded and tumbled all the way down the hill from the top of the Monument, Dagger had carried Frank out of the passenger seat and had placed her gently onto Dolly's back. The donkey huffed and puffed a bit, not because his rider was heavy, she just wasn't used to anyone getting up on board. Then, as the donkey got used to having a passenger, she suddenly spotted her best friend Lennie racing down the hill towards her with a huge grin on his face, tongue lolling and legs going at twenty to the dozen, so she suddenly set up a huge, wheezing, braying racket. Frank grabbed hold of her mane and held on tight just in case, but Dagger was holding the halter and talking affectionately to his beast.

"Give over, you mad old thing. It's Len. And look who else."

Frank gazed up towards the steep rise of the hill and gasped in delight. Shading her eyes against the sun, she called out in surprise and delight.

"Billy!"

Billy and the dog slithered to a stop at the side of the donkey, laughing and panting excitedly. Sue followed, slightly more sedately. Resting one hand on her knee the boy looked deep into her face, then brought his eyes to rest on the heavily bandaged lower leg. His eyes opened wide.

"Frank – what on earth are you doing here? I thought you were still in hospital!"

His friend grinned back at him, looking down at him from the donkey's back.

"They were going to keep me another day at least, Billy, but I was doing so well and I just had to get out. Hospitals are so noisy. And they stink, too. And it was so hot in there, and the weather was just gorgeous, so I thought…"

Dagger stepped forward. "Basically, she bullied them into letting her out early, Billy. But as she was making a good recovery, and because she's such a pest, they let her go. I only heard earlier," he informed them.

Frank grinned at them both, her blue eyes shining and reflecting the sky.

"And I knew you were going up here today. I didn't want to miss it, Billy. I had to be with you, but of course, I knew, I couldn't," she added with a shrug, waving her plastered ankle at him. "But my hero came to my rescue. Isn't that right, Dagger?"

Dagger grinned and raised his shoulders in a nonchalant shrug. "Well, Dolly needed the exercise, too. I knew this was important to Billy, so I thought we'd all go up to the top together. If that's OK with you, Billy?" Dagger raised his eyebrows questioningly to the lad, who simply grinned and nodded his head at them. He didn't feel like he could speak for a moment or two: memories and deep-seated emotions were running riot in his head just then, and if they spilled out before he was ready, he felt he might faint. Moving forward to take the halter lead from Dagger, he turned towards his gang of friends.

"Come on, then. Let's do this. Is everybody ready?"

"We are if you are, Billy," Sue told him, striding towards the path, leading back up to the top of the hill.

*

They made a funny little procession to the top. Other families with young children and dogs grinned as they passed them: the older, handsome guy in charge; the rather pretty, slim young woman, bringing up the rear; a crazy black dog, dancing with delight around them; and a boy, leading a girl with a broken leg on a chunky, cheerful donkey. They talked and laughed animatedly all the way up the hill, and once they reached the Monument, they all paused and went quiet, simply gazing at the massive structure, for a minute, in silence. Dagger broke the spell.

"Right, young lady. Hold on to me and I'll get you off there, for a bit."

Taking hold of Frank in his strong arms, he gently lifted her out of the saddle and carried her to sit on the edge of the base of the Monument, where some of the picnic items and Sue's bag were still lying, making sure he didn't knock her plastered lower leg as he did so. The donkey immediately wandered off to graze near the bushes at the side of the hill. Everyone joined Frank, sitting together in the warm sun, drinking water and eating the picnic items, which the seagulls hadn't found. Sue kept glancing at Billy, but he seemed thrilled to be up there, especially now that Frank and Dagger were with them, too.

"Frank's Nan rang me earlier to tell me they were chucking her out," Dagger began, eating a handful of crisps.

Frank threw a crust at him.

"Err, *discharging* me, I think you mean, Dagger," she told him sternly.

He laughed and continued. "And I knew you two were planning this trip, so I just thought it would make a lovely day out for Frank and me – and Dolly as well."

Billy offered Frank a sweet from the packet he was holding.

"Yeah," he agreed. "A family day out," he said quietly, to no one in particular. Sue and Dagger exchanged a small smile. Glancing across at Frank, Sue thought that she looked a little pale and pensive, despite the warmth of the sun on their faces.

"Frank, are you all right? Are you in a lot of pain?" she asked. Frank looked over, then down at her lower leg, dangling over the edge of the Monument.

"I am a bit, Sue. But I'll be OK, honest," she added quickly, not wanting to spoil the moment or the visit for everyone else. Billy turned to look at her with concern. Sue jumped down and stood in front of Frank.

"It's OK. We won't go down just yet, Frank." She knew what the girl was worried about. "Why don't you sit back and put your leg flat. Then it will be resting, while we're here."

Frank lay on her back, gazing up at the sky and a few soft clouds, scudding over the open roof of the Monument. Billy carefully lifted her head up and slid his backpack under her to act as a pillow. Sue caught Dagger's eye, and they grinned at each other over the top of the heads of the two youngsters. Soon, all four of them were lying back on the Monument, sunbathing and chatting amiably, their words and soft laughter drifting up into the blue.

"When I was little…" began Dagger, but Frank cut him off instantly.

"…The Monument wasn't even built…" She giggled. Billy laughed in delight, Sue chuckled.

"Oy," Dagger told her, a mock warning in his voice. "I'm not that old, you know." And he continued. "We used to come up here for a picnic and there were goats on the hill. My dad was reading the paper, while we were just rolling about, like you do, and a goat ate right through the front page of the Echo from the back."

"Get away, Dagger," Frank told him with a laugh.

Billy was intrigued. "What did your dad do?" he asked, lifting his head to look across at Dagger.

"Well, he wasn't best pleased, lad, I can tell you. The headline on the back page was Sunderland beating the Mags and he wanted to keep it in his scrapbook."

Sue chuckled. "Don't believe a word he says, Billy. He's full of… these tall tales," she added quickly. "Mind you, I once roly-poly-ed all the way down, when I was little, with my sister. Only to find we were covered in cow poo, when we got to the bottom. The bus driver wouldn't let us on the bus, so we had to walk all the way back to Fatfield."

"Surrounded by a little cloud of flies, all the way home." Dagger laughed, adding, "I could smell you two coming from the end of the road."

They chuckled on for a minute, Sue telling them about not being allowed into the house and having to strip their clothes off in the back garden, before being hosed down.

"Tell Billy your sister's name, Sue," Dagger said, still giggling.

"Pat, Billy. Her name is Pat." And she and Dagger carried on giggling for a bit longer. Frank laughed loudly at that, still lying on her back, chuckling up at the sky. "Silly cow," she giggled. "Silly cow pat." And off they went again, drawing curious glances from an older couple leaving down the wooden steps. When their laughter subsided, they all became quiet again, lost in their memories of life on and around the Monument in happier times, when they were younger and carefree, counting clouds and crows wheeling overhead. Sue sighed happily.

Suddenly, as if from nowhere, a small voice began, almost chanting, quietly at first, but getting louder.

"Eighteen, one hundred, fifty-three…"

It took each one of them a second or two to realise what was happening, but soon the two adults and Frank sat up, looking fearfully at each other and down at Billy, who still lay on his back, eyes closed, hands folded over his chest. The boy continued.

"Seventy, two…"

Oh no, not a panic attack, thought Sue. Not here, not up on his beloved Monument, in the sunshine, with the safety of good friends all around him? Sue, Dagger and Frank closed in on Billy, a look of puzzlement forming on each face. Each had witnessed Billy in one of his mad, chanting sessions before, but this one seemed different. They kneeled around him, looking down at his face with concern. Frank held one of his hands; Sue gently took the other, but Billy's eyes remained closed, his face calm and almost relaxed as he continued.

"Or, you could say, thirty, sixteen, twenty-one, two."

He stopped counting, and a small, soft smile crept onto his lips. He didn't seem to be panicking, just thinking deeply. Sue believed he wasn't even aware that she and Frank were holding his hands. Then, after another pause, his hands tightened their grip around those of his friends and his smile widened.

"Billy," Sue said softly. "Billy, are you OK, pet?" She glanced quickly at Frank, who was still looking down at him with worry. Dagger moved closer.

"Can you tell us now, Billy?" he asked softly. "What's that all about, then, eh, lad?"

Hearing Dagger's voice, Billy opened his eyes and sat up. Frank was happy to see that he didn't actually seem distressed. He just seemed to be miles away from them, his eyes staring out towards the city and the sea, glistening in the distance. He blinked once or twice and they thought he whispered the word 'dad'. Sue, Dagger and Frank sat beside him, supporting him silently, staying close to give him comfort and support.

"I used to come up here with my dad," he told them in a quiet voice, obviously deep in thought. "When I was little, like, and I still had my dad." The other three almost held their breath, not daring to move or interrupt Billy as his thoughts spilled out. As he spoke, quietly and calmly, Sue, Dagger and Frank gradually eased themselves into a more comfortable position, sitting close to Billy, so that he could feel their closeness and be comforted by them.

He took a deep breath, his eyes still staring away into the distance, and continued, "I used to think I could touch heaven, when I was up here with my dad. At first, I used to jump up and down, to try to reach the clouds, but then my dad would lift me up onto his shoulders and I'd try again. He used to say, never mind, Billy. You're still too little. But one day you'll come up here, when you're as big as me, and together we'll grab a cloud and pull it down. I'll wrap you up in it, Billy, and keep you safe for ever."

Frank glanced at Sue with a worried expression, but Sue held a hand up in warning, telling her to allow Billy to continue in his own time. She instinctively felt his deep-seated need to say this. Billy seemed to be lost in thought. His eyes travelled to the massive pillars supporting the Monument, then he studied the base and the hill for a moment, before continuing. Dagger watched in silent support, fascinated by the blue and green of the scene, being reflected in the lad's large, clear eyes.

"Mam never came up here. It was only me and Dad. Sometimes, he'd sit me up here with a bottle of lemonade and a sandwich, then I'd watch him running up and down the hill with his huge Bergen on his back, training; always running and training. It weighed much more than me, that bag. Never stopped my dad, though. He was as strong as an ox." He smiled here, a thin watery smile, then gulped and continued, not looking at any one of his friends, just out into the countryside around the Monument. The sun shone on, a bus rumbled by at the bottom of the hill, and the birds sang.

"This was *our* spot, *our* place – mine and Dad's. We even had a favourite pillar to lean against, when we had our picnic. We used to make up stories about a troll who lived behind the hill, but he was a nice troll: he lived in the bluebell woods, you see. I used to sometimes pick a bunch of wild flowers to take back to Mam, but they were always saggy and half-dead by the time we got them home. She always loved them, mind."

Billy paused and smiled for a moment, swatting away a fly, which had homed in on the group. Nobody else dared move a muscle. They didn't want the spell to be broken. A horse whinnied in the riding school field, and Billy smiled and glanced that way.

"One time, on the way down, we climbed the stile, but a couple of horses were standing in the way on the other side of it. Dad had to ask them to move, but he was a bit afraid of them, really. I laughed at him. I was like, 'come on, Dad, a big tough soldier like you. You can't be scared of these – they're not even that big!' But that's when he told me he was allergic to them. They made him itch and sneeze. So I asked them to move. I got hold of one and led it away by its mane, and the others just followed. I was the hero that day." He grinned and his face flushed slightly at the memory. The silence hung in the air between them.

Dagger shifted beside Billy, putting a hand on the boy's shoulder. "Your dad was a proper hero, though, wasn't he, Billy? I know what happened to him, you know. I found out recently."

Sue and Frank sat up and gasped, staring across at Dagger, shocked that he had possibly broken the dream for Billy. Billy turned his head to give Dagger a clear, knowing look, his eyes never blinking, then he looked to the front again and continued.

"We used to go to Mowbray Park in the town and I would climb on the stone lions, pretending to be Tarzan. We sometimes went fishing in the river as well. I liked that. Never caught much, mind. My dad used to go to the chip shop on the way home and buy a fish lot, telling my mam that he caught it ready-battered." He smiled again, remembering happy times, but then his face clouded over and his mouth tightened into a thin line. Sue and Frank glanced uneasily at each other, worried about what might come next. They felt sure Billy's dad had been killed in action and were scared the effect of relaying the bad news to them would have on Billy.

"But one day, when my dad was on leave, we went to the beach to look for fossils." Here he paused and gulped, but he ploughed on, regardless. Everyone watched him closely. "I was only about five at the time." Here, he actually looked at each of his friends in turn, making sure they were still listening closely, were still with him. They each nodded at Billy to continue. The movement down on the road, in the riding school and over in the park, all seemed to fade into the shimmering sunshine as they sat on the Monument, listening as Billy poured out his heart to them. He had to share; they knew that; no matter how painful it would be for him. Billy knew it, too. The time had come.

"We weren't on our soft, sandy beaches at home," he told them. "We went down the coast a bit, where it's really rocky and there are high cliffs. It's a bit like being on the moon, my dad said, and there was nobody around. Just us. It was brilliant, at first. I'd never been on a beach like that before – loads of shells and unusual shaped rocks with pretty colours." Frank actually held her breath, sensing something awful was approaching. Billy subconsciously began rubbing at his arms and knees as he spoke, his eyes still staring straight ahead. "I could see all these coloured bands in the cliff, with bits of rock sticking out, so I told dad that it was probably where the best bits of fossil would be found. So, we went over and started chipping away at the cliff. We found some really interesting things, like a flint-shaped bit and some shells, deep inside the cliff face. After a while, I was really thirsty, so dad said we should sit and sunbathe whilst we had a drink and something to eat. We sat with our backs to the cliff, just watching the tide coming in, feeding the seagulls, when all of a sudden there was this deep, rumbling sound. We didn't know where it was coming from, at first; we thought it might have been the men working in the harbour, just down the beach. But then, the cliff sort of cracked open." Billy paused, his eyes wide, obviously re-living the horror in his mind. "It split open, and sand and stones and mud started falling on top of me and Dad. He shouted something, but I didn't hear it because all the stuff had gone onto my head and was in my ears and my mouth. The ground was shaking like an earthquake and we couldn't get out of the way."

Billy gasped and paused, his eyes and mouth wide open, staring at this unseen terror. He began to tremble, wiping at his face and body, in memory of the accident. Sue knelt up to lean close to him. Frank had clamped her hands across her own mouth, in shock. Dagger waved a hand at the two girls, warning them to let Billy talk it out.

"The cliff covered us," he spat out. "It came slipping down on top of us. It all went dark. I was lying on my back, but I couldn't move. Something was pressing on top of me, holding me down, but because of it there was a tiny little gap where I could breathe, but not for long. I tried to shout but the words wouldn't come out. I knew I had to get out, but I couldn't. The tide was coming in, the water was getting closer, but there had been nobody else on the beach. I knew we were going to die in there. I was in hell, all alone, and I didn't know where my dad was."

By now the boy was sobbing and shaking, tears streaming down his face. Frank was crying silently beside him.

Sue looked at Dagger and said quietly but firmly, "Enough. We've heard enough now, Billy. It's all right. You know you're safe up here with us. Ssshhh." She put both arms around the boy and pulled him into a tight embrace, stroking his hair as she did so, trying to soothe away his pain with her soft touch.

Dagger moved forwards and gently lifted the boy's chin so that Billy had to look into the man's eyes. "Well done, Billy," he told him. "That was a very brave thing to do, to tell us what happened." The dog, who had been cheerfully snuffling about in the bushes, came forward to sit in front of Billy, sensing his distress. Lennie reached up and placed a paw on Billy's knee. Billy looked down at him and gave him a thin smile, patting the dog on the head.

Dagger gave the dog a rough, affectionate rub, telling Billy, "Look, Lennie's worried about you. Do you think it would be OK, if I told the rest of this story, Billy?"

Sue reached out to pass the boy a tissue to blow his nose, and Billy nodded at Dagger, snuffling and sighing deeply. He didn't look at anyone, but focused his attention on Lennie's deep brown eyes. "Yes, do," he sniffed.

Frank eased her broken ankle into a slightly more comfortable position, Sue continued cradling Billy, holding him gently in her arms, and Billy seemed perfectly content to lie in her soft embrace.

Dagger coughed gruffly and continued. He, too, stared out across the land in front of the Monument. Other visitors to the attraction wandered about, up and down the hill, but there was no one close enough to hear the story that was being shared.

"You're right. It was a landslide, Billy. There had been a lot of rain, but of course, your dad had been in a war zone – he wouldn't have known that. He was just home on two weeks' leave. And although there was nobody on the beach, they had heard it further along the cliff top. People did come running to help, but you wouldn't have known that. It took them a while to get to you, and for the emergency services to dig you both out. It was too late for your dad, Billy. But he was a hero: he saved your life, didn't he?"

Dagger paused, checking the lad's face to make sure he was OK with his telling of the story. Billy looked pale, and a stray tear trickled silently down his cheek. Beside him, Frank was crying, too, noiselessly, so as not to detract from Billy's anguish. Sue was simply sitting in silence, almost frozen in time, her eyes closed against the pain and shock of what she was hearing.

"Some locals came running. When they started dragging away at the sand and rubble of the cliff slide, the Police wanted them to stop digging in case more of the cliff came down. But they wouldn't have it. Someone *had* seen the two of them on the beach and realised that they were in there somewhere. They found them, after a while, but Billy's dad was dead. The rescuers could tell from his position that he had flung himself on top of Billy, was lying on him to try to protect him, but there was no hope for him."

Dagger shuddered here, rubbing his own face with the palms of his hands. Then he glanced at the three friends beside him, and carried on.

"They thought you were dead as well, son, didn't they? Billy was knocked unconscious and barely breathing. But we think that there had been a little pocket of air in the gap between Roy and Billy, and that's what saved him."

Sue and Frank glanced up sharply at Dagger, and then at Billy.

"Roy…" Frank said quietly. "I never even asked you what your dad's name was, Billy," she told him sadly, leaning into him. "Sorry."

Billy finally dragged his eyes away from the soothing green scenery all around him and smiled gently at Frank.

"S'alright, Frank," he told her quietly. "Sergeant Roy Higson of the Parachute Regiment. My dad. My hero. He saved my life, but lost his own at the same time."

Sue blew her nose loudly on her hanky, making a sort of honking sound, so that a pigeon, which had been sitting in the bush near Dolly, screeched loudly and flapped off, whiffling over the bushes and away from the group on the hill. This broke the spell a little and they laughed self-consciously, glad of the distraction. Dagger took a swig from a bottle of water and passed it to Billy, who took it with a grateful nod.

"This lad was in hospital for weeks, weren't you, Billy? Pretty much bashed up, eh, pet?"

Billy nodded thoughtfully. After a minute he told them, "Missed my dad's funeral as well. I couldn't even speak for about nine months after the accident. We left our little house and went to live in the tower block for a change, to try to help. But it didn't really help: nothing did. My mam was past herself. She tried everything. Social services got involved. The only thing that really made a difference was art – you know, my drawing and painting?"

He glanced up at Sue then, who had released him from her hug and was looking at him with deep concern. She smiled encouragement at him, so he continued.

"And the other thing that helped was looking at this Monument and remembering the great times I had up here with my dad. It gave me happy memories, which helped to fight off the terror I often felt. I couldn't come up here again, mind," he told them, looking at each of them in turn. They nodded in reply.

"I can understand why, Billy," Frank told him. "Did you never come back up here again, then? You know, after… what happened to you and your dad?"

Billy looked down at the grass near their feet and picked a daisy, before he answered her.

"Never, Frank – I just couldn't. But I still had all the books and pictures that my dad had given me about the Monument. Stacks of them, all in my room. And I could see it from my window. So, I learned *everything* I could about it." He actually smiled then, tilting his head backwards to gaze up at the pillars around him. "It's modelled on the temple of Hephaestus, the Thesion in Athens. It was built in 1844 – well, finished then. It stands at seventy feet high; the hill is 136 metres above sea level, which is 446 feet. It's a hundred feet long, fifty-three feet wide, seventy feet high and has eighteen columns, which are two metres in diameter."

He rattled off the facts all in one breath, then paused for effect, smiling at each of his friends in turn.

The light of recognition lit up Frank's face. Jumping to her feet she called out, "The chanting! It's all about this place!" Then she slumped down again, holding out her broken ankle and clutching at the plaster cast.

Dagger stood up and grinned down at Billy, before turning his gaze to take in the sweep of the Monument.

"It's the dimensions of the Monument, isn't it, Billy?"

Billy nodded, taking in the whole vista in front and around him.

"I come up here, in my head, whenever I get distressed," he told them, tapping at his temple with one finger. "It helps, you know? You might think I'm mad, but when I see this place in my head, my dad is always right here with me. And it… helps," he added with a shrug. Sue moved forward to hug him tightly to her again.

"Of course, it does, sweetheart," she told him, her voice thick with emotion. "Of course, it does, Billy. Now, it makes perfect sense. We can see it now."

Billy jumped back up onto the base of Penshaw Monument and went forward to wrap his arms around the nearest pillar. He leaned closely into it, closed his eyes and sighed deeply. His three friends stood back, smiling gently at him. Each was relieved to have finally learned the truth about the story of what brought Billy to them: his need to be up high to feel safe, when he felt distressed; for the reasons behind his panic attack and, seemingly, crazy counting. It all made sense. It felt to Frank as though a heavy, wide door had swung open for them and a newer, stronger and more confident Billy Higson could walk through it with his head held high.

The dog and the donkey were both getting restless, coming towards the four friends and snuffling at them, nudging them as if to say, come on you lot – we've been here long enough now. Dagger got hold of Dolly's halter and brought her closer towards Frank. He lifted her up onto the animal's back and turned to lead them back down the hill. Sue and Billy gathered up the remains of the picnic and stuffed everything back into their bags, calling to Lennie to join them. Billy walked alongside the donkey, resting his hand on Frank's knee to keep her and her broken ankle steady as they began to make their way down the hill. Taking one last look at his beloved Monument, where they had been sitting, he paused and called to Dagger to stop for a second.

"What is it, Billy?" Frank asked, twisting her head to look back over her shoulder. "Did we leave something behind?"

Billy stepped back to the spot they had just left. He picked something up and stared at it for a second, then a slow smile lit up his face. He stared up to the open roof of the Monument, then hurried to show Frank, sitting up on the donkey. Sue and Dagger came forward to see what it was he had found, puzzled looks on their faces. Billy slowly opened his fist to show them. A pristine white feather slowly uncurled on the palm of his hand.

Frank's eyes glowed at him. "I think that says it all, Billy, don't you?"

Sue wiped a tear from her eye; Frank just grinned at her mate, who flashed back a megawatt smile. Dagger simply sighed.

"Flamin' seagulls." Then he winked and led the little party back down the hill.

Chapter 36

At the foot of the hill, the little group stopped and looked back up towards the towering monolith. Sue was still shaking slightly, having been rocked by the story of what had happened to Billy and his dad. Frank was sitting on Dolly, gazing all around the hill, counting her blessings, whilst Dagger busied himself opening the doors of the battered little horsebox and getting Frank's crutches out of the front seat. Billy stood very still, holding onto the reins of the bridle, scuffing the grass at his feet, obviously still deep in thought. He sniffed occasionally and patted the donkey's warm, solid neck for comfort before leaning his head in towards her and sighing raggedly. Frank watched him, catching her breath. That poor lad, she thought, wondering what her own parents were doing at that very moment.

Dagger had opened the passenger door wide and was now standing next to Frank with his arms wide, waiting to lift her down and put her into the front seat of the horsebox. She glanced down at Billy: there was still so much that needed to be said, that she needed to know, that Billy would want to share with her. She glanced sharply at Dagger, an appealing look in her eyes.

"Dagger…" she began slowly. He was wise to her ways, though.

"What?" he asked, staring directly at her, with one eyebrow raised quizzically.

"Wouldn't it be great if me and Billy could walk home: me on Dolly and Billy leading me?"

Billy's head flashed up and his eyes widened in delight at the thought of it. His mouth opened to beg an affirmative answer from Dagger, but Sue came round the side of the horse box, shaking her head.

"No way," she told the two of them. "Sorry, kids – absolutely not. It's not safe. What if Frank fell off the donkey? She could do so much more damage to that leg."

Frank leaned forward, clutching Dolly's mane, and Billy leaned over her neck, both pleading with Sue.

"No, it'll be fine. I'll take great care of them both. Honest," he told Sue, earnestly. All three turned to look at Dagger for help, eyes flashing and pleading. He sighed and moved to stand beside Sue.

"Sorry, kids. I'm with Sue on this. It's not really safe…" He raised his hands in defence at their protests. "And it's not really fair on Dolly. It's quite a walk from here, you know, especially with that fat lump on her back," he joked, then jumped back, as Frank aimed a swipe at his head. Sue was full of remorse.

"Look, I know you two have lots to talk about, but you can catch up back on the riverside. There's not enough room for me and Billy in the horsebox, but we'll follow you down on the bus, maybe."

Dagger gave Sue a meaningful look, then, glancing down the road towards Sunderland, his face seemed to brighten. "Actually, I've got an idea which might suit us all." They all looked at him expectantly. "Why don't Frank and Billy get the bus down home, Sue and Lennie can come in the horsebox with me, and we can, er, get things ready at Fatfield and meet you off the bus? That way, you two can still have a proper catch up."

Sue heard some hidden meaning in that sentence and gave him a curious look, but Dagger merely nodded at her, flashing his eyes back and grinning at her. Frank's face lit up at the idea, and she, too, glanced along the road. A bus was just rounding the corner, laboriously heading their way, about half a mile back.

"Yeah, brilliant!" she exclaimed, opening her arms wide to allow Dagger to lift her down from Dolly's back and place her at the bus stop a few yards away. Billy hurried to grab her crutches and join her, flashing a grin at Dagger and telling Sue not to worry.

"Look, these buses drop right down for disabled passengers, so Frank will get on easily, and I won't let her fall. I promise."

Sue shrugged her shoulders in defeat. Taking Billy's backpack from him and giving him the bus fare for both of them, she looked up at Dagger.

"Okay," she told them, smiling as the two youngsters each put an arm out to stop the approaching bus. "We'll beat you home, anyway, and one of us will meet you at the end of the bridge. Be careful!"

She and Dagger made sure Frank and Billy were safely settled on the bus, waved them off, then made their way back to the horsebox, where Dolly and Lennie waited patiently.

"Right, you, Dagger," she told him, getting into the passenger seat. "You have some talking to do as well, don't you? And don't give me that innocent look – I know you too well. You're up to something." She arched her eyebrows at her neighbour as he started the engine.

*

Once Billy started chatting to Frank about his dad, it was as if a floodgate had been opened. She had the sense to sit quietly beside her friend as he talked and talked about his dad Roy, his memories of him tumbling out, telling her about the fun they used to have together. The roads and estates passed by unseen outside the bus windows, as Frank listened patiently and Billy spoke with happy passion. Occasionally, she would ask a question or clarify a point, and Billy would pause, his hands twisting slightly, before continuing his tale. Frank noticed the warmth and the worry Billy still held for his mam and a small, warm smile crept onto her face. Billy explained how school had always been a torment to him; how coming to stay with Sue and making friends had been such a life-changing experience for him; how even learning to live with the river made him feel more confident, normal and grown up.

"Your dad would have been so proud of you today, Billy," Frank told him, nudging him with her shoulder. "Isn't it so sad and ironic that a man like your dad – who spent so much of his time up in the air, in aeroplanes…"

"And jumping out of them," Billy interjected.

"Yeah." Frank grinned. "And jumping out of *perfectly good* aeroplanes, should end his life the way he did? It's an absolute tragedy. No wonder you ended up with a few issues, mate."

Billy turned to gaze into her beautiful blue eyes, which looked so sad and downcast, at that moment. She looked back at him.

"What?" she asked.

"*A few issues?*" he asked her. "Frank. I've been as mad as a box of frogs for *years!*"

Frank threw her head back and laughed. "But just look at you now, Billy!"

Billy grinned back at her and returned her shoulder-nudge. "Yeah. Now I've got good company: now I've got a friend who's as mad as I am!"

They talked some more, about their plans to continue displaying the birds in the trees, now that Frank was home from hospital, but that they might need a hand, so that nothing else could go wrong. As the bus trundled over Fatfield Bridge, Billy stood up to help Frank get to her feet and handed her the crutches. Billy had spotted Dagger and Dolly, standing at the bus stop to collect them, and glancing round the other passengers, he noticed, with a wry grin, that nobody seemed remotely surprised to see a big bloke and a chunky donkey waiting for the bus. Thanking the driver, they got off, when the bus dipped politely for them, and Dagger swept Frank and her broken ankle onto Dolly's back.

"Right, m'lady," he told her. "I think you've had quite enough excitement for one day. Let's get you back to your Nan's."

As they walked down the riverside road to Essie Bailey's house, with Frank swaying gently to the donkey's small steps, she asked Dagger, "So, Dagger, tell me. How did you find out about Billy's dad and the accident?"

Dagger stopped the donkey for a moment, glancing at Billy to see how the lad would take the explanation. He was gazing back at Dagger with a clear, open expression, and Dagger decided to tell the truth.

"Well, the other night, before your little accident, I noticed Billy's reaction to that jogger – my mate Bob's son."

Frank looked puzzled, trying to remember the jogger in question. Dagger told her, "The one with the spaniel and the maroon T-shirt?"

A light dawned in Frank's eyes and she nodded her head. Dagger continued. "I had seen some of Billy's art work, especially the one with the wings and the army boots, and that T-shirt made me think that it must be the same regiment Roy was in. We all just assumed Billy's dad had been killed in action, in a war zone, so I asked Bob to find out more from his lad from the regiment's archives. He told me later what had happened. And of course, I remembered it then from the local news at the time. It was a big disaster."

Billy hung his head for a second or two, and Dagger was beginning to think he'd upset the lad, when Billy told him quite clearly, "Sometimes, I think it would have been so much easier if my dad *had* been killed in Afghanistan, instead of at home, doing something he loved." He gulped. "When I was little, I used to think it was all my fault."

Frank gasped and reached out to him. "No way, Billy – it was a total accident. It could have happened to anyone that day."

"You were simply in the wrong place at the wrong time, son," Dagger told him, clicking his tongue to move the donkey on. "Come on, your tea's ready at Essie's."

At the gate, Frank was helped down, and Dagger tied the donkey up on the grass verge, near the river. Frank made her way up the path on her crutches to the open front door, where Sue was standing with a tea towel in her hand, clucking and fussing as she helped the girl over the doorstep. Leading her through to the back kitchen, she told Billy to go and wash his hands, whilst she got Frank settled in a chair. As he made his way up the stairs to the bathroom, he heard Frank ask why her Nan wasn't back yet. A few minutes later, as he came back down, he noticed through the open door that the front room looked quite different to usual. Curious.

Popping his head round the door, he looked into Essie Bailey's front room. It was comfortable and tidy, but instead of the settee, there was a single bed made up. A little jar of wild summer flowers stood on the table, near the bed, and a jug of orange juice with a glass. Ah, how sweet of her, he thought. She was going to just love having Frank home with a broken leg, so that she had someone to fuss over. He grinned to himself as he went down the passage to the kitchen. Sue and Frank were tucking into lemon drizzle cake and a cup of tea. Sue glanced up.

"Well, I'm happy to see that smile on your face, Billy. It's been quite a day for you, hasn't it, pet? Come and sit down."

Billy sat, noticing that Frank also had a huge grin on her face. "Your new bed is lovely, Frank," he told her, biting into a slice of cake. "Your Nan is going to smother you with kindness." Frank frowned at him and gave him a puzzled look.

"Your bed. In the front room," he told her, nodding his head in that direction. "It looks lovely in there." Frank's eyes widened in shock and she glanced quickly at Sue, who flashed a look back.

"Ah, that, yes. It's so she doesn't have to climb all those stairs every time, to go to the loo or up to bed, what with that leg of hers, you know." She was bumbling on, she knew it, but she had to keep the lad right.

Billy seemed completely happy with this, although he did say through a mouthful of crumbs, "Well, yeah, but there is a downstairs loo here, of course." Sue slurped her tea and nodded. Billy continued. "Anyway, where is your Nan, Frank? I thought she'd have come running up to the bridge to almost carry you home," he laughed.

Frank looked down the passage to the front door, and, putting her cup down very deliberately, she told him, "Actually, Billy, I think she's just pulled up. Why don't you go and give her a hand, getting the stuff out of the car?"

Billy sauntered down to the open front door. He could hear voices, Essie's shouting at Dagger, and him grumbling and laughing back at her. As Billy approached, Dagger had the front passenger door open and was talking to someone on the front seat, helping them out.

Essie Bailey spotted Billy and grinned like a Cheshire cat. "Billy! I see you've got my gorgeous girl home. And you'll never guess. When I went to the hospital to collect her, Dagger Dawson, here, had already beaten me to it."

Billy looked over at Dagger, who was standing proudly at the side of the car, a huge grin on his face. Essie continued. "So, I did the next best thing. I offered a lift to another patient."

At this, both she and Dagger stood back from the car, and Dagger waved his hand towards the passenger seat as he helped Billy's mam to emerge onto the path. She stood up slowly, carefully, holding tight onto Dagger's hand, grimacing with pain at first, then grinning from ear to ear as she spotted her boy.

"Mam!" he gasped, running forward to greet her. "Mam, you're here, you're out! What are you doing here?" He launched himself into her arms.

"Woah, careful, Billy, lad. Your mam is still a bit delicate. Don't knock her over."

Becky Higson gazed down at her son, squashed tight against her chest.

"Oh, Billy. Just look at you. Look at how tall and tanned you are! How I've missed you, you'll never know." She kissed his head, his eyes, his cheeks, until Dagger helped her over the threshold. Billy was left standing on the riverside path, gasping in delight, frozen for a second, before he dived into Essie's house after her.

They sat together in the kitchen, laughing, crying, drinking tea and telling stories, breaking the ice and getting to know one another all over again. Becky was amazed at the change in her boy, and was touched by the love that had been lavished upon him in her absence.

She took Sue's hand. "Look at him!" she whispered, staring hard at her son. "He's grown in so many ways. He's so relaxed and confident. You've worked miracles here, all of you. I can't ever thank you enough."

Billy was a bit shocked, not only by the fact that his mam was sitting with him in his friends' house on the riverside, but also by how pale and thin she looked. She was obviously still in a lot of pain. Frank spotted the worried look on his face.

"It's early days, yet, Billy. Your mam has been through a hell of a lot, but she's getting better all the time now."

Billy was still unsure. "It's lovely that you're here, mam," he told her. "But, how will you manage in our flat, if the lift is out of action? I mean, when are we going back there, now that you're out of hospital?"

Sue watched his face fall. It was dawning on him that his time on the riverside was coming to an end. Frank could tell what Billy was thinking, too: the end of his new confidence; the end of his freedom from all his fears; a return to the old way of life, the old Billy.

She spoke up to her friend. "No, Billy, it's not the end – more of a beginning, actually." And she reached across the table to hold his hand. Sue leaned back and smiled at him, looking from Billy to his mam.

"Actually, Becky, it's not just me who's made a change in Billy. This young lady, here, is more responsible than all the rest of us. She's the one who brought him out of himself. Frank is the one who released him from his fears."

Dagger joined in. "What Sue means is she's grateful for your thanks, Becky, but really, it was our pleasure. He's such a nice lad, your Billy. And for us, watching him grow and be set free from his troubles was all the thanks we needed."

Essie Bailey picked up a carved wren from her kitchen windowsill and showed it to Billy's mam with pride written all over her face.

"Our Frank made this out of a bit of wood she'd plucked out of the river, Becky. Great, isn't it?" She slid it over the table so that Becky could admire it, turning it carefully and stroking the smooth wood. Billy's mam smiled over at Frank.

"It's beautiful," she told her. "You're a very clever young lady."

Dagger reached forward and picked the bird up. "Oh, she's got loads more done, Becky. Wait till you see them. But one of her carvings was the cleverest of all, eh, Billy?" He cast a glance at Billy, who stared hard at his mate for a minute, then blushed slightly as the picture dawned on him. "Go on, Billy. Tell your mam your theory."

Sue and Frank looked at their friends, gathered around the table, as the afternoon sun moved round and settled on the back wall. The clock ticked and the fridge hummed in the corner.

Billy took a breath and said, shyly, "I think that Frank didn't just release the birds from the pieces of wood. She also released me. I think, for all those years I've been trapped, been imprisoned, I couldn't get out. I had too many memories and too much fear. I couldn't tell anyone about it. I couldn't *bear* to remember. But being down here, being with all of you, who knew nothing about what happened to me, that helped me come to life. Now, especially after today, I feel like I can cross rivers – and I could fly, if I wanted to. And that's all down to you." He dropped his head and smiled shyly at them all.

The silence hung in the air between them for a second or two, until Frank broke through it. Reaching forward to ruffle Billy's hair she told him, "Free as a bird, that's what you are, Billy. As free as a bird."

Dagger stood up from the table and took his mug to the sink. "And, speaking of birds…" he began. Frank and Billy turned to gaze at him, questioningly. "I have rounded up some help to get your birds up in the trees to finish off the display," he informed them, folding his arms and leaning against the sink.

"Good idea, Dagger!" shouted Essie, and Billy and Frank laughed as Becky jumped in her seat in alarm. "There's no way either of these bairns are climbing those trees again. Not after what happened last time."

Billy leaned over to his mam and told her quietly, "Don't be alarmed, Mam. She always talks to Dagger like that. I'll explain later."

Sue was smiling, too, as she asked Dagger, "Who is it, then? Who's going to help put them up in the trees, if these two are banned from doing it?"

Dagger wiped a large freckled hand over his face and grinned. "Well, there are a couple of local lads – or three – who have some apologising to do. They need to make amends for their awful tricks, and they are just the ones to get on with the job."

Frank's eyes opened as wide as her mouth, and she and Billy exchanged amazed glances at each other.

"Not… not Sid-the-snot-gobbler!"

"And his stupid Munchkins!" Billy added, smiling as he caught sight of his mam's face.

"I bet they won't do it," Frank said sullenly, folding her arms in disgust. "Bunch of numb-nuts," she grumbled.

Dagger was smiling. "Oh, yes, they will. That lad, Baz? Well, I know his mam, and I also know the leader of the cycling club, who ended up in the river the other night. And Baz is terrified of his mam. Well, they all are," he added. "So they *will* be helping out with the birds – and the boats on my side, too. That is, if they don't want the cyclists to know who ruined their bikes."

Everyone laughed, even Becky, who had no idea what they were all on about. She was so happy to see her boy settled and confident, sharing funny stories and experiences with these people. She twisted a little in her seat and winced in pain.

Essie Bailey noticed. "Right, young lady. Time we got you settled in for a lie down. You look done in. Must be about time for your next tablets, too," she announced, getting up from the table.

Frank pushed back her chair and stared hard at her Nan, defiance written all over her face. A lie down? Was she mad? "Nan, give over. Me and Billy were going out to the shed to check on the birds. And I don't need any more tablets 'til tonight. Honestly," she tutted, winking at Billy.

Essie Bailey pushed her chair in and came to stand close to Becky. "Not you, dafty. Billy's mam. She has to have a lie down. Now, Billy, get your mam's bag and carry it into the front room, there's a good lad."

Billy stood up and stood looking helplessly around the kitchen. Eh? What was going on? He didn't understand. Dagger stepped closer to tell him.

"That little bed in the front room isn't for Frank, Billy. It's for your mam."

Billy's head whipped round to stare first at Dagger, then at his mam, as she was helped to her feet. She smiled shyly back at him.

Sue put her arm around Billy and told him, "Your mam is staying here, Billy, just for a little while. She can't be on her own in that flat, whilst she's healing. So she'll be with friends. Us. We'll all be together for a bit longer."

Becky put her arms out to wrap them around her beloved boy, holding him close, pulling him to her to smell the sunshine and warmth of his hair and skin. She smiled softly into the top of his silky, sweet hair.

"I'm staying on the riverside until I heal a bit, too, Billy. Then the council are going to find us somewhere else to live. We're not going back to the flat in the city centre. I think we've both moved on from there, don't you think?"

Billy looked up at her, and grinned at his friends. His old life seemed to be ebbing out, away from him, like the turning of the tide. He knew they wouldn't stay on the riverside for ever, but as he walked his mam down the corridor to the front room, he was pointing out into the sunshine through the front door, telling her, "And that's where I'll be, look, mam – just over there. See, with the yellow bush in the front garden? You can just talk to me over the water and I'll hear you loud and clear. Now, Dagger lives just down there to the left, and he has a dog called Lennie Catflap. He's amazing, Mam, you'll love him. He dives out through a hole in the door. The first time it happened to me, I..."

Frank watched with a soft smile, as her friend guided his mam into her Nan's front room. He's nearly as tall as she is, she thought, happy that the two were reunited. And look at him, so calm and in control. No more numbers, panic and chanting for Billy. He had been *so* troubled; a couple of weeks should do it, she thought, but watching Billy now, she could see her friend was almost flying free, already.

*

The summer holidays had begun and life on the riverside became busy, with people enjoying the sunshine by the boating lake, fishing and having picnics. There was more traffic and movement, generally, along the once quiet riverside paths. Billy had grumbled about it to Frank, as they sat together at her front gate, simply people- and water-watching. It soothed Billy now, whereas not so long back, it would have left him stressed and shaking, desperate to bolt for the safety of isolation. Frank listened patiently to her friend, nodding her head occasionally, then she lay back on the grass and placed her hands behind her thick, glossy curls.

"Well, you know what, Billy? I think, yeah, it's a bit of a pain, having all these people wandering around, but it isn't forever. And if it's cheered them up to be here, by the river, if it's emptied their minds of any trouble and strife, well – that's got to be a good thing, eh? They'll climb on the bus, or into their car and head home, thinking, wow, it must be lovely to live down there. They leave with a smile."

Billy flopped down on his tummy, beside her, looking intently into her face, then glanced away at the water first, then up towards the Monument. After a moment, he, too, rolled onto his back. He mirrored Frank's position of hands up behind his head. Squinting up into the trees, he sighed in agreement.

"Yeah, Frank, you're right, actually. Look at what this place has done for me. I've been lucky enough to spend a few weeks here now, and look – I'm nearly normal!"

Frank rolled onto her front and threw a handful of grass into his face. Laughing, she told him, "You? Normal? I don't think so. But your mam is doing canny now, isn't she? I can see a big difference in her."

Billy smiled, thinking of how his mam wasn't quite so pale-faced anymore; how less of a shy little mouse she was, after a few days of mixing in with his riverside family; how she was able to stand and move without it being quite so painful anymore. He was just about to tell Frank about some possibilities for their new home, when a large figure blocked out the sun. They both opened their eyes and sat up suddenly, shading their faces from the glare of the evening sun.

"Hi, Dagger," Frank said, squinting up towards her friend. They both made to get up from their positions on the grass, but Dagger got down beside them, fairly clumsily, complaining about his knees.

"I'm getting too old for climbing that flamin' Monument," he told them, placing a cardboard box on the grass between them, then he, too, lay back in the grass, hands behind his head, and closed his eyes. "Aahh, this is the life, eh, Billy?"

Billy picked a dandelion, tore off the head, and threw it towards the water. "Well, yeah, for some people maybe, Dagger, but perhaps not for me."

Dagger and Frank sat up quickly, glancing first at each other and then towards Billy. His face had taken on a pained expression, like a flower closing before the rain, the one they used to see all the time, when he first arrived on the riverside.

"What is it, mate?" Dagger asked him, gently. Billy puffed out his cheeks and exhaled, gazing up into the trees and towards the water, rushing by not far from his feet.

"Oh, it's just the council have a few properties for us to start looking at, new homes for us. But I don't recognise any names or where they are, so they're not going to be round here, are they?" He shrugged his shoulders sadly.

Frank sat up on her knees and looked closely at him. "Now, Billy Higson," she began, taking his shoulder and making him look into her face. "If there's one thing you've learned by being here on the riverside with us, it's that there are plenty of buses..."

"...and taxis..." Dagger added.

"...and donkeys..." Frank grinned.

"...and bicycles... and boats..." Dagger was laughing now, and Billy was grinning, too.

"Seriously, Billy, if you *don't* come to see us *at least* once a week, we'll come looking for you! Honestly, Bill, I have to have you close to me here, or it'll be me being a right Billy-no-mates," Frank said.

Dagger told him seriously, "You'll be fine, Billy. Look at how much you have achieved in such a short time. You're like a different person now. You can do it, Billy – you can face anything now. After what you've been through, you should be proper proud of yourself. Isn't that right, Frank?" And he nodded at the box on the grass between them.

Billy looked from each of his friends and down at the box. He raised his eyes questioningly to them.

"Go on, Billy. Open it. It's for you, from us two."

"Yeah. I think the time is right. Open it, Billy," Frank told him quietly.

Billy reached for the box and gently peeled back the lid. Inside, nestled in soft straw, were two separately wrapped parcels, one on top of the other. Taking the top one out, Billy carefully and gently started to unroll the paper around it. He could feel a shape emerging beneath his fingers and held the gift carefully as he put the paper to one side. When it was clear of the wrapping, Billy held it aloft, turning it gently over in his hands, watching as the sun lit up the grooves and markings on it. He exhaled suddenly, as if all the wind had been knocked out of him.

"Oh wow, Frank. It's… it's just…" A knot formed in his throat and he couldn't speak. He kissed the carved bird and smelled the new thing in his hands, caressing it against his face, eyes closed.

"It's a swallow, Billy. The swallow of summer, my favourite little summer visitor."

Billy still couldn't speak. The bird was perfect in every detail – eyes glistening, soft apricot-coloured underbelly, and a tail of splayed out feathers to match its wingspan. Dagger reached out and gently took hold of it, for a moment.

"It's such an appropriate gift, Billy," he told him, handing back the wooden bird. "This little bird has crossed oceans to get here, has battled through storms and attacks from bigger birds all the way, just to get to this place it calls home. It's just like you, Billy."

And then he turned the bird once again in Billy's hands, pointing out something on the underside. In tiny lettering, carved into the tail feathers, were the words, 'Finally free'.

A small sob escaped from Billy's throat, and to hide it, he reached forward to put his arms around Frank. Drawing her close to him, he kissed her softly on her silken cheek.

"Thanks, Frank," he managed to croak.

"Now, the other one," Dagger told him, coughing deeply and looking away downstream. Billy carefully placed the swallow on the grass and gently unwrapped the second gift. He felt sure Dagger had carved him a boat, but it felt quite different in his hands inside the wrapping, not streamlined at all, more chunky and solid. As the paper revealed its treasure, a tear fell from Billy's eye and slipped down his cheek, even before the gift was fully uncovered. His face burned, his mouth worked silently, and he stared up at his friend with watery blue eyes, before flinging himself into the arms of the man beside him. Burying his head into Dagger's solid, rough chest, he coughed out, almost silently, "Thank you, Dagger. Oh, thank you so much. For this, and for everything."

Frank stared wide-eyed at the gift, too: a perfect miniature carving of Penshaw Monument, in all its glorious detail. The soft honey-coloured wood glowed in the sunlight, the pillars in perfect proportion, the shape of the steps leading up to the base. She picked it up gently, turning it over to look more closely.

"I thought you were building him a boat, Dagger. This is… just… wow! And look, Billy, look here."

Frank handed the Monument back to Billy, and together they leaned over it, heads and shoulders touching. On the underside, on the base, in little letters, perfectly formed, were the words, "Finally free." And the date that they had all sat on the Monument and heard Billy's story. They both looked questioningly at Dagger.

"It was what you said, Frank – the night Billy's mam came home from hospital. You said Billy was finally free. And that stuck in my head."

"Mine, too," she told him, grinning.

Billy wiped his eyes on the back of his hand and stood up, looking down on his two favourite people. "Well, you know what. If Frank sees me as a swallow, a summer visitor, battling the elements to get here, then this Monument is Dagger."

The other two got up to stand beside Billy, one on either side. Billy cradled it in his hands as he told them, gazing confidently from one to the other. "This Monument is Dagger 'cos to me it represents strength, solidity and respect. Local pride. I know the real Monument was built out of love of a special person, the Earl of Durham by his workmen, and I know that you, Dagger, have built this version of it out of love for me. But you are a very special person, too. So I will keep it and treasure both of these forever."

"Let's go and have a cuppa, eh, Billy?" Dagger suggested, as the three of them turned towards Essie Bailey's house. "We're so glad you like them. Like the swallow, we want you to keep coming back, and remember – like your beloved Monument – you will always have a place in our hearts."

The three friends moved towards the house, Billy in the middle, holding tightly onto his precious gifts, flanked on one side by the slim and beautiful Frank, with one arm around his waist. On the other, the broad and benevolent Dagger, with a protective arm around Billy's shoulder. People on the river banks were happily heading homeward now as the evening sun slipped westwards, behind the trees, and danced on the waters of the river.

THE END